KING KONG

KING KONG

A Novelization by Christopher Golden

Screenplay by
Fran Walsh & Philippa Boyens & Peter Jackson

Based on a Story
by Merian C. Cooper and Edgar Wallace

Pocket STAR Books
New York   London   Toronto   Sydney

An *Original* Publication of POCKET BOOKS

A Pocket Star Book published by
POCKET BOOKS, a division of Simon & Schuster, Inc.
1230 Avenue of the Americas, New York, NY 10020

ISBN-13: 978-1-4165-0391-0
ISBN-10:   1-4165-0391-9

This Pocket Star Books paperback edition December 2005

10 9 8 7 6 5 4 3 2 1

POCKET STAR BOOKS and colophon are registered
trademarks of Simon & Schuster, Inc.

Manufactured in the United States of America

For information regarding special discounts for bulk purchases,
please contact Simon & Schuster Special Sales at 1-800-456-6798
or business@simonandschuster.com.

KING KONG

1

In the midst of the Central Park Menagerie, a scrawny, dirty monkey sat scratching itself and gazed listlessly from within its cage, but there was little to see. It was so used to being alone that it was past the point of being troubled by the fact. In the midst of the Great Depression, the wonder and joy of the zoo had been all but forgotten by the people of New York, as though it belonged to another age.

On this unseasonably warm fall day, the city was a steaming jungle. The park had once been a vision of beauty and grandeur, but now it was a locus of squalor, strewn with rubbish and dotted with shantytowns set up by victims of the Depression, shed by the city. Homeless and jobless, they had fallen away from civilization and into a primitive state where each day began and ended with thoughts only of survival. Hungry, dirty, and ragged, these men, women, and children had slipped through the cracks in the crumbling economy of the 1930s, and no amount of willingness to work, no burning ambition, would be enough to bring most of them back to the world.

From the core of that filth and despair, from the

ramshackle shelters hastily erected in Central Park, each and every one of them could see the new skyscrapers being built in Manhattan. When they allowed themselves to dwell upon their circumstances, their eyes invariably turned to those new constructions, and their thoughts to the irony that such extraordinary investment in the world of tomorrow was being made during a time when so many had so little. And though it had been erected several years before, no building was more a testament to this disparity than the Empire State Building, the tallest and greatest structure in the world.

High above the city, in the lofty heights of its upper floors, the future was in the making. But for those the Depression had defeated, there would be no future at all. Only more of the same.

Or worse.

The city still bustled with life, but beneath it was a current of misery and hopelessness. Long lines snaked from the doors of unemployment offices, along sidewalks, around corners. Apple sellers and other vendors roamed the streets of New York, scraping for every penny, grateful to have whatever they could manage, which was so much more than those who slept above steaming vents and in garbage-strewn gutters. A man stood at the mouth of an alley, hat in hand, singing "I'm Sitting On Top of the World" in his best Al Jolson.

The song was all he had to offer.

And it was a lie.

*　　*　　*

Cymbals crashed and horns blew in the Lyric Theatre, but curtains and walls muffled the sound for those back in the dressing room. The smell of sweat and greasepaint was thick here, but to Ann Darrow it smelled like home. Her pulse raced and her skin tingled not with fear or anxiety, but with exhilaration. This was the moment, the chaos before she took the stage, the time when she could forget the world and everything in it. This was what she lived for.

Vaudeville.

Ann Darrow was part of a grand tradition, a parade of entertainers going back two hundred years. The stage was in her blood. Her mother had been a vaudeville girl and Ann had never known her father—had the impression Mom hadn't known him either—but she'd been on her own since the age of thirteen and somehow convinced herself she wasn't bothered by that. Vaudeville was her family. The theater people. The troupe. All the way back to Tony Pastor and Ben Keith, and through every performer from the Barrison Sisters and Ching Ling Foo to the greats, the ones who'd made it big. Benny and Brice, Cohan and Fields, Burns and Allen, and dozens of others. Distant cousins all.

Vaudeville had been all she'd ever needed. When her mother took off south after a song-and-dance man, the stage had been waiting. And when Fred Burliss had broken her heart, the audience had made it soar again.

So tonight, while she'd watched the jugglers and the trained dogs from the wings, she'd tried to ignore how quiet the theater had been, tried not to think about a venue that could hold five hundred but had pulled in an audience no more than a tenth of that number. Radio had struck the first cruel blow, and now, slowly but surely, the movies were killing vaudeville. Once the cinema started showing "talkies," that was the beginning of the end.

They didn't talk about it, of course; the performers. They just went on.

Ann struggled into the baggy pants of her costume and pulled up the suspenders, and she felt the familiar prickle of her skin. It was hot as blazes back there in the dressing room, but she barely felt it as the growing anticipation to get out there and bring the house down came alive. A thin smile touched her lips as she tugged on the oversized man's jacket to match the pants and then snatched the top hat off her dressing table. She'd been practicing the balancing of that hat for years until she had as much facility with it as the jugglers did with their pins.

The door was open. From down the corridor she heard the stage manager urgently whisper, "Where are they? They're on!"

Now any trace of a smile disappeared. Time to get down to business. Show time. They were never ready to go on stage early—it was bad luck. It was the adrenaline rush that made the performance great, the drumroll of the heart as they cut it close. Always close.

Ann hurried out of her dressing room, doing the button of her jacket with one hand even as she set the top hat onto her head with the other. The pants legs gave a hushed rasp as they rubbed against each other.

Like the sounds and the smells and the quickening of her heart, it was all familiar, all wonderful.

And it was all she knew.

Manny came out right after her, heading into the wings, into a sea of curtains and ropes. He was getting up there in years, but he still made it ahead of Harry, who had managed to stuff his rotund form into a dress and dolled himself up as the ugliest woman the world had ever seen. A smattering of polite applause could be heard from the meager audience and then the singers were coming off the stage. Ann, Manny, and Harry slid past them, waiting for the music cue to start their act.

"Ann!" Manny called in an urgent whisper.

She turned to find him already reaching for her. The seconds were ticking by. The stage was empty and it was ready for them. When she saw what Manny was doing, Ann held still. Quickly, he stuck a large, droopy black mustache to her top lip, holding it in place a moment for the glue to stick.

Her costume was complete.

In the seconds that she moved from wings to stage, Ann altered herself completely. Her gait became an odd cross between strut and saunter, her persona that of a slightly drunken Victorian gentleman. Scattered applause met her arrival and she smiled at the audience even as she launched into a song, the catchy tune matching the rhythm of her heart. Manny then joined her, whistling along with the melody. Harry began to hurry around the stage waving around a feather duster, the perfect picture of a fussy matron cleaning house.

When Ann reached the bridge of the song, she slid a

hip flask from her pocket. Manny continued to whistle beautifully, but Harry's mad dusting grew more frantic and Manny paused in his whistling to unleash a sneeze that rocked his body.

Ann's cue for a pratfall, as though the force of the sneeze or the startling noise had knocked her down.

And so the routine built. Ann sang, Harry dusted, Manny whistled and then sneezed, causing Ann's drunken gent to fall, again and again. How many times had they done this bit? A hundred? Five hundred? Once upon a time it had had them rolling in the aisles. Now there were only faint smiles, save for one man at the back who was laughing hysterically.

Ann should have appreciated the fellow, knowing that there was at least one person to whom the act was playing the way it was supposed to, but he was so over the top it was distracting. She forced herself to focus on the act, sweat beading on her face, throwing everything into her performance, not caring if she was bruised by her falls.

When it was over, there was a sprinkling of polite clapping. She told herself that it wasn't about the crowd, that the thrill of the performance was enough, but it sounded hollow even in her mind.

Afterward, Ann, Manny, and Harry retired to the dressing room and she forced away all thoughts of the nearly empty theater, letting herself be carried along by the energy and noise of the rest of the performers. Magicians and musicians, acrobats and dancers. They filled the place, all in various stages of undress, and the chatter of their voices, their excitement, worked its way into Ann until she began to realize that it really wasn't about the audience. It was about the *now,* right here, surrounded by people she thought of as her family, even though a few of them were strangers.

As Ann changed out of her costume, she glanced at Harry. He looked ridiculous in his wig, but with it off there was something so ordinary about him, so human.

"That's three nights in a row. Did you see him?" she said.

Harry raised an eyebrow. "Who?"

Ann smiled. "Laughing boy. I think he might be sweet on you."

"Really?" Harry asked, feigning excitement before making a sour face. "Uggghhh!"

Beyond him, Manny had a thoughtful look on his face. Then the older man screwed up his features and fired off a loud, comical sneeze. All business, he looked around at Harry and Ann.

"That's a funny one. Isn't that funnier?"

Ann gave him a doting smile and then slipped into a chair, focusing on her reflection in the mirror and the garish makeup that was necessary under the lights of the stage. It was the face the audience saw, but not her true face. With expert swiftness, she began to clean the makeup from her cheeks. A few moments later she was interrupted as someone moved into her light. She looked up as the young dancer Taps snatched up the book that had been lying open on the counter in front of Ann's mirror.

"What's this?" the kid asked.

She was about halfway through reading the book for the third time. *Isolation,* by Jack Driscoll.

"It's a play," she said.

"Annie dragged me to the theater once," Harry said as he pulled off his high heels. "Three hours long it was. And in the end everybody pegged it. I mean, who needs three hours to tell a story?"

"Shakespeare," Ann said dryly.

Harry shook his head. "Most depressing thing I ever seen."

"No. Twenty-four girls in feathers boas and fixed smiles prancing around like circus ponies—*that's* depressing." Ann dabbed at her makeup again.

The performers around them were starting to join in on the conversation. Maude, a gifted torch singer, lit up a cigarette and pointed it at Ann.

"I love a good chorus line," she said, not an argument but a fond declaration.

Manny nodded toward the book in Taps's hand. "Who wrote it, Annie?"

Taps was studying the jacket of the book. "Some guy, Driscoll. From the Federal Theatre."

Harry plopped heavily down in front of a mirror, his dress bunched up around his waist. "The Federal Theatre's nothing more than a haven for short-haired girls, long-haired boys, and weirdies of all kinds."

Maude blew out a plume of smoke. "Don't knock it, honey. At least they get an audience."

The comment seemed to still the air around them, a curtain of seriousness lowering.

"These things go in cycles. It'll pick up," Ann told them. "It always does."

But as they all went about their business, a bit more sober than before, she wondered why the cycle was taking so long to come round again this time, wondered if maybe the doomsayers were right, and *always* wasn't going to come to the rescue this time.

Then she put it out of her mind. It was too much to even think about.

Ann didn't have anything else.

When all the lights were down, the costumes hung, and their faces scrubbed of makeup, Ann and Manny left the dressing room through the door that let into the alley behind the theater. Manny still wore a studious look and from time to time would erupt with another sneeze. The truth was they all sounded pretty much alike to Ann, but the old fellow seemed to identify something unique in each.

As they stepped into the alley he let loose with a spluttering *achoo!,* a damp honk that did, indeed, sound a bit more ridiculous than the ones he'd been producing on stage.

"The trick is to start the build right at the back of your throat," he said. "Works well out through the nose, too."

Ann studied him. "Have you eaten today?"

Manny grew sheepish. "Oh, I'm not hungry. Don't worry about me."

"Hey, you're all I've got," she said, and slipped her

arm through his. "Come on, they'll still be giving out soup and biscuits on Third. Take me to dinner."

They walked down the alley arm in arm, and somehow, in spite of her circumstances, Ann felt content.

The following morning she found a needle and thread and mended a tear in the one dress that she felt still looked presentable. A life on the stage could lead to fame and fortune, but in Ann's experience that was rare as a lightning strike. Most performers were just getting by, and others not quite even that. Ann rarely had a decent meal, but she had been managing all right, so far.

On the other hand, times were lean and getting leaner, and the landlord was not the forgiving sort. At some point soon, she knew she would need a new dress, the fact that she could not afford one having no bearing on the impending necessity. Theater people by and large knew how to sew, and Ann was a passable seamstress—vaudeville had prepared her. But even if she sewed the dress herself, she could not afford the fabric. How she would find the money, she did not know, and did not like to think about, so while she sewed, she sang softly, under her breath.

When she was through she busied herself with her hair and makeup, and then at last slipped the dress on. Contented, she left the rooming house, pausing to exchange a pleasant word with the old man who ran the tailor shop on the corner.

For a time she wandered as though she had somewhere to go, but eventually she saw from the clock in front of a bank that it was time to stop by the theater and begin preparing for the evening's performance. The theater manager was supposed to be responsible for many of the preparations, but all too often things were forgotten and the troupe had begun to take such duties upon themselves.

It was mid-afternoon by the time she turned the corner two blocks from the Lyric and strode toward the dilapidated marquee. Ann had gone half a dozen steps, her eyes drawn to the workmen up on ladders on the sidewalk, before she realized they were taking the hoard-ings down. One man was putting letters onto the mar-quee. A single word.

CLOSED.

"No . . ." Ann whispered.

She hurried toward the venue, aware of the group of her fellow performers that had already gathered around the front doors, but unable to even acknowledge them. Their faces were a blur. The sidewalk was piled high with props and trunks full of costumes. The strength threatened to go out of her legs and she felt a woozy moment where she might have tumbled to the con-crete. When she spied the sign on the doors that read THEATER CLOSED TILL FURTHER NOTICE, a dark anger took hold.

Heavy chains were looped through the Lyric's door handles, tightly wound and locked. Ann reached out as though the chains weren't even there, grabbing the handles and tugging, rattling the doors.

"There's a law against this!" she called, turning on her heel to glare at the workmen. She glanced at the man on the ladder above her. "You're lucky we don't sue you for damages!"

The guy on the ladder only gave her a smirk. Ann backed away, giving him a hateful look, and then spun to face the other performers clustered around her on the sidewalk, nearly tripping over a prop umbrella.

"They're not going to get away with this," she snapped.

A few feet away, Maude bent to pick up an ornate fan as though it were a souvenir. She stood and glanced at Ann, her expression bleak.

"They just did," Maude said, and turned to go.

Ann could only watch as one by one, others did the same, claiming some item from the ground as though they were talismans of some magical power and then wandering off, dejected. Not one of them seemed to have any destination in mind: just anywhere other than here.

"Yeah, well, we'll see about that!" She turned again to glare at the theater, at the sign, at the workmen.

"Ann . . ."

She bent to gather up props: Manny's broom, Harry's parasol, her top hat.

"Ann."

Taking a deep breath, she turned to face Manny, whose eyes were filled with sad resignation. He was slumped down on top of a battered old leather trunk.

"It's over," he said. "The show . . . it's done."

She frowned and looked away.

"I'm done, Annie," he said. "I'm leaving. Going back to Chicago."

Ann stared at him in shock.

Manny swallowed visibly. "I'm sorry."

"For what?"

"Ever since you were small, people been letting you down. Some folks have it easy, but it's never been that way for you."

Ann glanced away, knowing it was the truth but unable to say it.

"It never stopped you, either," Manny said. "You should do it, Annie."

"Do what?"

"Try out for that part."

She shook her head. "Me? No . . ."

"Why not? It's what you've always wanted. You must have read that play a hundred times. Get yourself an audition."

Ann took a long breath. It wasn't that easy and Manny knew this. She looked at him warily.

"I know what you're thinking. Whenever you reach for something you care about, fate comes along and snatches it away," Manny said. He grabbed her hand. "But not this time, Annie. That's what you've got to tell yourself. Not this time."

She let the words swim around in her head a bit. Nearby, the loud rumble of an El train was thunderous. Manny's hand was like leather to the touch. Ann squeezed it tightly, thinking.

Thinking *maybe*. After all, she had nowhere else to go.

Ann had done it. She'd contacted the office of the producer, Mr. Weston, and sent him her résumé, hoping for

13

an audition. Days had passed—days in which she had chosen to use what little money she had left to buy food instead of paying her landlord—but she had not given up. Something good was bound to come her way, she told herself. It had to. The alternative was too horrible to contemplate. She passed the starving vagrants on the street and could not imagine becoming one of them, could not imagine it even as she ate the last of her food, hiding in her meager quarters at the rooming house, not answering the door when the landlord came to demand the rent.

Then, today—her stomach tight with hunger and afraid that any day, she would return to find herself evicted—something had been delivered for her, an envelope from Mr. Weston.

He had returned her résumé unopened.

What was she to do now? There was no work for anyone these days, least of all a vaudeville girl. Without this, she was lost. And the man had not even had the decency to open her letter.

Once upon a time she might have just gone away, given up on her ambition. But she had no choice. Without the theater, she was cast adrift. She had no family, no money, and today she'd had nothing to eat but some small bits of bread and cheese gone almost stale. Soon enough, she'd have nowhere to live. Not if things kept on like this.

And yet, in spite of her predicament, Ann's determination didn't come from having nothing to lose. It was more than that. She had simply grown tired of people disappointing her. If she was going to lose, it wasn't going to be without a fight.

Just after noon, she made her way to Weston's office, her stomach tight with hunger and her body taut with determination. She arrived just in time to see him exiting the building, a copy of *Variety* tucked under one arm. He was dapperly dressed in a charcoal pinstripe suit and a greatcoat and hat that looked brand new. It seemed the Great Deprssion had not touched him at all.

"Mr. Weston?"

The man glanced around, but the moment he saw her, he turned quickly away, set his shoulders, and started to move off. She heard him muttering something under his breath. Ann hurried and quickly fell into step beside him, the two of them angling through the people on the busy sidewalk.

"Look, miss, I told you already," Weston curtly began. "Call my office. Leave your résumé with my secretary."

He tried to behave as though that had finished the conversation but she kept pace with him. "Why would I want to do that when we can talk about it in person?"

Weston tugged the brim of his hat down a bit as though the sun was in his eyes. "Because that's what a smart girl would do."

"Come on," Ann said. "I sent you my résumé, and you returned it unopened."

Weston almost collided with an older woman of considerable girth, who shot him a withering glance as he brushed past her. Ann easily danced through the bustle of people.

"What can I say?" Weston replied. "Jack Driscoll's very particular about who he works with."

"An audition," Ann persisted. "That's all I'm asking."

The man grunted in annoyance. "Jesus, you don't give up, do you?"

"I know this role backwards, Mr. Weston. I can recite it in my sleep."

At last he looked at her, eyes narrowed with cynicism. "Well, that's too bad, because we just gave it to someone else. Sorry, kid, the play's cast."

He stopped outside the door of an Italian restaurant and Ann realized it was his destination—the only reason he even bothered with her now was that he wanted to be rid of her so he could go to lunch. Her stomach growled; she wondered if he could hear it.

Weston waved to someone inside the restaurant and then started to enter, leaving a crestfallen Ann just standing there. This was how it was going to be? Just go without another word? Then Weston looked back and there must have been some piece of him that was not pure cynicism, because whatever he saw on her face made him pause.

"Don't look at me like that," he said. "It's not like you ever had a shot at it."

A couple slid past them and entered the restaurant. As the door opened, Ann caught a glimpse of plates of sumptuous food and glasses of wine, the aromas drifting from the restaurant nothing short of torment. She glanced away.

"I know times are tough," Weston went on. "You want my advice, use what you've got. You're not bad looking. A girl like you doesn't have to starve."

Ann felt a flicker of hope as Weston fished in his

pocket and drew out a pen and a business card. On the back, he scribbled an address. But as he handed it to her, he wouldn't meet her eyes.

"It's a new place. Just opened." Weston straightened his jacket and then regarded her coolly. "Listen, princess, this gig ain't the Palace, understand? Ask for Kenny K. Tell him I sent you."

Ann looked at the address, not recognizing it. And she thought she knew the city pretty well. She shot him a questioning glance.

Weston grimly nodded. "Play the date, take the money, and forget you were ever there."

2

THE SCREENING ROOM WAS utterly silent save for the occasional cough from the film's investors and the whir of the projector coming from the booth at the back of the room. On the screen, black and white images flickered soundlessly past. Tigers roared. Handsome, square-jawed matinee hero Bruce Baxter stalked through the undergrowth in a pith helmet. A determined cast to his features, the actor on the screen raised his rifle and pulled the trigger. The gun jammed. Breaking character, Bruce turned to the camera, lips moving.

The angle shifted to take in a sleepy-looking lion. A piece of meat was being lowered into the frame and for just a moment, Carl Denham, the filmmaker himself, was visible on screen, attempting to use the lure of the meat to stir the yawning animal to life. The camera tilted back a moment to reveal the bars of the lion's cage. Then the film cut to the face of Denham's assistant, Preston, holding a clapper board. The number five was scrawled on the board, and Preston called it out, lips moving with no sound, and then clapped the board to mark the beginning of the take.

In the audience, Carl Denham paid little attention to the images on the screen. His attention was on the individuals sitting in the rows in front of him, the money men, who had financed the whole thing as an investment. Through the smoke that furled up from their cigars and cigarettes, he was trying to read the room, to get a feeling of how they were responding to the raw footage he had cut together on this picture. So far, he had no idea how they were taking it.

Denham wanted to shout at them for their inexpressiveness. At the same time, he was anxious about their reaction. He was an expeditionary filmmaker, used to scouring the world for sights and experiences unlike anything the American audience had ever seen. Now he was making a safari picture on a studio back lot, and there wasn't anything particularly special about it. Carl Denham was used to the extraordinary. Back lot filming was beneath him, but he couldn't very well tell them that. Not the gents who were footing the bill.

Mr. Zelman, head of the investment group, spoke to the screen, not bothering to turn around and address Denham directly. "How much more is there?" he asked, cigarette dangling from his fingers, bald spot pale in the flickering light from the projector.

Denham started to answer, but Zelman's assistant interrupted him from the back of the room.

"Another five reels," the kid said.

Zelman sighed. "Lights up."

The room was flooded with light that washed out the image on the screen a moment before the projectionist shut it down and the film went away entirely.

Poehler, a slick, cynical SOB in his own right, woke up with a start and a snort, glancing around mystified.

Zelman clearly had something to say, but Tom Farragher beat him to it. Farragher was a thug, plain and simple, and he made Denham nervous.

"This is it?" Farragher demanded. "This is what we get for our forty grand, Denham? Another one of your safari pictures?"

The filmmaker winced. He had made several of these films, but the majority of the footage had been taken on actual safaris, not on back lots. The fact that this genius couldn't tell the difference angered Denham. He was supposed to be a trailblazing filmmaker, not some errand boy. But he had to behave in this meeting.

He'd figured a way to give these men something more than the garbage they wanted from him—Carl Denham wasn't content to be relegated to the back lot.

It was time to change his circumstances. But to do that, he needed to keep their cooperation.

"You promised us romantic scenes with Bruce Baxter and Maureen McKenzie," Poehler piped up, his mouth a sneer.

"Come on, fellas," Denham replied. "You know the deal. We agreed to push Maureen's start date so she could get her teeth fixed."

Farragher clutched his cigarette between two fingers and gestured with it, the burning tip punctuating his words.

"It's not the principle of the thing. It's the money."

Zelman was all business, watching Denham carefully. "Carl, you've been in production for over two months."

"Trust me, Bruce and Maureen are gonna steam up the screen, once we get them on the ship."

Zelman furrowed his brow. "What ship?"

"The one we've hired to get to the location," Denham said.

The investors all exchanged wary looks.

"*What* location?" Zelman asked. "Carl, you're supposed to be shooting on the back lot."

"Yes, I understand that," Denham replied coolly. "But we're not making that film anymore." He rose from his seat and moved toward the front of the room, taking his place as the center of attention, making the investors his audience. The room was warm, so he had taken his jacket off and loosened his tie, but Denham figured that in just his vest and shirtsleeves, he looked more earnest, a hardworking man just trying to do his job.

"The story has changed, gentlemen. We are now on a different path. The script has been rewritten."

With a flourish he produced a tattered, folded map from his pocket. It was all the showman in him could do not to say *Voilà*!

"Life intervened," he went on. "I have come into possession of a map. The legacy of a dead man. A castaway, lost at sea."

"Whoa, Carl!" Zelman said, holding up both hands. "Slow down."

"I'm talking about an uncharted island," Denham pushed on. "A place that was thought to exist only in myth . . . until now!"

Poehler looked confused in the way only truly dim people ever did. "Is he askin' for more money?"

The thuggish Farragher just glared. "He's asking us to fund a wild goose chase."

"A primitive world, never before seen by man!" Denham said, wondering what it would take to get through to them. "The ruins of an entire civilization! The most spectacular thing you've ever seen!"

He indulged himself with a dramatic pause and then shook the map in his hand. "*That's* where I'm gonna shoot my picture."

Poehler's eyes lit up and Denham could practically hear the gears turning in the sleazy investor's head.

"Will there be boobies?" Poehler asked.

Denham gaped at him. "Excuse me? Boobies?"

"Jigglies, jablongers, bazoomers!" Poehler rattled impatiently. "In my experience people only go to these films to observe the . . . undraped state of the native girls."

"What are you, an idiot?" Denham snapped. "Didn't you hear a word I just said? You think they asked de Mille to waste his time on nudie shots? No, they respected the filmmaker, they showed some class! Not that you'd know what *that* means, you cheap lowlife!"

Denham was fuming, but he felt all the air go out of the room like a balloon deflating. The place fell silent.

After a moment, Zelman spoke, resignation in his voice. "Would you step out for a moment, Carl?"

The other investors avoided making eye contact with him. Denham thought about continuing, but knew when it was time to let the chips fall. With a shake of his head he left the room.

Out in the hallway, his assistant, Preston, stood to greet him, a glass of water in his hand. The fellow was of average height and build, but with a face that looked even younger than his years. He was a go-getter, loyal as could be, and Denham liked that. People who couldn't share his vision ought to just get out of his way. And it was time to find out who was with him, and who was against him.

"Gimme that, quick!" he snapped, reaching for the glass.

Preston handed it to him.

"You won't like it," Preston said dryly. "It's non-alcoholic."

Denham upended the glass, dumping the water into a potted plant in the waiting area. "Preston, you have a lot to learn about the motion picture business."

As quietly as he was able, he set the glass against the screening room door and pressed his ear against it, straining to hear the voices on the other side. Zelman was talking, just as he'd expected. He was the one they all looked to, and Denham figured Zelman would be his ace in the hole.

"Don't write him off, fellas. He's hot-headed, sure, but Carl Denham's made some interesting pictures," Zelman was saying. Denham smiled. That boded well. "He's had a lot of . . . near successes."

Denham's smile evaporated. Maybe not so well after all.

"He's a preening self-promoter," another voice

growled. That would be the thug, Farragher. "An ambitious no-talent! The guy has loser written all over him. It's pathetic when they can't see it themselves."

Denham froze, anger rising in him, but even more powerfully, a kind of panic. This was his *career* that the idiot was talking about. His true calling.

"Okay," Zelman said on the other side of the door. "So maybe he wasn't our strongest choice."

"Denham talks big," Farragher declared, "but he don't deliver."

Poehler chimed in. "He can't direct. He doesn't have the smarts."

What?! Outside in the hall, Denham flinched even as he restrained himself from bursting into the screening room with murderous intent. He adjusted his ear against the glass, not wanting to miss a word.

"I understand your disappointment. I'm feeling very let down myself," Zelman told them. "I thought he had something."

"Are you kidding me?" Farragher boomed. "He's washed up. It's all over town!"

Denham pulled away from the door, forcing himself to breath slowly and evenly. *So this was how it was going to be?*

Zelman's assistant, Sid Nathanson, was a twenty-one-year-old kid from the Bronx. More often than not, Mr. Zelman called him "Stanley," but Sid never corrected him. Working in motion pictures was his dream, and if the boss couldn't remember his name from time to time, he wasn't going to get heated up over it.

It was a tough business. Sid had known that going in, but he'd never really understood how tough until he had started attending meetings with Mr. Zelman. This one, though . . . it was brutal. Denham was intense and passionate, maybe a little crazy around the eyes, but obviously he knew what he wanted from a picture. Somehow, even though the man had been in the business for a number of years, he hadn't figured out that it wasn't about passion. It was about money.

Even as the thought crossed Sid's mind, Mr. Poehler spoke up.

"A man who doesn't recognize the value of boobies is a liability in this industry," the man said, lighting a cigarette.

Sid kept his face carefully neutral on the off chance that one of the investors would look at him. To do that, of course, they'd have to notice him, so it wasn't likely. Still, practiced neutrality was a valuable skill. That much he'd already learned.

"So," Poehler went on, "we scrap the picture? Cut our losses?"

Farragher reddened. "And flush forty grand down the toilet? This jumped-up little turd's gonna bankrupt us!"

"The animal footage has value," Zelman noted. He was the brains, obviously, and he was trying to figure out how to salvage whatever he could from this catastrophe. Sid had learned a lot from the man.

Poehler nodded. "Sure, Universal are desperate for stock footage."

"Then sell it!" Farragher said. "We've gotta retrieve something from this debacle."

Zelman nodded and gestured to Sid. "Get him back in."

Sid jumped up and hurried to the door. He wondered how bad the fireworks were going to get when they told Denham the news. But when he opened the door and stepped into the waiting room, it was empty.

Denham was gone.

Preston felt himself carried along in the wake of Denham's fury and determination. The moment when Carl had decided they were going to bolt had been abrupt, and before Preston could even think, the two of them were hurrying out of the building struggling under the weight of eight film cans, all the reels Denham had shot so far. Now they were rushing along the sidewalk laden with that burden, Preston trying to keep from spilling the cans into the street and Denham glancing nervously back over his shoulder.

"I want the cast and crew on the ship within the hour," Denham ordered, and Preston could see that he'd already moved on. The director had formulated a Plan B, and it was full speed ahead now.

"Carl," he said, "you can't do this!"

"Tell 'em the studio's pressured us into making an early departure."

Preston's ears burned with the heat of indignation. "It's not ethical!"

"What are they gonna do, sue me?" Denham scoffed. "They can get in line."

Preston caught the toe of his shoe on a sidewalk crack and stumbled a bit, only barely managing to keep hold of the film cans. Denham did not even slow.

"You realize none of the camera equipment's on board," Preston said as he hurried to keep up.

Denham wasn't paying any attention to him. Instead, the man was looking worriedly over his shoulder. Without warning he stepped off the sidewalk and started to cut across the busy road. Preston glanced back and saw Zelman and the other investors in the distance, an angry little lynch mob, and he set off after Denham as fast as he could manage with the film cans.

"We have no permits, no visas."

"That's why I have you, Preston." Denham raised a hand, imperiously flagging down a cab. It cruised up beside them.

"No insurance, no foreign currency . . . in fact we have no currency of any kind. Who's gonna pay for the ship?"

Denham yanked open the cab door and hustled Preston into the back, following behind almost before Preston had a chance to slide over to give him room. Preston sprawled across the seat in a pile of film cans.

"Step on it!" Denham told the cabbie as he slammed the door. He shouted out an address, but Preston barely caught the words.

A furious Poehler now took the lead as he, Zelman, and Farragher gave chase. He shouted after them, bellowing Carl's name as though they were in the army, and Poehler was some kind of drill sergeant. The rear window by Denham was partway open and Poehler grabbed hold of the glass. Carl quickly cranked it closed—the seedy investor yelped and withdrew his fingers.

"Don't worry, Preston. I've had a lot of practice at this. I'm real good at crapping the crappers."

The cab cruised through the crowded streets of Manhattan. Preston felt his stomach lurch as they rounded a corner, but somehow he managed to sit up straight and get all of the film cans piled in some semblance of order on the seat beside him. Meanwhile, Denham kept on talking about preparations for the film, and for the ship to sail. Preston pulled out his notepad and started scribbling.

"And two dozen of Mr. Walker's finest," Denham continued, listing the most vital of supplies for the voyage.

"Red label, eighty percent proof, packed in a crate marked lemonade," Preston confirmed, jotting it down.

"You got it. And tell Maureen she doesn't have six hours to put on her face. If she wants to be in this picture, she's gotta be on that boat."

Preston hated giving Denham bad news. *Plus he forgot . . . or maybe chose not to listen.* He hesitated for an eyeblink before plunging ahead. "She *doesn't* want to be in this picture."

Denham looked at him blankly.

"Maureen pulled out," Preston said.

"She pulled out?"

"Yesterday. I told you."

"You said we were shooting in Singapore, right?" Denham asked. "That's what you told her?"

"But we're not shooting in Singapore."

"Goddamn it, Preston!" Denham shouted. "All you had to do was look her in the eye and lie."

Preston didn't flinch. He'd grown used to being the object of his boss's ire. He was more interested in their destination, and now that the subject had come up, he wasn't going to let it go. Preston had given up a lot to become Denham's assistant, and he thought at the very least he'd earned the right to be in on the mystery.

"Where exactly *are* we filming, Carl? The Indian Ocean's a big place. I just thought you might have a land mass in mind."

A furtive look came over Denham's face. "You want to know what's going on? I'll tell you."

Surprised, Preston narrowed his eyes, studying Denham. Waiting.

"We've got three hours to find a new leading lady . . . or we're screwed," Denham said, voice edged with cynicism. "Is that enough information for you?"

The director looked away, muttering to himself. It was typical Denham. He lived in a world where he was the star, and everyone else merely extras. But there was passion for the craft in him, and a spark of true genius, that Preston couldn't help but admire.

"I gotta get to a phone, talk to Harlow's people," Denham said, mostly to himself, mind already a million miles away.

Jean Harlow? Preston thought. *Who was he kidding?*

"She's busy."

"Myrna Loy?" Denham replied, thinking, rattling off names as they occurred to him. "Joan Blondell? Clara Bow?" He glanced at Preston. "Mae West?"

"You'll never get her into a size four. You gotta get a girl who'll fit Maureen's costumes."

Denham's eyes lit up. "Fay's a size four!"

"She's doing a picture with RKO," Preston said, swaying as the cab took another corner. The whole vehicle rumbled, the engine badly in need of work.

"Cooper, huh?" Denham asked, his expression darkening. "I might have known . . ."

The cab screeched to a sudden halt in mid-traffic. Denham jumped out. Preston stared at him, utterly baffled. The director shot off instructions to the cabbie.

"I'm telling you," Preston called to him, "we've gotta delay the shoot. Shut production down!"

Denham's eyes were alight with cunning and mischief. "Not an option."

"Carl, there's no time," Preston insisted.

"For God's sake, Preston," Denham snapped, "think like a winner." He started to turn away.

"Carl!"

Denham looked through the rear window at him. "Call Driscoll. I need that goddamn screenplay!"

The cabbie had been silent throughout their frantic conversation. Now the driver glanced back curiously.

"He's lost his mind," Preston remarked to the inquisitive cabbie.

Denham leaned in the window, staring intently at Preston. "Defeat is always momentary."

He banged his hand on the roof of the cab and then

the vehicle was moving again. Preston could only stare dumbfounded back at Denham, who stood in the busy midtown traffic, watching him go, like some naval commander on the deck of his ship, ready to fight on no matter the odds.

Frustrated as he was, Preston couldn't help smiling.

3

EVENING WAS COMING ON, the sun setting over the buildings of Manhattan. The clock was ticking . . . and Carl Denham was getting desperate. He had no idea how long he was going to be able to stay ahead of his irate investors. If he'd just run off on his own, they wouldn't have cared, but he'd taken the reels of film that they'd financed and that was not sitting well with them. Chances were they'd already gone to the cops. Worse yet, he'd blabbed about arranging for a ship so he could go and finish the picture in the tropics.

Zelman might not just assume Denham would still be planning to sail, but he had to seriously consider the possibility.

Time was of the essence.

The problem was that Denham already burned precious minutes talking to a couple of casting agents upon whose discretion he knew he could rely, and came up with nothing. No respectable actress was going to just pack up and get on a ship headed out to the high seas or God knew where on a couple of hours' notice, and with no idea what kind of film she was really going to be making. The kind of proposition Denham was offering was sure to raise eyebrows, make any girl think the worst.

But he was now out of options, which meant that in his search for a respectable actress, he'd been forced to abandon both the "respectable" and the "actress." He needed beauty and he needed daring, and if he could get one with a little talent, that would be a bonus.

Denham strode along a busy sidewalk toward the third burlesque theater he'd visited in the past three quarters of an hour, and this one was the tackiest yet. On the wall outside the venue were photos of semi-naked women clad in only feather boas and peacock fans, gaudy banners proclaiming their names. Miss Lily Rose. Delaware Du Boise. Candice.

The sky had grown a bit darker just in the last few minutes. Dusk had seemed to give way to evening far too quickly.

This was it. Now or never.

He paused on the sidewalk and straightened his tie, trying his best to look presentable. Three girls came from the other direction, moving through the bustle of pedestrians. The girls were headed for the theater, obviously performers on their way to work. Denham appraised them quickly, a pair of big women and the third, petite. There was no way Bruce Baxter was going to be able to carry either of the bigger girls for long, so he set his sights on the smaller one. Denham went after them as they entered the theater.

He reached for the door handle . . . but something caught his eye. Denham could see himself in the reflection in the glass door, but behind him, the stream of humanity flowing around her, was another girl. Even in the reflection in that dirty glass, she gave him pause.

Denham turned to look at her, and he had to catch his breath. Her clothes were a bit tatty, but her face was *luminous,* her eyes bright even in the gathering gloom of evening, her golden hair falling around her face as though she was some kind of angel.

Carl Denham wasn't the kind of man who fell in love with any girl he bumped into on the street (although Lord knows there were plenty to go around). If he were honest with himself, Denham would have said he wasn't sure he was the kind of man who fell in love, period. What he saw in this one was something else, that indefinable aura, that spark that certain men and women had that let Denham know that on film, and through the camera's eye, they could be extraordinary.

The girl stood in the middle of the busy sidewalk, entirely unaware that anyone was watching her. She was focused on the burlesque theater, staring grimly at the hoardings, some kind of paper or flyer clutched in her hands. Her exquisite mouth twisted and her eyes gleamed with anger. Abruptly she crumpled the paper in her hands and dropped it in the gutter.

When she started away from the theater, Denham knew he had no choice but to follow.

All that Ann Darrow could think about was that she needed to get as far away from this hole in the wall as possible. There was a small part of her, a little voice inside, that warned her to turn around, to go in and get the job that Mr. Weston had told her about. *Take his advice. Take the money, and then forget all about it.*

She just couldn't.

There had been a lot of girls she had known to whom the leap from vaudeville to burlesque didn't seem very far at all, but to Ann it was the equivalent of vaulting across the Grand Canyon. With the life she'd led, Ann was hardly a prude—sharing a dressing room with dozens of different men and women made such a thing impossible—but she wasn't some floozy either. Ann might never have made it into legitimate theater . . . but there was too much pride at stake. She was an *actress*, dammit, not a burlesque girl. *Never* a burlesque girl.

No matter how loud her stomach growled—and it was indeed deafening tonight, the hunger pangs clutching at her belly—her basic decency just wasn't for sale.

But here she walked away from the burlesque theater and the promise of quick money, utterly directionless. Where was she to go? Any day now she'd be thrown out of the room she'd been staying in. She'd had so little to eat today that her legs were buckling from weakness.

Her eyes narrowed as she saw a fruit vendor's cart on the sidewalk ahead. People swarmed all around it, headed out on the business of their lives, to see family and friends, to dinner or a show, to do all of those things that seemed so foreign to Ann.

She fixed her gaze on an arrangement of semi-ripe apples piled on a tray at one end of the stall, and she thought of Manny, who'd always told her that the first rule of the stage performer's life was "survive . . . just survive."

Her body moved without any further thought, and she began to act. She lifted her chin and *performed,* taking on the role of a woman who was anything but starving, anything but a thief. The vendor was a foreigner, Greek from his accent, and he was hawking his wares to passersby as she approached, making herself appear carefree, just another girl in the throng.

His back was turned. She slowed down, eyeing the fruit. *Now.* Her hand thrust out and she swiped an apple from the tray, then slipped it into her pocket, quickly moving on.

A strong hand gripped Ann's arm. Her heart raced, panic shooting through her. She was spun around as the vendor pulled her hand from her pocket. Her fingers still clutched the stolen apple.

"Are you gonna pay for this?" the swarthy, angry man demanded.

Ann winced from his grip. "Let go of my arm, you ape!"

"You think it is okay to steal from me? Take my apples? Eat my fruit? You know how much money I make this week? Four dollar."

"That's a damn sight more than I have!"

The fruit vendor's hold on her arm tightened, but Ann didn't flinch this time, only stiffened her back and glared at him. She had learned young what it meant to look out for herself.

"What are you, a joker now? Let's see how you laugh when I call the cops!"

A few passersby had stopped to gawk at the scene, but she was used to an audience and refused to even glance at them. Then a man stepped out of the sidewalk traffic toward her and the vendor, a stout, dark-haired man with mischief in his eyes. He held up a nickel.

"Excuse me, ma'am," he said. "I think you dropped this."

The diner was one of a thousand in New York City named after its owner—Charlie's or Mike's or something like that—but Ann had been so distracted by hunger that she couldn't recall what it was. At first she'd been hesitant to accept an invitation to dinner from this Carl Denham character, being suspicious as to his motives, but the truth was he seemed kind enough. Ann's record of judging men's character was spotty at best, but she figured if Denham wanted something in return for covering for her out on the street, and now buying her dinner, he would have asked her back to his place already. That type of guy couldn't hide his nature very well.

And after all, there was that rule of Manny's. Survive.

If he was willing to buy her dinner just to listen to him talk for a while, that was a small price to pay. Her stomach wasn't going to accept any other opinions at this point.

Now she sat at the table with Denham, digging into

the plate of food in front of her, trying to be ladylike in spite of the fact that she was absolutely ravenous.

Denham watched her eat.

"Vaudeville, huh?" he said, picking up the thread of the conversation they'd begun.

Ann nodded, glancing up at him.

"I worked vaudeville once," Denham went on. "It's a tough audience. If you don't kill 'em fast, they'll kill you. Too brutal for me."

"Mr. Denham," Ann said in between bites, "I want you to know I'm not in the habit of accepting charity from strangers, or for that matter, taking things that don't belong to me."

"It was obviously a terrible misunderstanding," Denham said, and his eyes were so sincere she could almost believe he meant it. Except that she was positive it was more that he was simply agreeing with her version of events out of politeness.

"It's just that . . . I haven't been paid in a while," she offered.

Denham regarded her intensely. But then again he seemed the sort of man who brought intensity to everything. She took another bite.

"Tell me, Ann . . . may I call you Ann?" he asked, but didn't slow down to wait for an answer. "You wouldn't be a size four by any chance?"

Ann paused halfway through the mouthful of food she had just taken. Her appetite drained away as a chill passed through her. Apparently her ability to judge men had not improved.

She abruptly stood, her chair squealing against the tiled floor.

Denham's eyes widened in a kind of panic and he gestured as though to halt her. "Oh, no! God, no, you've got me all wrong! I'm not that type of person at all!"

Ann raised an eyebrow. "What type of person *are* you?"

"Someone you can trust, Ann," Denham replied with utter seriousness. "I'm a movie producer."

From his tone, Denham seemed to be expecting the revelation to work some magical transformation on her. But this was one line she had heard before and wasn't impressed.

"I make motion pictures," he forged on. "In fact, I'm making one right now. I'm on the level. I mean it, Ann, no funny business. Sit down, please."

He was just so damned sincere. Reluctantly, she sat back down and drew herself up to the table. There was a wild light in Denham's eyes, and when he spoke, it was as if he was looking right through her at some faraway place Ann couldn't see.

"Imagine if you will a handsome explorer bound for the Far East," Denham began.

"You're filming in the Far East?"

"Singapore," he said idly, then forged on. "On board ship he meets a mysterious girl."

"The size four," Ann wryly added.

"Exactly! She's beautiful, fragile, haunted . . . she can't escape the feeling that forces beyond her control are compelling her down a road from which she cannot draw back. It's as if her whole life has been a prelude to this moment, a fateful meeting that changes everything. And then, sure enough, against her better judgment—"

"She falls in love," Ann put in.

"Yes!" Denham cried, now slightly wild-eyed.

"But she doesn't trust it," Ann said. "She's not even sure she believes in love."

Denham's eyebrows went up. "Oh, really?"

The character Denham described was so much like her at this very moment in her life, and she wondered if he knew it, had concocted the whole thing for that very reason. Or if it was just kismet. And if that was the case, then Ann knew a little something about doubting love.

"If she loves someone," she told him, "it's doomed."

"I see," Denham replied. "Why is that?"

Ann studied his face. "Good things never last, Mr. Denham."

He stared at Ann, as though waiting for her to elaborate, but she was done with that line of conversation.

"Go on," Ann urged. "You were saying?"

"Oh, well, let's see. They're on the boat, they're in the middle of the ocean, when all of a sudden out of the blue, they see an extraordinary sight. Something amazing."

"What?"

Denham hesitated, then gave the tiniest of shrugs. "I don't know, yet. It's still being written. What do you think?"

"Well, I—"

"So you're interested? Good. I don't want to rush you but we're under some time pressure here."

"This person you've described. She's complicated. I don't pretend to understand her, but I do know I'm not the person you're looking for."

Denham pulled a face. "What are you talking about? You're perfect! Look at you, you're the saddest girl I've ever met. You'll make 'em weep, Ann, you'll break their hearts."

She shook her head. "No, see, I make people laugh, Mr. Denham. That's what I do."

And she did it well, of that much she was confident. Love might not last, people might take off when the going got tough, but dammit, you could always count on a laugh.

She stood again.

"Good luck with your pictures."

Ann walked toward the door and Denham followed her, an air of desperation around him now.

"Ann! Miss Darrow, please! I'm offering you money, adventure, fame . . . the thrill of a lifetime and a long sea voyage. You want to read a script? Jack Driscoll's turning in a draft as we speak."

She froze a moment, breath held. It just wasn't possible.

Could the world really be that ironic?

"Jack Driscoll?" she asked, as she turned toward Denham again.

"Sure, why . . . Wait! You know him?"

Okay, fine. She was impressed. "Well, no, not personally. I've seen his plays."

Denham was nodding with enthusiasm. "What a writer, huh? And let me tell you, Ann, Jack Driscoll doesn't want just anyone starring in this picture. He said to me, 'Carl, somewhere out there is a woman born to play this role . . .' "

He hesitated just a second. At first Ann thought he had sensed her interest, realized that Driscoll's involvement had hooked her and was trying to reel her in, but now Denham looked almost wistful.

"And as soon as I saw you," he said, "I knew."

Ann didn't like where this was headed. She'd been hungry and a little directionless, sure, but this was too much, too fast.

"Knew what?" she asked, uneasy.

"You're the one, Ann," Denham said, as though it was some epiphany, as though he really believed it. "It was always going to be you."

And for just that single moment, she could believe it, too.

One moment was enough.

The docks of New York harbor were extraordinary, like a city unto themselves, a veritable anthill of constant activity as ships of every shape and size arrived to be loaded and unloaded, sailors of every race coming and going. The loading cranes towered high above the water, the small waves lapped against the pilings, and the cargo and fishing vessels rolled in their moorings with a stately grandeur.

Then there was the *Venture*.

From the look of the wharf where she was docked,

a casual passerby might think the ship abandoned, perhaps even be surprised to learn it was seaworthy. The *Venture* was a rusty old tramp steamer whose captain and crew came recommended to Denham as men with certain expertise and little inclination to ask questions.

When Denham escorted Ann Darrow along the wharf and they came in sight of the steamer he saw her visibly stiffen when she realized it was their destination.

"Don't let appearances deceive you," he offered. "It's much more spacious on board."

He didn't think the size of the ship was really what had given her pause, but he also did not intend to let her hesitate. Hesitation meant indecision, and indecision meant see you later, Carl, and thanks again for dinner.

Denham's pulse was racing as he hurried with Ann toward the ship. He knew he had been lucky so far. Now he felt like he was holding his breath and wouldn't be able to exhale until they were at sea. Fortunately, Ann didn't mention having any business to wrap up before they left. In so many ways, she was the perfect find. He had set out against all odds to find a girl who'd run off on this mad adventure of filmmaking spectacle with him, with only the vaguest hope that he would be able to get an actress. She'd yet to prove herself in that area, but what the hell. Denham had a feeling about Ann Darrow.

Another girl, one with less gumption, would have

turned tail right then and run, but Ann was a tough kid. He'd seen that right off.

Now the two of them hurried past rough looking sailors working hard to get the boat under way. Activity was everywhere, crates being loaded, along with traveling trunks and all kinds of supplies. Smoke began to pour from the *Venture*'s stacks.

As they approached, Denham saw his assistant, Preston, hurrying down the gangway toward him. He'd expected urgency—had commanded it, in fact—but this was something else. Preston was worried, and that in turn made Denham worried.

They met at the bottom of the gangway. Preston glanced at Ann but didn't take the time for an introduction—a real breach of etiquette from such a well-bred fellow, Denham mused—and pulled his boss to one side.

"They're on their way," Preston urgently whispered. "I've just had word."

"Who?" Denham asked.

"Men in uniform. The studio called the cops."

A flash of fear rippled through Denham. Exactly what he'd been afraid of. And if Preston had a call, that meant they'd already figured out what dock the ship would be sailing from. Denham couldn't risk scaring Ann off, but they were out of time.

A short distance away, Captain Englehorn was supervising the loading of the ship, barking orders at a couple of dockworkers manning a crane. Englehorn was a sturdy-looking, blue-eyed, humorless German.

But despite his reputation as someone not to be trifled with, he was a man who got things done. It wasn't only his hat that identified him as the captain, but a definitive air of command.

"Englehorn!" Denham called, rushing over to him. "Hoist up the mainsail! Raise the anchor! Cast off! We've gotta leave!"

"I cannot do that. We are waiting on the manifest."

"What? In English, please!"

"Paperwork, Mr. Denham," the captain said dryly.

A thin smile came to Denham's lips. He leaned toward Englehorn, conspiratorially close. "I'll give you another thousand to leave right now."

"You haven't given me the first thousand yet."

Again, Denham glanced at Ann, who was observing the proceedings with a dubious expression.

"Can we talk about this later?" Denham remarked. "Can't you see we're in the company of a VIP guest?"

Preston and Ann had been sort of hovering, but now Englehorn turned to greet her.

"Ma'am," the captain said, as gallantly as Denham figured he was able.

"Ann Darrow," she said.

Englehorn regarded her. "So you are ready for this voyage, Miss Darrow? You are not at all nervous?"

Ann offered a small smile. "Nervous? No. Why? Should I be?"

"I imagine you would be terrified," Englehorn said.

Denham felt his pulse hammering at his temples. What was Englehorn trying to do, scuttle the whole trip before they even left the dock? Ann looked both startled and disturbed by the captain's words.

"It isn't every woman who would take such a risk," Englehorn added.

Before the captain could scare her off completely, Denham needed to get her on board. He shot Preston an urgent look.

"Why don't I show Miss Darrow to her cabin?" Preston suggested.

Ann went, though reluctantly. Denham waited a few seconds until she and Preston had started up the gangway, and then turned to Englehorn with a scowl, reaching into his jacket pocket for his checkbook.

"Will you take a check?"

Englehorn's expression was stone. "Do I have a choice?"

Ann felt like Alice through the looking glass. It was as though she had somehow been disconnected from her body, like she was seeing it all as an observer, not a participant. But she *was* a participant, and at her core it thrilled her. Just hours ago, she'd been cast adrift, directionless. Truly alone, with nowhere to go, and with no one who cared what became of her.

As Denham's assistant, who'd introduced himself only as "Preston," led her up the gangway and onto the deck of the *Venture,* sailors stared at them as they passed. Ann knew that she must be strange cargo for these men, unaccustomed as they would be to having a woman on board.

She didn't know if what she felt was fear or exhilaration, but Ann liked the feeling. This might be the best decision of her life, or it might prove the most foolish, but it would undoubtedly be an adventure. And if Denham wasn't an utter charlatan, she would at last speak words written by Jack Driscoll himself.

The fates were conspiring indeed.

4

IT WAS ONLY FRIENDSHIP that brought Jack Driscoll on board the *Venture*. If not for the fact that he loved Carl Denham like a brother, he would have ignored Preston when the kid came around pleading with him for the script. When he'd heard that Carl meant to sail this evening, Jack ought to have just rolled his eyes and washed his hands of the whole film.

But it was Carl after all, and Jack had a hard time saying no to Carl Denham. Everyone did. There was such passion in the man that it was easy to get carried away with his crazy schemes. Carl had vision, that much was true, and he had courage. He would race around the world like Phileas Fogg, and damn the eighty days, he'd do it in half the time . . . or at least boast that he could, and then do his best to make the boast come true.

Jack was the opposite. He was a writer, a thinker. Not that Jack didn't have vision, but he was content to set it down on paper and then let someone else worry about how to bring it to life. Unlike some of the writers he'd known, both in film and theater, he didn't have any interest in directing. To him it was all about telling the story.

Film was intriguing, though. Once he had looked down his nose at the medium, but Carl had changed his way of thinking. Theatre, with its live audience, could not be beaten for intimacy, but with film, a writer could touch people all over the country in a matter of weeks, even days. The appeal was undeniable.

He had first been introduced to Denham years before, when Jack was still a student at Columbia and Carl was just formulating his ambitions as an entertainer, preparing to embark on a trip to Africa as assistant to the director of several films purporting to be about cannibal tribes. Carl had despised the filmmaker for fabricating the cannibal angle just for sensationalism, and Jack had admired him for that. They'd been introduced by George S. Kaufman, a friend of the Driscoll family. A couple of years later Jack was in Berlin and ran into Carl again. As fellow Americans, they had become instant drinking companions for a few weeks, until Carl's next job took him back to the States.

When Jack had returned to New York, he and Denham had renewed their acquaintance. Once, Jack had taken Carl to the Algonquin for drinks with Dorothy Parker and her friends, but Denham had been too much for them, and it had been months before Jack himself was invited again.

He had declined.

There was only so much of the staid, intelligentsia that one man could take, even if he was one of them.

Carl Denham was the antidote.

But sometimes even Denham went too far. Which

was how Jack found himself sitting this very evening in Carl's cabin on board a dilapidated tramp steamer about to set out for God knew where.

He'd been there nearly an hour when the door rattled and then flew open, and Carl entered, looking a bit flustered. The director started a bit when he noticed Jack, put a hand to his chest.

"Jesus, Jack! You scared me!"

Carl crossed to a cabinet against the wall and nervously poured himself a drink. He looked like a man who needed one.

"If anyone comes to the door, don't open it," Carl warned. "You haven't seen me. Say I got depressed and committed suicide. Say I stuck my head down a toilet!"

Jack could only offer a thin smile. For a man with such passion, there were times when Carl didn't inspire much confidence.

The director held up a glass. "You want one?"

"I can't stay," Jack told him. "I have a rehearsal for which I am now . . ." he checked his watch. "Three hours late."

Frustrated, he tossed the few pages of script he'd written onto the table.

"What's this?" Denham asked, picking it up and leafing through it.

"The script."

"This is a script? Jack, there's only fifteen pages here."

"I know. But they're good. You've got fifteen good pages there, Carl."

Denham gave him a dark look. "I'm supposed to be making a feature-length picture."

Jack stared at him. Was this what filmmaking was? Could it possibly be this entirely disorganized, this haphazard? How was he supposed to turn in good work when schedules were changed with such apparent caprice?

"I thought I had more time," Jack told him, resigned. "Look, I'm sorry. You've got my notes."

He started to rise.

"Jack, no!" Denham said. "You can't do this to me! I have a beginning, but I need a middle and an end. I gotta have something to shoot!"

The whole ship rattled as her engines roared to life. Jack could physically feel the distance between himself and the theater where the rehearsal for one of his plays was taking place without him. If the engines were running, that was his cue to finally leave and salvage this evening. He stood up.

"Carl, I've got to go."

Denham looked forlorn and hopeless.

"I've gotta go," Jack repeated.

Denham looked dismayed. Jack just watched him, waiting for the argument that he was sure was coming. But what else did Carl expect? It wasn't like he could dash off the rest of the script in the next few minutes. For a moment it seemed Carl was looking past him, toward the porthole window.

Jack started to turn to see what had caught his attention—

"All right, fine," Carl said, his expression lightening. "We might as well settle up."

Jack was astonished to see Carl pulling out his checkbook. It wasn't like Denham to part with money so easily.

"You're going to pay me?"

"I'm not going to stiff a friend," Carl replied, seeming offended.

"I've never known you to volunteer cash before."

"How does two grand sound?" Carl asked, a magnanimous tone to his voice to mark his sudden largesse.

"Sounds great!" Jack replied. Playwrights weren't much better off than actors in the theater. Two thousand dollars would be a glorious windfall right now.

Carl scribbled out the check and handed it over to Jack with a little flourish. "Voilà!"

Jack glanced at it, and his forehead creased in a frown. "Carl, you've written 'two grand.'"

Denham took the check back from him and examined it, his expression apologetic. "So I did," he said, scrunching it up in his hands. "Let me tear this one up. I'll write you another."

Once again Carl's gaze shifted to that porthole window. Jack barely noticed, focused much more on the money. Carl even said it out loud as he wrote the check this time.

"Two . . . thousand . . . dollars."

As he finished, he glanced toward the porthole again. There was a rumbling and Jack could smell the smoke from the stacks. The engines began to groan, and Jack realized that the ship wasn't just preparing to depart—it was leaving the dock at any moment. He had to get out of here. *Now.*

Carl looked up at him. "What's today's date? The twenty-ninth?"

"Come on," Jack urged. "It's the twenty-fifth."

"Damn," Denham sighed. "Let me just . . . it'll just take a second."

He crushed the second check in his hands. The vibration of the engines increased, the whole ship shaking even harder. Jack shot Carl a withering look.

"Never mind! Pay me when you get back!" he snapped, and he headed for the door.

Carl raised his eyebrows, feigning innocence. "Okay, okay."

Preston knew Bruce Baxter's career as a matinee idol had been fading, but it was only when Baxter actually showed up on the docks, ready to board the *Venture*, that he realized just how much trouble the actor was in. Certainly the man could have gotten work with a major studio picture, but if any of them had hired him to play the type of lead role he had grown accustomed to, he would surely have balked at the abrupt rescheduling of departure for this voyage. For that matter, he would have asked to see a script a long time ago.

Bruce Baxter needed Carl Denham as much as Denham needed him. Preston thought this was a promising arrangement. Baxter was quick-witted, sophisticated, and charming, all of the things a good matinee idol had to be, but he was also used to being pampered. The picture business did that to actors.

So it was up to Preston to at least put on a good

show. "Your cabin's down here, Mr. Baxter. May I say how excited we are to have you back with us, sir?"

Jack Driscoll came sprinting along the corridor, a desperate look in his eyes. The ship's horn blew as the *Venture* began to move out of the docks. Preston thought to introduce Driscoll and Baxter, but the writer seemed wild and unfocused. Jack collided with the actor, then stepped back a pace.

Baxter thrust a suitcase at him, presuming that anyone on board the rusty tramp was subservient to the star. "Be a champion and lend us a hand."

Jack ignored him, instead looking out of the porthole, face etched with desperation. Through the same port, Preston could see that the ship was in motion, the dock sliding by the window.

"Oh, Christ!" Jack snapped.

He doubled back the way he'd come, bolting away as fast as his feet would carry him.

Baxter stared after him, equal parts irked and amused.

"Excellent," the actor said dryly.

Preston gave Baxter a look that said he shared the actor's dismay and puzzlement, then the two of them continued deeper into the ship. He felt he might collapse under the weight of the man's baggage, but made no complaint. Instead, he kept up the steady flow of inane conversation and acclaim, hoping to dull the effect of the moment when Baxter saw the cabin where he'd be staying for weeks.

It didn't help. When Preston opened the door, Baxter wrinkled his nose in distaste and even took half a step back, as though he might retreat. Of course, it was more the smell than the cabin's appearance.

"I know, that's not a nice smell, is it?" he said. He put the bags down quickly, hoping to make good his retreat. "I'm sure it'll disperse in a day or two. Did I ever mention how much I love your work, Mr. Baxter? I'm really quite a big fan. I've seen every one of your pictures, even the silent ones."

Baxter gave him a sour look. "I haven't made any silent ones."

Preston had made it out to the hall, and the actor closed the door in his face.

No, that hadn't gone well at all.

The interior of the ship was nothing short of a labyrinth. When Jack finally extricated himself from it, he practically hurled himself out onto the deck of the *Venture* and ran for the rail.

Where he froze.

The *Venture* had already left the dock.

Seven feet away. Then eight. He had to jump, it was the only way. Jack felt his muscles tense as he contemplated it. Nine feet.

"I keep telling you, Jack, there's no money in theater. You're much better off sticking with film."

He hadn't even heard Denham approach, but he should have smelled the man's pipe. Jack stared at the widening gulf between the ship and the dock, and knew that he had missed his chance to get off. He was going along on this voyage, an indentured servant to his good friend, Carl, with only the clothes on his back and the food of his imagination.

Denham stepped up beside him, one hand on the rail. He wasn't looking at Jack, though. The playwright shifted enough to see that Denham was watching two cars pull quickly up to the dock, passengers quickly disgorging as though they'd intended to be aboard the ship and only just missed it. The first was a police car. The second carried several men in suits, one of whom Jack was almost certain was Mr. Zelman, Carl's chief investor.

Something was going on back there on the dock. None of those men looked very happy. Yet there was something in Carl's face, an odd serenity, that was far more interesting to Jack than the arrival of the police.

"I don't do it for the money, Carl. I happen to love the theater."

"No, you don't."

Exasperated, Jack shot him a look, but Denham just casually tapped his pipe out on the ship's rail.

"If you loved it," Carl said, nodding sagely, "you would have jumped."

Jack sighed and shook his head, despondent, the result of his hesitation really settling in on him now. "I don't have to share with you, do I?" He managed a smile. "I draw the line at sleeping with the director."

5

THE *VENTURE* STEAMED AWAY from the docks, and for a time Jack could not tear his gaze away from the panorama of Manhattan at night. The lights of the city made it seem a wild kind of Shangri-la, a magical city like those in some of the pulp magazines he'd glanced through. Back there, among those lights, was an entire life he was abruptly and unexpectedly leaving behind. The rehearsal for his new play was going to go on without him. He ought to have been furious, and he *was* . . . truly.

But a part of him was anything but angry. Against his will, he was being spirited away on an adventure to a part of the world most men could barely imagine. As a writer, an observer of the human condition, how could he resist?

Jack smiled to himself. *You* can't *resist, Mr. Driscoll. You've been conscripted.*

Carl had gone off for a while, but just as Jack began to wonder where he was supposed to sleep on this rusty tub, and how he was going to survive the trip, the director returned with one of the crewmen in tow. Denham introduced him as Choy, apparently from China, though when the director said so, the sailor made no effort to confirm the fact. Carl simply announced that Choy would take him to his quarters, and that he would catch up with Jack soon. With a final urging to get to work on the script, the director had disappeared into the labyrinth of the ship's interior, and Jack was left to follow Choy.

The sailor would have been a font of information if he could have slowed down long enough to explain half of what he said. Apparently the captain was a gent named Englehorn, and there was a sailor named Lumpy who might or might not have been the cook. This Lumpy was a friend of Choy's, and Choy tended to quote Lumpy as though he had all the wisdom of millennia of seafaring men at his disposal. The man spoke with a thick Chinese accent, but it was the speed and erratic nature of his monologues that confused Jack.

They stopped in some kind of storage area to pick up blankets for Jack, and Choy extolled the virtues of those particular blankets, though to Jack they looked not merely ordinary, but threadbare. Choy, however, insisted they were the softest, warmest blankets on Earth, tempered, as they had been, by years at sea. The sea, according to Choy, made men hard, but made blankets baby soft.

He'd actually said "baby soft," though it was a phrase Jack had only ever read in magazine advertisements.

The sailor was pleasant and enthusiastic company, and though Jack had come to accept his fate, it was due to Choy that his good humor had begun to return.

In the midst of their traversal of the ship, however, he had somehow missed a vital part of the chatter coming from his erstwhile Asian companion's lips.

There was no cabin for Jack. The actors had them, yes. And the director of course. The captain and first mate. Most of the crew bunked together in large rooms. But nobody had counted on having the writer on board.

Jack was still trying to figure out where he was supposed to sleep when Choy led him deeper into the ship, down a long narrow stairwell, and toward the cargo hold.

"This room very comfortable. Plenty dim light. Fresh straw," Choy said, pleasantly.

Jack inhaled and nearly choked on the pungent, musty, animal stink that came from the dark room. Choy searched around the inside of a hatch, looking for a switch. When he found it, light flooded the place.

They weren't just near the cargo hold . . . they were in it. The air was thick and close and the dingy hold was strewn with straw, some of it still bound in bales. All around the hold there were empty animal cages. Jack felt his stomach twist with the stench and he forced himself to breathe through his mouth. He stared at the place in disbelief.

"What'd you keep down here?"

"Lion, tiger, hippo . . . you name it!" Choy proudly said.

Jack examined the nearest cage, then kicked at some of the straw. "Who do you sell them to? Zoos?"

Choy shrugged. "Zoos? Sure, why not?"

Jack started further into the hold and the sailor's benevolent expression turned to one of alarm. Choy reached out an arm to point at the floor beneath Jack's feet.

"Careful! Camel have bad accident on floor. Stain unremovable."

With the sick feeling in his stomach giving another twist, Jack looked down to find he was standing in a dark, viscous puddle of some unidentifiable gunk. He scowled.

"Yeah, zoos . . . circus," Choy went on. "Skipper get big money for rare animal. He do you real good price on rhite whino."

"Choy!" a none-too-friendly voice called, echoing in the hold.

The sailor's eyes went wide and he adopted a too-innocent expression as he turned to face the man who entered the hold. Just from the man's bearing and Choy's response to his arrival, Jack presumed this was the "skipper," Captain Englehorn. The man had a sternness of appearance and a bearing of command that was unrivaled in Jack's experience.

"My apologies for not being able to offer you a cabin," Captain Englehorn said, his mannerism the antithesis of what Jack was expecting. "Have you found an enclosure to your taste?"

Jack almost laughed at the question. The absurdity of it was enough to push his life all the way from drama to farce. They were animal cages. How could any one of them be to his taste?

And yet the truth, hard as it was to take, was that

there was nowhere else. He was stuck on this ship, and they had nowhere else for him to bunk. It was dry, at least, down in the hold, and few would bother him. It would be simple enough to write down here, and Carl's assistant had said there was an old typewriter Jack could use. For a fee, no less.

As a struggling playwright, Jack had slept in dingy rooms before. But never anything like this.

Englehorn surveyed a couple of the larger cages. "What are you, Mr. Driscoll? A lion or a chimpanzee?"

Jack opened the door of the nearest cage that was large enough to sleep in. "Hey, I'll sleep anywhere. This looks like me."

Choy nodded pleasantly. "Yes, warthog very happy there."

Warthog. Jack smiled and took the blankets from Choy, then went to a different cage. He pulled open the cage door and then jumped back in alarm as the jerking of the cage toppled a precariously balanced wooden crate. It thumped to the floor of the hold, and out rolled a large bottle with a medical symbol painted on the side.

Choy leaped away from it as though it might bite him. The bottle was rolling toward the sailor. Coolly, Captain Englehorn trapped it beneath his foot, ceasing its roll.

"I told you to lock it up," Englehorn said to Choy, his gaze dark.

"Sorry, Skipper!" Choy replied, and Jack was sure he sounded scared. "Lumpy said . . ."

"Lumpy doesn't give the orders. What are you try-

61

ing to do? Put the whole ship to sleep? Get it out of here!"

Englehorn picked up the bottle and handed it to the nervous Choy. Only then could Jack read what was written on the side of the bottle.

Chloroform.

Despite assurances to the contrary, Ann's cabin had not been ready when she had come on board. Preston had learned this from a sailor and, despite his obvious frustration, had been polite and diplomatic. Ann was impressed by the director's assistant . . . until he'd left her in the mess room by herself to wait. The business of setting sail had gone on around her and she had fidgeted for what seemed like an eternity before he finally returned.

Now, at last, Preston showed her to her stateroom. But the moment he opened the door for her, the stench from within made her wince and turn her nose away.

"I know. That's not a pleasant smell, is it?" Preston said. He nodded sympathetically. "I'm sure it'll disperse in a day or two. It's really very comfortable."

Ann wrinkled her nose and grimaced, but before she could voice her doubt, he went on. Preston gestured around the room. "Your closet," he said. "Maureen's costumes—"

He was interruptd by a knock at the door and then Denham stepped into the room wearing a magnanimous grin and holding a bottle of Johnny Walker scotch in one hand. With a flourish, as though this was the height of largesse, he thrust the bottle into Ann's hands.

"We can't have our leading lady deprived of the necessities of life," the director declared. Then he turned to Preston. "Do me a favor. Run a bottle down to Jack. It'll fend off his migraine."

Ann looked dubiously at the bottle, bemused by Denham's air of grandeur. She almost missed the significance of his words.

"They're still trying to find a place for him to sleep," Preston replied.

Confused, Ann looked from Preston to Denham.

"Mr. Driscoll . . . ?" she began.

"You told him my typewriter is available for hire?" Denham asked.

"Yes." Preston nodded. "He didn't take it well."

"He's on board?" Ann pressed.

Both men turned to look at her, as if they'd momentarily forgotten they were standing in her stateroom.

Denham once again adopted his magnanimous air. "Jack had his heart set on coming. Call me a softie; I couldn't say no."

Jack Driscoll. On board this ship. Suddenly Ann was more nervous than she had been since the first time she set foot on stage.

It had certainly been the longest and strangest day of Ann Darrow's life. Now she stood on the deck of the *Venture,* gazing at the Statue of Liberty and the lights of New York City as the ship slowly left behind the world she had known. Denham's enthusiasm and wild passion for this endeavor had carried her this far, overcoming her doubts and hesitations. Now that it was all really happening, she could not help feeling that she had shed the old Ann Darrow, husked away the life that had become a diminishing downward spiral of hard luck, and that she was now somehow free.

Whatever lay ahead, Ann yearned for it.

Plus, the thought of eventually meeting *the* Jack Driscoll excited her beyond words.

Silently, she said good-bye to the beautiful nighttime vista of Manhattan . . . even more beautiful *because* she was saying good-bye.

Beside her stood a member of Englehorn's crew, a gruff, odd-looking man whom everyone called Lumpy, and who was, apparently, the cook. He held a clipboard in his hand and in a Cockney accent had been asking her a series of questions, though she still hadn't worked out their purpose.

"Have you ever been seriously stricken with a contagious disease?"

Ann watched the Statue of Liberty shrink, silhouetted against the night. "No."

"Are you subject to fits?"

She glanced at him. "No."

"Do you have body lice?"

"Body lice!" she cried, horrified.

The odd sailor gave an almost imperceptible nod. "Nope." Then he studied his clipboard again. "Are you married?"

"Excuse me?" Ann said, reaching to try to get a look at his checklist.

Lumpy pulled it away and studied her closely. "Are you mentally ill?"

"I'm starting to wonder," she said. "I thought you were the cook."

"Correct, Madam. I am the cook, veterinarian, dentist, barber, and chief medical officer." He thrust the clipboard and pencil out to her. "Stick your moniker here."

Ann signed the form.

"Now," Lumpy said, apparently satisfied, "what can I get you for dinner?"

She found that for the moment she'd lost her appetite.

During her second morning on shipboard, Ann decided she wasn't going to let Carl Denham define her role aboard the *Venture*. The previous day he had come by her cabin twice, first in the morning and then in the evening. During his first visit he'd been at pains to let her know that sailors sometimes had superstitions about having women on board a ship, and that she might find them a little wary around her. On the second, he'd come by to share his enthusiasm about a scene he and Jack Driscoll had worked out that day.

Overall, the message she had gotten from Denham was that she ought to be quiet, keep to herself, and try not to interact with the crew until it came time to shoot the film.

The man just didn't know Ann at all.

Though she had wandered the deck for a time and of course gone to the mess to eat, she'd spent most of the first day trying to clean up her cabin as much as possible. After all, she was going to have to live in that cramped, smelly space for who knew how long.

Today, though, she was going to try to meet as many of the sailors as she could. Though some of the crewmen had given her doubtful looks, a smile and a wave had cleared their faces like a strong wind blowing storm clouds out to sea. These were rough men, and Ann knew she had to be careful, but she came from the theater, from vaudeville. She'd been around rough men all her life, and she knew that their gruff demeanor and often poor manners did not mean they weren't good men. The people on board the *Venture*, both the sailors and Denham's cast and crew, were going to be her family for weeks to come. For better or worse she wanted to know them.

Now, though, she had to rush. Ann wasn't sure how long Lumpy served breakfast, and she wanted to get there before he stopped. Most people, she knew, would not have been so anxious to sample whatever gruel he was dishing out that day, but she had eaten in enough soup kitchens and flophouses, and Lumpy's cooking was no worse.

Ann flung off a tatty old dressing gown and hurried over to the battered suitcase that contained all of her worldly belongings. Denham had taken her to her place by taxi before they went to the docks, and she'd just had time to throw a few things into the case. The couple of dresses she'd left behind were so threadbare as to be unwearable. Nothing else in the rooming house had belonged to her.

She pulled a dress from the suitcase and held it up against herself, checking her reflection in the mirror. Ann scowled. The dress was dowdy and ugly, and frayed at the hem. Awful. Looking at it made her wonder just how terrible the clothes were that she'd left behind, if she'd thought this one good enough to bring along.

Why are you so concerned? she thought. *The sailors aren't going to care if you have a nice dress.*

But the sailors weren't the only men on board. Jack Driscoll was here, too. How many times, reading his words, had she wondered what it would be like to meet him?

She flung the dress away and snatched up the next one, modeling for herself in the mirror. This second one was equally hideous. Frustrated, she let it drop. But as she turned back toward her suitcase again, she remembered the closet where they had stored her costumes for the film.

That is, the costumes of the girl who was supposed to play the part.

Ann smiled and went to the closet, grateful to the actress who had abandoned Denham. She reached in and made some space between dresses so she could get a look at one, then started quickly flicking through the others. The gowns were all glittery and formal, highly theatrical. Absolutely gorgeous, but not at all the sort of thing she could wear wandering around the deck of a tramp steamer.

Then again, compared to her other options . . .

She paused on an elaborate floral chiffon dress that made her smile even wider.

Tempting. *Very* tempting.

6

THE SKY WAS BLUE, morning light washing over the *Venture*, but Denham and Jack walked in shadows on the lower deck.

"Ann Darrow?" Jack asked, brow furrowing. "Who the hell is Ann Darrow? I never heard of her."

Denham's mind had been so occupied with other things—primarily trying to make sure Jack put together a great script for the picture—that he hadn't gotten round to bringing up the casting change before. In his mind, Maureen's quitting had created a problem, and once he'd solved that issue by finding Ann, he didn't have to dwell on it anymore. Ann was more than a solution. He believed she would turn out to be a real discovery. But that was Denham's way: solve a problem, and move on to the next one.

Of course, Jack was a little behind on the news, so Denham had to give him a chance to catch up.

"Well," Denham said, "she's not exactly famous."

"I'm not saying she had to be famous," Jack said, voice tight with frustration as they strode along the deck. "All you had to do was find a real actress!"

Denham would have laughed if he wasn't so irked.

Maybe Jack figured he had a lot riding on this film, on it being good, but did he actually think he cared more about the quality of the picture than the director?

"You haven't even met her. Give her a chance, for Christ's sake!"

They were just outside the mess room, the smells of breakfast wafting through the portholes, when Jack rounded on him.

"Half the theaters in New York are closed. You could have had your pick."

"Ann's from the theater!" Denham argued.

"Vaudeville," Jack said, like the word was a curse. "Give me a break! How do you expect me to write for a glorified chorus girl?"

Denham stiffened. "I cast Ann because she's special. She's right for this part."

Jack regarded him evenly. "That's what you said about Dolores. The blonde? You remember her, the one who couldn't act? She was in your last picture."

All right, so that part was true. But Jack was jumping to conclusions, now.

"That's a low blow, Jack. I learned my lesson. This is strictly on the level. There's not gonna be any funny business."

Jack shook his head as he pulled open the mess door. "Whatever you say, Carl. Just as long as she reads the lines."

The mess room was comparatively quiet when they entered. Most of the crew had already come and gone, though a few sailors were still finishing breakfast. Lumpy was still keeping some porridge hot, stirring it

69

from time to time, but he was doing double duty as cook and barber. He had a sailor Denham believed was called Judah in a chair and had lathered up the man's face for a shave. The incongruity of the two activities didn't seem to faze Lumpy or the other crewmen in the least.

Denham just took note, amused, and then went to a table where his film crew was assembled. Herb and Mike had been with him for years and over the course of several pictures. As far as Denham was concerned, they were true professionals. Herb was a genius with a camera, willing to hang from a tree, or to trust Denham's word that the animal wranglers wouldn't let the lion get too close. He was getting up there in age, but still capable. In his round glasses, bow tie, and wool cap, he looked more like someone's favorite uncle than a world traveler. Mike, the sound man, was younger and thinner than Herb, and more vocal. But Denham didn't mind his mutterings if it meant the job would get done well.

Preston hung back from the table just a bit. The kid had been with them for a while now, but still didn't seem to feel quite a part of the group. Denham wished he would just get over it, realize it was his own self keeping that distance. Something to do with Preston growing up rich, he assumed. Wealthy people always assumed folks with no money had a grudge against them. The funny thing was, the people with no money didn't have the luxury of holding grudges.

Jack and Denham wished everyone good morning, but then Jack went off to the other side of the mess room to examine the porridge and to fetch himself a cup of coffee. As Jack passed him, Lumpy started sharpening his straight razor, getting ready to shave Judah.

At the table, Mike adjusted his glasses, then started packing away his headphones and sound recording equipment. He'd been giving it the once-over, making sure it was all in working order, a stickler about keeping his equipment in perfect condition.

But Denham saw the way Herb and Mike were looking at each other; there was some unpleasantness there. Denham glanced at Preston, who gave a small shake of his head, as if to say he didn't know what to do about the problem. Denham, though, just wanted to know what the problem was.

"Mike?" he asked.

That was all it took. The sound man started in, complaining about the difficulties of recording on board the ship, particularly while it was moving. Denham tried to soothe him, but Mike had obviously built up a good head of steam on his pique, and he wasn't going to listen to platitudes. He wanted to know how Denham expected him to get quality recordings. At first the director was sympathetic, trying to be supportive, but that evaporated quickly.

"I'm gonna have the ship's engines all over the dialogue," Mike snapped. "Sea gulls, camera noise, wind, and Christ knows what!"

Denham didn't like being snapped at. "I don't care, Mike. You're the sound recordist, make it work!"

Out of the corner of his eye, he saw something pink.

Pink was a color that just didn't belong on this dingy, rusty steamer, and he glanced up curiously to see Ann standing in the doorway of the mess in a chiffon dress, clutching a handbag. She looked so out of place, and yet no more so than an angel come to Earth.

She hesitated, but Denham raised a hand and signaled for her to join them.

"Ann, come on over," he said.

With a smile, she entered, the dress flowing around her. All of the sailors looked up, but no one said a word.

"Let me introduce you to the crew," Denham said, knowing she would understand that he meant the film crew, not the ship's. "This is Herbert, our camera man."

Preston appeared behind her and pulled out a chair for her to sit, even as she shook Herb's hand. Denham had to say one thing for Preston: growing up with money had given the kid manners.

"Delighted to meet you, ma'am," Herb said. "And may I say, what a lovely dress."

Ann smiled and plucked at the dress, swaying a bit. "Oh, this old thing? I just . . . threw it on."

Preston leaned in toward Denham, the two of them watching Ann. "Isn't that one of Maureen's costumes?"

Ann overheard, apparently, and hurriedly changed the subject, glancing around. "What does a girl have to do to get breakfast around here?"

Denham grinned. "Lumpy, you heard the lady!"

Lumpy looked up from his dual duty, shaving the sailor with one hand while giving the porridge a stir with the other. "Porridge aux walnuts," Lumpy declared. Denham looked on in amazement. It was like some kind of twisted circus act.

When he glanced back at Ann, he found her staring at Mike. The sound man had taken out a notebook and was scribbling in it, working out some of his recording issues, no doubt. He had his head down, so focused that he hadn't bothered to look up when their guest joined them.

"Ann," Denham began, "I don't believe you've met—"

"It's all right, Mr. Denham," she said, all sweetness and light. "I know who this is . . ."

The way she was beaming, and the touch of quiet awe in her voice, confused the heck out of Denham for a few seconds. Then he saw the way she looked at Mike's notebook, the admiration in her eyes, and he put the pieces together.

Mike nervously glanced up at Ann.

"How do you like your eggs?" Lumpy called.

"Scrambled," the vaudeville girl said, completely deadpan. "No stubble."

Denham started to slowly shake his head. He glanced over at Jack, who was leaning against the counter and sipping from his coffee cup, watching the whole thing.

Ann reached out and took Mike's hand, giving it a vigorous shake.

"Thrilled to meet you," she said. "It's an honor to be a part of this."

Mike gave her a bewildered smile. "Gee, thanks."

"Actually, I am quite familiar with your work."

"Really?"

Denham winced and glanced at Jack, trying to figure out if it was too late for him to say something to prevent this from skidding out of control into utter embarrassment. He started to speak, but Ann wasn't paying any attention to him. Her focus was Mike, and that notepad.

"The thing that I most admire is the way you have captured the voice of the common people."

"Well, that's my job," Mike replied.

"I'm sure you've heard this before, Mr. Driscoll, but if you don't mind me saying, you don't look at all like your photograph."

Mike raised his eyebrows. "Excuse me?"

Denham couldn't let it go on any longer. "Wait a minute!" he said. "Ann—"

"Well, he's so much younger in person," she plowed on, giving a coquettish glance at Mike. "And much better looking."

Again, Denham winced, but at the same time he couldn't stop the quiet little chuckle of disbelief that rose in his throat, as he wondered what Ann would do when she realized she was flirting with the sound guy.

Jack started walking toward the table.

"Ann!" Denham said. "Stop! Stop right there—"

Mike wasn't even looking at her anymore. He was staring past Ann at Jack, who came up to stand beside Denham. Ann, though, just pressed on, unaware.

"I was afraid you might be one of those self-obsessed literary types. You know the tweedy twerp with his head in a book and a pencil up his—"

Jack interrupted with a cough.

Startled, Ann turned around. The realization hit her face like a bolt of lightning—Denham saw it all pass across her eyes in an instant. Ann made a kind of terrible groan and just stared at him.

"You must be Ann Darrow," Jack said.

She looked like she wanted to throw herself overboard.

On the lower deck of the *Venture*, Ann leaned on the railing and gazed at the churning ocean below. The thought of throwing herself overboard *had* occurred to her, but not in any serious way. She was too busy wondering if she was going to vomit, and all trace of strength had gone out of her limbs, so that she couldn't even have climbed the railing at the moment.

Preston had followed her out of the mess—and what a mess it was—and out to the railing. He hovered nearby, a comforting presence, as though he wished to cure her ills. Ann only wished he could.

"Help me, Preston," she said. "How do I get off this boat?"

"It didn't go *that* badly," he replied. Ann admired his ability to lie with such sincerity.

"It was a disaster."

"Jack's a writer," Preston said. "He's used to all kinds of personal abuse."

Ann looked at him doubtfully.

Preston gazed at her as though he was the most reasonable man on the planet. "He'll come round. Trust me."

* * *

Jack did not sleep well on board the *Venture*. Each time he woke in the darkness to find himself wrapped in blankets on a bed of straw inside a cage, it took him several moments to remember that this was not some vivid and horrible dream. The first night had been the worst. But after a couple of days, he found himself strangely quiescent about the entire thing. Jack had always secretly wished to go along with Carl on one of his great adventures, but had never been able to bring himself to ask. He was always busy with the life he'd made in New York, locked inside his mind with all the doleful observations about the state of the world that made their way into his plays.

Now that he was on this voyage, however, he knew there was nothing to be gained by trying to fight it. All of his responsibilities were back in New York. His only duty now was to make the most of his predicament, which meant working with Carl to make the best film possible. They had always talked about such a collaboration, but even when Carl had asked him to write this script, Jack had never imagined something like this.

So this morning he had woken with a changed attitude toward his circumstances. But soon after, his brighter outlook had been rewarded with the rise of the ocean, churning waves that rocked the ship roughly and knotted Jack's stomach with barely controlled nausea. He felt weak and pale, and from time to time his throat worked to keep the bile down, one more roll of the sea away from sending him into a corner to be sick.

Somehow, he managed to type.

Denham had brought him the typewriter, and Jack

had found that focusing on his friend and the familiar activity of tapping away at the keys, at feeding paper into the machine and hitting the return, helped to keep his mind off the rough seas and soothed his roiling guts just a bit.

On the bright side, Jack had gotten used to the animal stink of the cargo hold. He figured that meant he probably now smelled equally bad, but still chose to consider it a benefit.

Now Carl paced back and forth across the hold, puffing on his pipe, eyes glittering with the childlike excitement that had first endeared him to Jack years ago.

"We're killing off the first mate?" Carl asked.

Jack grimaced. "That's assuming she knows who the first mate is."

"Come on! It was an honest mistake. Ann's short-sighted. It could happen to anyone."

"Carl, I was joking."

"It's no joke, Jack," Carl said grimly. "Do you know how much Bruce Baxter cost me? Let's just call it a flesh wound." The director started pacing. "The point is, she's horrified! She's has to look away, and that's when she sees it: the island!"

Confusion overwhelmed Jack's queasiness. He stared at Carl. "We're filming on an island now? When did this happen? What's it called?"

"Keep your voice down!" Denham snapped in low rasp. "We're surrounded by sailors . . . they're very superstitious. I don't want the crew getting spooked."

Jack narrowed his eyes, studying Carl. "What's wrong with this place?"

A distant, sort of shifty look came over Denham's face. "There's nothing officially wrong with it because technically it hasn't been discovered yet."

Frustrated, Jack gave him a hard look.

"All right," Carl said with an air of surrender. "It has a local name, but I'm warning you, Jack, it doesn't sound good . . . Skull Island."

The cage doors swung and all the ropes hanging in the hold swung with each roll of the waves. Jack's insides twisted and he tried to force them to be still.

Before he could get any more information out of Carl, they had a visitor. Jimmy. The kid was maybe sixteen years old, the youngest member of the crew, and had introduced himself to Jack at breakfast, back before the idea of eating anything had become repulsive to him.

Jimmy walked into the hold carrying a tray that held bowls of some gray-looking stew, one each for Jack and Carl. He wore that navy blue cap that always seemed too big for his head and a kind of lost look that never left his face.

"Compliments of the chef," the kid said earnestly. "Lamb brains in walnut sauce."

He set a bowl next to Jack, who took one look at it—the kid's description of it still echoing in his ears—and squeezed his eyes closed, lips tightly shut as though that could keep the vomit down.

"Fend it off, Jack!" Carl instructed, seeing his distress. "You can make it to the end of the scene! Focus! Focus!"

Jack didn't know if Carl was really trying to help

him avoid getting seasick, or if he just wanted work done on the script. He chose to believe it was a combination of the two.

"Okay . . . all right," Jack managed. He started typing again. "We're sailing towards this place. S-K-U-L-L . . . Island."

Even as he said it, he realized what he'd done and looked up to see Carl glance nervously at Jimmy, who'd clearly heard and was intrigued.

"Let's stay with the action, Jack," Carl said quickly. "The first mate, he's been stabbed . . . he's screaming . . ."

"Screaming," Jack repeated. "Yes. He sinks to his knees."

"There's blood everywhere, lots of blood . . ." Carl prodded. "Can you write it?"

Jack started to nod, but then a small voice spoke up.

"When a man's knifed in the back, there ain't much blood," Jimmy said, and it was the sincerity in his voice that haunted Jack. Not just the knowledge, but the very ordinariness of the way he said it, like the average teenage boy talking about baseball.

"And he doesn't scream," the kid went on. "The only sound he makes is a rush of air, like when you puncture a ball. He drops fast, like a stone. It's the shock."

Quietly, Denham said, "It's just a movie, kid."

Jimmy was unfazed. "There's no such thing as a slow death, see? Not at the end. At the end it's always fast. The light in a man's eyes . . . one minute it's there and then it's gone. Nothing."

Jack and Denham stared at the kid. Jimmy's eyes were cool and expressionless.

"Just so you know," he said, and then he turned and walked out of the hold, leaving them staring after him.

The words haunted Jack, and the kid's matter-of-fact tone. Denham looked worried.

"We don't have to be factually accurate . . . do we?" the director asked.

The days passed, and the *Venture* steamed on, blessed with blue skies and calm seas rarely marred by a passing rain. Despite the hurriedness of their departure and the overcrowding on shipboard, Ben Hayes had never been on a voyage that had begun so well.

He didn't like it one bit.

Hayes was superstitious and suspicious by nature, a man who was used to having to bring order to chaos. So much so that it made him nervous when there was no chaos to make orderly. As first mate of the *Venture*, he demanded perfection from the crew, and more often than not, they delivered.

The military had drummed that into him. He'd once overheard a sailor who'd had too much to drink telling another crewman that he thought "the war made Mr. Hayes mean and he got all his anger bottled up."

The unwashed, grizzled seaman had been correct, to a point. But it wasn't his military service that had fueled Ben Hayes's anger. No, it was what had come after, and he was just furious at himself for hoping that there was justice in the world. From all he'd learned from his father and grandfather, Hayes had come to believe that the Great War would be like all those before it. In each war, his elders had told him, black men had fought alongside white men, and the trials they faced together had slowly eroded some of the hate and fear between races. In each war, black men had gained ground.

Not so in this war. Ben Hayes's war. The Great War had been a step back. And when he'd come home, expecting to feel some of that change that his father had promised, it had been in the wrong direction. The white men in his community had gone out of their way to remind him what he wasn't, to grind the pride he felt at having served into the dirt, along with his face.

One man in particular . . . well, if Ben Hayes hadn't taken to the sea, he was sure he would have had blood on his hands. He would have turned himself into a murderer, and would've ended up on the end of a hangman's noose for his crimes.

The only option he could see at the time was escaping, leaving America entirely. He set foot on American soil only when he was forced to by necessity, go gather supplies for a new voyage and load them. His family had tried to tell him that he had to keep fighting, but he had been in a real war, and understood when it was time to lay down his arms. He'd left them behind. Left it all behind.

And never looked back.

Hayes now put all of his energy into his duties on board the *Venture*. He was at his best when things were at their worst, which was why the calm seas and perfect days had troubled him. Even today, the ship steamed through placid waters, everything quiet enough that he'd seen men napping on the deck when not on duty.

He'd known it was all too good to be true.

When Hayes reached Captain Englehorn's cabin, he found the man relaxing, a piece of German music playing on the grammophone. Hayes strode into the room, charts in his hands and laid them out in front of him—he'd just come from the wheelhouse, and didn't like what he'd found. Englehorn was immediately at full attention.

"This heading puts us southeast of Sumatra," Hayes said, not bothering to hide the accusation in his tone.

"It's a new course, Mr. Hayes."

"It takes us outside the shipping lanes."

"What of it?"

Hayes stared at Englehorn, but the captain levelly met his gaze. There was no escaping the obvious—the further from traditional shipping lanes they strayed, the more difficult it would be to find help if they ran into trouble with weather or the engines.

The captain was smarter than that. Which begged certain questions.

"Captain, seven vessels have been lost in those waters."

"Lost in what?" Englehorn scoffed. "A bank of fog? A sea mist? I don't believe in fairy stories."

Hayes threw the chart on the table, trying to hold his anger in check. "How much did he pay you?"

A cloud passed over Englehorn's face. When he spoke, his voice was quiet. "That's enough, Ben."

Hayes grabbed him by the arm. "How much to compromise the safety of your ship and crew?"

Englehorn's eyes were like ice. "There are dangers in any job. More so for those who go to sea. That's how it is."

Hayes stared at him for a long moment, and then released him in disgust.

"Whatever you got," the first mate said, "I hope it was worth it."

For the first time that he could remember, Ben Hayes turned his back on his captain. He strode from the cabin without looking back, trying to remember his duty and why he had left America. He still believed Englehorn was a man of honor, but even such men could make mistakes.

He stormed down the gangway and out onto the deck. Fuming, he stopped at the railing and tried to let the sea calm him. As he stood, trying to regain his composure, Jimmy walked by him, carrying some thick ropes. He thought it was possible that the boy picked up his pace a little, not wanting Hayes to engage him. Normally, Jimmy wanted nothing more than to talk to the first mate, so Hayes wondered what the hurry was.

Then he remembered.

"Jimmy!" he called. "You got something for me?"

The boy froze, hesitated a moment, then reluctantly fished a battered school exercise book out of his back pants pocket. Hayes took it from him and flipped through the pages, noting that Jimmy's childlike scrawl had actually improved somewhat. In addition to what he'd written, the kid had pasted some pictures ripped out of magazines into his report.

"What do I always tell you?" Hayes demanded, looking him over.

"Do your best," Jimmy practically mumbled.

"And this is your best?"

"It is," the kid said, lifting his chin in defiance.

"So you've been practicing?"

"Yes, Mr. Hayes," he said, and then glanced away. The boy was lying, and it was clear he had just realized he'd been caught at it.

"Then where's the poem I set you to learn?"

Jimmy tried to weasel out of it. "What poem would that be?"

"The poem by Rupert Brooke. You were supposed to copy it out."

The kid had mutiny in his eyes. "What's the point? It's just a bunch of flowery words. It doesn't mean nothin'!"

Furious, Hayes cuffed him on the side of the head. "Brooke died a soldier, boy! Show him some respect!" he barked. And then he saw the hurt in the kid's eyes, and softened a bit. "Look, you don't want to be on this ship for the rest of your life."

Jimmy stared at him. "I do."

"No, you don't, Jimmy. You want to get yourself educated, give yourself some options. You've got to take this serious."

"I do, Mr. Hayes! I do! I been readin'."

Jimmy pulled a battered book out of his coat pocket. Hayes frowned and took it from him. There was a painting on the cover of a tramp steamer, along with the title and the author. *Heart of Darkness* by Joseph Conrad.

Hayes felt his chest tighten. "Where did you get this?"

"I borrowed it."

Hayes flipped the book open and saw a stamp on the interior of the cover. "Property of the New York Public Library."

"On long-term loan," Jimmy went on, carefully. "Have you read it, Mr. Hayes?"

"Yeah," Hayes said, chilled. "I've read it."

Jimmy pointed to a line printed on the back of the book. " 'Adventures on a Tramp Steamer,' see? Just like us."

Hayes handed the book back. "No, Jimmy," he said quietly. "Not like us."

He sure as hell hoped not.

7

CARL DENHAM WAS IN his glory. He stood on the deck of the *Venture* and watched another world come to life in front of him. The ocean was so calm it was like sailing across glass, the sky perfectly blue and the sunlight at just the right angle to give his actors the glow of ruddy health without washing them out on the black-and-white film.

Herb was the camera man, but often enough Denham took over the duty. At the moment he was behind the camera, with Herb on one side of him and Mike on the other, recording the sound track. Preston and Jack were around somewhere nearby, but Denham had nearly forgotten they existed. The only thing that mattered now was what was happening in front of the camera.

He marveled at the quiet on the deck. There were sailors gathered at a safe distance, observing the proceedings, but they were being remarkably silent. It pleased him profoundly. They all felt it—the magic of filmmaking.

In the frame, Ann leaned against the rail and gazed longingly out to sea. In full makeup and with her hair done, she looked absolutely, staggeringly beautiful. Even without all of the fuss, she was stunning, but that was the thing that made Ann Darrow the perfect subject for his camera: despite her breathtaking natural beauty, she had no idea how gorgeous she was. That lack of awareness gave her face a life and truth all its own.

On cue, Bruce sauntered up to her, every inch the matinee idol he had become.

"I think this is awfully exciting," Ann said. "I've never been on a ship before."

Denham silently cheered her. *That's it, kid, prove Jack Driscoll wrong.*

"I've never been on one with a woman before," Bruce replied.

Denham frowned. That wasn't the line. He imagined Jack wincing.

"I guess you don't think much of women on ships, do you?" Ann asked.

"No, they're a nuisance."

Bruce shook his head, breaking out of character. "That was applesauce. That last line . . . it ain't working." He looked at the director. "Denham, I got an idea. Let's go again."

Denham glanced over at Jack and saw the pained expression on the writer's face. Jack would hate it—the writers always did—but he needed to get through the scene, and if that meant letting Bruce switch some words around, he'd give it a try.

"All right, everyone," Denham said, "from the top."

"I think this is awfully exciting," Ann said, beginning the scene again. "I've never been on a ship before."

"It's a dangerous thing, having girls on ships," Bruce said, in character. "They're messy and they're unreliable."

Denham could practically hear Jack sigh, but he kept the camera rolling.

"Well, I'll try not to be," Ann replied, going with the line Jack had scripted for her.

"Just being around is trouble," Bruce said.

Ann flinched. "Well! Is that a nice thing to say!" Her tone changed, then, to a sweetness that had claws. "Why, I simply oughta knock your teeth down your gullet and learn you some real manners."

"Oh, you're all right," Bruce continued improvising, "but women, they just can't help being a bother. Made that way, I guess."

"Cut!" Denham called. He wasn't sure who was more likely to give Bruce a rap in the jaw, Ann or Jack, but if he let this go on much longer, they'd have to stand in line behind him.

"Great!" he said. "Wonderful work. Ann, stay right where you are. We'll move on to your close-up. Preston, get the filter box from my cabin. Bruce, my friend . . . you can take a break."

"What do you think, Driscoll?" the actor asked, sauntering over to Jack. "The dialogue's got some flow now, huh?"

"It was pure affluence," Jack said dryly.

"I beefed up the banter," Bruce replied.

Jack gave him a blank look. "Try to resist that impulse."

Denham wondered if he would have to step in. Bruce puffed up a bit.

"Just a little humor, bud," the actor said. "What are you, Bolshevik or something?"

When Bruce turned and walked off, Denham breathed a sigh of relief.

Jack shot him a look of utter frustration. "Actors! They travel the world but all they ever see is a mirror!"

Just a few feet away, Ann had been checking her makeup in a compact mirror. Jack clearly hadn't intended the comment for her, but she snapped the mirror shut and marched off, obviously offended. The two men watched her go. Denham knew he had to call her back. They had work to do. But he figured they'd all be better off with a few minutes to cool down.

Lumpy and Choy stood together beside the funnel, looking down on the proceedings on the deck. For a working-class dog like Lumpy, it was a strange sight indeed. He liked the movies well enough, he supposed, but to see it all happening in front of him . . . well, it looked an awful lot like just playing around. It wasn't real work, was it? No, not at all.

Still, there was something entrancing about it. And not just Miss Ann Darrow, either, though she was enough of an enchantment. Lumpy envied that Bruce Baxter. He figured it was probably Baxter's work in *Tribal Brides of the Amazon* that had gotten him this part, but what did Lumpy know? He had to admit, though, that Baxter seemed pretty good at his job. According to Judah and Toad, the guy knew how to tie a mean knot as well, so they had to respect him for that.

"What do I need to do to become a matinee idol?" he whispered.

Choy looked at him with grave sincerity. "Develop your chest an' you get body to be proud of. You get prettiest girl."

Bewildered, Lumpy looked at him. Choy grinned and pulled a battered Charles Atlas bodybuilding pamphlet from his pocket.

"Big muscle development. All over the beach," Choy assured him.

Lumpy shook his head. He never failed to be amazed by how enthusiastic Choy was about everything. Peeling potatoes and cleaning toilets were thrilling work, as far as Choy was concerned. His friend didn't like to talk about it, but Lumpy figured it went back to Choy's childhood in Northern China, when the warlords in that part of the country were under constant attack, slaughtering each other and being massacred by the armies of the southern government almost every day. Horrific stuff, but Choy was always in such a sunny mood. Lumpy had decided it was because compared to the things he had seen growing up, anything else was paradise—Choy had once said that he knew he was lucky, that he should have been dead, and anything was better than where he had come from.

"Choy," Lumpy said, "you are not and never will be Charles Atlas."

"This only day three!" Choy explained. "On day seven, I am a man!"

Lumpy could only grin.

*　　*　　*

Jack had watched the scene with trepidation, and now he was torn. Ann had cleverly surprised him—she had a lot of natural talent, and seemed to know just how far to push it for the camera. Baxter, on the other hand . . . now *that* was an ego to deal with there.

Ann had already returned, fully composed, ready for work. Denham was busy setting up for her close-up.

"Where do you want me?" she asked Denham, moving to a mark on the deck. "Here?"

Denham had the camera again and was peering through the viewfinder. "A little more to the left."

Jack had to move out of the way as Ann took up her new mark. He stepped back to give her room but she didn't so much as glance at him.

"That's good, Ann. Hold it there," Denham instructed.

"I have a question about the script, Mr. Denham," she said, ignoring Jack completely, despite the subject of her question. "If this is the beginning of a love story—"

Jack frowned. "Hold on a second. It's not a love story."

Ann raised an eyebrow but continued to ignore him.

"Jack doesn't do love stories," Denham told her. "He writes serious drama."

"That's not true. I can do love. I've done love. I've painted the stage with love!" Jack felt foolish the moment the words were out of his mouth, but there was no taking them back.

What was it about Ann Darrow that made him feel it was so important to say the right thing? She'd been insulting since the moment they'd met—though accidentally and charmingly so—and in the days since, they'd barely seen one another. He hadn't gone out of his way to be in her company, but when he had been there was a strange tension between them. He felt like there was something he needed to say to her. Could even feel his lips start to form words . . . but for once he had no idea what those words ought to be.

The strangest part was that whenever he saw her, he could swear she was feeling the same thing. It was frustrating, and it made being around her a test of aggravation.

Ann raised her chin, still focusing on Carl. "My point is, Mr. Denham, if he's so interested in her, why doesn't he want her around?"

"That's the thing," Carl explained. "He's attracted to her, but he doesn't want to show it."

Jack shook his head. "That's not the thing. That's not the thing at all!"

For the first time, Ann turned to look at him. "He's not attracted to her?"

"No," he said quickly. Then he gave a small nod. "Well, yes. He is. She's very . . . she's beautiful."

Her eyes were locked on his. Jack felt himself flush.

"And that's all she has to offer?" Ann asked. "I thought there was more to her than that, but perhaps I've read it wrong."

"No," Jack said quietly, almost mesmerized. "I think I wrote it wrong."

* * *

Preston rushed along the gangway to Denham's cabin, flung the door open, and hurried to a large trunk that stood against one wall. The director was caught up in the creative energy of making the film—the very intensity that had drawn Preston to want to work for him in the first place—but he couldn't find the filter box that he needed for the camera.

One day, hopefully soon, there'd be someone else working with them, some young guy with stars in his eyes, eager to run and get coffee, or filter boxes, just to have a chance to work in the pictures. When the time came, Preston hoped to be a more active part of the process, maybe shooting some of the footage himself, and actually working with the actors. But for now, he was Denham's personal assistant, and that meant doing whatever was necessary to help Carl get the job done.

He opened the trunk and started rapidly digging through it. Old scripts, outdated copies of *Variety,* story boards, empty whiskey bottles, reels of film, head shots of actors . . .

Preston frowned and stopped rummaging. There was something odd in the trunk, rough folded parchment paper that seemed like it would fall to pieces if he wasn't careful. He pulled the battered paper out.

Carefully he opened it fully before him and stared at it, puzzled.

It was a crudely drawn map. An island . . .

He instinctively turned it over to look at the back. Here someone had scrawled words, fragmented sentences in a spidery handwriting.

Whatever this was, Denham had never mentioned it. The parchment felt heavy in his hands. Preston studied the words, trying to read the scrawl, and as he worked out what some of them were, a chill danced up the back of his neck while his mouth dropped open.

His astonishment was interrupted by the sound of loud footsteps out in the hall. With a glance toward the door, Preston hurriedly stuffed the map into his pocket, even as Denham stormed into the room.

"Did you find it?"

Preston's heart skipped a beat. "What?"

"The filter box?" Denham prodded. Then he rolled his eyes. "Never mind. It's over here."

He grabbed the filter box from a shelf and Preston stood, watching him warily. When Denham gave him an impatient look and strode out, returning to the deck that was their impromptu film set, Preston sighed with relief.

But his mind was awhirl with dreadful curiosity. For now he had to follow the director, but later he would take a better look at that map.

The film crew finished shooting Ann's close-up and were setting up for another scene—a good time for her to take the opportunity and locate the nearest bathroom. As she made her way along one of the many interior corridors of the labyrinthine ship, Jack Driscoll rounded a corner up ahead of her, coming her way.

There was a moment in which they both hesitated. Ann noticed it only because she was just as guilty of the temptation to flee as Jack. They kept on toward one another and she tried to think of what to say, some meaningless pleasantry to pretend the butterflies in her stomach weren't real, that the tension between them didn't exist.

The sea had been calm all morning, but they must have been entering rougher seas, for the ship gave a sudden roll, the whole vessel swaying.

Jack was thrown forward, but Ann held her balance just fine.

"Good legs," he said.

She shot him a sharp look.

Jack colored. "Sea legs, I meant. Not that you don't have good legs. I was just . . ."

He let his words trailed off as she turned to edge past him in the corridor, not bothering to respond to his rambling.

". . . making conversation," he finished, when she was past him. Then he raised his voice. "Jesus! Miss Darrow!"

Ann was surprised at the intensity in his tone. She'd learned rather quickly that Jack was a thinker, and that was where his passion lay. But now she stopped and turned, wondering at his outburst.

"About the scene today," he began, "with you and Bruce—"

Of course. He wanted to talk about his words.

"I know," she said, working both an apology and a bit of disdain into her voice. "It wasn't what you wrote. But Mr. Baxter felt very strongly that if a man really likes a woman, he ignores her, and if things turn really hostile . . . then it must be love."

She gave Jack a pointed look, but it was obviously lost on him.

"Hmm. Interesting theory . . . not quite what I had in mind."

"I'm sorry, I should have . . ." she began, but then paused. What should she have done? Insisted that Bruce stick to the script as written? Surely, that was someone else's job. Mr. Denham's, or Jack's. If words were all he cared about . . .

"I was just very nervous," she managed, wondering why she felt the need to make excuses at all.

But then he looked at her, searching her eyes, and there was charm and warmth there that seemed uncharacteristic for Jack Driscoll. Ann liked that. She liked it very much. Too bad she had made such a mess of things when she'd met him. Ann had daydreamed about what it would be like to meet Jack Driscoll, how perfect it would be, but fate had obviously had other plans.

"Well," he said, looking at her with a kind of curiosity, as if she was some kind of animal he'd never seen before, "it wasn't what I intended. But you made it your own. It was funny, actually. *You* were funny."

Ann gave the tiniest of shrugs. "Yeah, but you meant for it to be serious."

"I have a tendency to do that."

"Mister Driscoll, you don't have to say anything."

Jack looked at her closely. "You don't have to be nervous."

His voice was barely above a whisper, so gentle that it froze her in place. The air between them seemed to crackle with electricity. Ann searched his eyes. There was something there, and it drove her crazy that she didn't know what it was. The man infuriated her and compelled her all at the same time.

He had to know, didn't he? Had to realize from the way she'd behaved that she had created this whole story in her mind, this whole idea of how this journey was going to unfold? Her great adventure at sea with Jack Driscoll, whose words had created such passion in her.

And now she'd discovered Jack Driscoll was just a man. An ordinary man, who hid whatever passion he had behind veiled eyes and dry intellect. And she herself had been revealed to be nothing more than a fanciful, dreaming girl.

Did he really understand all of that? How humiliated she felt?

"I guess . . ." she began, and then faltered. Ann shook her head, feeling the absurdity of it. But there was kindness in his gaze, and that drew the truth from her. "I just had this stupid idea that maybe, this one time, things would actually work out. Which was really very . . ."

A tremor went through her.

". . . foolish."

She saw Jack, noticed the way he was looking at her, felt that charged air between them again, and a realization went through her.

Maybe she hadn't been as foolish as she'd feared.

8

THE NEXT FEW DAYS passed pleasantly enough, though for Jack, living on shipboard was taking more than a little getting used to. As a playwright, he was certainly not rolling in money, but he'd done well enough that living in Manhattan was a pleasure. There were thousands of restaurants in the city, or so it seemed, and one could begin on New Year's Day, eating in a different spot every breakfast, lunch, and dinner, and still not have touched them all by year's end.

Lumpy's cooking didn't quite measure up.

But the culinary deprivation was minor in comparison to other basic niceties. Laundry, for instance. He had nothing to wear save what he'd had on when he came aboard and whatever he could beg, steal, or borrow from the sailors and the film crew. Also, it seemed to him that no matter how vigorously he scrubbed with the laundry soap, washing his shirts and drawers by hand never quite got them completely clean.

Still, these were small things.

The truth—and it was difficult for him to admit, even to himself—was that being cast adrift like this, cut off from all that he knew of civilization, Jack felt more alive than he ever had in his life. The *Venture* steamed on toward the East Indies under blue skies and at night the sun burned orange as it set upon the ocean.

And for those days, Jack wrote.

With Denham breathing down his neck, he produced several new scenes for the as-yet-unnamed jungle adventure the director was orchestrating. But time and again he found himself going back to another project, a brand new play that had taken root in his creative consciousness and was demanding to be written. Ever since he had met Ann Darrow, something had been niggling at his brain, some idea playing there. And once he'd seen her filming her scenes with Bruce Baxter, seen the natural humor and charisma she brought to her performance, it had begun to take form.

Ann was a comedienne. Jack had denigrated her vaudeville roots when Denham had first told him about her, but now he saw that there was more to vaudeville than simply buffoonery. Ann was a genuinely funny person. It was in her delivery, her facial expression, her confidence. When she wanted to be archly comic, it flowed from her naturally, a part of her no less than her beauty. And that was another thing; she seemed completely unaware of how stunning she was.

The fact was, he just couldn't get Ann Darrow out of his head. As prickly as she'd been with him, she was damned charming as well, particularly when she was embarrassed or uncomfortable.

Jack's nature in contrast could be pretty dour. He wrote drama, investigated the human condition and at times all sorts of other depressing subjects. But for the first time in his life, he wanted to try his hand at comedy, to understand it. Ann had triggered in him a fascination with the comedic form.

So he stayed down in the filthy hold and wrote. Now, here in the morning hours, he sat in his singlet and boxer shorts, typing madly while his clothes hung to dry from a makeshift clothes line he'd rigged above the cages. He had no idea if what he was writing was funny, but when he imagined Ann speaking the lines of the female lead, they made him smile, so he thought that was a decent start.

Bruce Baxter was troubled. Ann was a sweet girl, but she was an amateur, and from what he could tell so far, just about every man on the ship was falling for her. Wife, girlfriend, mother, daughter, sister . . . she just touched a nerve for all of them, somehow.

Not that he was immune, either. She was a decent enough actress, he supposed. Her sharp wit gave him something to react to on camera. That was more than he could say for some of the wooden actresses he'd worked with in the past.

But he wondered if perhaps she was a little too good. Denham was enchanted with her. Not romantically— Bruce didn't know if Denham had an ounce of romance in his soul, and there was always that little thing between him and the rest of humanity . . . the camera. He always viewed the world from the other side. But Denham was nevertheless caught up in Ann's allure.

Driscoll, too, and maybe even more so.

Where did that leave him? Bruce was the hero. The star. He'd signed on to play the lead in this picture, and he wanted to make sure Denham and Driscoll didn't forget that fact. Bruce had too much at stake. His last few pictures had not performed to expectations, and studio executives were apt to just move on to the next handsome young man. If he wasn't careful, he'd be playing second fiddle by year's end, or worse yet, the heavy.

He could fight, though. And by God he would. He'd come from nothing, grown up down South in a hardscrabble backwater town, and when he came to Hollywood, he'd risen the hard way. Bruce didn't like to let it show. He was a star, after all, and had an image to consider.

But he was a scrapper, and when it came to his career, with this picture he was fighting for his life.

One of the posters in his cabin had fallen down. The moisture had gotten up under it and loosened it from the wall. Now Bruce took pains to hang it up again. His favorite poster . . . *The Dame Tamer*. That was the circus one with the lions. Bruce had enjoyed the heck out of that one. He'd also hung the posters for *Rough Trader* and *Tribal Brides of the Amazon* in his cabin, just to remind him who he was, and what he was doing out here in the middle of the ocean, making this picture.

Fighting for his life.

At dusk, Denham stood on the deck, hoping to catch the light exactly right for the shot he wanted. Ann

101

wore a cream-colored dress that shimmered and sparkled with beads, the picture of glamour. But it wouldn't have mattered if she was clad in rags; the woman was radiant on film. In a certain slant of light, she gave him all a director could ever want of a woman's soul up on the screen. He just knew that men all over the world were going to fall in love with her when they saw this footage.

He stepped back from the camera and wiped sweat from his brow. Herb moved in and checked focus. Mike had his headphones on and he gave Denham a thumbs up to say the audio was recording just fine.

Denham glanced at Preston, who had seemed extremely distracted the last couple of days. The assistant caught his look and gave him a curt nod, then looked away. Something was going on with the kid, but Denham didn't have the time or patience to find out what.

He had a film to make.

"All right, Ann. Let's move on," he said, and then he began directing her through a series of emotions. He was building up a reel of reaction shots that he could edit into the film wherever they were necessary, helping to punctuate the story.

Pensive. Sorrowful. Angry. Giddy.

Out of the corner of his eye, Denham saw someone moving along the deck. He glanced over and saw Jack approaching. The writer held loose pages in his hands and was reading them even as he walked.

"Laughing, Ann!" he called. "You're happy."

She spun around, blond hair flying around her shoulders as she turned, her whole face illuminated by her laughter and the golden rays of the setting sun. When she saw Jack, she froze for a moment, staring at him, distracted, as though she had completely forgotten where she was.

Denham glanced over and saw that Jack was staring back.

Then Ann broke the look and started to turn again.

Well, well, Denham thought, smiling to himself. *Isn't that interesting?*

When Denham was done with her for the day, Ann started back toward her cabin. She hadn't gone twenty feet when she heard the music begin. A smile immediately blossomed on her face and she went back out onto the deck in search of the source.

There was laughter and the clink of bottles. Some of the crewmen who weren't on duty had brought out bottles of whiskey and were passing them around. But the alcohol didn't interest her at all. It was the music that drew Ann, a blissful tune she recognized but couldn't name, something from the Highlands of Scotland.

There was a flute and some kind of percussion and other instruments, so that it felt to her almost like a little orchestra pit, there on the deck of the *Venture*. These rough, unshaven men were the soul of the sea, and they had at last let down their guard entirely with Ann. The music drifted out over the ocean and Ann laughed to hear them and to see the pleasure in their eyes as they played.

Standing to one side, she saw Jimmy. The boy was kind and his eyes bright, but there was also a shadow over him at times and from what she knew of him, it was there for a reason. He had lived through dark times. Indeed, they all had.

When he saw her looking at him, Jimmy shyly glanced away.

Ann shook her head, letting him know he wouldn't be allowed to be bashful with her, and she went over and pulled on his hand, tugging him into a circle of sailors who hooted and clapped.

Even as they began to dance, Choy started to sing. He had a strangely beautiful voice, but none of his shipmates seemed surprised. They clapped all the more for him.

Ann's heart soared. For the first time since her vaudeville troupe had been disbanded and the theater closed, she felt the rush of giddiness that she always got in the company of close companions. Right then, she didn't think she could ever wish to be anywhere but there on the deck, with Choy singing, dancing with Jimmy, and laughing.

With a mock serious face, Ann snatched the cap off a sailor's head and put it on. She strutted in it a moment, and the crew laughed at her antics.

She caught sight of Jack, watching her. Their eyes met for an instant before Jimmy spun her, whirling her away. For a kid, he was a good dancer.

As she whirled about, she caught sight of other members of this strange new "family." Preston had been keeping to himself of late and he stood off to the side, quite alone. Further along the deck, Denham stood against the railing, scanning the horizon with a pair of binoculars. Englehorn was beside him, a chart held in his hand.

It crossed her mind for just a moment to wonder what they were looking for, but then Jimmy was spinning her again, and all such thoughts left her. The music went on, and the singing, and dusk turned to evening turned to darkness. After a time, Ann wandered away from the cluster of sailors and at last went back to her cabin.

There was still laughter and music up on the deck, but members of the crew had begun to drift off, returning to their duty, or to sleep, or other pursuits. Denham stood in the mess room, leaning over charts that Preston had brought to him, spreading them out on a table. He tried to be as inconspicuous as possible, but Lumpy, sometime cook and jack of all trades, kept shooting dark, disapproving glances in his direction.

There were footsteps and Denham looked to see Mr. Hayes entering the mess, with Jimmy in tow. The kid had a guilty sort of look, fairly confirming Denham's long-held suspicion. The director had certainly overheard the whispers and gotten strange looks from the crew.

The kid had heard Jack that day in the cargo hold when he and Denham were talking about their final destination, and he sure as hell hadn't kept it to himself.

A confrontation was coming, and Denham—master of avoiding confrontation—could see no way around it.

Hayes strode over to the cook, who was wiping down a bench top. "Lumpy, if someone was to tell you this ship is headed for Singapore, what would you say?"

Lumpy sniffed, clutching a rag to his grubby paw. "I'd say they were full of it, Mr. Hayes. We turned southwest last night."

Denham tried to focus on the charts, to pretend he wasn't hearing them. But then he felt someone behind him and looked up sharply to find Hayes standing over him.

"Gentleman, please," the director said calmly. "We're not looking for trouble."

"No," Jimmy said softly. "You're looking for something else."

Denham glanced around at the men gathered in the mess, then stared a moment at Jimmy, whose loose tongue had forced this moment. There was no getting around it now.

"Yes we are," he admitted. "Skull Island is going on the map. We're gonna find it, film it, and show it to the world. That's the hook: for twenty-five cents, you get to see the last blank space on earth."

Lumpy had gone over to the whetstone near the kitchen and now lifted a large knife. "I wouldn't be so sure of that," he said, and set the blade to the stone.

"What do you mean?" Preston asked, a quaver in his voice.

"Seven years ago . . . me and Mr. Hayes, we were working our passage on a Norwegian barque," Lumpy replied, and glanced at Hayes.

"We picked up a castaway, found him in the water," the first mate said, continuing the tale. "He'd been drifting for days."

"His ship had run aground on an island. Way west

of Sumatra," Lumpy went on, his Cockney accent thickening. "An island hidden in fog. He spoke of a huge wall, built so long ago, no one knew who had made it."

Denham knew they were hoping to frighten him, but the words had the opposite effect. A tremor of excitement went through him. He glanced at Preston.

"What did I tell you?"

"A wall, a hundred foot high," Lumpy said. "As strong today as it was ages ago."

Preston stared at the cook, mystified. "Why did they need to build a wall?"

The mess room went silent a moment. The sailors exchanged a glance that chilled Denham.

"Have you ever heard of Kong?" Hayes asked.

"Kong? Sure," Denham said offhandedly. "It's a myth. A Malay superstition. What is he, a god or a devil? I forget."

Lumpy held up the sharpened knife to punctuate his words. "The castaway, he spoke of a creature neither beast nor man, but something monstrous living behind the wall."

Denham waved the words away. He'd heard a thousand such tales, and so had every one of the sailors aboard the *Venture.* Typical island legends. "A lion or a tiger," he said. "A man-eater. That's how these stories start."

But Preston was spooked. "What else did he say?"

"Nothing," Lumpy replied, glancing at the blade in his hand before regarding them all gravely. "We found him the next morning . . . he stuck a knife through his heart."

Preston's eyes went wide and his face was ashen. Jimmy looked even worse, pale as a corpse.

"Sorry, fellas," Denham said, trying to break the grim mood. "You've got to do better than that. Monsters belong in B-movies!"

But Hayes and Lumpy were implacable.

"If you find this place," the first mate said, expressionless, "if you go ashore with your friends and your camera . . . you won't come back.

"Just so long as you understand that."

Late morning, the day after the merrymaking on board the *Venture*, Bruce Baxter made his way back to his cabin for a wardrobe change. Denham was taking reaction shots of him and wanted him in a variety of different getups.

On the way along the claustrophobic corridor, he bumped into the boy, Jimmy, who was always tagging along after Mr. Hayes, the first mate. The boy didn't even excuse himself and when Bruce shot him a look, there was something shifty in Jimmy's eyes.

But then he was at his cabin and his thoughts were already drifting back to the film. Until he opened the door and stepped inside.

Someone . . . and he was sure he knew who . . . had drawn a thick black mustache on his face, on each of the movie posters that hung from the walls. Bruce gritted his teeth and felt himself flushing with anger. His fists clenched at his sides and he tensed, about to start after the little hooligan, teach him a lesson.

He started to turn away, but then caught sight of himself in the mirror. The view gave him pause. Bruce glanced at the poster of *Rough Trader,* at himself with a mustache, and then he studied his reflection again.

Maybe he *did* look good with a mustache, come to think of it.

Try as he might, Jack just couldn't stop thinking of Ann. He had felt the connection between them, an electric circuit that ran from him to her and back again. Not that he claimed to understand it. The Driscoll men had never been known for their outward displays or professions of affection, nor had Jack himself spent much time giving any consideration to the subject.

All he knew was that he was drawn to Ann . . . and so far it had been somewhat frustrating to wonder if she felt the same way.

That night, unable to sleep, he'd sat up typing late into the night, working on the comedy play that he was writing. The current title was *Cry Havoc,* but he wasn't sure if it would stick. Right now, the story was more important, the feeling. The humor.

All through the next day he'd pretended to be working on Denham's script but instead made progress on *Cry Havoc.* By nightfall, Jack had a first act he was mostly pleased with, but the only way he was going to know if it was any good was to have someone read it. And not just any someone.

Ann Darrow.

Without giving himself a moment to hesitate or to

wonder if what he was doing was appropriate, he went to her cabin. Night had already fallen and the dim lights on shipboard cast a gauzy yellow pall on the walls that made shadows all along the dingy corridor.

Taking a deep breath, he knocked.

"Hold on," Ann called out from within. Seconds went by and Jack clutched the sheaf of papers in his hand. Then he heard her voice from the other side of the door, asking who it was.

"It's Jack Driscoll, Miss Darrow."

There was a long, quiet pause before she opened the door.

"Good evening, Mr. Driscoll," she said, so fragile in her pajamas and a shawl for warmth against the chill of night on the ocean. "To what do I owe the honor?"

She wasn't cold, as he'd feared, or even distant. Instead, Ann was pleasant enough, and curious.

"I've been working on a new play," he said quickly. "I was wondering if you'd be interested in reading it. A writer gets lost in his own head sometimes, and it would be helpful to have your opinion."

Ann's eyes shifted to the manuscript in his hand and she smiled, then stepped back to open the door wider. "I'd love to."

She snatched the pages from him and went to her bed, where she folded herself up cross-legged, reading without any further effort at welcome or hospitality. Jack was simultaneously pleased and nervous. He'd never written anything even remotely like this play before. Normally he didn't like to show anyone anything until it was completed, for fear that it would impact the course of the work. But on this, he wanted Ann's thoughts.

For long minutes he remained silent while she read, flipping pages, a broad smile growing upon her face. Several times she laughed softly. Eventually, she glanced up at him.

"This is funny," she said, and with her tone, she clearly added, *I didn't think you had it in you.* "You're writing a stage comedy."

"Yeah. I guess I am."

"You know who would love this?" Ann said, getting excited now with the possibilities. She came up off the bed, flush with the energy of her enthusiasm. "The Eastside Theatre."

"I'm writing it for you," he said flatly, before he could stop himself.

Ann looked at him, obviously taken aback. A troubled expression crossed over her face, and he saw now that at least a part of it was doubt. Though whether it was about his words, or her own feelings about them, he did not know.

"Why would you do that?" she asked.

"Why would I write a play for you?"

"Yes."

Jack could only stare at her, unsure how to respond. Wasn't it enough for him to show her how much he was thinking of her?

"Isn't it obvious?" he asked.

"Not to me," Ann replied.

"Well, it's in the subtext," Jack went on, growing frustrated now. What did she want from him? Couldn't she just accept it and be happy?

"Then I must have missed it."

"Look, it's not about words," Jack insisted.

Ann gave him an uncertain look. She understood. She had to. Jack moved toward her, reaching out to hold her arms.

"Sometimes," he said, "you have to be brave."

And he pulled her into his arms, and kissed her.

She made no effort to push him away.

9

THE DAYS WERE BEGINNING to blur one into the next for Bruce. It had rained several times, though mostly in the early morning. Otherwise they'd had almost miraculously beautiful weather. It had reached the point where the perfection had grown a bit boring. Denham was running out of bits he could film on shipboard and seemed to be more and more distracted as time passed. Bruce presumed that the director was just as bored as he was. They all wanted to reach their destination so they could get on with the process of shooting the film they came out here to make.

One morning at breakfast, several days after Jimmy had drawn the mustaches on his posters—and hadn't Captain Englehorn gotten an earful about that?— Bruce was sitting in the mess room picking at his food.

His only company at the table was Herb, Denham's camera operator. The sailors all ate early, and Bruce rarely dined with more than a few of them. Denham was at an adjoining table, alone in his thoughts, perusing through an atlas spread out in front of him.

Herb had come in a few minutes after Bruce, and just around the time Bruce was about to start eating, the camera man had plunked a hideously gray prosthetic leg onto the table and set about tending to it with an oil can and screwdriver.

Bruce had tried to ignore it, but it was as though the leg was a magnet for his eyes. He poked at his breakfast and eventually gave up and simply stared at the prosthesis and Herb in turn until the other man noticed him.

"It's my spare," Herb said. "Needs an overhaul."

Bruce raised his eyebrows. He hadn't even known that the camera man was an amputee. Herb tapped his trouser leg and the substance beneath made a hollow sound.

"Sea lion up in Nova Scotia," Herb said.

"Your leg was bitten off?" Bruce asked, appalled.

Herb leaned closer and lowered his voice to a conspiratorial rasp. "Not just my leg."

Up at the counter where the food was prepared, Lumpy was cracking walnuts. With the image of Herb's leg and . . . parts . . . bitten off by a sea lion, the sound was obscene.

"That's tough," Bruce said.

"Tough? It was a tragedy." Herb shook his head. "Mr. Denham should have won an award for that picture. Best footage we ever shot. You see . . . Mr. Denham doesn't care about his personal safety. It's not about the individual. You have to expect sacrifice and loss. That's what he taught me."

Herb looked Bruce straight in the face. "The only thing that matters is bringing back the picture."

Bruce was simply aghast. The tragedy was that

Denham hadn't been recognized for his brilliance, and here was Herb without a leg? No wonder the director and camera man worked together—they were made for each other.

Bruce tried to go back to his breakfast, but his appetite was all but gone now. As he glanced again at Herb, he saw Preston come into the mess. *That* kid, at least, seemed to have his head screwed on straight. Or, at least, Bruce normally thought so. But this morning Preston was disheveled and looking more than a bit anxious.

Preston walked right over to Denham. The director hadn't touched his breakfast; instead he was entirely focused on the atlas.

"Carl," Preston prompted. "We have to talk."

"What about?" Denham asked, not bothering to look up.

"The weather," Preston replied.

Bruce forgot all about Herb's missing leg. The tension radiating off of Preston was palpable, and it was obvious that Denham felt it, too, and heard it in his assistant's voice. The director raised his head. Preston pushed his glasses up the bridge of his nose, quite self consciously.

"More specifically," Preston went on, "the likelihood . . . of fog."

Denham was up immediately, anger and frustration etched into his face, and he hustled Preston out into the corridor in the blink of an eye.

Bruce stared after them, wondering what the hell *that* was all about. But not for long. Whatever their problem was, as long as it didn't interfere with the making of the film, he figured it was theirs to worry about.

None of his business, as long as it didn't affect him.

Denham felt his every nerve ending fraying, energy coursing through him and he didn't know what to do with it. He nodded, almost bouncing on his feet, and his hands at his sides curling into fists and uncurling repeatedly.

"You have something of mine."

Preston shook his head, but it wasn't a denial. It was clear he just couldn't summon the words he wanted to say. Edgy and evasive, at last he flattened himself against the corridor wall and gazed at Denham, his eyes full of a question he didn't want to know the answer to. And maybe with a little disappointment as well.

"Twelve men died, Carl." Preston pulled the map— the same map Denham had been trying to find for days, worried about whose hands it had fallen into— out of his pocket and waved it under his employer's nose. "On *this* island. The one that's hidden in fog. The one *you're* looking for . . ."

Denham pressed his lips together in frustration, hands up, angrier than he had been in a very long time. He ought to have been relieved that it was Preston who'd taken the map, but it wasn't something he could appreciate at the moment.

"The fella who drew that was out of his mind!" Denham said. "He was found half drowned in the middle of the ocean. It's the ravings of a madman!"

"His crew," Preston said coldly. "They were mutilated."

"I'm telling you, he was delusional!"

Preston just stared at him. "Didn't you read the small print? Something tore them apart."

Denham sighed. "See what happens when you get upset? You're starting to unravel."

"You're putting our lives at risk . . . it's not . . . it's just not . . . you can't do this—"

Denham wasn't going to listen anymore. He was done with this. A hysterical assistant was something he didn't need. He reached into his pocket and brought out a piece of candy. Something to placate his assistant. "Preston, you're perspiring. I think you should have a mint."

But the kid ignored him. "What about Jack? Ann? Herb and the others? They're your friends."

Denham sniffed. "Yeah, they're my friends. And they're all on the goddamn payroll."

"Well, they trust you, Carl!" Preston replied, voice rising. "And you're using them!"

On the deck of the *Venture,* Ann stood leaning against the rail with fresh script pages in one hand and a half-eaten apple in the other. Though the sky today was still mostly blue, from time to time a gray cloud would pass by overhead, casting a shadow on the sea below, or across the deck of the steamer. Though they were now in tropical waters, when the breeze shifted just right it brought a chill that made her shiver.

Lost in her reading of the script, she nearly dropped

both the pages and her apple when she heard an angry shout through the porthole behind her.

"That's bullshit!"

The voice belonged to Carl Denham. Ann frowned and turned to look with surprise at the porthole. Denham was a driven man, used to barking orders and to declaring his passions. But so far she'd never seen him angry.

"Tell them the truth!" a different voice replied, with equal vehemence. It took her a second to identify it as Preston's.

"Are you kidding me? They'd walk!" Denham declared. "I don't need you spookin' the cast!"

Ann felt a dreadful shiver go through her. What were they talking about?

"They *should* be scared!" Preston snapped. "*I'm* scared!"

"I don't care if you're crapping your pants! Keep your mouth shut, understand?" Denham said.

Ann stared at the porthole, growing uneasy with every word.

Preston saw the anger flaring in Denham's eyes and he nearly flinched from the fire he saw there. For just a second he thought Denham might actually hit him, but instead, a look of calm detachment settled on the director's face.

"Do you know why I took you on, Preston?" Denham asked, as though he were about to share a secret. "Think about it. Why would I want to hire some messed-up kid who failed to make it through law school? The truth is . . . I felt sorry for you."

Shocked, Preston didn't know how to respond. He had given up everything for this man, had worked his heart out, and now Denham was going to slap him down? The only thing worse was the possibility that he was speaking the truth. Preston didn't know if he could handle that.

"You may come from money," Denham went on, "but fundamentally, you're a charity case."

Preston was gaping at Denham, trying to summon some kind of snappy comeback, but at those words he had to look away. Whatever Denham's faults, Preston looked up to him for his passion and his art. To Preston, Denham was a giant. And that giant had just crushed him underfoot.

He felt Denham tug the map from his fingers and didn't even try to hold on to it.

"Funny thing is," Denham said, his tone very different now, "you proved me wrong. You're good, Preston. You're more than good. You are one hell of a personal assistant. You're smart. You're loyal. You have good instincts. You could go far in this business."

Slowly, unsure, Preston raised his eyes to study Denham.

"But here's the thing you need to decide," the director said sagely. "Are you afraid . . . or are you a *filmmaker*?"

That night, the fog rolled in. Up in the wheelhouse, Hayes stood and watched Captain Englehorn steer, trying to see through the thick white mist. Hayes didn't like it. Not at all. They were so far from the shipping lanes now that if the *Venture* had trouble, no one was ever likely to run across them. The captain had made his choice. Whatever his motivations for going with Denham's chosen course, Hayes wasn't privy to them. Unless it was just the money, and Ben Hayes hoped to God there was more to it than that.

The tension between skipper and first mate had been growing for days. But Hayes would say nothing more out of loyalty. It was Englehorn's error to make, and Hayes's job was to follow instructions.

They proceeded at half-speed, moving through the darkness and the gloom. As quiet as it was in the wheelhouse, Hayes started when the radio operator stood and went to the captain, handing him a note.

"Message for you, skipper," the man said.

Englehorn read it quickly, his brow furrowing deeply.

Bad news.

Preston didn't like the fog, and after so many perfect days and nights out on the ocean, he would have expected not to mind so much. But it was claustrophobic enough on the ship, in the corridors or down in the hold. The fog made it just as bad on deck. Plus he was still smarting from this morning's brutal tongue-lashing.

He needed a drink.

Now he stood in Mr. Denham's cabin—the night and the fog outside the porthole windows—and smiled softly to himself as he poured two glasses of scotch. Denham was holding the new script pages loosely in one hand, staring off into nothing. Preston offered him a glass.

"No, not for me," Denham said, waving him away. "I'm off it. Can't afford to get smashed."

Surprised, Preston studied the man. Obviously, whatever was troubling Denham went deeper than just script pages.

"Preston, when I ask you to do something," Denham began, then faltered a moment. His expression was inscrutable. "Have I ever said 'Please?'"

"No," he replied after a moment of reflection. "I don't think you ever have."

On the table, next to Denham's drink, was the map. A finger of dread traced its way down Preston's back as he glanced at it. He reached out and picked it up.

"But that doesn't mean I take you for granted, right?" Denham continued.

"Right," Preston echoed, distracted by the map.

Still lost and distant, off in his own mind somewhere, Denham absent-mindedly picked up Preston's scotch from the table, apparently having forgotten that he was "off the stuff."

"Because you know . . . I would never jeopardize your personal safety . . . or the safety of anyone on this ship."

Preston was no longer paying attention. All of his focus was on the map. He'd noticed something written in a strange, barely legible script.

"Carl," he said quietly, "have you seen what's written here?"

"I wouldn't do it," Denham muttered, staring into

the scotch, swirling it in the glass. "I would never betray a friend."

"Kong . . ." Preston read, recalling the warnings of Hayes and Lumpy that day in the mess room. "It says, 'Kong.' "

"When all this is over, I'm gonna make it up to you," Denham said firmly. "I swear."

The director gestured for him to drink up, but Preston ignored him. He stared at Denham, unnerved and growing deeply worried. He'd thought they were talking about two entirely separate subjects . . . but now he wondered if perhaps they were talking about the same thing after all.

"Carl, what are you really looking for?"

Denham downed the scotch in one gulp.

"Carl?" Preston prodded, his dread growing deeper with every breath.

Denham opened his mouth to speak. Then his troubled expression turned to one of anger. For an instant, Preston thought the director would be cross with him again, but then he felt it, too.

The thrum of the ship's engines had begun to die down. To slow.

Denham stood abruptly, face etched with fury and panic and shock.

"We're turning around!"

10

DREADFUL EXPECTATION HAD CURLED up into a tight ball within Denham's gut. He stormed up to the wheelhouse, riding a surge of fury and desperation. Nothing was going to get in the way of his making this picture. Carl Denham was a man out of options. If he came back from this voyage empty-handed, he was finished.

His hands shook with the desire to hit something and his skin prickled with horrid anticipation as he marched to open the door.

When Denham burst into the wheelhouse, Englehorn was at the helm. The tightness in the director's gut turned to ice, for he knew that the captain himself had ordered the reversal of direction. The first mate, Hayes, and the radio operator both looked up warily as Denham stood glaring at their skipper, chest rising and falling with each angry breath.

"What's going on, Englehorn? Why are we changing course?"

The captain's expression was blank, but hard. He handed Denham a cablegram. "It's from the bank. They're refusing to honor your check."

A spike of panic went through Denham's heart and his pulse quickened even further. This wasn't going to happen now. He wouldn't allow it.

He made a show of reading the message, though Englehorn had already told him all he needed to know.

"Look, it's a stupid mistake!" he said.

Englehorn's nostrils flared. Curtly, he spoke one word. "Outside."

Denham felt the corners of his mouth twitch as if he might smile, but it was hysteria, not amusement. This was not going to happen. Englehorn led the way out onto the narrow bridge that ringed the wheelhouse. The fog had grown thicker and the wind was whipping against them. Denham glanced around, but there was no one to overhear them. No one but the boy, Jimmy, up in the crow's nest high above, and given the glimmer of illumination up there, it was clear the kid was busy reading something by flashlight rather than doing his job.

With a grunt of anger, Denham pushed his black, unruly hair away from his face and glared at the captain.

"There's a warrant out for your arrest, did you know that?" Englehorn said, quiet, reserved. "I have been ordered to divert to Rangoon."

Denham felt the blood drain from his face. He shook his head. No way.

"Another week, that's all I'm asking," Denham said. All his life had been one negotiation after another. This was no different—it was only the consequences that were greater. "I haven't got a film yet. I've risked everything I have on this."

It wasn't quite pleading, but it was as close as Denham's pride would allow him to get.

"No, Denham. You risked everything *I* have," Englehorn replied scornfully.

A strange calm settled over the director, as though he were sailing into disaster and there was nothing he could do about it.

"What do you want?" he asked. "Tell me what you want? I'll give you anything."

Englehorn gave him a look of cold, detached indifference.

"I want you off my ship."

In the mess room, Jack poured Ann a cup of coffee. His stomach knotted in revulsion as the thick, steaming, black sludge plopped from the pot into the mug. He passed the mug to Ann a bit reluctantly and watched in fascination as she took a sip. The grimace she made at the taste came as no surprise.

"Too hot?" he said hopefully.

"I think it's just taken the enamel off my teeth."

Jack raised his own mug in a mock toast. "Here's to drinking bad coffee in the middle of the Indian Ocean."

Ann arched an eyebrow. "Happy days."

Lumpy had been puttering around the galley and Jack had wrongly assumed he couldn't hear them.

"Throw it out!" the cook called as he entered, carrying a huge bucket of sloshing liquid. "We'll restock the perishables in Rangoon."

Jack frowned. "Rangoon?"

"Very tropical," Lumpy said. "You'll like it there."

Ann wore a puzzled expression that Jack figured was a mirror of his own.

"That's where you're getting off," the cook explained as he dumped the bucket in a slop sink. "The skipper thinks Rangoon is the ideal place for Mr. Denham to finish his film. You couldn't have picked a nicer spot, providing you stay indoors and you're sensibly armed."

Alarmed, Jack glanced at Ann, whose face blanched as her mouth opened silently. Lumpy seemed not to have noticed the effect of his words. He hefted a crate of cabbages and headed for the door.

"Mind you, it's not getting into the place that's hard. It's finding a safe passage out . . . good luck with that," the cook said, and then he was gone.

Jack reached for Ann's hand, certain she was thinking precisely the same thing that he was.

It was time to have a little chat with Carl.

Jack stood on the deck of the *Venture,* the night closing in around him. The ship sliced through black water with an almost conspiratorial whisper that was audible above the rumble of the steamer's engines.

He stared at the map in his hands, at the crude drawing of an island. The writer and Carl had a friendship going back many years, so because of that, Jack was trying to figure out a way to look at their present situation and not want to slug Denham.

"Englehorn's in on it!" Carl raved, wildly pacing. "That bastard German! Him and the bloody Norwegian!"

Jack scowled at him. "What Norwegian? What the hell are you talking about?"

"The fella I bought the map off—the skipper of a freighter. He picked up a castaway. The guy was barely alive, the only survivor of a shipwreck. Before he died he gave the Norwegian skipper that map. I'm telling you, Jack, they're trying to get rid of me! They're gonna dump me in Rangoon and claim it for themselves!"

"Claim what?" Jack said, throwing up his hands. "For Christ's sake will you listen to yourself? You dragged us all out here on the pretext of making a movie—"

Denham snatched the map from his hands.

"This *is* the movie, goddamn it! Do you have any idea how huge it could be? The last remnant of a dead civilization. It's gonna vanish, Jack! This island is sinking . . . it's gonna disappear from the face of the Earth! Don't you get it?"

For just a moment Jack was intrigued by the idea. If Denham was right, if this was some ancient civilization about to be lost beneath the waves like some miniature Atlantis, it would be an extraordinary find—and a once-in-a-lifetime backdrop against which to shoot a picture.

But his interest was swallowed by anger.

"No," Jack said. "No, I don't. You know why? You never told me. Buddy . . . pal . . . friend?"

"Damn right, I didn't," Carl replied, expression hardening. "You think I was born yesterday? I learned this business the hard way. No one had the guts to back me, so I backed myself."

"On the basis of what? A scrap of paper?"

Denham grew quiet. He held up the map. "This is real. It exists."

Drawn in by the man's certainty and overwhelming charisma, Jack took the map from Carl again, held it up and stared at him. A shudder went through Jack, though he couldn't have said why.

Then he looked at Carl, eye to eye. "Then perhaps it's not meant to be found."

Anger still burned in Captain Englehorn, but as he stood in the wheelhouse, peering out into the night through moisture-spattered glass, he found he had other, far graver concerns. His first indication of real trouble came when he glanced at Hayes, who was at the wheel, but bent over to peer at the ship's compass.

Englehorn didn't like the nervous expression on Hayes's face. Not in the least. It wasn't like the man at all.

The captain moved to the compass and looked down. Its pointer was swinging wildly to and fro as though the ship were caught up in the midst of some magnetic storm, with lightning throwing it off.

Englehorn took the wheel from his first mate. "Check our position, Mr. Hayes. Use the stars."

Hayes picked up a sextant and stepped through the door out onto the bridge, little more than a narrow walkway around the wheelhouse. He looked up at the sky and his face hardened with concern. Watching him, a tremor of apprehension went through the captain.

Hayes ducked his head back through the door. His facial expression was nearly as ominous as his tone.

"There are no stars, captain."

The captain handed the wheel over to another crewmember, Pierrault, and stepped out to join Hayes on the bridge. He kept a grim, stony façade, but his heart had begun to hammer with alarm. The ship, and all aboard, were his responsibility.

Englehorn stared into the murkiness ahead, wondering what, precisely, they had sailed into.

Denham leaned on the rail, looking out to sea, the map clutched in his hands. He was so lost in his thoughts that he barely noticed Jack pacing in frustration, the thick fog rolling in. Now, though, the writer came striding back toward him.

Jack called his name, but Denham didn't stir. His friend's voice seemed far away.

"Carl! Hey, Carl!" Jack said, getting his attention at last. "What happened? What the hell is going on?"

Denham was about to respond, but he glanced down at the map again. That dark smudge on the paper caught his eye. He rotated it in his hands, studying it more closely.

And in the scrawl of barely legible words on the map, only one gave him pause.

Kong.

Beside it there was that image. With a little imagination, and perhaps the superstitions of sailors working on his mind, it *did* look like a face: the terrible, snarling, bestial face of a gorilla.

His fascination was interrupted by the foghorn blaring up on the bridge. Slowly, Denham glanced up from the map, a spark of hope fanned to life in his chest. As he looked up, he saw Jack's concern: the thin mist that had lain on the surface of the water was being enveloped by a much larger, denser bank of fog, like one cloud swallowing another. This new fog bank was a wall of gray-white roiling above the inky water—and already the prow of the ship was disappearing inside.

Another blast of the foghorn echoed across the ocean.

At the wheel, Englehorn barked at Pierrault. "Station the for'ard lookout, and get me the depth by lead line!"

The helmsman hurried away. Englehorn's pulse was racing as he tried not to imagine the *Venture* bottoming out on some reef or shoal. The compass wasn't working. They could see nothing at all in the fog. And he had already heard the stories of the island Denham had wanted to bring them to . . . of the fog that shrouded it and the men who'd died when their ships were scuttled on the rocks.

He couldn't think about it. His crew would drop lead lines, measure the depth of the ocean bottom that way, and he would keep his ship out of shallow waters. No other choice.

"Reduce speed, steerage way only," he ordered.

Hayes swung the levers on the telegraph. "Dead slow ahead, both," he replied, and the engines went from growl to purr.

They were blind, now, but they were still alive. Still running.

*   *   *

Jack gazed around the deck, still astonished at the thickness of the fog and the utter lack of visibility. He could barely see Denham in front of him, or the door that led belowdecks. Sailors hurried all around him, shouting to one another in the jargon of their occupation, half of which he didn't understand. One of the men threw a line overboard.

"Thirty fathoms! No bottom!" the man cried into the echoing fog.

Preston came out the door onto the deck, the fog caressing him. He looked like a drunken man, staggering a bit, staring around wide-eyed. Jack expected his expression was no different.

Hayes discovered he was holding his breath, and took a sip of air, exhaling slowly as he stared out at the fog. It slid over the windows of the wheelhouse like some preternatural thing, as though they were not so much sailing through it as being consumed by it.

Anxiously, he turned to Captain Englehorn, whose grip on the wheel was white-knuckled.

"You should stop the ship," Hayes said, biting off each word. It was the smartest course—they could wait out the fog, or wait out the night, but with both, they could not proceed without risk.

And he knew the tales of the island as well, and the men who had died in a fog so much like this.

Englehorn spun the wheel. "Fifteen degrees port."

Hayes silently urged him to listen to reason.

"We're getting out of here, Mr. Hayes," the captain assured him. "We'll find clear conditions."

From out on the deck, the shout of a crewman rang clear in the fog. "Twenty-five fathoms!"

Cursing, Hayes rushed out of the wheelhouse onto the bridge and looked down at the sailor on the deck with the lead line. There was a wild look of fear in the crewman's eyes.

Driscoll and Denham were also down on the deck looking around, anxious and helpless, as the crewmen rushed around them. A ripple of bitter fury went through Hayes. It looked like Denham was going to get what he wanted after all. The director walked away from his writer, pushing past his assistant, Preston, as he went.

"We have seabed!" the sailor with the lead-line shouted. "Twenty-two fathoms!"

Hayes turned and rushed back into the wheelhouse. "We're shallowing!"

Englehorn only stared ahead at the thickening fog, despair in his eyes. He started to spin the wheel. "Twenty degrees starboard!"

"Captain, you don't know where the hell you're going!" Hayes shouted.

Englehorn glared at him. "Get me another reading!"

High in the crow's nest, Jimmy had put aside *Heart of Darkness* and his flashlight the moment they'd entered the dense fog bank and the horn had blown. No use trying to read now. And now with the shouting from below, he knew something had gone terribly wrong.

He peered into the fog, trying to make out anything

ahead. Nothing. Just gray, damp mist roiling in the darkness.

And then there it was.

Jimmy leaped to his feet, terror seizing him. In that moment, heart hammering in his chest, every childhood fear he'd ever entertained came back to him, every monster who'd ever lurked under his bed. For out of the fog loomed a huge face, carved of rock, glaring down at him with utter malice.

No, not just a face. Something else. Impossibly huge.

"Wall!" he screamed. *"There's a wall ahead!"*

11

WHEN HE HEARD JIMMY'S panicked shout, Lumpy was sitting on the deck in the fog, scrubbing mold off of a basket full of dodgy-looking vegetables. If the sailors moving past him in the dark got a good look at them, they wouldn't have touched a vegetable for the rest of the voyage. That was saying quite a bit, considering these gents weren't the most discerning when it came to their cuisine.

Lumpy chuckled to himself in amusement at Jimmy's alarm. He knew they were in shallow water—all the shouts from the crew had told him that much—but a wall?

"Gotcha, Jimmy! Did you hear that boys?" he called without looking up from his task. "There's a bleedin' wall in the middle of the Indian Ocean!"

Lumpy shook his head, grinning, and kept at the moldy vegetables. The fog closed in around him.

In the wheelhouse, Captain Englehorn was seeing for himself this impossibility—a gigantic obstruction that loomed out of the night and the fog before the ship as though the Great Wall of China had appeared suddenly before them. The wall was two hundred feet high, at least, dwarfing the *Venture*. In the misty darkness it was impossible to get a clear view of its monstrous structure, but it looked jagged and spiny, as though meant to keep anyone from coming near.

As if anyone would have sailed up to it by choice.

From above, he could hear Jimmy still shouting in the crow's nest, voice tight with fear.

"Wall!" the boy cried. "Dead ahead! Look!"

Englehorn spun the wheel hard to starboard. "Stop engines!"

Hayes slammed the telegraph to the stop position. The order went through the ship and the thrum of the engine began to subside. Below, in the engine room, the engineer was shutting the power down.

Through the windows of the wheelhouse, the captain could see Denham move to the railing at the prow, staring up in awe at the vast wall that towered above them.

"Ten fathoms!" shouted the crewman with the lead line.

Englehorn gripped the wheel and held his breath. The *Venture* slowed . . . slowed . . . but its weight carried it forward, and with a grinding crunch, the prow struck the wall.

"Give me some power!" he shouted at Hayes. "Half astern, both!"

At his hands and beneath his feet, as though he were one with his vessel, he could feel the *Venture* lolling without power in the heavy swells that swept up against the wall. There came the heavy throb from below as the engines regained their strength, and the reverse propellers kicked in. The ship began to pull away from certain doom, but at low power and with the swell of the ocean, Englehorn still didn't have adequate control of her.

They were at the mercy of the sea.

Ann careened along the corridor, the rolling of the ocean casting her from one side to the other, and she kept her hands up to protect herself as she was thrown from wall to wall. When she reached the door she hung onto the frame and then stepped out onto the deck. Her heart hammered with fear, and she gazed around at the panic that had gripped the sailors, who ran to and fro in wild attempts to get the vessel under control.

Then she saw Jack. He stood at the rail, holding on and staring into the darkness and the thick fog. She started to go to him, and then paused, looking past and above him, as a huge, jagged peak thrust out of the fog off the starboard bow.

"Rocks!" Jack shouted, pointing, turning toward the wheelhouse, trying to warn the crew.

"Rocks to starboard!" came a voice from above. Ann looked up and saw Jimmy, practically hanging from the crow's nest as he pointed. "To port!" he said, looking around wildly. "Rocks everywhere!"

Ann said a silent prayer.

Englehorn rushed to the wheelhouse door. "Take the wheel, Hayes!"

He burst onto the bridge, the moist fog heavy on him. With horror he stared around at the rocks looming from the shroud of night and mist, and he realized the *Venture* was trapped in the midst of a huge reef. His ship was out of control, and in every direction lay her destruction, and perhaps the death of all aboard.

The *Venture* tilted in the water. Ann reached out and grabbed hold of the railing at the top of the stairs from the lower deck to keep her balance. Steadied, she let go, and even as she did the sea rolled again and she reeled with it, staggering across the deck and careening into Jack Driscoll. His arms encircled her at the instant the ship scraped the rocks with a shriek of metal.

Then the *Venture* was rising on another wave and it was clear the rocks had not done any real damage. Not yet.

"Are you okay?" Jack asked.

Ann was stunned into silence by fear and shock, and she could see that Jack was just as horrified by their fate.

She nodded to him. They just held each other for several seconds, not speaking. Then the ship gave another lurch and they were torn away from one another.

For those few moments she'd felt safe in his arms, as though everything would be all right, and Ann grabbed at the space where he'd been, wishing to feel that again. But Jack was beyond her reach.

The *Venture* was in a slow, long spin. As the captain had tried to get control of her, to maneuver her, he'd been unable to give it enough power to really get moving in one direction. The rocks were just too close on all sides to risk it. As another wave rolled by and the ship dipped into a low trough after it, more rocks were revealed all around the hull. Any second they might tear right through and scuttle her.

Jimmy figured they were all going to die. The thought was strangely comforting. If he was going out, this was as good a way as any—with Mr. Hayes and the crew of the *Venture*. He'd never expected to be a part of anything, really, so to be part of the crew . . . if this was the end of things, that wouldn't be the worst thing that could happen.

But he wasn't giving up just yet.

Frantic, he tried to see through the rocks that loomed up seemingly on all sides. It was as though the ocean bottom had thrust up gigantic fingers of stone to clutch at the ship, maybe to drag them down to a watery grave. The fog churned and the night shrouded the reef, but there had to be a way out. Somehow, trying to pull away from the wall, they'd managed to sail into the reef, and if they'd gotten in—

There was an opening ahead, a place where the cloak of night was blank, swirling with the whiteness of the fog and nothing else.

Jimmy smiled, heart skipping a beat. "It's clear ahead!" he cried. "There's a gap!"

Englehorn heard the boy and for a second wondered if he'd imagined it, wished the words into being. But no, Jimmy's voice echoed in his head. He turned to the wheelhouse.

The ship rode another swell and it sent him staggering through the door. He raced to the telegraph and slammed it forward, heard the engines roar as they responded, and felt the *Venture* surge toward the gap.

"Full ahead!" he shouted.

Hayes looked at him, and Englehorn had never appreciated his first mate more, for he was the only man now on the ship who did not have fear and desperation in his eyes.

The captain took the wheel.

The ship rose on the surf, engines and ocean carrying it toward the gap in the reef, and Englehorn gripped the wheel tightly, knuckles white. The impact threw him forward, slamming him into the wheel.

A sickening groan of metal and a creak of stress upon the hull met his ears, then a grinding noise from below. The *Venture* shuddered as Englehorn closed his eyes and cursed whatever gods there were.

The *Venture* had run aground.

Denham had been thrown to the deck of the marooned ship. Now he picked himself up and staggered to the railing. The waves were still slamming the hull all around the ship, and it dipped and rose a bit with each swell, but it was not high enough to lift the *Venture* off the rocks.

The engines churned and joined with one last ocean surge, pushing at the vessel, and it slid further up onto the rocks, lodging even more firmly there. Even as it did, Denham looked up into the fog shrouded around the ship, at the walls of stone that were all too close, and then he spied a face . . . an outcropping that had been hewn into a huge, stony face. Weathered, eroded, made by the hands of some ancient people, the face looked down on him with a blank, baleful gaze, and Denham stared up at it in awe.

The engines shut down, and the *Venture* settled on the rocks, stuck fast. Englehorn had taken the first chance presented to turn the ship around, and yet fate's irony had delivered them here regardless.

Denham thought back to the map that had led him here. There could be no doubt. In his heart he had been sure, and the fog had been proof enough, but now there was utter certainty. The words written on the map had given a name to his destination.

"The Island of the Skull," he whispered to himself.

Pandemonium erupted on deck. Sailors were shouting at one another, running around to make sure everything was tied down, slipping below decks to check the damage, and those who weren't occupied dashed to the railing to survey for themselves just how dire their situation.

And dire it was. They weren't going anywhere without a hell of a lot of effort and a whisper of a miracle, and maybe not even then.

Dawn was not far off. Through the fog, which now began to melt away, Denham saw the eerie silhouette of a small island. Jagged peaks rose from its rocky shoreline. On barren cliffs along the coast in either direction there were crumbling ruins, some clinging to precipices high above the water. It was without a doubt the most inhospitable landscape he had ever seen.

There was no opening, no cove in which a ship might set anchor. There were only the ruins and cliffs, the rocky reef, and in the mist off to port, that strange wall of rock and earth and wood, shafts like spears jutting out of it from every angle.

It wasn't a place that invited visitors.

Denham sensed someone approaching and turned just as Preston arrived. He was startled to find the younger man carrying his Bell & Howell movie camera. Preston presented it to him as though it were some sort of prize, and in this instance, perhaps it was.

"Like you said," Preston told him, "defeat is always momentary."

A feeling of relief and gratitude swept through Denham. The kid had had him worried for a while—Preston had seemed to lose his way, to forget what being a filmmaker was really all about. But if Denham needed any proof that he was thinking straight again, here it was. They were aground off the coast of the very place Preston feared, the whole crew was focused on repairing the ship and freeing her from the rocks, and Preston had the camera all prepped and ready to go.

To do the job they came for.

Denham smiled.

A door swung open across the deck and Bruce stepped out. He was dressed in his pajamas, unshaven and yawning, stretching as though he'd just woken up. And obviously he had, for he glanced at the shoreline of Skull Island with an air of utter indifference.

"So this is Singapore, huh?"

Dawn had arrived, but Hayes hadn't seen a glimmer of it. He was in the engine room, sweat running in rivulets down his face and the back of his neck. Metal plates had been riveted to the hull to cover holes torn by the rocks—some of them he'd installed himself—but still jets of water were shooting through cracks between the plates. His boots were in several inches of water and the situation was getting worse.

"Faster! Come on, open those valves! Without those pumps—"

He let the words hang there. The crewmen down in the engine room with him were not novices—they knew the consequences if the damage couldn't be repaired, and if the water couldn't be pumped out.

The stokers were frantically working to open valves on the pumps, getting the water flowing faster out of the *Venture,* a race against the water leaking in through the riveted plates. Hayes snapped at a few of the men, who were holding mattresses up against the leaks.

"Shore up those holes!" he shouted, frustrated that they could not keep the mattresses in place. Hayes looked at one of the stokers. "Get extra pumps in here! Now!"

As the sailor ran to fulfill this command, Hayes saw Captain Englehorn step into the engine room with an expression grim and knowing.

"She's taken a pounding," Hayes told him.

Englehorn gave a small nod. "What about the prop?"

"Shaft's not bent, far as we can tell," Hayes replied,

the only piece of good news, though even that was complicated. "But she's stuck hard against the rock . . ."

He was interrupted by a loud groan as the ship shifted on the reef.

Jimmy suddenly burst into the engine room, eyes wide and wild. "Captain! You'd better come quick!"

Hayes narrowed his gaze. *What now?*

Englehorn went to follow Jimmy up to the deck, Hayes following out of curiosity. When they emerged, he was somewhat relieved to find that the fog had thinned considerably and that morning had already come while he was below. The landscape around them was the most forbidding he had ever seen, even in war, but there was something about even this diffuse daylight that lifted an invisible weight from his shoulders.

With morning there seemed hope.

Hayes and Englehorn followed Jimmy to the railing and the boy pointed toward the island. There was no mistaking what had gotten Jimmy so anxious. A whaler, one of the smaller lifeboats, was being rowed away from the *Venture* toward the shore, where a tiny inlet appeared to be the only real access to the island that didn't involve scaling craggy cliffs or that impossibly huge wall.

They'd made a good distance already, but by the dawn's light, Hayes could see Denham at the prow of the whaler, along with Driscoll, Miss Darrow, and Mr. Baxter, and the sound and camera men who worked with the filmmaker. Four sailors were ferrying them to the shore, all of them packed into that little boat.

"What the hell does he think he's doing?" Hayes asked, unable to comprehend the scene.

Englehorn lifted one corner of his mouth in sarcastic sneer. "It looks like Mr. Denham's mounting a one-man invasion."

Hayes looked at him. "And why would he want to do that?"

"He doesn't need a reason, Mr. Hayes. He's an American."

Several crewmen ran past, and Englehorn turned to bark orders at them. "Have you checked the fo'c'sle and cargo holds? Come on, move it!"

Hayes kept his eyes on the diminishing lifeboat. "You want me to bring them back?"

Englehorn fixed him with a dark look. "I don't give a damn about Carl Denham. I want this ship fixed and ready to float on the next high tide. We're leaving, Mr. Hayes."

12

THE SURF LAPPED THE sides of the whaler, sea spray dampening all of those Denham had either hired or shanghaied for this trip ashore. After the long night of fog and terror, Ann felt grateful for the return of the sun, though there was still a sheen of light mist that she thought might always cloak this spot, this strangely ancient place called Skull Island.

The sailors who were ferrying them ashore worked in grim silence. Bruce, Jack, and Denham's film crew were all equally subdued, and Ann wondered if they were as breathless as she, staring up at the great stone ruins that jutted out of the water all around them.

What kind of ancient civilization was this? she wondered. *And what happened to the people who once lived here?* The accomplishment of the statuary alone spoke of an advanced society, far from the primitive culture she would have expected from a remote, tropical island centuries in the past.

And that wall.

More than anything, it was the wall that chilled her, the wall that she was sure gave them all pause. It was a feat of construction no less extraordinary than the great pyramids, towering hundreds of feet in the air. It began in the water and ran up onto the shore, creating a barrier that effectively cut this part of the island away from the rest. It ran inland from here, and disappeared into the jungle, but it stretched as far as she could see, possibly all the way across the island.

The overall effect of the intimidating environment was that they were all sober as judges, and silent. All except Carl Denham, who seemed like a boy on Christmas morning. When he looked at Ann, she saw his eyes sparkling with excitement. He seemed to jitter in place, ready to jump out of his skin . . . or out of the boat, impatient to reach shore.

Can't you feel it, Mr. Denham? she thought. *Don't you have the same chill that's touching the rest of us?*

Denham balanced himself in the front of the boat, camera on his shoulder, filming as the sailors rowed them ashore. Herb was the camera operator, at least technically, but Denham almost always preferred to do the filming himself, leaving Herb to act the squire to Denham's knight.

"Can you believe this, Jack?" Denham quietly asked. "It's a godsend!"

Jack was staring up at the ruins. Ann followed his line of sight and saw a sea snake writhe from one of the gaping holes in the weathered edifice and slither down into the water. She shivered and drew her rain slicker a little closer around her, then slid a bit closer to Jack. In the midst of this strange new world, surrounded by these surly men, she reached across the private space that separated her from Jack and curled her fingers into his hand. He glanced at her, eyes searching and grave, and gave her hand a reassuring squeeze. But she didn't see that hope in his gaze.

Wind whistled through the gaps and holes in the ruins, an eerie moan that mixed with the deep boom of the waves crashing against the wall to create a mournful requiem.

Ann studied the faces of the statues—the idols—carved into the rocks all around the lifeboat. She glanced ahead at the shore of the small inlet and then her sight drifted along the water until she found herself looking over the side of the whaler, wondering if they were near enough yet to see the bottom.

She uttered a tiny gasp as she saw, beneath the water, a hideously distorted face staring back at her. The head of a fallen statue, tumbled by entropy.

The boat lurched forward and the image was washed away. Ann looked up and focused on the shore again. At the bow, she saw Denham look up from filming to glance shoreward, and the rapt expression on his face was beatific, as though he'd waited his whole life for this moment.

Ann felt as though she—all of them, in fact—were simply being swept along in the wake of Denham's quest. Yet she wondered what the object of that quest was, and whether or not even Denham truly knew.

The tiny inlet they had discovered led to a narrow, stony beach. A little ways in from the shore, sheer cliffs rose straight up. The carved faces of stone statues glowered down all around them. They'd run the whaler right up onto the little beach and then begun to unload the equipment for the film. It was as though the ancient civilization that had once called Skull Island home had created this place just for them, as though it was some macabre theater or forum.

Though the ocean lay to one side and the sky was wide above, Jack Driscoll felt more than a little claustrophobic on that narrow strip of beach. With those graven images and the closeness of the cliffs, he felt as though they were surrounded by the ghosts of the ancients here.

And then it occurred to him that it was more than that; the island itself was a kind of phantom remnant from another age.

As Denham got all of his people into place, Jack found a spot just a bit away from the others to watch. Ann and Bruce hit their marks, Mike and Herb took their places around Denham. Preston stood by, ready to do the director's bidding. Several times he rushed forward to make an adjustment to the actors' wardrobe, or to give Ann a quick turn so that her best profile was to the camera.

The sailors had helped unload, but now they stayed by the whaler, watching the proceedings with the curiosity of those who have seen a film and never imagined the mundane work that went into its creation.

"You're feeling uneasy, Ann," Denham called to his leading lady.

Her expression reflected his direction, and watching her face, whose beauty took Jack's breath away, he marveled at her ability to summon emotion from deep within herself. She was a natural actress, and he was certain that emotions she was dredging up had been hard won.

"Tilt up to the statue, Herb," Denham said. For once he was allowing the camera operator to do his job.

Herb did as instructed, and Jack tried to picture in his mind what the images would look like on screen. The beautiful, anxious girl with dread in her eyes, the imposing, almost grotesque features of the towering statue.

"The feeling is growing," Denham told Ann, "washing over you. You're trembling, Ann. You're overwhelmed."

The director pointed to Baxter. "Comfort her, Bruce!"

The matinee idol went into action. He slipped his arm around Ann's waist and swept her backward, practically dipping her, and leaned in to kiss her in a clinch so typical of the silver screen.

What the hell? Jack thought, face growing warm. *Denham said comfort her—*

"Wait a second! Stop! Stop! That's not in the script!" Jack barked.

Baxter looked up at him with what seemed genuine surprise and innocence. "I was improvising."

Jack sneered. "That wasn't improvising, pal, that was molestation. She would never kiss you. She's not available . . . emotionally . . . to men. Isn't that right, Miss Darrow?"

Ann inclined her head just a bit. Jack was talking about her character, but they both knew his reaction was about more than that.

"It did feel a little . . . premature," Ann agreed.

Bruce looked at her as though she'd grown a second head. "What are you talking about? I told you I loved you on page fifty-three!"

"That doesn't give you a free pass, Bruce," Denham chimed in. The director paused for just a moment, forcing actors, writer, and crew alike to turn to him. "You're sitting this one out."

Baxter's eyes went wide and he gave a little shake of his head. "I know what's going on here. And it's time we all acknowledged the truth of the situation."

Jack tensed. *Here it comes.*

"You can dress it up any way you want but there is no escaping this one singular fact," Baxter went on.

They all stared at him, awaiting his revelation.

When the actor finally spoke, it was with dreadful gravity.

"My part is getting smaller."

Jack arched an eyebrow and regarded him coolly. "I'm sorry. There's nothing I can do about your small part."

He let the double entendre and the accompanying insult hang there like bait, but Baxter either hadn't gotten the jibe or didn't go for it.

"From day one there has been an unusual amount of focus on the female's side of the story," the actor said, almost petulantly. "I'm telling you, Denham, this clam is trying to sideline me!"

Jack took a step closer, ready for an argument. Baxter was a pompous ass, badly in need of a career boost, but he was used to having films built around him and

150

obviously didn't like sharing the spotlight. He needed a good punch, just to shake him up, get him to see that the world didn't revolve around him, and that some scripts—those written by Jack Driscoll, at least—had more going on than some bullying tough guy.

But Jack didn't get a chance to say anything. Carl Denham was the director of this picture, and he clearly didn't like the fact that Baxter had seemingly forgotten that.

"For Christ's sake . . ." Carl began, about to give Baxter a piece of his mind.

But the actor wasn't done. "I won't play second fiddle to a girl! It's screen suicide!"

That did it.

"You don't have a say in this!" the director snapped, irate, as if lecturing a schoolboy. "Shaddup!"

Even Jack blinked at the vehemence in Denham. They all looked at him in shocked silence. Carl shook his head in exasperation and then fixed a hard stare at Baxter.

"You can't run a film like a democracy. If it's not a dictatorship, it falls apart. Now let me finish this goddamn picture so I can have a nervous breakdown!" he shouted.

Then he took a breath and turned, quite calmly, to the camera operator. "Herbert. Roll camera."

As the boys argued, Ann was at first amused, but as she stood listening to them, her mind began to wander. As they had made their way to shore, the imposing presence of the statues had chilled her. The memory of that face beneath the waves lingered, and she was sure it would bring nightmares. It was as though each of those terrible images was filled with some dreadful intelligence.

She glanced around at them again now, unsettled. Ann turned to the primitive, ancient faces carved in the rock behind her, and it was as though she could hear in her head the chants of whatever primeval tribe created them. A strange thrumming sound filled her head. As if entranced, she walked to the base of one of those idols and put her hand against the rock. The sound in her head intensified.

The quiet dread raced through her, one that she could not have even described. The urge to return to the whaler and rush back to the *Venture* was overwhelming.

Then Denham called her name. Quietly.

"Ann," he said. "Look up slowly, Ann."

It was his director's voice, and suddenly she was back on film again, in character, trying to feel all of the emotion he wanted to extract from her, to bring it up from within her and reveal it with only her face and her eyes.

She did as he asked.

"That's it, "Denham said. "It scares you. You can't look away. You're helpless. You want to scream, but your throat is paralyzed!"

The dread she'd felt, that thrumming in her head, the haunted gaze of those ancient faces, all grew stronger in her now. Denham seemed to be speaking to her from another place, another world, and she knew her fear was real.

"What do you think she's looking at?" she heard Preston whisper, but the voice was far away.

"There's just one chance," Denham continued. "If you can scream. Try to scream, Ann! Try!"

And she wanted to. It was as though she'd been wanting to scream all along, ever since she'd seen the idol in the water, ever since she'd set foot on the shore, and now Denham was giving her permission to put voice to the terror inside her.

She opened her mouth, but only a small sound came out, the shriek dying in her throat.

"Throw your arms across your eyes and scream!" Denham shouted. "Scream, Ann! Scream for your life!"

Her lips parted, drew back, and she let loose with a scream that came up from deep within her, from her terrified center, eyes wide and staring at some unimaginable horror, the source of her nameless dread. Ann screamed with all of the fear she had ever felt.

As the sound died, she looked at Denham, at Jack beyond him, and all of the others. They were staring at her, concern and surprise on their faces, as though they were truly fearful for her. But it was acting, of course. Ann told herself that now, tamping down the tension and the dread of this place.

Only acting.

And then, as the last echo of her scream disappeared, there came another sound.

An unearthly, bestial cry that was part scream itself

and part roar came from somewhere deep within the island's jungle interior. The sound was inhuman and yet she had no doubt it was a reply to her own primal scream.

For several moments, those gathered on the beach could only stare at one another, frozen into silence by that terrible cry.

On the deck of the *Venture,* Hayes was standing with Jimmy and Captain Englehorn, discussing the efforts to repair the ship, when they all heard that bestial scream. The three turned as one toward shore. From deep within the island they saw a flock of startled birds rise into the air, panicked.

Running from something, Hayes thought. *But what?*

That scream, more like a roar, came from the jungle.

Bruce Baxter was fighting for his professional life. Carl Denham was supposed to have helped revive the actor's dwindling career. But every step of the way, he'd been able to see both Denham and Driscoll conspiring to make the film more about Ann's character, or at least more about the relationship, than about Baxter's heroic male lead. That was dangerous.

Bruce could do just about anything. Ride a horse. Fence. High dive. And better than almost anyone. Looks, talent, and brains. But he couldn't compete with Ann.

All of that had been going on in his head while he watched her act, right up until that scream. Then he heard the roar, that terrible sound from the jungle, and he wished he was a little boy again, to crawl under his bed and hide.

Suddenly his career didn't seem so important anymore—not nearly as important as his life.

"What was that?" Bruce asked. "A bear? That was a bear, wasn't it?"

All eyes were scanning the cliffs. Denham hurried to the far edge of the cove.

"Herb! Get the camera!" the director commanded.

Denham had found a way up inside the cliff. Some kind of entrance. Bruce took a few steps nearer to get a better glimpse. It was a ruined stone stairway, leading up into the darkness of some kind of tunnel. Whatever ancient culture had carved these idols and built the wall had made this as a passage to whatever lay above in the ruins.

Denham gestured to the others to follow him, and started into the blackness, up those stairs.

"Where are you going?" Bruce asked, incredulous. "Fellas? Is this a good idea?"

13

TWO OF THE SAILORS stayed with the whaler back on the rocky beach. Everyone else gathered round the foot of the ancient staircase that Denham had discovered. Carl led the way, with Herb and Preston right behind him. They entered the darkness and started up the stone stairs—hewn from the cliff face—without waiting for the rest.

Bruce, Mike, and the other two sailors—Pardue and Young—were the last to reach the tunnel. Jack and Ann beat them to it.

At the base of the stairs, Jack paused to peer up into the dark silence. The tunnel had high, vaulted ceilings, as though the stairs had been constructed inside a natural cavern. Far ahead and above he could see daylight at the top of the stairs. Now that his eyes were adjusting to the dark, what little illumination there was allowed him to see the handiwork that had gone into making this passage. Primitive symbols had been engraved in the walls, the stairs themselves were a remarkable feat.

He started up. Ann was following and he glanced

back in time to see her hesitate, a troubled expression on her face.

"Ann?"

"I want to go back," she said, clearly rattled.

Jack moved toward her, reaching for her arm. This was entirely unlike the Ann he knew, albeit briefly. "What is it?"

"I don't know."

Distracted, she glanced around a moment before meeting his gaze. Jack saw that she was truly skittish, like a young deer, ready to bolt at any threat. He found the island pretty unsettling himself, and was more than a little concerned about the condition of the *Venture*. But he was fascinated by Skull Island as well. The archeological and anthropological value of this place—the ruins of an ancient civilization—was immense.

He was surprised Ann didn't feel the same. Yet he was also not going to downplay whatever had her so disquieted. She was not some delicate flower, given to general anxiety. And if she wanted to go back, he would take her.

Jack turned and called up the stairs. "Carl!"

He started up, and he could sense Ann reluctantly following. Denham, Herb, and Preston were far ahead now and he could make out their silhouettes against the light at the top.

"Jack, you're not going to believe what's up here!" Denham called back down. "It's incredible!"

"Hey, wait up!" Jack gave Ann a regretful look and

continued up the stairs. Carl being the director, it was up to him to decide if Jack would be allowed to take Ann back to the ship.

Carl turned to look back at those still coming up the stairs through that tunnel. He had a beatific smile on his face, as though angels had just lifted a weight from him.

"I owe you one, buddy," Carl said to Jack. "That goes for you, too, Ann. Herbert . . . Preston . . ."

"Carl!" Jack tried to interrupt.

Denham wasn't listening, however. He was so enraptured by his surroundings and what they meant for him that he was lost in his own thoughts. Overwhelmed with emotion, he now shook his head, grinning.

"Sorry, Jack, I gotta say it. You believed in me. All of you. I want to thank you for standing by the picture. It means so much to me. Seriously. You saved my life." Carl paused, swallowing hard, overcome. "I love you guys."

Jack stared at him, stunned. In all the years he'd known Carl Denham the only emotion he'd ever revealed so nakedly was his passion for the cinema. On either side of the director, Jack could see Herb and Preston gaping at him with the same obvious amazement. He could only imagine that behind him, Bruce and Mike were doing the same.

Then all that emotion shut off like a movie screen going dark, and Carl's eyes sparkled with exuberant purpose once more. The director was back.

"Ann—let's get a shot of you at the top of the stairs."

Ben Hayes rushed along the deck of the *Venture*, shouting at the crew. They were already frantic, but he didn't mind adding to their hurry. They had to be ready to float by high tide so they could get the ship off these damned rocks and away from this island.

"They need more shoring timbers in the engine room!" he shouted at a couple of the younger lads as they ran past. "Quick! Now!"

Away from this island. He glanced up at the carved head that towered above the *Venture* like some mythical monster or vengeful god. Hayes scowled. They never should have come here in the first place. He had told Englehorn that very thing, but the captain had taken Denham's money—or at least the check that the bank said was no good—and wouldn't hear of it. All of the men had been in peril. Now that it seemed the worst was over, Hayes was ready to call them all lucky and return to the sea. Perhaps they could pick up cargo somewhere still, so the trip would not be a total loss.

He spotted Lumpy further along the deck, talking to Choy, and was about to tell them both to go down to the engine room and help out. But then he spied a pale face looking out from a place behind one of the lifeboats.

Jimmy was there, tucked away, out from under the running feet of the crew, reading his book.

Hayes sighed and started for the boy. Jimmy looked up just as he arrived and tried to clutch *Heart of Darkness* protectively against his chest. But Hayes reached out and slid it from his hands and the boy let it go, reluctantly. He had a finger holding his place, and Hayes took it and opened it to that page, looking down at the words there, at the ideas and images that were touching Jimmy's mind even now. At a tale of a boat, and a jungle, and a man obsessed. Hayes remembered the story well.

"We could not understand, because we were too far," Conrad had written, *"and could not remember, because we were traveling in the night of First Ages, of Those Ages that are gone, leaving hardly a sign and no memories. We are accustomed to look upon the shackled form of a conquered monster, but there, there you could look at a thing that is monstrous, and free."*

He handed the book back to Jimmy, who closed it and held it to him again, an ashen expression on his face.

"Why does he keep going up the river?" the boy asked. "Why doesn't Marlowe turn back?"

Hayes had no idea the true extent of the horrors that the boy must have seen and lived to end up in an animal cage, filthy and bruised, and think he'd found a fine home. But he knew Jimmy would be struggling for a long time to understand men, and to figure out what sort of man he himself would be.

"There's a part of him that wants to, Jimmy," Hayes said with a shrug. "A part deep inside himself that sounds a warning. But there's another part that needs to know . . . needs to bring light to the mystery and defeat the thing that makes him afraid."

Even as he spoke, Hayes was thinking of Denham, another man who felt the need to bring light to the mysteries of the world. There was nothing Denham loved more, and his obsession for committing such things to film had nearly gotten them all killed. Hayes wondered how it could be that Denham didn't understand that every time he put a mystery on film, he was destroying it, making it no longer an enigma. Denham seemed to have a hunger to prove himself more than an ordinary man by exploring, uncovering . . .

Hayes had read about Joseph Conrad in an article somewhere. The author had supposedly loved maps, loved the blank spaces on them, the regions unknown, and hated that as he got older those blank spaces were filled in, the mystery erased. How was it that Conrad had seen it, and Denham could not?

Ben Hayes had abandoned his homeland, venturing out to sea because, among other things, he longed to remain in those blank spaces upon the map, and it was getting so that the sea was the only one left.

Jimmy had grown thoughtful as he considered the first mate's words. After a moment he said, "It's not an adventure story, is it, Mr. Hayes?"

Hayes studied the boy's eyes, saw the light of understanding there, and imagined just what must be going through the boy's head. "No, Jimmy. It's not."

Together, they turned to look up at the grim, graven features of the statues, and for a time, neither said a word.

The top of the stairs gave way to a landing with a vaulted, cavernous ceiling. The daylight that Denham had originally thought meant the end of the tunnel came from a hole high above them, but it provided enough light to continue on, enough illumination to see what they had entered.

Ahead, there was some kind of ancient burial chamber.

The smell of the sea permeated the place, but beneath that there was something else. The dust of centuries. The withered bones of another age. Denham led the way along the path and in the dim light they could make out tombs in the walls on either side. Some of them were broken, and in the burial niches inside he caught glimpses of mummified skeletons, remnants of skin like parchment paper and small tufts of wiry white hair still clinging to mud-colored skulls.

The dead seemed to watch in silence as they passed, as though they were the guardians of this place. To Denham, it felt as though they were traveling on a journey through time from present to past.

He came to a break in the path, a crevasse in the solid rock of the cliff. A bamboo bridge spanned the gap, and he wondered how long ago it had been constructed and whether or not it was possible that it would still hold everyone.

No time to hesitate. If Denham allowed his companions or the sailors to see him pause, they might question the safety of that bridge. And nothing could stop him, now. Not when he could see more stairs ahead, and the true light of day at the top of them, streaming in from somewhere close.

He had to see what was out there—the monstrous roar that had come from the jungle still echoed in his ears.

Denham led them across the bridge, which creaked and strained but held firm. They followed him up those stairs and soon the burial chamber was left behind. At the top of the stairs, the exit had once been elegant, vaulted and arched, carved from stone with the same skill and craftsmanship as the idols that were all over these ruins. But some time ago, it had caved in and huge blocks of stone now were piled in their path.

But there was enough room to climb through.

Denham began to make his way up and the others followed. Carefully they moved over the blockade, quiet and tense. On the other side, the sky was gray, hung low with heavy clouds and some dark and threatening rain. He took a few steps forward, heard the others clambering down the collapsed rocks behind him, and held up a hand to caution them to silence.

Thunder rumbled overhead and he could feel it in his bones. One by one, Herb, Preston, Jack, Ann, Mike, Bruce, and the two sailors who'd accompanied them made it over the rock fall and emerged from the ruined tunnel mouth. They were on the crest of a hill. The cliff behind them was a sheer drop to the rocky beach, but ahead it sloped down at an angle, still intimidating but not impossible.

Cautious, keeping low, Denham hurried to an out-cropping of stone to get a vantage point from which he could see what lay down that slope. The others followed, but by then Denham had nearly forgotten they were there.

The rest of the plateau spread out in front of them. The burial chamber in the tunnel they had just emerged from was only the beginning, or perhaps even some spillover, for what lay below was a true necropolis, an ancient burial ground with stone mausoleums and tombs that were huge and intricate, clearly of the same period as the ancient culture responsible for the ruins, and like the final resting place of the last souls of that civilization.

Many of the tombs had been smashed open, others reduced to rubble.

It was not the dead that made him catch his breath now, though.

Spread amongst the necropolis was a crude shanty town, a village of meager huts crafted from bamboo and grass. Denham was well-traveled, and could tell this culture was indeed far more recent, and devoid of any of the sophistication of the civilization that had once thrived here. It was also devoid of any sign of life.

"It's deserted," Preston remarked.

"Of course it's deserted," Denham hastily replied. "Use your eyes, Preston. The place is a ruin! It's been abandoned for hundreds of years. Nobody lives here."

Denham was puzzled. The question of the fate of the ancient tribe of Skull Island was put aside for the moment in favor of the more pressing mystery . . . how had this other village sprung up? They weren't descended from the ancients, for they would have had to devolve. All he could think was that they might have been some kind of amalgamation of peoples who had been shipwrecked here in more recent centuries, maybe all of them coming together to create a new tribe, a new culture.

Surely, the people who built ramshackle grass huts could not have built the wall that even now he could not help but stare at. On the far side of the plateau, it rose skyward, towering over the village and the ruins of the graves of ancients—a huge structure that bisected the island, running off into the ocean on one side and into the jungle on the other.

A wide staircase ran through the village up a slope to an enormous door in the wall. All along the top of the wall there were hundreds, perhaps thousands of huge bamboo spikes that jutted out from the structure. From a distance, Denham had not been able to make out what they were, only that they had been spiny, like the quills of a porcupine. Up close it was plain they were spears of bamboo, though he could not guess at their purpose.

He would relish hearing a real anthropologist's or archeologist's take on all this one day.

Another bestial roar rose from the jungle, somewhere in the heart of the island. Denham glanced over the top of the wall, momentarily distracted.

When he lowered his gaze, he nearly leaped backward in fright.

A small child stood on the dusty path before them, a girl with ebon skin, clad in a dark, heavy garment that covered her front and back, but was open at the sides, held only by a few strings. The girl had strange, almost feral eyes. She slowly raised an arm and pointed at the group huddled behind the rocks, as though frozen in fear of them.

Denham stood up. "I'll handle this."

He moved out from behind the rocks and started down the path into the not-so-deserted village. The child stared at him but Denham reached into his jacket pocket and withdrew a bar of Hershey's Chocolate. His own mouth watered at the thought of the candy, but it was no longer for him. Thunder boomed above once more and he could feel the electricity of the storm brewing in the air, the cool dampness of the rain about to fall.

Then he felt the first drops.

He waved the candy in front of the child. "Look, chocolate. You like chocolate?"

Her were wide and unblinking, drilling into him.

The rain began to fall.

"Good to eat!" Denham said, thrusting it at the child again. "Good to eat! Take it . . . take it!"

The girl stepped back. Denham felt a flash of concern. He wanted to be understood. Getting off on the wrong foot here could be dangerous. He reached out and grabbed the child by the wrist and attempted to press the chocolate bar into her hand.

She struggled to break free from him, crying out.

Denham froze at the sound, knowing it would bring

others. Sure enough, villagers begin to melt out of the shadows of huts and tombs alike, gray ghosts in the rain, old and young, their flesh glistening oil black. They wore very little, mostly scraps of animal hide. Some had faces etched with decorative scars or punctured with sharp bones that jutted from their skin. Others wore bits of bone around their necks or in their matted hair.

A ripple of panic went through Denham and he struggled with the child, trying to explain by gesture if not by word. Hollow-eyed women stared at him balefully.

The girl sank her teeth into his wrist, snapping like a wolf. Denham let out a yell of surprise and pain, releasing his grip. The child ran off and for a moment he could only look at the villagers who had started to gather before him. Retreat was considered and then discarded. There was no way he could, or would, walk away from this.

Instead, he turned and gestured for Jack, Ann, and the others who were watching from the rocks, to come forward. They stared at him as they nervously emerged and came up to join him.

"It's all right," he assured them. "It's just a bunch of women and kids."

Ann, Jack, and Preston were in the front, but suddenly Mike lurched past them, as though in a rush to join Denham. Ann glanced at the sound man, concern etching her features.

"Mike?" she began.

The sound man gasped, staring around at them with

a fearful, helpless expression, and then he fell face forward onto the ground, revealing the jagged spear that jutted from his back.

Denham cursed inwardly and his breath caught. He had thought the situation in his control and it had just been torn away from him. He and Jack both spun to see where the deadly attack had originated from.

Ann stepped back in horror and screamed.

The terrifying jungle roar filled the village as if in answer to Ann's cry, an echo of her once more. But it was louder and closer this time, as though whatever creature had uttered it had been summoned by her and was even now drawing nearer.

Then all hell broke loose.

Native men sprang from behind rocks and in the shadows of tombs, raced out from amongst the women and children and from the huts. Ann cried out in alarm, but there was nothing any of them could do as they were quickly swept into a maelstrom of rough, powerful hands and jabbing spears, pushed and pulled by the primitive mob. Denham was tossed into a churning, stormy ocean of anger, and then spun around as all motion ceased.

An old woman now appeared, painted with strange symbols and decorated with bones and feathers and small artifacts Denham did not recognize. There was a crown on her head that looked like it was made from small finger bones, and her skin was like worn leather. In the rain, her thin, white hair plastered to her skull, she had the aspect of a witch out of Shakespeare. Her fingernails were like claws, yellow with age. The crone wore a cloak partially made of feathers, and around her neck hung the skull of some large bird.

With the deference the rest of the villagers paid her, it was clear she was some sort of matriarch, a figure of power amongst them. In Denham's experience, primitive tribes often had a shaman, a being supposedly in tune with mystical power and nature, but they were always male. Still, this woman seemed to hold a similar place here, and so he instantly thought of her as some sort of . . . sha-woman.

The matriarch ignored Denham and focused on Ann. She muttered what had to be curses and spat, her eyes burning with dark fury. Ann began to back away from her, and many of the old villagers began to rock and wail in unison. They bent to gather mud from the rain-spattered earth and smeared it upon their faces, across their screeching mouths. Denham could only imagine he had found himself on an island asylum, a place filled with only the mad and the damned.

Bruce shouted at some of the natives, struggling as they held onto him, dragging him forward as though about to offer him to the sha-woman as some sort of prize. Jack reached for Ann and pulled her close, trying to protect her. Denham was heartened by the sight, but it was bittersweet, for he knew there was nothing any of them could do against these numbers, not with only their fists as weapons.

Denham started shouting at the sha-woman, at the natives, trying to make them understand that he and his friends had come in peace. They only wanted to talk, and if they were not welcome, they would leave. Yes, it was most certainly time to leave now.

But it was also clear that was not in the plans.

Denham's head thundered with the shrieking of the natives, their language gibberish to him. The rain pelted him, cold and cruel, and the ground darkened with it.

He heard someone shout his name and turned to see one of the sailors, Pardue, dragged through the rain. In the blink of an eye, Pardue was forced to his knees, his head pushed down on a flat stone slab, and then even as Denham realized what was happening, the natives clubbed the sailor to death, shattering his skull, pulping his entire head.

No! This wasn't happening. They were supposed to be shooting a film! This was a nightmare . . . this couldn't be!

In the churning confusion, the sha-woman continued to scream at Ann, voice rising, becoming hysterical.

"Larri yu sano korê . . . kweh yonê kah'weh ad-larr . . . torê Kong!" the sha-woman chanted, pointing at Ann and darting her head forward in a menacing, mocking sort of dance. *"Yu tore. Kweh norê dahah ad-larr Kong-ka!"*

Denham had no idea what she was saying, but through gesture and intonation it was clear that the villagers thought Ann had done something. From the way they looked fearfully at the wall, and the stress upon the word, he had an idea that whatever it had been built to hold back, they were afraid it was coming.

What was she saying then? That Ann, somehow, had summoned it?

Then he remembered Ann's screams on the beach, and the horrible, beastly roars that had answered back. And the last one, which had sounded so much closer. Even then he'd thought it was as though her screams had called to the beast from the jungle on the other side of the wall.

Two men were dead, their murders ghastly and savage, and the survivors were all about to share their fate. But Carl Denham could not resist wishing he could see what it was they all feared, what they thought Ann had called.

Then the islanders tore her out of Jack's grasp, and he cursed himself for a fool for even thinking such thoughts. Jack fought them but the natives only pulled him away. Ann struggled and Denham found himself silently hoping she would not scream again.

The sha-woman continued her accusatory chant. Denham abruptly tried to free himself from his captors. His arms were twisted, his muscles burning with pain. But in the same moment, Jack tore loose and he rushed toward Ann. Denham felt a surge of hope and struggled as well, hoping to help him, but as Jack attacked the islanders, fists flying, one of them loomed up behind him and clubbed him in the back of the head.

He dropped like a stone, sprawled on the ground, moaning.

Ann screamed at last, and it felt to Denham as though every one of them, islander and visitor alike, froze, holding their breaths. Fearful glances turned toward the wall.

In the distance, the beast roared. But not so distant at all, really. Far closer even than before. And from the way the sha-woman rounded on Ann, then, fury in her eyes, he knew he had been right. They *were* blaming her. And they were all terrified of whatever it was on the other side of that wall.

Denham tore his hand free and slammed a fist into the face of an islander. But there were so many of them that new hands grasped him, gripping him, forcing him to stagger forth until he stumbled and went down on his knees.

He twisted his head to one side as they thrust him forward and he caught the copper scent of blood a second before they pressed his face against the hot, gory mess left behind by Pardue's murder. Denham struggled, shouted at the villagers, at the heavens, at the beast beyond the wall. It was over. He was going to die here.

Clubs rose into the air.

A gunshot echoed off the wall and the ruins and the rain.

Hands released him and Denham spilled over onto his side and started scrambling away from his captors. Englehorn and Hayes led a group of armed sailors down into the village. The natives were at first

172

stunned, but then they scattered, disappearing into the rain and the shadows from which they'd emerged.

Captain Englehorn strode over to Denham and roughly hauled him to his feet. His words were a snarl, an unfriendly rescuer.

"Seen enough?"

14

THIS WAS THE MOMENT. Englehorn could feel it. The *Venture* was like an extension of his own body, his own flesh and blood, and as she swayed with the crashing waves and scraped on the rocks below, shifting . . . shifting . . . he knew that they had reached a critical point.

The captain stood on the deck of his ship in the dark, with stars strewn across the sky above and the tumultuous sea below. His pulse drummed in his temples.

"Lighten the ship!" he called, shouting to be heard over the howling of the wind and the waves pounding the hull. Members of the crew hurried from belowdecks, carrying anything they could lift. He'd been shouting at them for several minutes, but he wasn't about to stop now.

"Anything that's not bolted down goes overboard!" Englehorn roared.

Lumpy, Jimmy, Choy, and every hand he could sacrifice to the effort were on deck now. They went to the railing and tossed ballast over into the churning sea. Tables, chests, even kitchen equipment went into the water. Englehorn grimaced, for he knew how difficult it must be for them to part with some of the things that were being lost. Lumpy himself had thrown a heavy mixer from the galley into the surf.

But they had no other choice. As each wave struck the *Venture*, she groaned and scraped and shifted against the undersea rocks upon which she was stuck. The aftermath of the previous night's storm had made the tide higher than it would ordinarily be, and even that wasn't enough. They had to lighten the ship. If they didn't get off the rocks *right now,* he didn't know how many days it would be before the conditions were so favorable again.

This was the moment.

Alone in her cabin, Ann pulled a robe tightly around her, covering the satin slip she had put on after washing up. Jack was still unconscious but Lumpy had assured her that he would be all right. Jimmy had offered to stay with her, but she didn't want to be spoken to or to discuss the day's events. She needed solitude.

Or so she'd thought.

Now she wished she had not insisted. It was worse, being alone. She would have been better off with a distraction. If things were not so chaotic, if they were not all working to get the ship off the reef, she would have gone up to the mess to laugh and joke with the sailors.

Anything not to think about Skull Island and poor Mike. She remembered so clearly his sweet befuddlement on the day she'd first met him and confused him for Jack. But that memory was scarred now, scribbled over with an image of his dead eyes wide with shock and . . . what? Sadness? Disappointment, that his life should end like this. Those eyes now haunted her waking hours.

The island had gotten under her skin from the moment she saw it, and that had grown worse when she set foot upon the shore.

Silently, she exhorted Englehorn and his crew to work faster, to do whatever was necessary to get them off the rocks. To get away from this damnable place. The faces of the natives were seared into her brain, of the sailor who'd had his brains dashed out upon some kind of sacrificial stone, of Mike . . . but perhaps worst of all, the ancient, withered crone with those ugly, gnarled fingers and that crown of bones.

She could not shake from her mind the question of what would have happened if the captain had not come along when he did. Once again she tightened the robe around her, wishing she had something warmer. In her heart, though, she knew it was not just the temperature that made her cold. The worst of the chill was coming from within. She pressed her eyes tightly together.

In her mind, she could still hear that terrible roar from the other side of the wall, deep in the jungle, that echo of her own scream. Her eyes opened. There was no way she was going to be able to sleep tonight, even if they managed to get away from this godforsaken place.

Ann looked down and noticed that her hands were trembling.

Out in the dark, they moved in silence. The waves crashed upon the rocks and the salty spray spattered their lithe bodies, but nothing interrupted the rhythm of their progress. The chanting in the village still resonated in their ears, punctuated by the screams of the girl and the roar of Kong.

They knew what had to be done.

Clutching long, bamboo poles they vaulted from rock to rock over the stormy seas. Effortlessly, in fluid, unhesitating motion, they crossed wider and wider gulfs between the craggy monoliths that jutted from the turgid water. Waves leaped as if to dash them into the sea, but they danced across the rocks, planted the ends of the poles, and sailed through the darkness over the roiling surf.

The ship loomed ahead in the dark, grounded.

Captive prey.

Jack woke to a loud, metallic creak and a hell of a headache, like someone was crushing his skull in a vise. He squinted his eyes tightly closed and softly groaned. For a few seconds he had no idea where he was or what had happened to him. Then he remembered following Denham up through that burial chamber, the village, that bizarre sha-woman, all of it. Mike was dead. At least a couple members of the crew.

And you nearly joined them.

The memory of his fear grew quickly in his heart so that it was as though he was still surrounded by those angry natives with their hate-filled eyes. How had it come to this? How had Denham's dream led to such a brutal end?

His vision was out of focus. He rolled onto his side and blinked several times, and slowly the world swam back into focus. He was on a bench in the mess room, which made sense, given that the cook was also the ship's doctor. But if Lumpy had been tending to him, where was the man now?

Where was everyone, for that matter? He had a vague recollection of faces looking down upon him, of being in the whaler as they rowed back here, of voices talking to him and being hoisted up onto the deck of the ship.

Of Ann.

He thought again of the sha-woman, of the way she'd looked at Ann, screamed at her in that accusatory tone, and he remembered the roar from the jungle. Jack had no idea what could create a sound like that, or what the sha-woman had been talking about, and he hoped never to learn.

Ann. He had seen her terror, had tried his best to protect her. Half-conscious though he was, he had seen her when they brought him back to the ship, so he knew she had not been badly hurt. But that did not mean she was coping well with the horror of their experience on the island.

He had to go to her, see how she was.

Once again he tried to force his vision and his thoughts to clear. Just the tiniest motion sent hammer-strikes of pain thudding through his skull. He reached around to touch the back of his head, the point from which the pain radiated, and found something hot and sticky. When he withdrew his hand and glanced down at it, he saw that his fingers glistened with his own blood.

Denham took a swig from his hip flask. The storm battered and crashed outside and the ship swayed. Herb and Preston stood gloomily, watching him as he strode about his cabin, but Denham was having none of that.

"It was close," he told them, "but we got it. We got away. We have to be grateful for that, gentlemen."

It was a good thing Englehorn had a change of heart and came along when he did, Denham mused. *Talk about divine intervention.*

"What about Mike?" Preston asked quietly, face slack, still traumatized. "He didn't get away. He's still there."

"Mike died doing what he believed in!" Denham said sharply. "He did not die for nothing. And I'll tell you something else, I'm gonna finish this picture. For Mike! We'll finish it and donate the proceeds to his wife and kids, because that man is a hero and he deserves no less!"

Herb nodded. "Hear, hear!"

The cabin door banged open and a pair of sailors bustled into the room.

"Lighten the ship! Captain's orders!" snapped the first one. "We're floating her off the rocks. Everything goes overboard!"

Denham gestured around the cabin with his flask. "Help yourselves, boys."

One of the sailors picked up a small table, the other a chair, even as more of the crew slipped into the cabin and grabbed hold of other pieces of furniture.

Denham toasted their efforts and glanced at what remained of his film crew. "The sooner we get out of this godawful stinkhole, the better!"

"We got some great stuff though, didn't we?" Herb said proudly.

"Herbert, we shot Skull Island," Denham replied, swigging from the flask. "All we have to do is finish up the film with Ann and Bruce, somewhere warm, sunny, and safe."

He smiled to himself and took another swig. As he did, he glanced around the room and a frown creased his brow.

Something's not right here . . .

"Where's my camera?"

Gone.

He dropped the flask and ran for the door.

Denham hurtled along a corridor, fury and panic warring within him. Up ahead he saw Choy's head bobbing as the little man ran for the door. A swell rocked the ship and Denham stumbled as he was thrown to the right. He crashed into the wall, spun, and then let the rocking of the ship add to his momentum as he threw himself forward again.

Choy flung open the door with one hand. With the other, he clutched the Bell & Howell movie camera, which he carried on his shoulder like a rifle at arms.

"No!" Denham roared as Choy disappeared.

He reached the door and threw it open, gaining on Choy. The camera bounced on the sailor's shoulder as he raced for the railing, ready to throw it overboard. Denham's heart thundered in his chest and he wanted to snap every bone in Choy's body. His camera was *not* ballast. They'd be better off throwing all their food stores overboard than the camera—it was their one chance of making a profit off of this voyage.

"Not that!" he shouted at Choy, still in pursuit. "Stop!"

But Choy wasn't slowing down. Denham, instead, sped up.

The wind whistling around him, a silent figure sailed through the night, steadied upon a bamboo pole he had used to push off from the top of the carved stone head of an ancient god. Little more than a silhouette, darkness against darkness, he dropped down to the deck of the ship, alighting noiselessly. Swiftly he set the pole aside and raced to press himself against a wall, unseen.

There were shouts all around, the crew in a frenzy as the ship rocked in the stormy sea, but no one had noticed the intruder. Quickly he slid along the wall, creeping along until he came to a door and slipped inside.

Jack staggered onto the deck at the aft end of the ship, skull still splitting. He'd dabbed at the back of his head and the bleeding seemed to have stopped.

There was dried blood in his hair but now wasn't the time to think about it. Nothing mattered until he'd seen Ann, made sure she was all right, and then he'd hunt down Denham and Englehorn and find out what was going on.

Still somewhat disoriented, he couldn't tell how much of his stumbling was due to the rocking of the sea and how much came from the blow to his head. He felt the ship roll and reached out to clutch the railing to steady himself.

He took a breath and glanced down.

On the deck was a crude necklace of small bones and feathers, with the skull of a tiny monkey as its center piece. A sick feeling churned in his gut and horror swept over him as he bent to snatch it up from the deck, his dizziness worsening.

No, he thought. *They can't be on board. Why would they—*

Then the answer struck him, so obvious he felt like a fool. They'd wanted Ann for whatever dark purpose, and been insistent about it.

Jack silently cursed and looked around just in time to see Jimmy running along the deck, intent upon some errand or other. Whatever it was, it was nothing compared to this. Jack grabbed him by the arm as he ran past.

"Where's Ann?" he demanded.

The boy looked at him, eyes a bit wild. "In her cabin."

Jack let him go. The boy had duties to attend to. Teeth gritted as he pushed the pain in his skull away,

Jack steadied himself by sheer force of will. Sailors continued to scurry all around him, carrying anything that wasn't vital to their survival and flinging it overboard.

He pushed through them, making his way to the nearest door that would take him belowdecks. Once inside, it was even more crowded in the corridor. He shoved past crewmen, ignoring their shouts and the frantic climate of the moment, trying to get to Ann's cabin.

Ann sat on her bunk, clutching a blanket in her hands. Her knuckles were white. On the island she had been struck with a terrible foreboding, and now here it was again. Her heart sped up, pulse throbbing in her ears and thudding in her chest. Her throat felt constricted and her lips were dry. She tried to wet them and found them rough. Ann glanced around the room as though the shadows themselves were alive. It was foolish, but she could not escape the terrible dread in the pit of her stomach.

A wave crashed against her window and she spun around in fright, lips pressed tightly together to contain a scream.

She told herself to stop, to take it easy. They would be away from the island soon. But it did nothing to calm her. Ann stood and went to the window to look out at the churning seas. The ship swayed worse than ever, rocking as though the water god Poseidon himself had them in his grip. With a thump and a bang that made her jump, her closet door swung wide and costumes spilled out onto the floor.

For an instant she stared at the closet door swaying

back and forth. Then something out of the corner of her eye caught her attention, some small motion. She looked at the door to her cabin . . .

. . . and sucked in her breath, eyes widening as she stared in horror at the handle, slowly turning.

The door began to open.

Denham caught up with Choy only a few feet away from the railing. Fueled by panic, the director reached out and grabbed hold of the camera with both hands and tore it from Choy's grasp, a surge of triumph rising in him. The ship pitched again and he stumbled a bit but managed to stay on his feet, the Bell & Howell safely in his hands. He glared at Choy, about to berate him.

But Choy wasn't even looking at him. Denham turned to see what had his attention and saw Captain Englehorn striding toward them, face etched with the mad obsession of Ahab.

"Throw that thing overboard before I break your neck!" Englehorn barked. "No more filming. No more pictures. Men have died because of you!"

Denham stared at him, enraged. The man really was mad. Didn't he realize the camera was the only chance they had of this voyage not being a total and complete failure, an utter disaster?

"Don't threaten me!" he said. "If you come any closer, I'll be compelled to defend myself."

Englehorn lunged for the camera. Denham wrenched himself back, spinning it away from the captain's grasping hands. Then something just snapped in Englehorn and the man came at Denham, swinging wild, roundhouse punches.

Startled by the man's crazed fury, Denham staggered backward and lost his footing. As he fell, the camera flew from his hands and slid across the deck.

Denham caught himself with one hand and lurched back to his feet. He turned just as Englehorn came at him again, raising both hands in pugilistic fashion. The captain was thin but well muscled. Denham was not a fighter, though he'd had his share of scraps. But Englehorn was out of control and Denham was both fast and lucky. He swung a left hook into Englehorn's stomach.

The ship tipped violently on an ocean swell as Englehorn doubled up in pain from the blow. The deck heaved and an enormous wave came up over the railing, washing over the deck and knocking the captain off of his feet.

Denham grabbed the camera. He looked up into the night as the ship twisted upon the rocks and stared into the eyes of one of those carved, ancient gods, which was looking dispassionately down upon them like a Roman emperor overseeing the bloodshed at the forum.

The vessel shuddered and there came a scraping noise of metal upon stone, louder than anything they'd heard thus far. And then the ship began to move.

The *Venture* floated free of the rocks.

The ship was moving again, but in the wrong direction, the raging seas pushing it even closer to the reef. He looked at Englehorn and saw the same realization in the captain's eyes.

Englehorn turned and ran for the wheelhouse.

"Start main engines!" he shouted as he ran. "Start main engines!"

The *Venture* lurched and shook violently, and Jack lost his footing, sprawling onto the floor of the corridor. He reached a hand up to steady himself against the wall, starting to rise. Even as he did he glanced down the length of the corridor and saw the door to Ann's cabin hanging open, swinging wide.

He hauled himself to his feet and ran the rest of the way, careening off the walls as the ship rolled on the churning sea. Jack grabbed the swinging door and held it open, then staggered inside, carried by the next rise of the ship.

Inside, he froze, staring around in shock. The cabin was abandoned. The privacy curtain by the bunk hung down, torn loose from its hooks. The bedclothes were strewn upon the floor. The chair in front of the vanity had been tipped over, clothes spilled about. Even her hairbrush was on the floor. This wasn't just from the pummeling of the ocean.

There had been a struggle here.

Ann was gone.

He clutched the primitive necklace tightly in his hand, bones digging into his palm for a moment, then turned and raced from the cabin. He glanced around, mind awhirl. They would have taken her whichever direction they were less likely to run into crewmen. No one was to the left, and he ran that way.

Jack was nearly hyperventilating. He was without thought; he wouldn't allow himself to think for fear of what would come, and let his legs pump along with his heart.

He went through a door and arrived at the bottom of a set of metal steps. Here lay a dead man, a member of the crew he'd passed a few words with but whose name he did not know. Jack forced himself not to look at the crewman's face, not to be given pause by his murder. He stepped over the bloody corpse and raced up the stairs.

At the top there was another body that he nearly tripped over. This time he couldn't help looking down. The pale, bearded features of another crewman, Schlesinger, stared up at him, wide-eyed.

Jack shook it off, thinking only of Ann.

As Englehorn took the wheel, Mr. Hayes took up the helm. The captain felt the familiarity of the wheel in his grasp, and he forced himself to breathe deeply, to calm down. This was where he belonged, up in the wheel-house at the command of his ship. To hell with the raging seas or the howling wind or that idiot Denham. This was his element.

He aimed the *Venture* toward a gap in the rocks ahead.

"Half ahead both," he commanded. "Easy, Mr. Hayes."

A voice rose to starboard. "Rocks!" cried a helmsman he'd placed on lookout there.

"Hard a port!" Englehorn shouted.

The ship's prow turned just a few degrees. The sea rose up, propelling her. The *Venture* plowed between the jagged rocks and then slid into open sea.

A rousing cheer went up from the crew.

Englehorn scanned the waters, tense and on edge. They had approached the island in fog and he wasn't confident enough of the shoreline to assume they were entirely clear.

"Clear to starboard, captain!" called the helmsman on lookout.

"Clear to port, captain!" shouted Jimmy, down from the crow's nest for once.

Englehorn allowed himself to exhale. The *Venture* was his responsibility, and the lives of every member of his crew were in his hands. He had feared the worst but been unwilling to surrender to that fear.

They were free now. Safe.

Time to set a course for home, and to hell with Carl Denham.

"Wheel amidship . . . full ahead, both engines!" he shouted, and then he turned to his first mate. "Well done, Mr. Hayes."

But even as the words were out of his mouth they were muffled by another voice, shouting urgently from the deck.

"Stop! Stop! Turn back! We have to turn back!"

Englehorn went out of the wheelhouse, the wind whistling in his ears and whipping at his face. He looked down to the lower deck and saw Jack Driscoll staring intently up at him.

"They've taken Ann!" Driscoll called.

The captain saw Denham on the deck, clutching his damned camera as though it were a much loved child. The director's assistant, Preston, was approaching. At Driscoll's words, Denham turned and shoved the camera into Preston's hands and started for the wheelhouse, eyes locked with Englehorn's.

A terrible weight crushed down upon the captain, then. He glanced back at the island, feeling as though it still had him in its grip, even though the ship had been freed from the rocks. They were away from the reef, but they were not loose of this strange trap. Not yet.

On the island, he could see the orange glow of firelight emanating from the native village.

Ann's throat burned with sea water. Her eyes stung. She tried to breathe and swallowed another mouthful of ocean. The edges of her vision were black and she knew that she was drowning by inches.

The islander's powerful arms were wrapped around her. He had attacked her in her cabin, a terrifying figure with spikes of sharpened bone pierced through his chin, nostrils, and the bridge of his nose, and with a pattern of ritual scars on his forehead. In that first instant, she had thought him some kind of demon. Her scream was cut off quickly as he grabbed her with strength that belied his thin, bony frame. He had slung her over his shoulder and leaped from the deck of the ship, splashing into the stormy seas below. Maybe she was about to die, she would be dashed against the rocks and disappear beneath the surf.

Then the islander had grabbed hold of her again, tugging her through the water, and she had given up struggling, thinking that he was her only chance of survival. Somehow he had gotten his hands on a waiting rope in the water, and only then did she realize that her abduction had been far better planned than she imagined.

They were dragged along in fits and starts. Waves crashed over her. Ann tried to hold her breath but the sea pulled at her, exhausting her, and she could not help gasping. The ship was barely visible in the swell of the ocean and the spray of waves crashing around her.

Then she and her abductor were being dragged up onto the shore by a gathering of other islanders, hauling on the rope.

Ann choked, some of the water she'd swallowed spurting from her mouth. But it was not being half drowned that defeated her. It was despair. Their hands fell upon her and she did not even have the strength to scream.

Hayes surveyed the faces of the crew, there in the darkness of the deck. To a man, they were horrified. Ann was not merely a woman to them, not just an actress in Denham's film. She had become a member of the crew, and more than that, she was a bit of laughter and beauty on a dreary voyage. Precious to each and every man aboard.

All of the men were looking to Englehorn, waiting for the order. Doubt flickered on the captain's weathered face.

Hayes frowned. "Captain?" he quietly prodded.

Englehorn gave him a hard look. He hesitated only a moment and then, at last, he gave the nod.

"All hands going ashore report to stations!" Hayes shouted at the gathered sailors. "Jump to it!"

Then they were in motion. The panic that had ensued while trying to get the ship off the rocks had been replaced by grim, quiet determination. The entire *Venture* crew was mobilizing for the rescue effort, though only a handful would actually be sent ashore. The two whalers were swung out and lowered to the water. Equipment and rifles were loaded onto them.

Hayes scowled and pointed down at the men in the whaler. "What the hell are you doing? You want that boat to sink? Stow those rifles midships—come on, hurry it up!"

The rifles would help, but they had other resources as well. Even now, Lumpy and Choy would be in Englehorn's cabin, pulling the cushions up from the captain's window seat to get to the secret compartment below. Inside, there were the weapons they *weren't* supposed to be carrying. Thompson submachine guns.

Hayes had no idea if they'd need the Tommy guns, but he was glad to have them.

He spotted Denham and Preston attempting to be inconspicuous as they boarded the whaler. Hayes considered having at the man right then, finally giving him a beating he so richly deserved for causing this entire mess, but he had seen the expression on Denham's face when the director learned that Ann had been taken. For all of his faults, all of his ambition, it was clear that Denham had been truly shaken and afraid for her, and that bought him a reprieve. For now.

When Hayes went to supervise the loading of the other whaler, he saw that Jack Driscoll had joined the crew and was helping out just as though he was one of them. The first mate nodded in approval. He'd never have imagined the writer to be much of a scrapper, but Driscoll was tougher than he looked. The man was loading a box of ammunition, but paused a moment to look toward the island. Hayes followed suit and saw what had distracted him.

On the island, the fires were still burning. If anything, the flames were higher now, smoke swirling away into the night.

Seconds later, the two whalers were being rowed away from the *Venture*, packed with sailors. Denham, Preston, the actor fellow Baxter, and the gent with the artificial leg were on board one of the lifeboats, and Driscoll was in the other. Hayes knew the director and writer were friends, and he wondered if this separation was coincidental, or if Miss Darrow's abduction had driven a wedge between them.

It was only a passing thought. The truth was, he didn't much care, as long as it didn't interfere with getting Ann back on board and getting the hell away from Skull Island.

Hayes hurried to round up Lumpy and the others to get the next boat off toward shore. The captain had taken the first group to get there quickly. Hayes would be bringing the reinforcements—both men and firepower.

He hoped to God they would make it in time.

15

DESPITE THE TORRENTIAL DOWNPOUR, the top of the wall was hellishly ablaze with torches when they dragged Ann into the village. She hung in their grasp for several seconds at a time and then struggled for a few moments, but it did no good. Even if she could wrest herself free of their grasp, where could she run?

The men who held her captive were silent, but all of the other villagers around her were far from it. They were a frenzied throng gathered at the base of the wall. Many of them were chanting in the same language she had heard the old sha-woman speak in before. Sometimes the words were punctuated by that one syllable, the one that seemed so heavy with fear and dread.

Kong.

But there were those among the villagers who were not chanting, not lighting torches, not surrounding her as they dragged her toward the wall. Instead, they wailed and beat at the ground, wide-eyed with terror, as though the end of the world was at hand. Others shook their fists at her with anguish and fury.

Ann's throat was still raw from swallowing sea water and from screaming. Her legs were weak and her whole body felt shaky, from being dragged through the ocean and out of fear. At first she'd thought that her heart would burst and she would fall dead of fright in the midst of her captors, and then when she realized that she would not, she began to wish it were so. Whatever fate they had in mind for her, a heart attack would be far more merciful.

Shock was setting in, she presumed, and found that even that only made her feel more hollow.

Eyes wide, staring around at the hideous painted faces of the islanders, it was almost as though she had stepped outside her body. Her mind swirled with horrid images of rape and mutilation, of torture and depravity, as she tried to imagine what they had in store for her, but in time Ann closed off such thoughts.

It was best to be numb. That way, perhaps there was a chance she would see some opportunity to run. Surely by now Jack and the others on the *Venture* would have noticed her missing. They wouldn't just leave her here. They'd come for her. And if it looked as though things were going to turn even uglier, that they were about to kill her, then she'd fight—*anything* to stay alive until they came for her.

They will *come,* she told herself. *Someone will come.*

If Ann couldn't hang on to that belief, her last bit of sanity would go with it.

She looked at the villagers surrounding her, screaming and chanting and wailing in fear. A fear that was directed at the wall. But it wasn't the wall itself, of course—they were afraid of whatever was behind it, whatever it was the wall had been built to keep out.

She stared at the wall, that towering structure of stone, and the latticework of wood that had been built around it, with spears jutting out all around. It was breathtaking, hundreds of feet high, and as far as she could tell it cut all the way across the island.

What are you? she thought, as though she could touch the mind of the thing that had answered her screams, that had been summoned by her. *What kind of creature exists in the world that requires a barrier such as this to keep it out?*

The question alone was enough to make her tremble again. But then the men who were dragging her toward the wall stopped and part of the chanting throng parted. A withered old crone—it might have been the one she'd seen earlier, but she couldn't tell—came forward. Her eyes were red and glazed as though she was drugged. As she threw her head back, rain pouring on her face, all of the bone jewelry she wore rattled as she shook her whole body and began to speak in a guttural language that seemed different, even, than that of the islanders.

Speaking in tongues—that was what Ann thought of. It was as though the woman was possessed by some spirit, or perhaps by the ghosts of the ancients who had carved the statues that were in ruins all around, and who had constructed the wall that kept out the monster.

The old woman continued to rave, red eyes locked on Ann.

The men who'd abducted her forced Ann to her knees and abruptly the mad woman lunged at her, splashing some kind of foul liquid in her face. Ann re-coiled in disgust, the stink of it up her nose, the rancid taste upon her lips. Several younger village women came forward and tied bracelets to her wrists and hung a necklace of bones and other trinkets around her head, and only then did she understand that the filthy liquid had been splashed upon her as some kind of anointment.

Ann was being prepared for some kind of ceremony, some ritual.

When they grabbed hold of her again, she tried to fight but it was useless. Her captors herded her like an animal up a long walkway and up steps that took her to the top of the wall. Even then it was not enough. They dragged her to its very highest point, and there they bound her by her wrists to a pair of upright bam-boo posts, facing into the night-black, mist-shrouded jungle from which those horrible roars had come.

Ann ignored them all after that, was numb to every indignity. All that consumed her mind was the jungle and the memory of that roaring. She peered into the darkness, into the trees and the mist, searching for some sign of what it was that awaited her there. The flames of the thousands of torches along the top of the wall flickered into the darkness, but the light did not penetrate deep enough to reveal the jungle's secrets.

Her heart ached with every beat, a fist pounding her chest from the inside, as she stared out at the dark tree tops.

The chanting and screaming continued and now several of the islanders carried fiery torches to pools of oil that had been poured into channels cut into the stone of the wall. With a touch of fire, those pools ignited and flames raced along those channels, brightening the area around the wall as though some midnight sun had just risen.

For the first time, Ann could see clearly below her. The wall was sheer and its vertical drop ended in a rocky grotto that spread out from its base toward the tangled jungle of Skull Island.

The flames surrounding her seemed to dance to the frenzied, ritual beating of drums.

Villagers stepped forward and knocked away wooden plugs that had kept the burning oil confined to the channels atop the wall. Now liquid fire sluiced down other channels roughly hewn into the wall itself, like the gutters of some great cathedral, racing along those chutes into pools carved in the walls of the grotto far below. The grotto lit up with dancing fire, illuminating chambers at the base that were carved with the faces of ancient gods.

The jungle was a hellish nightmare of shadows and dancing firelight. She could see the tops of distant trees tremble, the canopy of the jungle swaying as if pushed by some unseen force. Her legs weakened and she sagged against the bonds that held her to the bamboo poles.

Horror grew in her like rising mercury until she could stand it no longer. No longer numb, Ann began to struggle against her bonds, trying desperately to free herself. Her wrists chafed raw on the ropes, but it was useless.

An islander painted and adorned with bones began to beat a new rhythm on a log drum. Off to one side Ann saw the old sha-woman, arms out, chanting wildly, her red eyes rolled back in her head. All along the top of the wall, villagers fell to their knees, a moaning wail rising from them in unison, even as the drumming grew frenzied as though building to a climax.

And it suddenly ceased.

In that moment Ann felt herself dragged forward. Panic seized her and she froze as though paralyzed. The posts she had been tied to were moving, pulling her toward the edge of the wall, toward that sheer vertical drop down to the fiery grotto below.

Her mind screamed. This was it—if she didn't get free somehow, she would surely die. She dug her heels in and tried to hold back, but was now pulled forward, not strong enough against the force of those posts. Ann was dragged over the side of the wall . . .

Into thin air.

Screaming, she fought against the flaxen rope, but then she let herself hang free, realizing that the rope was the only thing keeping her from falling to her death. Her arms felt as though they would be torn from the sockets; the bones in her wrists shifted and the skin burned as all of her weight dangled from those bonds.

Ann glanced back and saw villagers holding onto ropes, releasing them slowly, and she realized they were lowering the entire structure, topped with those bamboo posts, down over the grotto.

Over, but not *into* the grotto.

The whole framework swung out over the chasm with Ann dangling from it, and lowered her toward a rock promontory between grotto and jungle. The grotto seethed with heat from the burning oil and she squirmed against her bonds. But it was not the fire she feared.

As her feet alighted upon the promontory, she could see trees swaying violently ahead of her. Above the crescendo of the native drumming and chanting, terrible, *familiar* roars could be heard from the jungle.

The chants assaulted her senses.

Kong.

The whalers were tossed upon the raging seas. Englehorn shouted orders and the sailors tried their best to follow them, attempting to steer the lifeboats toward the narrow cove they'd found before. The little boats bounced off of rocks and statues, but they would hold. He had to believe that.

When they reached that cove and the boats were beached, the sailors dragging them up onto the rocky shore, Driscoll leaped from his perch and raced for the tunnel Denham had found earlier, for the great staircase through the burial chamber that would lead to the village and the wall high above.

They could hear the drums and the wailing and the chanting from the village, and Englehorn imagined each of them had terrible pictures in his mind of what might have become of Ann.

Driscoll might have been the first one up the stairs,

but the rest of them were close on his heels, weapons at the ready.

Ann twisted her arms, still trying to tear her wrists free, but she was tied fast to the bamboo posts. The rock promontory upon which she stood was flat and she could not escape the thought that it seemed almost like an altar, upon which she had been placed as a sacrifice.

It was as if the gates of Hell had opened. Heat prickled on her skin from the fire that lit the grotto behind and on either side of her. Burning oil lit up enormous, hideous faces carved in stone, and it was as though they were the audience for her fear, and her fate.

Oily smoke from the fire billowed up around her, swept up into clouds by the breeze. Her view of those terrible faces was obscured and even twisting round and glancing up she could only vaguely make out the shapes of the chanting villagers high atop the wall. Though she choked on the stinking smoke she found herself grateful not to have to see any more what was around her.

Then the trees began to rustle in the jungle again and all such thoughts dispersed. She squinted, heart hammering in her chest, breath coming in short gasps as she tried to see through that black, greasy smoke.

The night was filled with a loud, splintering sound.

The islanders who lined the top of the wall ceased their wailing and chanting, falling entirely silent.

Ann's breath came in hitching gasps and she shook as she tried to see what moved through the smoke ahead of her. She caught a brief glimpse of something huge and dark moving toward her, but her vision was obscured by the smoke.

It was close enough that she could hear the bellows of its breathing.

Then all sound ceased. Through the smoke she could see a massive, dark silhouette leaping through the air. The ground shook beneath her with the force of the impact as it landed. If she hadn't been tied to the posts she would have been thrown from her feet.

Ann could only tremble and stare in disbelief as a breeze blew up and the swirling cloud of black smoke began to dissipate. Through it she could see a gigantic, leathery foot.

Every muscle in her body was taut with terror unlike anything she had ever known. Her lips parted, but she was too scared even to scream.

A sudden gust of wind cleared the rest of the smoky veil and she looked up, gaze following from the foot and up toward the face of the monstrosity. Her mouth was agape as her mind tried to accept the impossible.

Kong.

He stood before her, a twenty-five-foot gorilla, massive upper body hunched as he rested on his fists. The thick fur on his arms ruffled in the night wind. His entire body was covered in battle scars and his face was etched with them, including a large crescent-shaped slash over his right eye that gleamed in the firelight. One fang jutted up from the right side of his lower jaw, even when his mouth closed. The huge gorilla's barrel chest rose and fell, and he snorted, the sound like a steam engine.

Ann stared at him, and the giant stared back, leaning forward on his knuckles, chest rising and falling as he breathed deeply, as though inhaling her. The intelligence in his eyes was remarkable and she was completely entranced, unable to turn away.

Suddenly, Kong stood to his full height, massive fists beating against his chest as he let out a deafening roar that seemed to shake the very ground.

At last, Ann could scream—she shrieked in terror and despair.

Her anguish brought a response from the islanders up atop the wall. They began to wail again, screaming down at her and at Kong in that guttural language.

All the strength went out of Ann. She did not lose consciousness, but still she could not even hold herself up. Numb in both mind and body she fell slack against the ropes and just hung there between the posts.

Faint, half-conscious, she barely flinched when Kong reached out a huge hand and ripped her bonds away from the posts, roughly clutching her and carrying her off. She saw the faces of those ancient idols, lit by oily flames, watching, but the faces receded as Kong took her from the altar.

The night echoed with the sudden eruption of gunshots on the other side of the wall.

Bitter sorrow rose in Ann's heart.

Too late, she thought. *You're too late.*

*　　　*　　　*

The islanders scattered as the men from the *Venture* came down from the ridge, firing warning shots in the air. The gunfire echoed off the wall, the whole plateau lit up by the fire that burned along its top like a scene from Dante. Jack could hear Englehorn shouting orders at his men and knew the captain was nearby, but he wasn't paying attention.

All he cared about was Ann.

The villagers cleared a path, ducking into their huts or hiding in the ruins as several more shots were fired. Jack ran for the wall. From beyond it came the distant sound of Ann screaming.

Then the night was shattered by a roar so loud it shook the wall and the earth beneath his boots.

Englehorn came to an abrupt halt a few feet away, staring up at the top of the wall.

"What in God's name was that?" Englehorn asked.

Jack had no answer.

The islanders continued to melt into the darkness, vanishing as fast as they had appeared earlier in the day. Even those who had been ranged across the top of the wall were disappearing, coming down by stairs and ropes and ladders. Ahead of Jack, the way was clear.

Jack rushed to the wall and began to climb. As he did, he glanced down and saw Carl Denham hurry up to the massive, heavily fortified gate. Carl pressed his face to the gate, trying to peer through the latticework of sharpened bamboo.

From the way he flinched and took a step back, Jack knew Denham had seen something. He kept climbing, desperate to reach Ann.

When he reached the top of the wall, he raced across and peered over the edge, but there was nothing to see there, no trace of Ann at all. There was a primitive altar and a grotto whose walls were carved stone faces, ancient and grotesquely leering, beyond that was the jungle, the nearest trees lit with firelight, but then only darkness.

"She's gone!" he shouted down to the others, unable to keep the disbelief from his voice.

Denham had seen it briefly, but still wasn't sure he believed it. The gorilla that had carried Ann into the jungle was without a doubt the biggest animal he'd ever seen, at least twenty-five feet tall. In all his life—in his entire career as a filmmaker—he'd never seen anything so fantastic. It was as though he'd gotten a glimpse of the remnant of another world, of an age when the impossible strode the earth.

If he could put *that* on film, audiences around the world would storm movie theaters for that same glimpse, a window into the extraordinary. Not only would his discovery become legend, but his own name would go down in history.

His mind raced, fueled by both fear and by possibility. Ann was in the clutches of that monstrosity. But in his heart he knew that even if she had not been in peril, he would still have had to give chase. He'd been waiting all of his life to brush against the incredible, and his moment had finally arrived.

The first mate, Mr. Hayes, had come ashore with a second wave of sailors. They dragged boxes of ammo and guns had been carried up from the beach. All around Denham, sailors pried open the lids and started distributing ammunition.

Jack hurried down from the wall. "She's gone!" he called again, coming up to Denham, who quickly looked away.

"What is it, Carl?" Jack asked, staring at him. "You saw something."

"You can have Hayes and fifteen others," Englehorn said, his expression grave.

Denham was barely listening. His pulse was racing.

"I don't believe it," he said under his breath. Preston and Bruce were nearby, but the only one close enough to hear him was Herb, who looked at him with concern. Denham felt his stomach twisting into knots of despair. "I just snatched failure from the jaws of success. How did I do that?"

Herb frowned. "What?"

"The camera equipment . . . I left it on the boat," he said, despondent. How could he have been so stupid?

"No, you didn't, Mr. Denham," Herb said. He reached down and pulled aside a rain slicker to reveal the box that the Bell & Howell came in. "I always bring the camera. You should know that."

Joy lit Carl Denham up like it was Christmas morning. He could have kissed Herb right then and there. Then he saw Hayes watching him with a grim expression, and tried to contain his excitement. This was a somber moment, after all, and if he wasn't quite as somber as he ought to have been, he could at least fake it.

"What was it, Denham?" Hayes pressed, even as the sailors unpacked the rest of the weapons. "What did you see?"

They were all watching him now, Jack and Englehorn, Herb and Bruce, Preston and Hayes. And the sailors had begun to gather around, armed and ready. Lumpy, Choy, Jimmy, Chet Trask, Hal Shannon, and a small army of others. Denham was a showman and he craved the spotlight, but not in moments like this.

"Jesus, I don't know," he said. "It was dark. I only caught a glimpse. It was some kind of . . . ape."

From the man's expression, it was obvious Hayes did not like this news at all. Denham glanced away, not liking the disapproval and distrust in Hayes's eyes.

Jack slung his pack on, shot Denham a look of utter disdain, and strode toward the gate. He grabbed the bamboo barricade and tried to pull it away by himself. It was foolish. No one man was going to get through the barricade without help.

"Step aside, Driscoll," Hayes said, raising the barrel of a Tommy gun.

Denham's eyes widened in appreciation. He hadn't been aware the weapons were on board, but he was glad to have them.

Jack leaped out of the way and Hayes fired a stream of bullets into the bamboo, neatly slicing a splintered path through it.

Hayes thrust the smoking Tommy gun into Jack's hands. "Can you be trusted with this?"

Denham almost laughed out loud—Jack held the gun with all the familiarity of an apartment-dwelling writer, a true city boy. But something in his eyes must have satisfied Hayes, for the first mate didn't take the gun back from him. Instead, he turned to survey the other men who had either volunteered or been chosen by Englehorn to go along.

The kid, Jimmy, was among them. He loaded a rifle with what seemed like expert swiftness to Denham's untrained eye, then checked its sight. Hayes's expression grew stormy and he marched over to Jimmy and grabbed the barrel.

"Not you, Jimmy," the mate said.

The boy was visibly upset. To Denham, he looked insulted. "Come on, Mr. Hayes," he protested. "Look at 'em. None of them knows which way to point a gun. You need me. Miss Darrow needs me!"

The most troubling thing about the kid's argument was that he might be right. That didn't matter to Hayes, who pulled the rifle out of his grasp.

"She needs you coming after her with a gun like she needs a hole in the head. You're staying here."

Denham turned away, letting the two of them get on with their argument unobserved. None of his business, after all, and he had more important things to attend to.

He went to where Herb and Preston were double-checking the contents of the camera boxes and crouched down between them. They looked at him expectantly. Both men knew him well enough to know there was no way he was going on this expedition without the Bell & Howell.

"Bring the tripod," he said in a hushed voice. "And all the film stock."

"You wanna go with the six inch lens?" Herb asked.

"The wide angle will do just fine," Denham replied.

The ground crunched with the tread of boots and Denham turned to see Englehorn scowling down at him with contempt.

"This is a rescue mission, Mr. Denham," the captain said tersely.

Denham stood and met his gaze. "Correct, Mr. Englehorn. I am fully committed to saving Miss Darrow . . . and whatever is left of my failing career."

He turned his back on the captain and gestured to Herb and Preston, who hastily repacked the camera equipment and began to pick it up. Bruce was nearby, talking to one of the sailors, a rifle already in his hands. Aside from Denham's people and Jack Driscoll, there were Hayes, Choy, Lumpy, and eight or nine others. A sizeable rescue party.

Englehorn gave Denham a final, disapproving look and then surveyed the group. He turned to Jack.

"You've got guns. You've got food. You've got ammo. And you've got twenty-four hours," the captain declared.

That gave Bruce pause. The actor stared at Englehorn. "Twenty-four hours?" he asked, incredulous.

"This time tomorrow, we haul anchor."

Some of the men looked as though they might hesitate, even argue the point. But Jack just slung his rifle over his shoulder, turned and started through the now open gate.

After a moment, the rest of them followed.

16

BRUCE BAXTER HAD PLAYED at adventure his whole life. He was, in every way, a pretender. But there was nothing make-believe about what he had stumbled into now, and nothing at all wonderful about it either. Real adventure, he was quickly discovering, was filled with fear and peril.

As a young man attempting to enter the world of motion pictures, Bruce had often been afraid, often faced situations that were fraught with certain perils. On soundstages and back lots, in front of the camera, he had made of himself a hero, afraid of nothing. More often than not he had done his own stunts, risked his neck a thousand times to get a good shot. Bruce Baxter laughed in the face of danger.

At least he did when the threats were props, when the wild animals were old and tired or even caged.

Now he was living the very sort of tale he'd so often pretended to, and only the embarrassment he'd have suffered if he showed his cowardice in front of the other men kept him from going back to the ship with Englehorn.

You're selling yourself short, pal. That's not the only reason you're out here.

He was scared, true enough. But when he thought about Ann Darrow and how terrified she must be, he knew there was no way he could go back to the ship. He had a gun and a dozen other men alongside him. She was alone, and from all accounts, in the clutches of some jungle beast.

If she's even still alive.

The thought drove him on, forced him to grip the rifle tighter and grit his jaw. As anxious as he was—as afraid as he was—he couldn't just leave Ann out there in the jungle. They hadn't even gotten along that well, and he'd been worried all along about her stealing screen time from him. But her life was in the balance, and he was no coward. He wasn't leaving her behind.

Even at night, the jungle was warm and humid. They walked through clouds of tiny insects that stuck to the light sheen of sweat on his face until he brushed them off. Branches scratched his arms, but Bruce had spent long days and nights exploring the forests and swamps around the house where he'd grown up, and so the jungle itself did not trouble him.

It was the sounds that were unnerving, the shifting and hissing in the deep brush and up in the canopy of the trees above. He reacted to every unknown noise, but he wasn't alone. Most of the sailors were on edge, not to mention Denham, Preston, and Herb, who had paused several times to shoot some quick footage, but with the air of dread hanging about them. Only Driscoll, blinded by his fear for Ann, seemed not to notice. Mr. Hayes certainly took note, but the man was unafraid.

The island was supposedly volcanic. Denham had said or speculated something about it sinking into the ocean. Bruce wasn't a geologist—he hadn't had enough science to last out the eighth grade, so he certainly didn't understand how such a thing could be, unless the earth was just so unstable underneath the island that it was being swallowed up.

He just hoped it didn't sink—or erupt for that matter—before they were well away from here.

The volcanic history of the island made its terrain strange and imposing. Previous eruptions had left a jagged, tortured landscape of rock outcroppings, deep crevasses, and towering cliffs. The soil was rich and dark, and thick vegetation grew wildly all around them, so that even during the day, Bruce imagined it was quite dark in the depths of the jungle.

Ancient gnarled trees twisted out of the ground. Thick lichen and long mosses hung from branches and tangled vines. Steam rose from festering swamps, superheated by the volcanic magma far below the surface.

Hayes led the way through all of this formidable terrain. Lumpy, Choy, and a couple of other sailors were near the front with him and Driscoll. Bruce traveled with Denham, Herb, and Preston, the remnants of the film crew sticking together. Herb carried the movie camera, stumping along on his artificial leg with an obvious limp but no less quickly than the rest of them. The rest of the sailors brought up the rear.

The atmosphere amongst the men was tense, heavy with dread. Unseen creatures scurried away from them, moving out of their path through the underbrush.

Up ahead, Hayes paused, holding up a hand to indicate that they should all be silent and follow suit. Everyone froze, watching him a moment, and then a strange, low moan echoed from the surrounding jungle. Bruce glanced around, trying to see in the impenetrable darkness of the jungle. The men all stared into the jungle, watchful and on edge.

There came a sudden noise, a cracking of branches and the thud of heavy footsteps. Bruce raised his weapon, wondering if this was it, if they had found the gorilla Denham had supposedly seen.

His fingers gripped the rifle so tightly they hurt.

He had no idea who was the first to fire, but suddenly guns were blazing. The staccato burst of firing from the Tommy guns ripped the darkness, muzzles flashing as several of the sailors panicked and shot blindly into the jungle. A couple of them raised their rifles and fired. Bruce was itchy to fire as well, but he kept his eyes on the landscape around them. There weren't many rounds in a rifle and he didn't want to expend them shooting at nothing.

"Cut it out!" Hayes shouted. "Hold your fire!"

Military, Bruce thought. *He's definitely a military man.*

Hayes ignited a flare, instantly flooding the clearing with a sickly red light. They could see far better, but the crimson illumination cast such a hideous pallor over the jungle it was somehow worse than the dark.

Something moved and Bruce swung the barrel of his rifle toward it, then backed off a few steps, cursing loudly as a dead creature, thirty feet tall, toppled from the jungle like a mighty tree being felled. It crashed through the gloomy foliage and thudded to the ground in front of the men.

Bruce could only stare. The thing possessed enormous legs and had obviously stood upright, bent like a kangaroo. It had a long tail, a narrow head with a beaklike snout, spikes along its shoulders and sides, and horn-covered oval plates like armor all over its green, mottled hide. On its head was a sort of fin.

Dinosaur, Bruce thought. *Impossible, but what else could it be?* He was almost giddy with disbelief and relief that it was dead.

"Gimme that camera," Denham said excitedly to Herb. "We gotta get this."

Before any of them could move there came a violent, thrashing noise from the jungle. Branches splintered, leaves shook.

Another of the fin-headed lizards crashed into the clearing, blood streaming from a bullet wound in its side. It shrieked in pain and fury as it ran at the men, and they all scattered, trying to keep out of its path as it charged wildly among them.

"Watch out!" Jack shouted.

The creature was thirty feet high, but its tail was nearly half that length and it whipped it through the air, knocking several sailors off their feet. Then the dinosaur spun, about to attack again.

A sudden flash of gunfire erupted, lighting up the clearing. Bullets riddled the dinosaur and it staggered, then dropped to the ground amidst the smell of cordite and the copper stench of blood.

Hayes stood nearby, finger still on the trigger.

There was silence for a moment. The men began to gather around again, slowly approaching the dead dinosaurs.

Preston, his boyish face pale and drawn, stared at the creatures. "Aren't these things supposed to be extinct?"

The grizzled English cook, Lumpy, scratched at his stubbled face and spat on the ground. "They are now."

Choy started to back away from the dinosaurs. Bruce couldn't blame him, but he was less concerned about the dead ones at their feet than what else might be out there in the jungle. Rattled, he looked around at the darkness, even as the flare began to fade.

"What the hell kind of place is this?" he rasped.

Ann focused on just breathing. The giant gorilla clutched her so tightly that her ribs felt as though they would break. Her tears were gone. No longer was she trembling with fear. Her initial terror had been sublimated by the primal need to survive.

Kong carried her through the jungle, and everything blurred past her eyes so quickly that she had to close her eyes or she would have vomited. With her legs and her head exposed, she keenly felt their vulnerability. If he struck her against a rock or a tree, she would be broken, or even killed.

For a short time Ann attempted to imagine herself somewhere else, anywhere but in the madness of her predicament. But she smelled the hot, earthy scent of the gorilla and heard the locomotive sound of his grunting, and she could not transport her mind elsewhere.

Her terror had been assimilated—fear ran in her blood now, made up the stuff of her flesh and bones. It whipped into a frenzy in her mind, a storm of thought and instinct, but little by little Ann pushed it down. If she couldn't think straight, she was dead.

Kong's leathery fingers loosened slightly and she drew a wonderful sip of air, and her mind cleared just a bit. She looked around in the darkness as he slowed and saw shafts of moonlight playing across the faces of grotesque statues set into a mossy cliff up ahead.

What's he doing? she wondered. There was obvious intent to his actions, if he hadn't killed her already. This was a path he had traveled before. Huge as he was, he was not a demon or a creature of myth. Kong might be monstrous, but he was no monster. He was simply an animal.

She wondered if there were others. The terror racing through her veins grew even worse as she imagined entire jungles filled with gigantic gorillas. But there had to be more than just the one. That wall was centuries old and Kong couldn't possibly have lived that long. There had to have been others before him, and it only made sense to think there were more now. *God help me.*

So where's he taking you?

And beneath that, another question was niggling at her brain. Even as Kong carried her through the jungle, sometimes hanging her down low and other times holding her clenched in his fist, pressed greedily close to his chest like something precious, she couldn't escape it.

What had Kong—and his ancestors—done with the others that had been given up to them from that altar?

The cliffs loomed up ahead, lit by the moon, and Kong came to a small plateau below them. His grip on Ann tightened and she felt the bones in her chest once again grind together. She grunted, eyes welling with the pain. A fresh wave of fear coursed through her.

Ann pressed her eyes tightly closed and images of her life in New York flashed across her mind. Of the vaudeville stage and her whole family there. Of her tiny apartment, of music and dancing, of the laughter of an audience. She'd thought Denham's crazy dream a grand adventure.

Now it had become a living nightmare.

Ann dangled in the great ape's hand as he climbed, fearful for the first time that he would simply drop her and she would plummet to her death. Almost at the same moment, Kong reached the top of the plateau, clutching her tightly, and he stopped.

Ann's heart seemed to skip every other beat and in her mind she could hear a tiny voice repeating *no, no, no*.

Kong squatted, lifting her up to study her in the moonlight. For the first time she was able to get a clear view of his face at rest. He was very old . . . far older than she had imagined . . . and now she saw even more clearly the terrible scars upon his face. Whatever else lived in this jungle, it was clear that Kong had fought to survive the long years of his life. One of his eyelids was badly mangled and his jaw was crooked, which caused one of his huge, yellowed lower incisors to jut up, over his upper lip.

He stared at Ann and she was rigid with fear of

what would come next. She dared not move, but her breath came in rapid little gasps of air.

With a single, fluid motion, Kong swung her upside down. Ann tried to scream but no sound would come out. He shook her violently, her limbs flying round as though she were a rag doll. The ceremonial necklace the islanders had put around her neck fell to the ground below and as she watched it fall, watched it strike the earth, she heard a clink of bone upon bone and saw that dozens of other necklaces littered the clearing atop the plateau.

And amidst the necklaces, larger bones. Skulls. Human remains. This was it, then, the fate of those who'd been offered up to Kong in the past. Brought here and killed, crushed to death or battered against the ground.

A whimper rose up in the back of Ann's throat and escaped her lips.

Kong lifted her up and studied her again, lips curling in a slow, guttural snarl. She could only stare into those enormous eyes.

His grip tightened in the moment before he would kill her.

Then the snarl began to slacken, the eyes to widen slightly in what might have been curiosity or confusion.

Kong hesitated, grip loosening slightly.

In Ann's heart, terror gave way to instinct, to self-preservation. Kong's fingers opened just slightly as though he wanted to examine her more closely. She threw herself from his grasp, dropped a dozen feet and

landed at his feet, falling and rolling amongst grinning human skulls, shattered rib cages, and scattered
bones.

She leaped to her feet and ran like hell.

Kong rose up with a roar of surprise and fury that
shook the trees, leaves falling and night birds fluttering
up into the sky. Ann did not turn to look back, fleeing
into the deepest part of the jungle, wanting to get lost,
to be hidden from her captor.

Desperate, she pushed through dense undergrowth,
threw herself over fallen logs and through tangled
vines. Her heart was hammering, but this was a different kind of exhilaration. The fear was still there, but
there was hope now as well.

From behind her she heard the crash of trees falling
and Kong smashing through the undergrowth, splintering branches and tearing vines down, plowing down
small trees.

She stole a glance back, and in that instant went
over the edge of a small slope, losing her footing. Ann
fell, rolling through the foliage.

From the distance she heard the sound of gunshots
puncturing the night. She was up in an instant and
running in the direction of the shots, and now she
could hear more gunfire and shouting voices.

Jack. He and the others had come for her.

"Help me!" she called out, so they could find her by
her voice. *"Help!"*

Though he'd tried to hide it even from himself, Jack
had feared the worst. The moment he heard Ann's

screams off in the jungle, it was as though he came alive again.

"Ann!" he shouted.

He took off, running through the jungle toward the sound. Hayes, Denham, and the others all followed, shouting after him, some of them calling out for Ann. Jack barged through tangled vegetation, passing between two huge stone columns, now covered with moss. He'd no idea what they had once supported and didn't give it a second thought.

An enraged roar echoed through the jungle.

Once again, he shouted her name.

Hope sparked in Ann's heart as she heard Jack calling for her. She pushed herself through the dense jungle and the dark of night, lit only by streaks of moonlight slipping through the canopy high above. The pounding of Kong's pursuit shook the ground.

"Here! Over here!" she called.

A tree crashed through the jungle off to one side and she darted in the other direction, going down another slope, leaping and rolling almost blindly in the near dark. Up ahead, a rock jutted up at an angle almost like the prow of a ship and she ran onto it, trying to get a view of the mist-shrouded valley below.

"Jack!" she cried, and her voice echoed back from the night and the mist.

Then, close by, she heard the sound of snapping twigs. Slowly, she turned and peered into the jungle.

"Jack?"

From the darkness above, with astonishing agility

and grace, Kong swung down from the trees and scooped her off the rock. Ann barely had time to cry out as he carried her off, moving with eerie quiet, deeper into the dark heart of the island.

Ann's scream resounded through the jungle. But despite its intensity, it meant Ann was alive. Jack had heard her voice, calling his name. He was never turning back.

The entire search party picked up speed, moving through tangled vines that hung down all around them. Moments later they emerged from the densest part of the jungle to find the glimmer of dawn on the horizon. In the depths of the jungle it was still dark as night, but morning light touched the top of the low plateau where they came out of the foliage.

In the clearing, they found piles of human bones.

It was a killing ground.

The men spread out to search the carnage. Jack used the toe of his boot to kick aside several necklaces of shells and bones and carved wooden trinkets. Most were faded with age.

But one of them looked quite new.

He bent to pick it up and found a lock of blond hair still tangled within the strands.

Ann.

But she was not here. The gorilla, or whatever Denham had seen—whatever it was that they'd heard roaring—had not killed her. Yet. There was still time.

"Christ, it's a bleedin' boneyard!" Lumpy said as he stared around at the human remains. "They've been ripped from limb to limb."

"Ann!" Jack called into the jungle, even as dawn's light spread fingers of morning in amongst the trees.

He looked over at Denham, but Carl wasn't paying any attention to anyone at all, nor to the bones. Instead, he was looking at a huge gash in the forest where trees had been knocked down, trunks splintered, and the web of vines had been torn away.

Something had smashed a path through the jungle, here. Something huge.

"What took her, Carl?" Jack asked, walking up behind him.

Denham hesitated before answering. "I told you it was dark."

Jack stared at him. Carl was a friend, maybe one of his best friends. But just then he wanted to break the man's jaw. "I know you're lying. I just don't understand why."

Hayes felt a chill up his spine as he stared at the human remains strewn across the clearing. He'd seen death up close, seen men massacred in war, but still there was something haunting about this scene. Brutal and gruesome.

The sailors in his charge were wandering about a bit aimlessly, waiting for orders. They were going to keep after Miss Darrow, but this had given them all pause, seeing the potential savagery of the thing they were chasing.

Hayes prepared to give the word, he did a mental head count of the men he'd brought with him. One of the sailors, short and slight, was turned away from him, a woolen hat pulled down over his head.

Hayes's stomach gave a sick twist.

He marched over to the sailor, who'd stepped away from the grisly remains, and batted the hat off of his head. The sailor whirled, eyes wide with surprise and alarm.

"Just keep walking, Mr. Hayes. Pretend you didn't see me."

"Jesus, Jimmy!" Hayes snatched the gun from his hands.

"I need that!" the kid said, defiant.

"I'm not giving you a gun," Hayes snapped.

"You were younger than me when they gave *you* one!"

Hayes shot him a withering glare. "You're not in the army. I was trained . . . I had a drill sergeant!"

Jimmy narrowed his eyes. "I got a drill sergeant. He orders me around all the time!"

Hayes stared at him a moment and then exhaled, all the tension going out of him. He was afraid for the kid, but what else could he do? He handed the gun back, holding Jimmy's gaze fiercely.

"Don't make me regret it," Hayes said.

"I just wanna help bring her back," Jimmy said.

Before Hayes could reply, Carl Denham strode over to them.

"That's what we all want, kid," Denham said.

The other sailors had gathered around, along with the actor, Baxter, and the fellow from Denham's crew.

"Ain't gonna be much to bring back, if you ask me," Lumpy said.

From the edge of the clearing, away from the rest, Jack Driscoll glared at Lumpy. "No one asked you."

"Come on, fellas," Denham said, looking around at them all. "We all want the same thing. To see Miss Darrow's safe return." He shot a look at Driscoll. "Isn't that why we're here?"

Something was going on with Denham and Driscoll, just as Hayes had earlier suspected. But as long as it didn't interfere with the search party, it wasn't his problem.

"You heard the man," Hayes said to his sailors. "Get moving!"

Giving the kid one last, cautionary look, Hayes tossed him the gun he'd taken away. Jimmy caught it, surprise on his face. But before he could say any more, Hayes was already moving.

There was no turning back now.

Not for any of them.

17

As THE MORNING WORE on and the search party continued slogging through the rough jungle terrain, Jack knew that the sailors' nerves were fraying. They were all on edge after the grounding of the *Venture*, the efforts to get it off the reef, and then Ann's abduction, now followed by a night without any sleep and the terrors they'd encountered in the tangled interior of Skull Island. With the arrival of the morning, the temperature had risen twenty degrees or more, and the jungle was humid and filled with annoying insects that buzzed around their heads and bit at bare flesh.

Though the sailors and the film crew talked to one another about the island and the creatures—the dinosaurs especially—that they'd run across, they studiously avoided discussing Ann, and their chances of catching up with her. They'd all heard her screams and her shouts for Jack. With the sun climbing toward noon, their conversation grew more and more sparse until they were hiking through the jungle in grim silence.

Hayes led them, as he'd done from the outset, and his ability to track the monster that had taken Ann was impressive. From the killing ground they'd stumbled upon, he'd unerringly followed the pattern of broken branches and felled trees.

After their disagreement, Jimmy followed close behind Hayes, but the first mate seemed to ignore his presence.

Dread hung heavy upon Jack and in time he found he could not bear it in silence any longer.

He caught up with Hayes. "What do you think? About Ann?"

"You mean do I think she's dead?"

Jack flinched at the question . . . then again, as gunfire erupted behind them. Hayes, Jack, and Jimmy all spun around, guns at the ready, to find Lumpy shooting wildly at a creature that seemed to fly or leap in amongst the trees. The other sailors raised their weapons as well, ready to fire, but instead just stood and stared at the thing. It took Jack a second to realize that despite being the size of an average dog, it was some sort of huge insect.

He understood the revulsion etched in Lumpy's features, and the gunfire as well.

Hayes took two threatening steps toward Lumpy. "Conserve your ammunition!" he growled.

Lumpy shot him a petulant look, then glanced back into the jungle. The bug thing was gone. Hayes set off and once again they were on their way. Jack kept stride with the first mate, with Jimmy just behind them. Hayes's words had made Jack curious. He had been concerned about Lumpy drawing attention, but Hayes had only been worried about the cook wasting bullets.

"You were in the army?" Jack asked, watching him.

Before Hayes could respond, Jimmy piped up. "The Harlem Hell-Fighters!"

Hayes gave Jimmy an irritated frown, then turned back to Jack. "369th Infantry."

"Mr. Hayes led the charge across the Rhine," Jimmy added proudly. "The 369th was the first U.S. division into France. They saw continuous battle for one hundred and ninety-one days, longer than anyone—"

"Zip it, Jimmy!" Hayes barked.

Jimmy fell back, eyes downcast, obviously smarting.

Jack studied Hayes again. His skin gleamed like polished ebony whenever they would pass through a shaft of sunlight coming through the jungle canopy, but his expression was grim. Always grim.

"369th, huh? What did they give you guys, the Congressional Medal of Honor?"

Hayes glanced at him for a long moment before replying. "The French gave us the Croix de Guerre." A pause. "*You* didn't give us a goddamn thing."

Troubled, Jack looked away. Hayes was a good man, smart and fearless. His unit had been vital to the war effort in Europe, but they'd been ignored because of the color of their skin. Jack was embarrassed for his country . . . and his race. If he'd been writing for the papers, it would have been a story he *had* to tell. But writing about it would have made the unpleasantness of it somehow more bearable—perhaps it was better to have to hold onto that story instead of setting it down.

"We'll find her," Hayes added a moment later, his tone softened.

Hopeful, Jack turned to him, but the look in the first mate's eyes was cold and hard.

"Alive or dead," he said, "you bring them back."

The gun was light as a feather in Ben Hayes's hands. Trekking through dangerous territory like this, it felt a part of him, just the way it had when he'd faced the German infantry across blood-soaked turf. The jungle was nothing like the battlefield he'd known, but with the murderous things that lived on this island, it was quite a lot like war.

He was wary as they emerged from the thick jungle at the edge of a ravine. The sun beat down on him and he wiped away the trickles of sweat that beaded up on his skin. The jungle had been sticky and humid with very little breeze, and though there was a light wind here, without the shade it was an inferno.

The terrain ahead sloped down into a ravine. It was too narrow to be considered a valley, less than seventy-five feet across, and the sheer cliffs that rose up on either side made it the perfect place for an ambush. But of course the enemies they faced in the jungle wouldn't be lying in wait for them. As much as his instincts told him the ravine was far too exposed, he knew that here, if anything was going to try to eat them, at least they'd see it coming.

He silently hoped he wasn't leading them all to their doom.

Hayes paused at the top of the slope as the others filtered out of the jungle. Lumpy stumbled out from the trees, feet sliding on vines, hunched over by a fit of hacking and spitting, his smoker's cough ravaging his lungs.

Jack came out of the jungle, seeing Hayes and other sailors standing there. His eyes widened.

"Which way?" he asked.

Hayes stepped nearer to Jack and spoke quietly as he looked around, still getting his bearings. "I have no idea."

Jack stared at him a moment and then sighed in resignation.

"Great," Lumpy remarked, overhearing them, "we're lost."

Denham and Preston moved along the ridge of the ravine, away from the sailors but not out of sight, to set up the Bell & Howell camera. Thus far in their mad dash through the jungle, there had been only mere moments to stop and catch anything on film, bits and pieces really, and Denham was getting itchy. He felt as though he had a kind of fever about him, a compulsion to really get the camera rolling. This jungle was a primordial wilderness that he had to bring back to the civilized world. It was his duty, really. They'd seen dinosaurs, for Christ's sake! If he didn't fully commit Skull Island to film before it was lost to the predations of time, he'd be failing in an obligation to science . . . and to audiences everywhere, of course.

As they were getting the tripod properly placed, Denham waved to his leading man. "Bruce, over here! I want to get a wide shot of the valley."

Preston scratched at the back of his neck. He looked

at Denham and shrugged. "Carl, shouldn't we think about conserving film stock? I mean, we're going to want to finish Miss Darrow's scenes . . . when we get her back. So my thought is to save what we have and . . . temporarily suspend photography."

Denham gave him a sharp look. "You want me to stop shooting?"

"It's a plan," Preston replied carefully. "What do you think?"

"Preston, let me tell you something," Denham said with a scowl. "All you know about movies, you could stick in a cat's ass."

He picked up the tripod and camera and moved uphill a ways, gesturing to Bruce to follow. Herb fell in behind the actor, pausing a moment as he passed Preston.

"You don't get it, do you, kid?" the camera operator said. "Look at this place! Look at what we've got in the can! It's gold! It's not about her anymore."

The words carried enough that Denham caught them and he felt a small twinge of conscience at the truth. He wanted to rescue Ann as much as the next guy, but the glory of what he was capturing on film didn't really rely on her. Whatever happened to Ann, he would still have his movie.

Denham turned up the slope, climbing higher above the valley below with Bruce and Herb in tow. When he reached the top of the slope, he heard a strange noise off to one side and turned to discover its source.

His eyes widened in amazement, his mouth hanging agape.

*   *   *

Jack knelt on one knee and stared at the soft ground of the slope leading down into the valley. There, plain as day, was the impression of a gigantic footprint.

He didn't hear Lumpy come up behind him.

"Bloody Nora!" the cook cried.

The rest of the group had already been rising, preparing to continue their pursuit of Ann, and now they responded to Lumpy's exclamation, quickly gathering around Jack and the print.

"Is that what took Miss Darrow?" Jimmy asked.

"There's only one creature capable of leaving a footprint that size," Lumpy said sagely. They all turned to look at him before he continued. "The Abominable Snowman."

Jack thought the statement amusing—there wasn't any snow on Skull Island for love or money. Still, a ripple of fear spread through the crowd of superstitious sailors.

"And I, for one, have no desire to meet it face to face," Lumpy went on. "Believe me, fellas, against something this big, we've got no chance."

Rattled, the sailors began to mutter among themselves. Some of the men obviously agreed, and others even talked about turning back. Hayes pushed through them and knelt beside Jack, examining the print for himself.

"It's got to be, what, twenty? Twenty-five feet?" the first mate asked.

Anger rippled through Jack as he looked at the man. "Carl saw it," he said grimly. "Let's ask him."

Hayes glanced over his shoulder. *"Denham!"* When he received no answer, he looked around. "Where'd he go?"

Jack rose and started up the slope, following the path he'd seen the director and his crew take earlier.

"Carl!" he called. But he received no reply.

Denham could barely breathe. His skin prickled all over, not with the heat and humidity or the itch from insect bites, but with the flush of true awe unlike anything he'd ever felt. This was transcendence. This was sublime.

Preston had stayed with the sailors down where they'd emerged from the jungle. Bruce and Herb, however, had followed Denham to the top of the slope that led down into the valley. Denham had set up the camera immediately and now all three of them stared, transfixed, even as Denham cranked the Bell & Howell, capturing the impossible on film.

Ahead of them, a herd of twelve brontosaurs grazed in a wide clearing, long necks swaying as they nibbled the tall grass. Brontos were one of the few dinosaurs Denham was familiar with from museum trips and books, and as a boy he had never quite decided whether he believed in their existence or not. He wanted evidence, wanted to see with his own eyes the same way he strived to bring the wonders of the world to others, so they could see with theirs.

Here was all the evidence he'd ever need.

Denham spoke, his voice low. "Walk forward, Bruce."

The actor blinked several times, as though waking from a trance. "What?"

"You're the star of this picture," Denham reminded him. "Get into character and head towards the animals."

Nervously, Bruce shuffled forward. "Are you sure about this, Denham? Don't we have a stand-in for this type of thing?"

Denham sighed, hating having to explain himself. "I need you in the shot, or people will say they're fake."

Something moved in his peripheral vision, off to the left of the herd. Denham turned to see what it might have been. Nothing. He brushed it off, assuming the wind had swayed some branches in the trees at the edge of the clearing.

Then the brontosaurs began to stir. Their feet shuffled and their heads rose slightly, as though they were listening for something. They were suddenly edgy and restless, these huge, lumbering animals.

"You're making them nervous," Denham whispered harshly, stopping Bruce in his tracks. "No sudden movement."

The actor shot him a dark look. "I'm not moving."

A low, rumbling sound began. Denham tensed, glancing around for its source before realizing it came from everywhere. The ground began to tremble. Denham thought for just a heartbeat that it was an earthquake.

Then the brontosaurs turned toward the film crew, on the run.

"Mother of God!" Bruce shouted, and fled back down the slope.

Denham and Herb looked at each other, and the director reached for the camera.

A full-on stampede of dinosaurs was headed this way.

Hayes started the group down the slope into the ravine. Jack wasn't worried about Carl; he knew the man wouldn't stray for long and the moment he returned to the place where they'd come out of the jungle, he'd be able to see everyone working their way down into the valley. Carl would catch up easily enough.

Jack wiped a hand across the back of his neck, rubbing at the grime and insect bites there. He grimaced but did not slow, keeping pace with the sailors. Hayes was up ahead. Lumpy and Choy were talking about something in low voices, just behind him.

Without warning, a piece of the cliffside to their left gave way, rocks tumbling down into the ravine. The men got out of the way easily enough. Jack frowned and looked up to the place where the cliff had broken loose, wondering what caused it.

Then the ground began to shake.

The sailors glanced around nervously, most of them watching the cliffs on either side now, wondering how bad the coming rockfall would be and where they could take cover.

As the crewmen pressed on, passing him by, Jack heard a noise from behind him, and turned to see Bruce Baxter running down the hill, a decidedly unheroic expression on his face.

"What is it?" Jack asked, as Bruce reached him. "Where's Carl?"

Bruce slowed down, making an obvious effort to calm himself. "He's . . . um, well, he's up there." He gestured back up the slope. "Filming."

There was a slight curve in the slope, and a rise, and the two topographical elements combined to keep the upper portion from view now that they were deeper in the ravine.

A loud roar echoed down toward them.

Bruce bolted like a startled rabbit, sprinting after the sailors. Many of them began to run now as well. The sound of that roar chilled Jack—though it wasn't the same one they'd heard in the jungle before. But he couldn't just leave Carl and Herb behind—he started cautiously uphill toward the source of the loud rumbling, a part of him questioning his own sanity as he moved.

The director and his camera operator came toward him over the rise in the slope, running for all they were worth. For a fellow with an artificial leg, Herb was making good speed, keeping up with Carl, practically hopping along. The rumbling grew louder, the ground shaking wildly.

Then Jack saw what they were running from.

A herd of dinosaurs now came over the rise, long necks bobbing up and down as they stampeded right toward him, following Herb and Carl. Jack froze, his heart skipping a beat. But no time for astonishment.

"Holy Christ!" Jack yelled.

Hayes and some of the sailors had hung back as

well, wondering what was up. Now the first mate screamed to the rest of them.

"Run!"

As if anyone needed to be told.

Jack was a native New Yorker, played baseball in city parks and stickball in the streets. He had run a lot as a boy, and he wasn't a kid anymore—yet his body remembered. He was lanky, long-legged, and fleet of foot, and he ran like hell, the wind in his hair, passing by some of the sailors who were rugged but not swift.

Something made him look back, concerned for Carl and the limping Herb. Even as he glanced over his shoulder, he saw Denham trip and fall. The stampede stormed down upon Carl there in the narrow valley. Carl was paralyzed on the spot. He'd been carrying the camera apparatus over his shoulder as he ran and it had gone flying from his grasp as he fell. Now as he started to rise, Jack saw the way Carl seemed mesmerized by the camera.

Fool! Jack thought.

He started back for Carl, even as the man went after his camera, which lay right in the path of the stampede.

"Leave it!" Jack shouted as he got a grip on Carl's clothes, trying to haul him away, to set him running again.

"No!" Denham snapped.

Carl lunged, got his hands on the equipment, and then he turned, the two old friends running again, side by side now. Carl cradled the camera and tripod in his arms as the brontosaur herd bore down on them from behind. Rocks calved off the cliffs and slid down, crashing nearby. The ground shook like an earthquake—they were nearly thrown from their feet by the tremors of the stampede.

Jack had lost track of everyone now. Herb, Hayes, Jimmy, Bruce, Lumpy, Choy . . . he was just running. Only Carl's presence beside him seemed solid and reliable. The rest was a blur.

He glanced over his shoulder again, and he discovered the reason for the stampede. He'd assumed somehow Carl's filming had set the dinosaurs off, but now he realized that was not the case at all. The brontosaurs were herbivores, eating only plants.

But not all dinosaurs had such a fussy diet.

Sprinting along after the bronto herd, running at speeds that were startling, was another breed entirely, some sort of Hunter-lizards. They were perhaps fifteen feet tall, much smaller than the brontos, but these were predators nevertheless. Huge, gaping jaws, snapping, gnashing, bearing razor teeth. Their upper arms were thin but ended in long talons with wicked looking claws, their lower legs were huge and muscular. Each of the Hunter-lizards had a wide red stripe down the back of their leathery hide.

They were closing in at incredible speed. One of the hunters leaped onto the back of a brontosaur and tore into it with both talons and the hooked claws on its powerful feet. The bronto faltered and slid to one side, crashing into the cliff. Two more of the predators leaped onto the fallen brontosaur, three of them tearing, slaughtering their prey as the rest of the herd streamed past.

Jack's view of the carnage was suddenly blocked out by a forest of thundering brontosaurus legs as the stampede caught up to them.

Jack and Carl were engulfed by the herd, surrounded by huge legs like giant redwood trees pounding the ground around them. The Hunter-lizards were in amongst them, snapping and snarling at the mammoth legs. Jack had been so terrified, so sure that his life was about to end with a crunch of bone as he was pulped underfoot, that it hadn't occurred to him that these predators were even more dangerous.

Until one of them noticed him—its eyes narrowed, tracking Jack.

He and Carl had instinctively been trying to move toward the edge of the herd, to escape the stampede, but now Jack grabbed Denham's arm until his old friend saw what he'd seen. Their only hope of survival was to stay within the stampede, to take their chances with the thundering tree trunk legs of the brontosaurs, so that they could stay out of the flesh eaters' reach.

Up ahead, in the sea of legs, a sailor tripped and tumbled to the ground and was crushed underfoot.

Others had not yet noticed the predators—Jack saw two sailors jump clear of the stampede only to be set upon and torn apart. Their death cries were drowned out by the thunder of the brontosaurs' flight.

Now the others saw this new peril, and all were running madly, trying desperately to dodge the stampeding legs of the brontosaurs and the lunging, snapping jaws of the red-striped predators. One of the things still focused on Jack. He saw it eyeing him, but then the writer's attention was diverted as a huge leg swept toward him that he quickly avoided.

In the same moment, the vicious Hunter-lizard found its opening, darting and weaving in between and ducking under the brontosaurs until it came up right behind Jack. It lunged, jaws snapping inches from his head.

Desperate, with death all around him, there was only one option. He stopped, and slammed his shoulder into the hunter, knocking the slavering dinosaur with its gore-stained teeth under the trampling feet of a brontosaur. Its body was pulped and bones shattered, but Jack was already in motion, dodging again, making sure he didn't share the thing's fate.

Jack and Carl had made their way toward the front of the stampede again. Up ahead, along the floor of the valley, Bruce was still sprinting. Somehow he'd managed to stay ahead of the stampede, ahead of the Hunter-lizards, outpacing everything and everyone.

Even as Jack spotted Bruce, one of the predators did too. It darted out past the front of the herd and headed for the actor, powerful legs pistoning, driving it forward with unstoppable force and speed.

Panic swept over Bruce. He brought up the Tommy gun Hayes had given him, bringing the barrel around to aim at the predator . . . and at the stampede beyond. Jack saw impending disaster.

"No!" he screamed.

Bruce fired, missing the Hunter-lizard, and hit the

lead brontosaur in the chest. The massive, lumbering dinosaur collapsed at top speed, tumbling end over end, huge neck and tail thrashing out. The other brontos plowed into it, tripping and rolling.

Jack and the others were caught in the crash, in that massive pile-up of heaving dinosaur flesh. A couple of sailors were crushed as the brontosaurs came down on top of them; one of the flesh eaters was trapped between two brontos that collided, shattering the hunter.

A rock jutted from the path and Jack rolled up against it as brontosaurs crashed and tumbled all around him. Nearby he spotted Carl throwing himself to the ground, wild-eyed as he tried to shield his precious movie camera from harm, willing to sacrifice his own life to keep it intact.

The lunatic.

In the space of seconds, the mighty herd of behemoths was reduced to a vast heap of dead and wounded animals. The Hunter-lizards immediately went to work, leaping onto the brontosaurs and ripping open their fleshy stomachs, snouts darting, stained red with blood and viscera.

Jack crawled past huge, heaving bellies and twitching legs, staggering out of the mountain of flesh, and then turned back quickly at the sound of loud hissing.

One of the predators was climbing over a dead brontosaur, gleaming eyes intently watching Jack. It leaped at him, about to deliver the killing blow. Gunfire ripped the air, riddling the hunter with bullets, and it fell dead at Jack's feet.

Numb, Jack looked up to see Hayes hurrying toward him, Tommy gun clutched in his hands.

"Go! Go!" Hayes shouted.

He got them all moving up a steep, rocky incline, the survivors slipping and sliding on slimy, moss covered rocks. But Jack didn't follow—he looked around, panic mounting. Where the hell was Denham now?

"Carl?" he called. "Carl!"

Denham limped from somewhere out of the mound of dead and dying brontosaurs, bloodied and covered in dust. The camera was cradled in his arms. Intact.

Unknown to the director, another of the Hunterlizards was pacing him. Hayes pulled the trigger and bullets tore it apart. It toppled backward into the wreckage of dead history.

"Run!" Hayes shouted.

Denham needed no further encouragement.

18

DENHAM DIDN'T HAVE A clue what these predator dinosaurs were, but he didn't want to get a closer look. He'd once seen the skeleton of a *Tyrannosaurus rex* at a museum, right next to the brontosaur, and these vicious monsters seemed like a cross between a T. rex and a kangaroo, small in comparison, but built for speed, powerful and sleek. Their snouts were thick, their yellow eyes gleaming with cunning and ravenous hunger that he was sure was never sated.

Denham didn't want to die, but he *had* to save the camera. Period. Without it, without a record of this place and the extraordinary events that had unfolded on this voyage, he might as well die here on Skull Island. He wouldn't have a life to go back to, otherwise.

The Bell & Howell camera was all-important, more vital than his own survival.

Now that he'd retrieved it, though, surviving wasn't a bad idea at all. Some of those vicious predators were thrusting their heads up from ravaging the dead and dying brontos, their attention turning to the fleeing sailors. Now *that* was bad.

Denham reached the steep, rocky incline that the

others were already scrambling up. He cradled the Bell & Howell in one arm and used the other to climb, dammit. Some of the men carried packs, guns, and other equipment just as heavy as the camera, or more so, and he quickly caught up to them. They were slipping and sliding on the wet moss that covered the rocks. He assumed that Preston and Bruce were far above him. He could see Jack and Herb just a short way ahead, Herb having difficulty climbing with his artificial leg.

One of the men above Denham, a sailor named Brandon, was staring back down the mossy, rocky slope, making a strangled noise in his throat. Denham turned to find that four of those carnivores had finally torn themselves away from the brontosaur feast and started up after the group.

Some of the sailors panicked, choosing their footing too hurriedly, and sliding backward. The carnivores slid as well, but their powerful legs worked furiously, propelling them higher and higher, closer to the flailing sailors.

Brandon shouted in fear as he lost his grip, falling, rolling down the slope, banging off the rocks, tumbling with such speed that he passed two of the carnivores. Then a third darted out its snout, jaws snapping down, and snatched the sailor in its teeth. Brandon screamed in agony.

Denham grabbed hold of a rock, climbing faster. All around him sailors held onto weeds, rocks, moss, whatever they could to steady themselves, avoiding Brandon's fate. Hayes shouted from high above, a triumphant noise, and Denham glanced up to see he'd reached a network of narrow fissures between huge rocks, almost like the sword of some ancient god had slashed into the stone. If they could get into those fissures, the dinosaurs would not be able to follow. Hopefully.

He gripped the camera tightly, breathed evenly, and focused on not falling. If he was too slow, he would die . . . but he had a better chance if he was careful than if he lost control, falling to his death in those bloody jaws. Control was all that mattered now.

Curses and shouts came from all around and above him. Herb had slowed down even further—he scrabbled against the stone and moss as best he could, but he could never be sure of his footing with a false leg, could not trust that prosthetic limb. He was too damn slow.

Denham moved up toward him, inching sideways, bracing himself with his feet, camera cradled in his left arm as he tried to reach for Herb with his right.

"Herb! Come on!"

"Mr. Denham," Herb gasped. He was as brave a man as Denham had ever known, fearless in the pursuit of the perfect camera shot, but now there was a bleak desperation in his eyes that chilled Denham.

"Come on, Herb, grab my hand. Do as I say! Grab it!"

Herb strained to reach for Denham's hand, but too late. His artificial leg gave way beneath him, slipping from its foothold. Herb rolled down the slope, right into the path of a ravening carnivore. All of the predators fell upon Herb with a sick ripping of flesh and cracking of bones.

Denham stared in utter horror at the grotesque tableau below him. He glanced at his empty hand, the one he had tried to grab Herb with, as though he did not understand why he had failed. Inside, he was hollow.

Someone shouted his name from above and he started climbing again. While the monsters were busy with Herb, he made it to the fissures in the stone and slid through, still careful not to damage the camera.

They were safe.

Those who had survived.

Hayes kept them all moving. Jack felt exhaustion overtaking him and tried to fight it, but he needed a rest. Still, Hayes kept them going through the fissures in the rocks and over the top of the next hill. For twenty minutes they moved over treacherous terrain, and eventually found themselves clambering down a jagged rock face into lush subtropical vegetation.

This looked more like swamp than jungle. Even in the midst of his exhaustion and his fear for Ann, Jack found a moment to be amazed at the differences in terrain in just a small section of this volcanic island. This death trap.

The group gathered slowly, one by one the survivors climbing down from the rock face. Bruce Baxter. Preston. Carl with his damned camera. Jack was relieved to see that Jimmy was alive, for he'd not caught sight of the kid throughout the bloody stampede. Lumpy and Choy, that odd pair, had also survived. And Hayes, of course. Intrepid Hayes. But the first mate now had a much smaller search party to command than before. Aside from the kid and Lumpy and Choy, there were only a handful of other sailors remaining, none looking very interested in taking orders from anyone at the moment.

Cut, bruised, covered in dust, the bedraggled, dispirited group gathered in a clearing at the edge of the misty swamp that spread out before them. Sheer cliffs rose up out of the swamp on both sides of the shore. Jack very quickly realized that most of their guns and many of their other supplies had been lost.

The sailors slumped to the ground in the clearing, utterly demoralized and terrified, some staring around at each other, and others avoiding eye contact with anyone.

"Do a head count," Hayes instructed Jimmy. "I want to know how many injured, and how bad—"

"Injured?" Lumpy remarked. "Four of us are dead!"

Denham and Preston came further into the clearing, apparently looking for a spot to set themselves down to rest. Lumpy glared at Carl, who quickly looked away. The director dumped the camera gear, obviously out of breath and unsteady on his feet.

Only Jack was close enough to hear the film-maker and his assistant as they spoke quietly to one another.

"Carl?" Preston ventured.

Denham responded with quiet despair. "What are we doing here, Preston? How could it end like this?"

Carl was one of Jack's closest friends—or at least had been when all this madness began. Jack knew he ought to try to raise the man's spirits, but he had seen the desperation in Carl's eyes, had seen him risk his life and jeopardize others for that damned camera, for a film that would make him a household name, and he didn't feel like offering Carl Denham comfort at the moment. He had always known the director was obsessive, but until now he hadn't understood how deep that obsession ran.

Instead of addressing the mixture of rage and pity he was currently feeling, Jack walked away from them, went toward Hayes. He kicked mossy debris off a fallen tree, studying it. They had to keep *moving*. He was determined to find Ann, and equally determined to get everybody back to the ship without anyone else getting killed.

"How much rope have we got?" he asked Hayes, kicking the moss off another fallen tree and seeing the potential there.

"Are you out of your mind?" Lumpy barked. He gestured at the swamp. "We can't get across that!"

A number of the sailors muttered their agreement.

"Don't wanna go no further," said a squat, grizzled sailor.

"It's over," agreed another. "She's dead and so are we."

Lumpy shrugged. "Bugger this! I'm off!"

Jack stared at him. He looked around for support and was surprised to see that Bruce was guarded and tense.

"He's got a point," the actor quietly said. "Englehorn sails in nine hours."

Jimmy rounded on him. "So? We've gotta find Miss Darrow!"

"Didn't you hear me?" Bruce asked the boy. "We're gonna be stranded here."

"I heard you, and I ain't going back!" Jimmy snapped.

"Yeah?" Lumpy sneered. "Well, you were never destined to have a long and happy life."

Like a match to a fuse, that set Hayes off. *"Shut it!"* he flared.

Lumpy quieted, but Bruce was not through with Jimmy. Jack heard the actor's next words with numb horror blooming in his heart.

"She's dead, Jimmy," Bruce said.

Jack kept his breathing steady, but could feel the fury radiating from within. When Bruce became aware of Jack's glare, he shifted self-consciously and cleared his throat.

"Miss Darrow was a great gal, no question," Bruce said, looking around at the others. "A wonderful person. We're all gonna miss her."

When Jack spoke, his words came out a growl, through gritted teeth.

"I always knew you were nothing like the tough guy you play on screen," he said, his eyes staring daggers. "I just never figured you for a coward."

Bruce brushed him off. "Hey, pal, wake up. I'm an actor. Heroes don't look like me. Not in real life. In real life they've got bad teeth, a bald spot, and a beer gut. They're normal."

"Are you done?"

Bruce slung his gun over his shoulder. "Go ahead. Make me the bad guy. I've played 'em before and let me tell you what I learned. There *are* no bad guys, Driscoll. Only bad writers."

He took several steps away, setting himself apart from the group.

Jack watched him a moment and then turned to regard the rest of the group. Hayes was also surveying them with a wicked look.

"Anyone else?" the first mate demanded.

A couple of sailors shuffled over to join Bruce. Lumpy set his pack more firmly on his shoulder and looked expectantly at his closest friend.

"Choy . . ."

The Chinese man grinned, but Jack saw a glint of determination in his eyes. "Not me. I stay with the boys. I got Charlie Atlas training!"

Lumpy groaned, rolling his eyes.

"I complete the course!" Choy declared. "Perfect manhood very hard to kill."

Jack saw Lumpy's expression, and knew that the man's determination to leave had been defeated. He wasn't going anywhere without Choy.

Without further support, Bruce's efforts at mutiny were doomed to failure. They were all going on, no matter what their fate.

Preston was more than a little concerned about Carl Denham. The man had a lost look in his eyes. He'd grieved after Mike had been killed by the islanders, but this was different—Herb's death was haunting him. Carl stared into the swamp as though searching for some sign of the ghost he thought ought to be there. His confidence, his certainty, had been shattered.

While the others were debating who would go and who would stay, Denham turned to him.

"I think I lost my way, Preston. Somewhere back there, we took a wrong turn."

"It's not your fault, what happened to Herb. It's no one's fault."

"When there are no rules," Denham rasped, "who's to say what is right?"

Preston looked him in the eye. "You *make* the rules, Carl," he said firmly. "You're the director."

Denham flinched, eyes widening slightly. He stared at Preston.

"Isn't that the way it works?" Preston asked.

The Carl Denham he'd come to know and admire—for better or worse—was a man who was not accountable to anyone or any system of moral judgment. Right or wrong had always been a gray, amorphous thing to the director, dependent only upon what would benefit his ambitions as a filmmaker.

Now Denham's eyes lit up. Preston saw it all turning over in his head, as though he was suddenly waking from a dream. All he'd done was remind Denham who he really was, but it was enough to free the director from his indecision.

"That's absolutely the way it works," Denham said softly, nodding. "And I'll tell you something else. Herbert didn't die for nothing. He died for what he believed in . . . and I'm gonna honor that."

Preston studied him. "Really?"

Denham stood a bit straighter and when he spoke it was with the grandeur of the showman he'd always been. "He died believing there is still some mystery left in this world and we can all have a piece of it . . . for the price of an admission ticket! Goddamn it, Preston, we're gonna finish this film for Herb . . . and donate the proceeds to his wife and kids."

Preston blinked, stunned. But only for a moment. He had always known that it wasn't about money for Carl Denham. It was about spectacle. About being extraordinary.

"That's fantastic," Preston said.

Denham had been clutching his flask throughout their conversation, but now he raised it in a toast.

"Here's to the motion picture business," he said, taking a swig of whiskey. "The greatest fantasy of all."

Amen to that, thought Preston. *Welcome back, Carl.*

Kong propelled himself through the jungle with ease, barely disturbing the forest, moving with grace along a route that seemed well used and which Ann imagined must be familiar to him. She was held fast in his grip, flung wildly around as the great ape bounded across chasms and leapt over rivers. The jungle spun and blurred by and Ann did her best to brace herself against Kong's fingers. She was not strong enough, and the constant jostling knocked her around like a rag doll.

All she could focus on was the jungle and that grip, though thoughts of what would become of her when the gorilla reached his destination did flit through her mind. He'd certainly taken her to the place where he'd killed the previous sacrifices taken from that altar by the ancient wall, but *Ann* had been spared.

Whatever happened now, it would be new territory for both of them. Ann had no idea how she would manage to escape, to stay alive, but she was sure Kong would have no idea what to do with her now, either.

Even as these thoughts entered her mind, there came a blur from the green around them. Kong was knocking trees aside, and a pair of massive lizards leaped from the brush. Ann screamed, certain they were after her, looking to steal away Kong's prize, to prey on his capture.

They clung onto Kong's arms, clawing furiously, snapping at Ann. Saliva flew from razor-sharp jaws. They weren't merely giant lizards, but actual *dinosaurs,* and she screamed again as they continued toward her.

Kong effortlessly thumped his arm against a tree, crushing one of the creatures. Ann clung to Kong's fingers as he reached out and strangled the second beast with one hand, snapping its neck with a bone-crunching sound.

The most stunning aspect of this entire scenario was how casual it all played out, how almost *routine* it seemed for Kong, as if this was just a recurring theme in this incredible animal's day.

Then Kong swung Ann roughly upward and bounded off into the deep jungle interior, her in one hand and the dead dinosaur in the other.

It wasn't long before they came to an ancient ruin of the sort she'd seen in various places across the island. Whatever the civilization was that had originally settled here, they had sprawled across the surface of Skull Island.

As he ambled into the ruins, Kong dropped Ann into a heap on the ground, plopping the dead dinosaur beside her. Kong would have to decide what to do with her. New territory.

Ann lay completely still, unmoving, pretending to be unconscious or dead. Kong circled around her, prodding her roughly with an enormous finger. Ann gritted her teeth, forcing herself to give no response.

Kong growled, prodded again, but Ann lay still.

The towering gorilla scratched his chest, but then seemed to become distracted and moved away. Kong sat on the edge of the ruin, surveying the jungle.

Ann slowly opened her eyes and looked warily toward Kong. He didn't seem to be paying any attention to her . . . but still she was cautious as she tried to survey her surroundings. Her whole body hurt. Exhaustion and the battering she'd taken as he'd rushed through the jungle with her took their toll, but she didn't think anything was broken inside her. Not yet.

If she was going to escape, she didn't know how many more chances she'd get. Ann had to assume this would be the last.

Surreptitiously, she glanced around. The ruin was a small courtyard—its walls were cracked and split by encroaching jungle creepers. Kong sat with his back to Ann, in the crumbling remains of an enclosed entry area, but the walls around her were still intact, which meant he was blocking the only way out.

She lifted her head, risking a quick look around. The walls were too steep, but it turned out there was another way out after all. Across the courtyard was a narrow stairway leading down into the jungle.

Inch by inch, Ann edged forward, crawling on her stomach toward the stairs. Kong abruptly shifted his weight, half-turning.

Ann froze, let her muscles go slack, and closed her eyes to slits, attempting once more to look lifeless and praying he wouldn't notice that she'd moved several feet.

The instant he turned away, she started to move forward once more. Her breathing came evenly, her pulse was steady—by focusing only on the task at hand, she remained calm.

Then, inches from her face, strange, unfamiliar insects crawled out of a crack in the flagstones. She flinched. No way could she drag herself over *those*.

Only a few feet from the stairwell, she rose as quietly as possible and started toward freedom. It felt as though her heart would burst with tension, but then she had made it into the narrow passage, out of sight of Kong. She glanced only once over her shoulder as she hurried down the stairway.

Ann paused at the bottom, listening for sounds that would indicate her escape had been discovered. All was quiet as she glanced back up the stairs. No sign that he'd noticed her departure. Gathering her strength, Ann emerged from the passage and bolted across the clearing around the ruins toward the cover of the jungle.

Her only warning was a strange *whoosh* of air, then Kong's fist slammed into the ground in front of her.

Ann gasped and tried to change direction, but even as she did the other fist thudded to the ground, blocking her route.

Kong growled angrily, glaring down at her.

Ann was cornered. She spun to face him and he snarled at her, furious and deadly, the stink of raw meat on his breath. She darted under his arm in a last ditch attempt to escape. Halfway across the clearing, she tripped and fell, crashing face-first to the dirt.

Kong bounded over to her, slapping his hands on the ground as though he were pounding a drum, uttering a guttural growl. Ann lay flat, eyes shut, lying still, praying the ruse would work again.

Kong circled her, suspicious. As before, he prodded her a couple of times but again she gave no response. And as before, Kong moved on. Through slitted lids she saw him lumbering away, and she opened her eyes.

He spun around and caught her watching him.

Despair and panic shot through Ann and she sprang to her feet. For a desperate moment, she stared at the gorilla and wondered if she should run. But her heart sank as she forced herself to accept the truth. She would never make it, never escape. Trembling, she had to do whatever it took to survive.

Ann's stumbling had made him curious before, had distracted and confused him. It had also hurt like hell, but that had merely been an accident. Her life in vaudeville had allowed her to master the artful fall.

What the hell—let's see if it works again . . .

Ann did a pratfall, there in the midst of the clearing, arms and legs flying as she flopped crazily onto the ground. It hurt, but not nearly so much as when she'd struck face-first.

Kong cocked his head, brow furrowed with interest. He bared his teeth a bit and made another circle around her, studying her closely.

She climbed to her feet, stood for a few seconds, and then repeated the pratfall. Kong slapped his hands on the ground, shook his head and growled, but he did not move closer. Instead, he watched to see what she would do next. She had to make him see her as something new, something unique.

What, she thought to herself, *you're going to make him laugh?*

Perhaps not, but she might amuse him or, at the very least, intrigue him.

Her breath came in tremulous gasps and she tried to

steady herself, forcing herself to breathe evenly. She closed her eyes to slits and tried to remember the stage and the audience, the music and the smell of greasepaint, and it all seemed a lifetime ago. New York City was another world, another age.

As Kong watched, mesmerized, Ann began to sway drunkenly, falling into character as the English gentleman she'd played with Manny so many times. Voice low, she sang an inebriated little ditty, and then fell, but this time let herself roll into the fall and spring up again immediately.

Kong grunted and slapped the ground, but remained where he was, staring at her.

Ann kept on. She began to dance, a bit of softshoe, there on the rough ground of the clearing. A song rose from her lips, but it was a mask that she hid behind, carefully watching the reaction of her audience, making certain her performance was striking home. She went back to her routine, swaying drunkenly and falling, then bouncing back up, working her timing around Kong's reactions. All along, she observed him, and saw that he grew increasingly engaged.

Panting from exertion, body bruised and bones aching, she forced herself to continue. She bounced up, beads of sweat trickling down her face. Her gaze darted between the jungle and Kong, hope rising once more that she might find the right moment to flee, might lose herself in the jungle.

But Kong was nothing but a demanding audience. The moment she hesitated in her private show, he became impatient. He reached out, knocking her off her feet, the poke of that massive finger like a punch to the gut. Ann fell to the ground, winded, sucking air.

Kong slapped his hands on the dirt again and let out an excited growl. He thumped with his fists, and shook his head. At last he was amused, but Ann quickly realized he had come to see this as a game. She would stand up, sway a bit, and fall down again. And he hadn't tired of the game yet.

Instead, he was delighted with it.

Wary, Ann tried to get up, but Kong pushed her over once more. This time she stayed on the ground, breathing heavily, fear roiling in her chest. She had felt like a rag doll in his hands before, but now he really was treating her like some child's plaything. But if he played too rough, he might just kill her out of sheer amusement. How many times could he knock her down before something broke inside her?

Grunting, he thumped the ground several times in rapid succession. He reached out and tried to prod her into getting up. Ann slapped his huge finger away and Kong pulled back his arm, startled.

"Stop!" she gasped, one hand clutched to her aching chest.

Kong cocked his head and beat the ground again.

"Stop," she repeated, staring up at him as she tried to stand.

But her performance had severely depleted her. Her legs went out from under her and she collapsed. This time, it was no act.

Kong rose to his feet and beat his chest, towering

over her. He raised a huge fist then slammed it down toward her. Ann closed her eyes, frozen, as Kong's fist thudded into the ground inches from her. He drove his other fist into the dirt on her other side.

When she did not move, Kong went berserk. He beat his chest, a roar erupting from him and echoing all through the jungle. Flocks of birds took flight from the trees above. Things skittered through the underbrush at the edges of the clearing.

Kong wanted an encore and Ann's failure to provide one had driven him into a rage. Even if she tried now to stand and continue, it was too late. Fury overcame him—Kong ripped a tree from the ground and threw it, cracking other trees and branches in his display of anger.

In this place, he was the master. The undisputed *king*. Whatever he demanded would come to pass, or he would shatter and destroy. This was the nature of the male of the species—Ann knew enough about the animal world to understand that.

Ann had angered the ruler of this domain, and now fully expected to die.

The ground shook with his fury. Ann rolled onto her stomach and lifted her head. For a brief moment they made eye contact. Incensed, Kong charged at her. Eyes blazing, teeth bared, he snatched her off the ground.

Ann screamed.

Kong's fingers tightened around her and she shut her eyes, cowering, raising her arms to shield her head. It was useless to fight, and she accepted her fate.

But death did not come.

259

Slowly, Ann opened her eyes, and found Kong staring at her, this small figure in his hand. Something about his face had changed. All of the anger drained from his features, and his eyes had softened. There was almost a sadness there, as though he had a rudimentary thought or memory about something that touched him.

From the moment she had escaped Kong at the place where he had killed the others, she had struggled to make him notice her, to see her as something other than an object. Perhaps it had happened at last, but what it was that reached him, what soothed him or saddened him, she could not know.

Very slowly, Kong opened his palm and allowed Ann to slide from his grasp. Tense, wondering if at any second he might change his mind, she slipped through his fingers and landed heavily on the ground.

Hesitant for the first time since he'd come for her, Kong stepped back from Ann. He stared at her, that look of utter confusion making him seem somehow lost, as though some of his power had been diminished, as though he was now no longer master of all he surveyed.

Slowly, he backed away, then faster. Suddenly he turned and left the clearing. Ann could only watch as Kong loped off into the jungle. He pulled himself up and over a ruined wall and in a single motion disappeared from sight.

Ann stood, finally free of her captor, but somehow troubled, both by the encounter, and by the uncertainty of her own fate.

Without Kong to protect her, she feared she would not survive the journey back to the shore. And even if she were so lucky as to find her way, and get there alive, hours had already passed and it was unlikely the *Venture* would still be waiting.

She started off, and could only pray she had chosen the right direction. Exhausted, her throat parched with thirst, she moved through the jungle as fast as she was able, pushing through thorns and tangled vines.

Ann was completely unsure if Jack and the others had indeed stayed around to rescue her—she silently hoped so. But first, she had to make it out of here, and for the time being she could only rely upon herself.

19

THERE COULD BE NO turning back now. As the sailors used long branches to pole the two makeshift rafts they'd built across the surface of the murky swamp, Jack felt the weight of their fate upon his shoulders. Everyone had pitched in to build the rafts, heading across the swamp in the direction that Hayes gauged the monster had taken Ann.

Yet Jack knew that if he had given up, not a man among them would have gone on without him. His unwillingness to give up on her, to turn back, sustained them. In some way, that made him culpable for whatever destiny awaited them, a responsibility he keenly felt.

The lead raft carried Hayes, Denham, Bruce, Lumpy, and several other sailors. Jack was on the second, along with Preston, Choy, Jimmy, and the rest of the party.

Dead trees thrust out of the water, draped with vines and dried moss. Fog drifted lazily over the fetid swamp, air stuffy and close. The insects were clearly more numerous here than in the jungle, yet they didn't bother with the sailors much. Small flying lizards flitted among the stumps of trees that had rotted and been torn down by storms.

Dinosaurs. Jack still had difficulty with the truth, though he'd seen them up close . . . too close. Somehow this place had survived in its primordial state from prehistoric times. Conan Doyle had once written about a Lost World, and here it was in all its glory. Skull Island.

Under other circumstances, he would have thought it a wonder. Instead, the island itself seemed savage, preying upon their group, taking them one by one, even as they strove to save Ann from whatever strange secrets it had.

An ape, that's what Denham said he saw. But what sort of ape left tracks like those they'd found? Could a gorilla truly grow that large? If he hadn't seen those dinosaurs, Jack would never have believed it.

He shifted the ammo pack that hung heavily upon his shoulders, gaining little relief. Miraculously, Carl had given Preston the camera to hold onto, and the director's assistant clung to it almost as avariciously as Denham had, as though it were made of gold. At the front of the raft, Jimmy peered nervously down into the water.

Up ahead, something rippled under the surface. Jack frowned and shifted his position, trying to get a better look. Even as he did there was a thump ahead and Hayes's raft jolted, rocking in the water. The men muttered anxious grunts and looked over into the murkiness, trying to see what they'd struck.

"What the hell was that?" Lumpy snapped, twisting around to try to get a glimpse.

On the raft behind them, Jack and the others did

the same. The water rippled again and a large, dark shape moved beneath the surface of the swamp, swiftly creating a wave that rolled toward Jack's raft.

Without warning, it burst from the water, a monstrous thing that seemed part fish and part serpent. Its huge jaws gaped wide with jagged rows of vicious teeth, like some kind of piranha-serpent. It reared out of the swamp and smashed down upon the raft, shattering the fallen logs into kindling, tearing it apart. Men shouted in terror and alarm. Jack heard Lumpy swear and Hayes call out to Jimmy, even as he saw the boy go under the black water.

Then Jack was splashing into the swamp as well, plunging deep, with thick, filthy water choking down his throat. Long reeds waved in the depths of the swamp like tentacles. The ammunition pack weighed Jack down, dragging him deeper, and he sank like a stone to the bottom.

Out of the corner of his eye he saw motion in the water, and knew it had to be that monster, that prehistoric piranha. *Piranhadon,* he thought, the writer in him needing to name the beast.

And he wondered if there were others.

For just a moment, Ben Hayes felt hope leave him. Watching Jimmy sink into the swamp was like drowning himself. He was responsible for all of these men, but for Jimmy most of all. Preston, Denham's right hand, had managed to cling to the last vestiges of the shattered raft, still clutching the damned camera. But the others had all gone under.

Then one of the sailors was splashing in the swamp just inches from his own raft, and Hayes was in motion. He dragged the sailor aboard.

"Get them out of there!" he shouted. "Come on, help them!"

Choy was floundering in the water, trying to reach for a shattered log.

"Swim, you dopey bugger, swim!" Lumpy yelled to him.

But Choy sank beneath the water. He emerged again, spluttering and gasping, but it was clear he was going to drown. Lumpy called his name in panic, then dove into the murk and swam for Choy.

Hayes kept on shouting, wondering how many of them would be left when they reached the other side of the swamp.

If they reached the other side.

Underwater, Jack frantically looked around. He thrashed his legs against the long reeds that seemed to want to wrap around them, to drag at him. The water was dark and filthy. Another sailor, Carnahan, sank down nearby. He was also wearing an ammo pack. Jack wanted to go to him, to help him toward the surface.

The Piranhadon emerged from the gloom. Its body flowed back and forth, propelling it toward them, twenty-five feet long at least. Carnahan tried desperately to undo his heavy pack. Jack tried to stop him, signaling to Carnahan to head to the bottom of the swamp. The creature would be drawn toward the thrashing at the surface. But Carnahan ignored him— the sailor slipped the ammo pack off of his back and floated free, pulling for the surface.

With frightening grace, the Piranhadon swept the sailor up in its jaws.

Blood blurred the water.

Jack dove down, into the swirling weeds, using the weight of the pack to propel himself along the bottom of the swamp. His lungs burned and blackness played at the corners of his vision, oxygen deprivation taking its toll. His heart clenched as he looked back to see the Piranhadon pursuing him, Carnahan's mangled body still in its jaws. It closed the distance with terrifying speed.

With a desperate effort, Jack heaved himself between the tangled roots of a swamp tree, just as the creature lunged toward him. It scraped against the tree roots, denied its prey, and then turned back toward the raft and the sailors still trying to get out of the swamp to safety.

Lungs ready to burst, Jack kicked for the surface. He came up from the water, gasping for air. Hidden among the roots of the swamp tree, he glanced around and immediately saw Preston clinging to the remains of the destroyed raft.

From the surviving raft, Denham shouted to him.

"Hold on, Preston! Don't let go! Whatever happens, don't let go of the camera!"

Concealed in the shadows of the tree's roots and the

swamp, Jack felt a twist of disgust in his gut. Carl had already lost two men. Yet still all he could think about was his film. *Damn him.*

The monster reared out of the swamp in a spray of water and muck. Carl raised a Tommy gun and let loose a torrent of gunfire that punched the water between Preston and the creature. The Piranhadon disappeared below the surface and Denham looked around wildly, waiting for it to rise again.

Jack took that as his cue. He swam out from the roots of the swamp tree, straight for Preston. When he reached the shattered bit of broken log that Preston clung to, he grabbed hold of the wood and the two of them began to struggle together toward shore.

Nearby, the swamp monster broke the surface again and began to circle around, coming back for Preston and Jack.

From Hayes's raft, upon which the others were swiftly working, trying to pole it toward shore, Carl fired the Tommy gun again.

"Stop!" Hayes shouted.

The Piranhadon veered away from Preston and Jack and headed straight for the remaining raft. Carl had wanted to get its attention, and he'd done the job too well. It dove under the water, disappearing again. Carl ignored Hayes and let out several more bursts of gunfire, bullets striking the water, chasing the wake of the creature.

The thing swam beneath the raft. Carl kept firing, bullets splintering wood and severing the rope that lashed it all together. As Hayes shouted at him, the raft began to break apart beneath them, and then Jack and Preston watched as all of the men began to tumble into the swamp.

Heart pounding, throat ragged, gasping for breath, Jack kicked toward shore. Preston worked just as hard, silently, clutching the precious camera in his hands, keeping it atop the remnant of raft they were using to stay afloat. Jack waited, every second, to hear the screams of sailors dying or the splash of the creature thrusting from the water again. His every nerve was on edge, but none of those things happened.

Finally, he and Preston could touch the bottom with their feet, and they were staggering up out of the water onto dry land. Moss and vines hung down around them, and the humid swelter of the day clutched at their sodden clothes, but at least they were out of the swamp.

Moments later the first of the others reached land, eyes dull with shock and exhaustion. Carl and Hayes were among the first. Jimmy, Hayes, Bruce, Kelso, Lumpy, and Preston soon followed. Other stragglers joined them. Choy came up and sat down beside Lumpy.

Carl ignored the others, even Preston, and went straight to the camera. He picked it up and cranked it, the mechanism whirring.

Lumpy rounded furiously upon him. "Turn that bloody thing off!"

"Just a quick check," Carl replied, without so much as looking at him.

The last of the crewmen, Hal Jablonski, waded toward them in the shallows.

"It's working," Carl said, his relief palpable, turning the camera toward Jablonski.

The placid surface of the swamp exploded as a huge shape reared out of the water. The Piranhadon snatched Jablonski up in its jaws, then drew back, vanishing into the water as quickly as it had appeared. There hadn't even been time for Jablonski to scream.

Everyone stared numbly at the place where the man had been only a moment before.

Lumpy turned to Denham. "Get that, did you?" he asked grimly, a gallows smile on his lips.

Slowly, they gathered up what little they had left by way of weapons and supplies. Hayes looked at the sun, turned to gauge the distance and location of the peaks that were behind them, and then chose a direction. He started off and the others followed.

Jack paused and looked at Carl, who stood frozen, staring at the swamp, camera still whirring.

They trudged on. Once more they had entered thick jungle, and the underbrush was like barbed wire, branches and thorns tugging at them as they made their way through. Hayes kept his eyes out for more signs of the passing of the giant ape or whatever it was that had taken Miss Darrow. He was sure he was headed in the right direction. The largest of the hills and mountains that rose up from the heart of the volcanic island were still ahead, and he navigated by line of sight now.

His clothes were nearly dry, but they were stiff and clung uncomfortably. From the moment they'd set off to rescue Miss Darrow, he'd been thinking of the war, but now it was on his mind more than ever. Slogging through trenches and across battlefields, waiting for the next explosion or attack, the next horror to present itself.

There was only one thing to be done in such situations.

Continue onward.

The men followed in line, strung out behind him. Hayes ducked beneath a hanging vine and pushed through some dense undergrowth. He glanced back and saw the men in glimpses through the thick, damp green of the jungle.

Something moved, up ahead.

Hayes had no time to react as a streak of gray and red burst from the undergrowth, jaws open wide, tail whipping behind it. It leaped at him, and in a fraction of a moment, the space between heartbeats, he knew he was dead.

A gunshot punctured the air, stopped the vicious dinosaur dead in its tracks, and it crashed to the ground at Hayes's feet, lifeless and bleeding.

Hayes stared at the thing's lower legs, at the single toe on each foot that was like a gaffing hook and would have torn him open from gullet to groin. He felt cold inside.

Hayes turned and saw Jimmy standing a few feet away, gun in his hands, looking quite proud of himself.

That was all he needed, Jimmy getting overconfident and getting himself killed.

"Don't go thinking you're so smart," Hayes told the boy. "Just because you got off a lucky shot."

Jimmy scowled. "There's no danger of that."

Hayes glanced at a couple of the sailors coming up behind him. "Kids," he said. "They grow up too fast. You listen to him and he knows it all."

The words made Jimmy drop his gaze to the jungle floor. "I know you don't think much of me," the kid said quietly. "I know I won't ever measure up. That's about it."

Jimmy turned and walked off, shoulders squared. Hayes could only watch him go, a sick feeling in his stomach, knowing he should call Jimmy back, try to explain, but unable to find his voice, or the words.

Lumpy watched the exchange between Mr. Hayes and the kid. He caught only some of the words, but the expression on Jimmy's face as he stormed off was clear enough.

The kid paused to steam for a minute and Lumpy stepped up beside him. When Jimmy looked at him, Lumpy made a point of glancing at Hayes. He nodded in the first mate's direction.

"You're lucky," Lumpy said. "I never had that."

Jimmy looked at him, confused.

"A father who cares," Lumpy went on. "He thinks of you like a son, you know. He loves you, Jimmy . . . Gawd knows why."

Jimmy flinched, taken aback. The kid wanted so badly to be a man that he mistook Hayes's concern for a lack of faith in him. Kids could be blind like that. Lumpy'd seen it a million times.

Doesn't have a clue how lucky he is, Lumpy thought.

Having said his piece, Lumpy walked on, Jimmy staring after him.

20

ANN HAD ENTERED A kind of fugue state, where the world blurred around her. Her senses were acute, on alert for possible threats from the jungle, but the details were lost to her. All she knew was the ache in her legs from trudging through the jungle, the trickle of sweat upon her brow and chest, the itch of insect bites on her arms, and the need to keep moving. In the back of her mind she knew that she might have gauged her direction incorrectly, might not be heading back toward the shore and the *Venture* at all, but she would not allow this thought to fully form. If she had, despair would have utterly defeated her.

She kept on. Many times she heard things scurrying through the branches overhead, or crunching through the underbrush nearby, and she froze and waited until the sounds had faded.

In time, with the sun making a humid oven of the jungle, she came to a ridge overlooking a valley. The line of the ridge seemed to follow her general direction and so she stayed along it rather than descending into the new terrain of the valley.

In a small glade Ann found a rocky outcropping, the

stone face covered with moss, and a small rivulet of fresh water running down from a spring somewhere higher on the mountain. With her hands cupped, she caught a few drops, and only when she drank the cool water did she realize how parched her throat was. Ann stayed until her thirst was quenched, and when she moved on her legs felt all the more sluggish for the rest.

But she continued, forging her own path through the jungle. Once again the details blurred around her as she focused only on watching and listening for any sign of danger.

A sound. She froze and cocked her head, listening, even before she understood what it was she had heard. Then she spun around, pulse quickening with equal parts hope and fear. The sound was unmistakable. Footsteps, coming through the dense jungle.

Jack?

She started moving toward the approaching footsteps, trying to fight against the hope that rose in her, afraid to believe that they may have stayed behind and found her at last.

Jack signaled for the group to freeze. His own heartbeat thrummed in his ears from exertion. The other members of the search party—the survivors—saw the tension in him, saw that he was listening for something, and remained absolutely silent.

Then they all heard what brought Jack to a stop. There was a crunching noise in the jungle, footsteps, something moving toward them through the brush at a run. Tired and tense with fear, several sailors brought

Tommy guns up to their shoulders and aimed into the thick of the foliage, tracking the sound of the approaching runner.

Ann hurried through the dense brush of the jungle, still following the ridge above the valley. Water from another stream coming down the mountain had turned a patch of ground to mud and she fell when her heel struck it, her foot slipping out from under her. She tumbled down a muddy hill, careening through trees, fell over a log, and crashed into a thicket of palms.

Jack saw Lumpy cock his gun, saw his finger twitch by the trigger and the anxious fright in his eyes, and he knew what was about to happen. Fear and exhaustion had made them all skittish and dull. Lumpy aimed at the jungle, directly at the sound coming their way.

A loud crash, just to the left. Lumpy swung the barrel of his gun, tracking the sound. Panic surged through Jack.

"No!" Jack shouted.

Lumpy pulled the trigger, firing a burst of bullets into the trees. Jack stared, gape-mouthed, wondering if he was due a miracle, if somehow those rounds—so many and so tightly grouped—could have missed their mark.

For a moment, silence reigned. The jungle itself went quiet for a single beat, and then from the brush came the thud of a falling body. Jack felt an icy chill come up from deep within. Carl and Hayes and Jimmy and the others all glanced at one another and then looked at Jack, only now realizing why he had wanted Lumpy to hold off.

Tentatively, Jack pushed through the undergrowth and the others joined him. Choy, Lumpy, and Carl were right with him as he entered a small clearing. Hayes, Preston, Jimmy and another sailor followed. A couple of them hung back, still on guard.

On the ground in the clearing was a large, flightless bird, thrashing around in pain, wounded by Lumpy's attack. Lumpy walked over to the wounded creature and fired a round into its head. The bird went still.

The men stared at it numbly, but without comment. Jack registered how strange their silence was, how quickly they'd all come to accept the impossible in this place. Nothing shocked them, now.

One by one, they moved off into the jungle, following Hayes. Jack hesitated only briefly before setting off after them.

As Ann picked herself up from the nasty spill, seemingly none the worse for wear, she glanced out over the valley and saw in the distance a plume of smoke rising into the sky. It was difficult to judge accurately, but she gauged it to be at least four miles away. The sight heartened her. She had been headed in the right direction after all.

She hesitated, wanting to keep trekking toward that smoke. But those sounds in the jungle could be Jack and the others. Ann stood very still and listened, tilting her head to peer into the brush. The footsteps were getting closer and closer, but a tremor passed through her now. The snapping of branches and the weight of those steps concerned her.

No, she thought. *Too heavy. Not Jack.*

Quickly, she ducked behind a thick tree and peered around the trunk just in time to see a dinosaur step into the glade ahead. It was smaller than the others she'd seen, perhaps only eight feet high, but the predatory grace of its movement and the size of its jaws left her no doubt it was a carnivore. And hungry.

The dinosaur paused as though it had sensed her. In all her life Ann had never really prayed. The way she'd been raised was that the only prayers that did not go unanswered were the ones she tended to herself. But now, almost unconsciously, she let her thoughts go to prayers for salvation.

The carnivore twitched its nostrils, trying to catch a scent. Ann peeked out from behind the tree, but then something shifted behind her, a twig snapped, and she spun to see a second predator emerging from the trees just a few feet away.

Adrenaline surged through her and Ann bolted. The plume of smoke from the village—from the wall—was directly ahead. She ran right past the dinosaur in the glade and leaped over a fallen tree, crashing into the undergrowth. The two monsters pursued, jaws gnashing as they dashed through the jungle.

The glade opened just ahead and a huge tree towered above Ann. At its base it opened into a tangled root system that was above ground and exposed. Desperate, Ann ran for it. In the back of her mind she'd been hoping for an easy tree to climb, as the dinosaurs would be unable to follow, but they were gaining on her, right behind her now, and this was better.

One of the carnivores lunged. Ann glanced back, saw it coming for her, and threw herself forward as its jaws snapped above her head. With a grunt she struck the ground, rolled forward, and scrambled into a hollow under the huge rotten tree.

Frantic, the carnivores clawed at the tree, trying to get at her. Ann lay beneath the roots and pulled her arms and legs tight around her, gripped by terror as they dug and tore. She tried not to imagine what they would do if they could reach her. All she could see from her hiding place was their legs and slavering snouts as they rammed their jaws into the narrow gap.

Then the legs of one of her pursuers lifted right off the ground, its taloned feet thrashing in mid-air. The second carnivore turned and fled into the jungle. Stunned, and horrified by the dawning realization of what this new development entailed, Ann watched the twitching legs of the first dinosaur shudder and flail. The sound of bone crunching, then the carnivore's legs spasmed and went limp.

This was the nature of Skull Island, then. No matter how vicious and brutal a predator was, behind the next tree or over the next hill was something far worse. Ann lay completely still. She heard something breathing heavily and a low rumbling, but could see nothing of the thing yet, though it was inches from her hiding place. If she could only remain still, it might go away. The blood of the small dinosaur it had killed might block her own scent.

Or so she hoped.

There was a tickle on her bare leg—something was crawling on her flesh. She twitched. Slowly, she turned and peered into the hole behind and below her, at the base of the rotted tree, inside the exposed roots. Long, segmented legs covered with coarse hair probed from a hole, slowly uncurling, finding a foothold on her skin. Its size was impossible—the legs were two feet long at least—but it was a spider, a huge thing that lived here in the darkness.

In utter panic, revulsion prickling her skin, Ann scrambled away from the spider and rolled out the other side of the tree. She was about to sprint toward the thickest part of the jungle, when she looked up. The spider was the least of her troubles.

Towering above her with the dead carnivore hanging limply from its huge jaws was a gigantic dinosaur, nearly as large as Kong himself. Its mottled, leathery flesh dripped with the blood of its fresh kill. Tiny arms seemed almost useless, but its massive, muscular legs and thick tail were formidable. She had seen drawings of dinosaurs like this in magazines and newspapers. They called the *Tyrannosaurus rex* the king of dinosaurs, but this thing was even bigger than the bones she'd seen in a museum. All she could think was that this was the T. rex's evolutionary counterpart in this living hell.

With its huge head, those rows of dagger teeth, and killer, gaping jaws, this thing was something even worse than historians had ever imagined. Not a T. rex, then, but more vicious. And voracious, with those gnashing jaws.

V. rex? Ann thought, and it seemed as good a name as any.

Ann fled. The dead carnivore dropped to the ground and the V. rex crashed after her. It did not roar, did not grunt, it simply came on, silent and hungry, a killing and eating machine. She raced through the jungle, dodging trees, leaping over fallen logs, smashing through bushes, but she knew escaping this thing was hopeless. If she climbed a tree, it would tear her from the branches; if she hid beneath something, the dinosaur would knock her shelter down.

The V. rex pounded in pursuit. Close, now, too close. She had been in the presence of death before, had seen dead men and women, had lost friends to its cold clutches, but her own death had never been so intimate and near. Ann felt its hot, sour breath blowing on the back of her neck. The huge jaws of the beast were open just inches from her head.

Her chest ached, her lungs burning, heart about to burst, but she knew she had only the smallest effort left to give before she would simply collapse and it would be upon her, those teeth tearing her flesh. Ann looked for any escape. She spotted a fallen tree that jutted out over a small cliff and scrambled onto it, clinging onto the mossy log and crawling toward the end. The V. rex could not follow her without falling over the edge of the cliff to the sharp rocks below.

With an almost delicate movement, the V. rex nudged the log with its massive head, causing it to lurch. Ann let out a small shriek and clung desperately to the log as the huge, slavering dinosaur pushed harder, knocking the log sideways to the ground. Ann fell, twisting away from the log. She screamed as the V. rex positioned its head for the final lunge, gaping jaws opening impossibly wide.

A familiar bellow thundered through the jungle.

From the trees, Kong charged.

The V. rex turned and attacked, the two monstrosities colliding at full speed. Kong swung his fist, pummeling the V. rex's head, knocking it to the ground. Ann threw herself against a tree as the dinosaur crashed onto the ground beside her. Savage with fury, Kong leaped onto the carnivore, gigantic fist rising and falling as he pounded the V. rex.

Ann was awash in conflicting emotions. Kong had come to her rescue. Death had been so close. She had imagined herself bitten, flesh torn, ripped apart, and Kong was protecting her from that. But even if he destroyed the V. rex, once he had his hands on her, she would never reach that plume of smoke on the horizon, never get back to the beach, never see Jack or home again.

She watched as Kong hammered at the V. rex. Then, suddenly, a second V. rex burst from the jungle into the glade, responding to the roars of the first. It charged in a single, swift motion, and its jaws snapped down on Kong's arm. Ann flinched, fresh terror filling her, and she decided Kong was her only hope now. Her only choice.

Kong roared, ripping his arm free just as a third V. rex strode into the clearing. The first V. rex scrambled back to its feet with a roar. It shook its head and blood showered from its snout, though its own or its recent kill's Ann had no idea.

When Kong reached for her and plucked her from the ground, she went willingly, relieved. He held her protectively as he braced himself for attack. The three dinosaurs circled around him. Ann shuddered, staring out from Kong's grip at the gnashing teeth and gleaming yellow eyes of the dinosaurs.

They lunged, as if in response to some silent signal—all three of them moved in on Kong. His free arm was like a battering ram, hammering at the creatures as they tried to pluck Ann from his grasp, or to tear into his flesh. He fought on all three fronts, spinning, swinging, cracking bone and breaking teeth off in his own flesh. Again and again he transferred her from one hand to the other as the dinosaurs snapped at her heels.

He moved her again, now holding her in his foot to free up both hands to deal with the dinosaurs' onslaught. Ann screamed over and over, and then her throat was so raw she could not scream any more.

Kong wrapped an arm around one carnivore's neck, twisting hard and falling back, flipping it onto the ground. With a roar, eyes wide with primal fury, Kong drove a second V. rex to the ground and then he was down, crushing his weight upon it. For just a moment, he had to let Ann free to defend himself against the third as it came at him. Kong batted it away.

Ann rolled across the ground and climbed to her feet, surrounded by this war of gargantuan horrors. Then one of the V. rexes dove for her, dodging, running past Kong. The gorilla brought his fist down on its head and it staggered away. The melee thundered all around her.

With a swift, decisive action, Kong tore a jagged tree trunk out of the ground and rammed it into the mouth of the nearest V. rex, shoving it so deep that it burst out of the back of the dinosaur's head.

As the second V. rex fell upon him, Kong locked his arm around its neck and twisted, hauling it off its feet, flipping its body in the air. Ann gasped as Kong suddenly reversed direction, breaking its back with a sickening crunch.

The last of the dinosaurs got to Ann. As its jaws descended upon her, Ann screamed. Its breath enveloped her in a cloud of noxious fumes, its teeth sliced the air, and then it took her in its teeth, pressing into her and lifting her up. She felt the twitch of its muscles as it was about to bite down.

She felt so cold. So tired. So far from home.

The bite never came. With a roar, Kong grabbed the V. rex's jaws in both hands, keeping it from clamping down. He forced it to the ground, slammed it onto its back, thick fingers prying at its teeth with Ann still wedged in its mouth.

Ann stared into Kong's face, into those yellowed eyes, saw every line and scar. With a grunt, teeth bared, Kong forced the V. rex's jaws open. Ann pushed herself from its maw, bruised but not cut open, not gutted, not dead. She dropped to the ground and turned to see Kong forcing the dinosaur's jaws further apart.

He ripped them apart at the hinge with a wet tear of flesh and a loud splintering of bone.

The V. rex sprawled on its back, dead.

Kong stood, panting heavily. He had been bitten, clawed, and cut but he was utterly victorious, and now he stomped his foot on top of his final conquest, the blood streaming out of its gaping, torn jaws. With a loud, long bellow, Kong raised his arms and began to beat his chest triumphantly. He did not even look at her, as though she meant nothing to him.

Then, to Ann's amazement, Kong turned and began to walk off.

Ann hesitated. There might be another V. rex nearby. What were her odds of surviving another hour in this jungle, never mind another day? Kong moved slowly, as though to give her time to catch up.

She set off after him.

He must have heard her footfalls for he glanced back, grunted, and then continued on, still slowly, giving her time to follow. Something had been agreed between them.

The air echoed with gunshots. Ann flinched. She had been convinced that her fate lay with Kong, but those sounds were so close, so full of hope that at first she thought she had imagined them. More gunshots filled the air, not far away.

Kong roared angrily, looking around, chest heaving. If there was another threat, he would destroy it just as he had the V. rexes. Kong lifted Ann and placed her on the top of a ruined thirty-foot stone column that stood at the edge of the glade, another remnant of the ancient civilization that had once called the entire island home. She clung on to the top of the narrow pillar, safe above the jungle but unable to move.

Kong turned toward the sound of the gunshots, deadly intent in his eyes. Ann could only watch helplessly as he disappeared into the jungle.

21

HAYES HAD LOST THE trail hours ago. There was nothing to be done for it. They had two choices; go back to the ship, leaving Miss Darrow in the hands of a monster, or forge ahead as best they could manage and hope he could find some indication of the ape's passing. He wondered how many of his men would have taken the first option if they knew he was navigating their course using his own sense of direction and his memory of the path before. There was guesswork as well. Above the jungle he could see one mountain towering above the others, odd shapes flying around its peak. It was directly in the path Ann's abductor had been taking before Hayes had lost track of them.

It was a hunch, that was all. But they had nothing else to go on.

Or they hadn't, until just now, when they had come onto a wide path that seemed to have been made over the course of many years. Flora had been trampled underfoot and branches had been snapped from trees. It led straight toward that peak in the distance, and he had found a trace of a recent foot print.

The ape had come this way.

Hayes hefted the pack on his back and gripped his gun. Somehow the heat and the sweat trickling on his forehead and neck had ceased to bother him. All that mattered now was moving forward, pushing himself beyond physical limits and just getting the job done. It felt like war again, and though it troubled him to admit to himself, war felt good. Simple and pure. The mission was all that mattered.

The terrain appeared to change up ahead. Before he continued on, Hayes wanted to check on the others, make sure no one was straggling too far back. Jimmy was just behind him, the others trailing along. Denham, Driscoll, and Preston walked together, though there was tension amongst them. The actor, Baxter, had been curiously silent since his mutinous speech a couple of hours earlier. He kept to himself now, but seemed as determined as the rest to soldier onward. Lumpy and Choy led the remaining sailors. Hayes tried not to let himself count how many had already died on this mission, and instead focused on the men still alive, and trying to make sure they stayed that way.

Hayes glanced at Jimmy and then turned to forge on. As he'd suspected, the terrain drastically changed ahead. Another fifty yards and they arrived at a dark vine-entangled chasm, spanned by a single, massive, fallen tree. Weak sunlight filtered through the dark canopy above, casting a sickly green hue over the place.

If he let them, the boys would hesitate. Hayes wasn't about to give them the chance.

"Single file," he called back to the others. "Jimmy, you follow me."

He started across, with Jimmy close behind, leading the group across the slimy moss covered log. The going was treacherous.

"Don't look down," Hayes said.

Denham was behind Jimmy, struggling with the damned camera. Hayes wished the thing would just slip from his fingers and fall into the chasm below. Jack was behind Denham, and following him was Lumpy, who was mother-henning Choy, then Bruce and Preston. They were all on edge, but managed to put one foot in front of the other. The others were straggling, with a sailor named Turcotte coming last, just starting onto the makeshift bridge.

Hayes continued across, picking up his pace carefully. He was focused so much on his footing that he nearly missed the sound of something shifting in the jungle on the other side of the chasm. He stopped, muscles tensed, and scanned the opposite side. There were dark ruins in the foliage across the chasm, much like those so common to Skull Island. Whatever civilization had lived here in ancient times had spread its influence all across the rock.

He stared into the ruins and the trees with their spiderweb of hanging vines, and he knew something was watching them from the darkness. He could feel its eyes upon them.

"What is it?" Jimmy asked, his voice low.

Hayes motioned for Jimmy to be quiet. He tried to get a glimpse of whatever awaited them there in those foreboding ruins.

"Mr. Hayes," Jimmy whispered.

Warily, Hayes tore his gaze away and turned to look at the boy. "If anything happens, you run. Understand?"

"I'm not a coward," the kid said, indignant. "I ain't gonna run."

"It's not about being brave, Jimmy. I want you to make it back."

Jimmy gave him an uneasy look, but Hayes had nothing more to say. He kept one eye on the ruins as he continued across the log. With every step, he tried to get a look at what was hiding there, waiting for them. If they could get off the log quickly enough and spread out, with the guns they still had, they would probably be all right. The question was, would they have that kind of time?

Hayes stepped off the log onto the safety of the other side. Now that he had a different vantage point, he saw that part of that ancient structure had collapsed, stone columns tipped toward one another or tumbled down to create a kind of tunnel into the darkness.

A pair of gleaming eyes shone from within, and the moment he set foot on the ground, they were moving, rushing toward him.

"Go back!" Hayes shouted.

He bolted back toward the log. The men still crossing the chasm froze and then started to back away, slipping and sliding on wet moss. Hayes turned as he ran and shot into the darkness behind him, even as the watcher emerged from the ruins.

* * *

Jack saw the giant gorilla run at Hayes. It was as tall as the trees. The beast—the same one that had taken Ann?—was old and horribly scarred, but its teeth looked vicious and its fists were huge. All throughout this nightmare journey, he'd had the chanting of the villagers in the back of his mind. *Kong! Kong! Kong!* And as he stared at the monstrous ape, he was certain it was not just a word, but a name. This giant. Kong.

With one sweep of its massive hand, it snatched Hayes up into its fist.

Jack faltered, watching in horror. Jimmy started to run toward the monstrous beast, but he held up a hand and the kid paused. Kong stared at them both, about to attack.

In the gorilla's grasp, Hayes shouted. "No! Look at me! Look at me!"

Slowly, his hands still free, Hayes began to raise his gun. Disturbed by his captive's angry shouts, Kong glanced down at Hayes, tightening his grip.

"You've got to run, Jimmy. Go back across. Do as I say," Hayes commanded, voice deadly calm as he locked eyes with the beast. Then he spoke to Kong. "Keep looking at me!"

Hayes did not dare even glance at them, did not dare break the contact with Kong. "Go with Jack," he instructed the boy.

Then he raised his gun and aimed at Kong's face. "Run!"

Jack and Jimmy ran. There was one single shot from Hayes's weapon, and then gunfire erupted all around, echoing back from the chasm below. Most of the shots went wild as the sailors tried to maintain their balance on the mossy log.

Jack looked up just in time to see Kong hurl Hayes through the air. He flew over their heads, tumbling, smashing against the far wall of the chasm with a sickening crunch.

"No!" Jimmy cried.

Kong roared. The desperate sailors scrambled and slid, trying to make it back across the chasm, to get off of that log. But not Jimmy. The boy wept tears of grief, and his eyes were wide with rage as he moved forward, toward the giant gorilla, fists bunched as though he might attack it with his bare hands. Jack had no doubt that he would.

Kong was at the edge of the chasm. Jack grabbed hold of Jimmy, forcing him down onto the log, pinning the both of them there. The gorilla roared as he brought a huge, leathery fist down onto the tree bridge, missing them by inches.

They had nowhere to run.

As that fist hammered down again, Jack grabbed Jimmy and rolled the two of them right off the log. He reached out and wrapped his arm around a thick vine that hung beneath it, saw Jimmy scrabbling for a handhold and catching another vine, and then the two of them were just hanging there, under the log. If they let go, they would plummet toward certain death in the chasm below.

Denham felt like he was flying. Nothing seemed quite real. The chasm yawned beneath him and the safety of solid ground seemed so far away, but a part of him felt no fear, as though he didn't need any log to hold him up. It was that strange confidence he always had in his dreams, the certainty that whatever happened, he'd be all right. The sunlight streamed down through the break in the canopy above, casting a strange light upon the vines that dangled from the trees overhanging the chasm, adding to the dreamlike quality of the moment.

Hayes was dead. He'd heard the man's bones break.

But Carl Denham was more alive than he'd ever been. Terror was exhilarating. He ran along the log, skated on the moss, and he kept his eyes on the other side of the chasm.

Then he stumbled and went down hard on his stomach. His camera slid out of his hands and struck the stump of a broken branch. It jammed fast, wedged in the fork of the stump.

The dream shattered. Shock or hysteria, whatever it was, he was over it now. His breath came in a ragged gasp and he keenly felt the approach of death. Up ahead the rest of the panicked sailors had stopped and were shooting wildly, but fear and lack of balance threw their aim off. Denham wanted to scream at them to just run, to get off the log. Hayes was dead, they couldn't help him now.

Denham scrambled along the log toward the Bell & Howell, but up ahead of him, Lumpy was the nearest of the sailors. He was practically on top of the camera.

"Grab it," he called. "Don't let it fall!"

Lumpy glanced down at the camera. Denham nodded at him. Lumpy raised his foot and very deliberately booted the Bell & Howell into the chasm.

Stunned, Denham watched the camera tumble into the depths below.

And the log began to rise.

Denham was already on his belly. He grabbed hold of an upturned chunk of bark as he glanced back to see the gigantic gorilla—the same titanic creature he had seen carrying Ann into the jungle—lifting the end of the log. He saw Jack and the kid, Jimmy, hanging onto vines as they were raised higher.

The sailors near Denham started shouting.

The titan twisted the log. Men scrambled to hold on. The creature gave it a hard shake. Denham heard cries of terror and two of the sailors slipped and fell from the log. One of them struck his head on the wood as he tumbled down into the chasm. The other kept screaming the entire way down.

Choy shot a desperate look at Lumpy and threw himself down, scrambling for a handhold. The violent twisting of the log threw him then, and he too slipped away into the abyss. Lumpy screamed, and all Denham could do was watch.

Preston was nearest to the far side, to the edge from which they'd set out. He leaped and managed to catch hold of some hanging vines, hauling himself up to safety. Denham was about to shout to him, but in that moment, Kong roared again, a final sort of frustrated sound, and then he thrust the log sideways, over the edge, and the entire thing began its final descent into the chasm.

Denham couldn't hold on any longer, and they all fell.

Bruce Baxter refused to die. He'd come close a hundred times on film sets, where the stunts were badly planned or executed, or where the animals weren't as tame as producers claimed. Oh, he'd die eventually. But not here. Not now.

As the log tumbled into the chasm he felt it flipping over. The momentum of its turn threw him off, but he leaped at the same time, controlling the direction as best he could, and he managed to grab hold of a ledge halfway down into the chasm. It jerked his shoulders nearly out of their sockets and something gave way in his left wrist. But it wasn't broken. And he wasn't dead. Not today.

Jack held onto the vine, falling with the log, all sense of his surroundings gone. The log struck a curtain of vines that arrested its descent for an instant before momentum toppled it away again. Jack was flung clear. He saw other men twisting in the air but could make out only flailing limbs before he struck soft, slick mud that cushioned his impact.

As he sat up, it sucked at him and he had to pull himself free. He could only gaze down at his own body in disbelief—he was scraped and bloody, chafed raw where the vine had been wrapped around his arm, but he was otherwise uninjured. Alive. Unbroken.

Jack staggered to his feet, caked with mud. The bottom of the chasm was another jungle entirely, thick with moss and vines, overgrown with strange, twisted trees unlike anything he'd ever seen, and shot through with caves and damp vents in the ground that might have been burrows of some sort. It was strangely cool down there, and yet even more humid than it had been in the world above.

Denham lay nearby. He and Lumpy had both also struck the mud, and been saved by sheer luck.

But not all of them had been so fortunate.

"Choy!" Lumpy shouted.

The cook crawled toward his friend and comrade. Choy lay in shallow muck, his body splayed at an awkward angle. Jack flinched at the anguish in Lumpy's voice, all of his bluster now gone. He could not look away.

Choy gasped for air. Quaking, he managed the hint of a smile. "What you think he say about this?"

Lumpy stared at him. "Who?"

"My guy . . . Charlie Atlas." Choy twitched and swallowed hard. The way his body was twisted around it was clear he was shattered inside. "Training, see? Training make all the difference. Anyone else . . . after a fall like that . . . be curtains for sure."

Jack finally averted his eyes, but he could still hear Lumpy's reply.

"Yeah, I used to think it was a waste of time. But you held up." His voice quavered only a little.

When Jack looked to them again he saw Choy nod and smile. Lumpy turned away, then, so Choy would not see the anguish in his face.

"Hey, don't worry. It's oh-kay," Choy said.

Lumpy kept his back to Choy as he nodded. He wiped tears from his eyes and managed a blank expression before he turned toward his friend again.

By then, Choy was dead.

Jack couldn't watch anymore, allowing Lumpy to grieve alone. Instead he began to search for the others. Jimmy wasn't far away. Unlike Choy he had landed at the edge of the thick mud, near enough to avoid serious injury. Yet the kid just sat there, knees drawn up to his chest, staring vacantly into space.

"Jimmy?" Jack said, kneeling down beside him.

The boy was unresponsive. He clutched his battered school exercise book in his hand. Jack took it gently, holding a finger in the page to which Jimmy had opened it. On the page was a poem written in the boy's spidery handwriting.

Jack glanced around at the remnants of his search party. Denham was opening his eyes, rubbing his head. Lumpy cradled Choy's body in his arms as though he held his own son. Not far off, he saw the corpse of Ben Hayes, lying where it had fallen on some rocks at the base of the chasm.

His gaze drifted back to the poem, and he read:

Today I have been happy. All the day I held the memory of you,
And wove its laughter with the dancing light of the spray,
And sowed the sky with tiny clouds of love,
And sent you following the white waves of the sea.

Jimmy looked up at Jack, tears filling his eyes. He fell into Jack's arms, softly sobbing. Jack held the boy tightly, heart breaking for the loss of Hayes, for the dreams unfulfilled, but not only for that. For all of them.

Past Jimmy, he saw Carl sit up. The man had been one of his closest friends. He had tested that friendship over and over these past hours, and even the days before, but looking at him now, Jack knew he still cared for Denham. He just couldn't help him.

Carl stared forlornly at the wreckage of the camera, which lay smashed and broken on the chasm floor. A thin, shiny thread of black film trailed from the smashed Bell & Howell body like spilled innards. Carl reached out and touched the exposed film, his dreams destroyed.

Motion out of the corner of his eye caught Jack's attention. A huge slug-like thing, like some sort of giant maggot, was squirming from a hole in the ground. It was as long as Jack himself was tall, and crawling toward Lumpy and Choy.

"Look out!"

He snatched up a long stick and put himself between Lumpy and the maggot, using it like a spear to fend the creature off. Lumpy began to drag Choy's body away, trying to get it somewhere it wouldn't be disturbed, but the entire cavern floor came alive with life. From beneath rotted stumps and fallen trees, from under rocks and out of burrowed holes, the insects came.

Not merely insects, these. Monsters. A pair of creatures the size of dogs set after Lumpy and Choy. A giant thing that seemed a cross between crab and spider scuttled toward Jack and he jabbed it with his makeshift spear. Even as he tried to save his own life, he heard Lumpy screaming, heard the terrible sounds of flesh being rent by pincers and mandibles. When he forced the crab-spider back a step, he saw Lumpy and Choy's body being consumed by the nightmarish bugs.

Jack looked wildly around for Denham.

With a roar, Carl ran at the bugs. Something had given way inside of him and now he wielded a short stick like a club, smashing huge insectile monsters in a psychotic explosion of rage, pulverizing their bodies into the dirt.

Jack shouted his name, but too late. A blind, probing thing like some kind of hideous worm slithered out of a hole and bit Carl's leg. Denham smashed it to pieces even as dozens of other insect things descended on him. Jack desperately swung at the creatures with the stick, batting at them and stabbing them. All around them, monstrous freaks of nature emerged from dank burrows and crawled toward Jack and Carl, huge insectile mutants that seemed twisted combinations of spiders, crabs, mantises, and centipedes.

They were surrounded. No escape.

The chasm erupted with gunfire.

Around Jack and Carl, giant insects were blown apart. Chitinous shells shattered and legs were shot off. Jack spun around, confused, and then tracked the shots upward.

Bruce Baxter swung down from above, clinging to a vine, Tommy gun rat-tatting in his hand. Giant spiders swarmed out of holes in the cliff face. Again bullets ripped the air and tore them apart, but these shots didn't come from Bruce. Up on the lip of the chasm, Englehorn and a couple of sailors fired down into the gap.

Agile and strong, Bruce dropped to the bottom of the chasm and swung the barrel of the Tommy gun in an arc.

"Nobody get in my way! I'm an actor with a gun and I haven't been paid!" He pulled the trigger and laid waste to the bizarre creatures, bullets blasting apart crab-spiders and giant centipedes and flying things, giant dragonfly things with tails like wasps.

Those not blasted apart scurried away back into the darkness.

As Jack stared at Bruce in amazement, a length of rope landed beside him with a thud.

"Up here!" called a voice.

It was Preston, clinging to a crumbled ledge twenty feet above them.

"Grab it!" he said.

Jack grabbed Jimmy and pushed him to the rope. The kid was in shock but he grabbed hold and began to climb. Jack turned to Carl, but the man didn't move. His gaze was distant, lost. Jack was about to say something, to urge him on, when Carl began to quietly speak.

"Just as you go down, for the third and final time, as your head disappears beneath the waves and your lungs fill with water . . . do you know what happens in those last precious seconds before you drown?"

The man was raving. Jack let him speak for a moment, then started tying the rope around Denham's waist.

"Get out of here, Carl. Grab the rope."

Denham frowned. "Your whole life passes before your eyes. But if you lived as a true American . . . you get to watch it all in color."

His smile was sublime.

Englehorn clenched his jaw as he reached down to pull Denham up the last stretch of the rope. The voice in the back of his head was screaming at him, telling him what a fool he was for not leaving when he'd said. He never should have come into the jungle to search for them. But there had been too many of his own men on that expedition. If it had just been Denham and his foolhardy foot soldiers, perhaps he would have left them behind, somehow convinced himself that Ann Darrow was already dead so he could sleep at night knowing he'd left her to the predations of this savage land.

But in his heart he'd known he wouldn't be able to go, and he cursed himself for it. Particularly now that he saw how few had survived. Of the members of his crew that had followed Jack Driscoll into the jungle, only the boy, Jimmy, was still alive.

Baxter and Preston were sprawled on the ground nearby with Jimmy. Denham fell to his knees at the top of the chasm, gasping from exertion.

"That's the thing about cockroaches," the captain said, glaring down at him. "No matter how many times you flush them down the toilet, they always crawl back up the bowl."

Englehorn turned away in disgust as Denham stood.

"Hey, buddy!" the director called, voice brittle and on edge. "I'm outta the bowl! I'm drying off my wings and trekking across the lid!"

"The pity of it is, you didn't die with the others," the captain said through clenched teeth.

He turned toward Denham to continue, but then he spotted Driscoll. The madman was climbing toward the top of the chasm on the other side.

"Driscoll, don't be a fool! It's useless! Give it up!" he called.

But as he reached the top and stood on the opposite edge of the chasm, the writer turned and raised his hand.

"I'll be seeing you."

Englehorn gave him a hard look. "She's dead."

Beside him, he heard Denham speak softly, as if to himself. "She's not dead. Jack's gonna bring her back."

The captain turned to glare at him, but Denham had an almost beatific look upon his face that gave Englehorn pause.

"And the ape will be hard on his heels," Denham went on. "We can still come out of this thing okay, if we put aside our differences. More than okay."

Englehorn looked at Denham and laughed. "You want to trap the ape?"

Denham spread his hands, as if his suggestion was the most reasonable thing in the world. "Isn't that what you do? Live capture? You've got a hold full of chloroform we could put to good use."

The captain stared at him. "I don't think so."

301

"Don't tell me you're afraid. I heard you were the best."

Denham rose and turned to look across at the solitary figure on the opposite side of the chasm. Driscoll stood there, bloodied and torn.

"Jack!" Denham raised a hand in salute. "Look after yourself!"

"Keep the gate open," Driscoll replied, voice echoing down in the chasm.

"Sure thing, buddy!" Denham called. "Good luck!"

Driscoll turned to go.

"Jack . . ."

Driscoll looked back over his shoulder.

"I'm sorry," Denham said.

Jack looks puzzled by this, Englehorn thought. But the man said nothing more as he turned and disappeared into a dark tunnel formed by the collapse of ancient ruins in the midst of the jungle.

Kong moved swiftly and powerfully through the jungle with Ann held close against his chest. Before he had carried her like an object or a toy, but now he was more gentle and protective. The blood from his wounds was already drying and he moved with such determination that he gave no sign of having been injured. Ann looked up at him, studying his face, and for the first time she saw a kind of dignity there instead of pure ferocity. The tension went out of her body and she relaxed in his grip. Strange as it was under the circumstances, for the first time since coming to Skull Island, she felt safe. She had chosen to remain with him for her own protection and while that meant she was not free, at least she knew Kong would not harm her . . . and that he would keep her from harm.

From what she could see of the route he was taking, both the path on the ground and the way certain tree limbs had been broken off, she thought he had passed this way many times before. Ann could only presume he was taking her to his lair.

She let out a tiny noise of surprise when Kong clutched her a bit more tighter and launched himself across a narrow chasm. With his free hand he reached out to grab thick vines that hung on the other side, but the vines gave way, tearing, and Kong fell backward, Ann still clinging to his chest.

The giant gorilla landed hard, impact shaking the ground. Ann was rocked by the fall, her head snapping forward, teeth clacking together. She shook it off even as Kong scrambled to his feet, growling. He placed Ann on the ground, pushing her protectively behind him. She tried to peer around him, confused, wondering what had set him off.

Looming up at the edge of the chasm was a huge statue of a gorilla, a fierce, powerful figure that might have been some ancestor to Kong. Ann stared at it a moment, her fear giving way to comprehension. She stepped out from behind Kong and moved nearer to get a better look at the towering statue, another remnant left behind by that ancient civilization.

As she passed him, Kong gave a low, warning growl.

"It's all right," she said, glancing up at him. "It's okay."

Ann reached the statue and began to pull away more vines and creepers. The statue had been eroded by weather and entropy, but it was quite lifelike. If not for the scars and the jutting tooth, it might have been the very likeness of Kong.

Excited, she turned and smiled at Kong. "Look, it's *you*. Kong," she said, pointing at the statue and then at him. "See? *You*. Kong? This is *you*."

Kong looked from Ann to the huge statue. He took a step back, glancing between her and the giant stone carving, and Ann saw that he was troubled by the comparison. She was dwarfed by the stone monolith, and it seemed to her that he did understand, that he had seen the carved figure as a threat to her, and now that he realized it was an image of himself, on some fundamental level Ann realized that to her, he was monstrous.

Kong looked down at his hands as if he was seeing his gnarled, leathery fingers for the first time. Ann moved toward Kong and when he looked at her she was certain that she saw fear and sadness in his eyes.

It was a full minute before he reached his hand down to pick her up once more, and when he did she climbed into his grasp willingly, wishing she could communicate with him. He cradled her gently as he started off through the jungle again.

The daylight was fading toward dusk as they arrived at a tall mountain Ann had noticed many times during their odyssey. Kong reached up and began to climb the steep, craggy face, higher and higher toward that vertiginous peak, carefully cradling Ann in his hand. A sudden flap of wings and a flickering of shadows came from the twilit caves in the cliff face, and Kong pulled her close to his chest. From the darkness lunged a huge flying creature whose upper body was batlike, but whose torso, legs, and tail reminded her of drawings she'd seen of mangy jackals. Its wingspan must have been eight feet from tip to tip, and its feet had sharp, wicked talons. The creatures were scavengers of some sort, hovering in the skies around the mountain like vultures.

Protected in Kong's grasp, she was safe from the bat-thing.

Into the shadows he carried her, through an opening in the mountain face and into a vast, rounded cavern whose depths she could not see in the last traces of daylight. At the mouth of the cave was a broad ledge that jutted out high above the jungle.

Kong carried Ann out onto the ledge and she looked across the vastness of Skull Island and marveled at its beauty, struck by the irony that such a terrifying and brutal place could be so magnificent. Over the ledge was a dizzying drop of at least a thousand feet down to the jungle floor. In the dying of the light she could see the *Venture* moored off the tip of the island. Despite the distance they'd traveled to get here, the ship seemed no more than three miles away. Whatever route they'd taken, with all of the terrors that had impeded their progress, must have been circuitous, for surely they'd traveled farther than that.

No matter, three miles or three hundred, it was a lifetime and a world away from her now. Her hope of survival was in the hands of her captor.

Kong gently placed Ann on the ground, then moved away and sat to one side of the ledge. The horizon was a fiery orange as the last of the sun went down, silhouetting the massive figure of Kong against the light.

Ann gazed at him a moment and then looked around at her strange surroundings. It took a few seconds for her eyes to adjust to the deepening shadows. Then, in the recesses of the cave, she saw something that made her catch her breath. Far to one side there lay a giant gorilla skull and the skeleton of a creature that would, in life, have been at least as large as Kong himself.

So much made sense to her now. He truly was alone. Here on the cave floor were the bones of his ancestors. Kong had not always been alone. But it was clear he had been by himself for a very long time, without any family at all. And now, suddenly, that had changed. He had protected her. Ann had always made a family of those around her, from vaudeville to the *Venture*, but this was not like anything she had ever imagined. She felt oddly touched, and somehow, no longer afraid.

A sudden flutter came from the dark recesses of the lair, a sinister sound. Ann glanced worriedly into the shadows and hurried back out onto the ledge to join Kong.

She gazed at him expectantly but he would not look

at her, his eyes distant, looking out at the jungle but also, somehow, at nothing.

Ann danced a few tap steps, hoping to amuse him again, to bring him back from wherever his mind had wandered. But Kong gave no response. She leaned down and picked up a stone, rolling it up and down her arm like a juggler's ball. Still Kong did not turn to her. Ann knelt at his closed hand. There were things shifting in the cave that frightened her, but more than that, she could not escape the feeling that he was sad, and she wanted to comfort him. She tugged on one of his fingers, wanting to connect with him, but he brushed her away.

"Look at me," she said. "Look at me."

Slowly, he turned to meet her gaze. Kong crooked his finger, she wrapped her arms around it, and he gently pulled her to her feet. Kong held her gaze temporarily and then he turned and looked out over the jungle canopy. Ann followed his gaze, taking in the rugged landscape, bathed in last evening rays of sun.

She stared out at sea, a rain cloud casting shadows over the ocean, and she wondered if he was not sad after all, but simply at peace after a tumultuous day.

"It's beautiful."

Kong only sat, quietly staring out over the jungle.

"Beautiful," she said, and he looked at her. Ann placed her hand over her heart. "Beau-ti-ful."

Kong's hand unfurled beside Ann. She hesitated, then climbed into his palm. Kong gently lifted her up and for a moment he just stared at her. He lifted one enormous finger and touched her hair. Cradled in Kong's hand, she looked into his eyes without fear.

They sat there together, content in each other's company, high above the jungle, as the last of the dusk light faded to dark.

22

FATE HAD PLAYED A hand in all of the events leading up to this moment. Jack was certain of that. So many men had died in the attempt to rescue Ann, and he felt the weight of their deaths upon his shoulders. Yet if Kong had not returned to attack them at the chasm, he wasn't sure he would ever have been able to track the great ape back to his lair.

Instead, once he reached the other side, he had seen the broken tree limbs that lined the path the giant gorilla had taken, and soon enough he'd come to see the signs of Kong's passing, and to realize that this was a well-trod path. Even in the failing light of day he had been able to look into the sky and see the trail led directly toward the tallest peak on the island.

Night had fallen, but the evening sky was clear enough that above the darkness of the jungle, the mountain was still visible. Things moved in the undergrowth and in the branches above him, but they seemed almost unwilling to venture onto the path, as though afraid of incurring the wrath of Kong.

Jack had no such hesitation. All he could think of was Ann.

His thoughts felt crisp, his mind awake and alive, but he knew that was an illusion. In truth he was far past exhaustion, his muscles sluggish, his nerves on edge. Only adrenaline fed him now, and he wondered how long it could keep him going.

It seemed to take an eternity for him to climb up the cliffside to Kong's lair. The going was not terribly difficult, the rock was craggy and provided many handholds, but it was steep, and one misstep would send him tumbling to his death.

In time, though, he reached an opening in the cliff face that led into a vast cave. Moonlight streamed into the cave and he kept to the walls, moving in silence. The chamber was huge, its ceiling so high that in the dark he could not make it out. A short distance from the opening through which he'd entered was another, that led out onto a broad ledge overlooking the jungle.

Jack froze.

Kong lay upon the ledge, asleep. The giant gorilla's massive chest rose and fell and his breath rattled in a light snore.

Jack hurried across the stone floor to take cover behind a large rock. He scanned the cavern for any sign of Ann, but could not see her. His pulse raced, his every muscle tensed to spring if Kong so much as twitched in his sleep. The old bones of a large gorilla lay on the other side of the cave.

With no other choice, Jack moved toward Kong. He kept to the shadows of the rocks. Huge bat-things fluttered, agitated, up in the eaves of the cavern, sensing an intruder. Jack froze and looked up at them. During the day he'd seen dark things flying around this peak. Now they rustled up amidst the stalactites that hung from the roof.

He winkled his nose at the smell of them. The bat-things were rather pungent, and once more the writer in him was temptd to name creatures that were strange to him. He'd been schooled in Latin, of course, and now the name came to him. *Terapusmordax,* perhaps? Latin for "pungent-bat."

And God, the stench was awful.

Jack crawled forward onto the ledge. He crept close to the back of the sleeping giant, whose shoulders rose gently with each breath. Jack crawled past Kong's feet and looked up at the gorilla. His eyes widened and he stared in amazement.

Ann lay in Kong's hand, fast asleep.

Kong growled.

Jack spun, hands up, ready to bolt. But the gorilla's eyes were still closed. Kong was merely rumbling in his sleep.

Ann was only eight or ten feet away from him. Jack stared at her, wondering how to approach without waking Kong, when her eyes opened. For an instant she gazed blankly at him, almost as if she had been dreaming and now woken. She blinked, and he saw the realization strike her.

Jack had come for her. She stared at him with obvious disbelief.

He put a finger to his lips. Neither of them dared to move or make a sound. Very slowly, Jack approached. He gestured for her to stay motionless in Kong's palm.

There was more rustling and leathery fluttering in the cave, and then some of the terapusmordax flew out of the cave and began to fly around the ledge.

Kong might still be sleeping, but Jack's arrival had disturbed the other things that lived here. Whatever fear they might have had of Kong, it was clear the presence of Jack and Ann was too tempting to resist. More of them fluttered about.

On the ledge, Kong stirred.

This was the only chance he and Ann were going to get. He extended his hand toward Ann. She reached out. Their fingers touched.

Kong's eyes snapped open.

Time seemed to slow. Jack attempted to grab Ann's wrist, but Kong's fingers closed around her with stunning speed. Kong rolled to his feet, pulling Ann away. Kong snarled at Jack, who stood helplessly before him. The bat-things now swarmed above Kong in a predatory frenzy.

"Jack! Run!" Ann cried.

Kong swatted at Jack with his free hand. Ann struggled and kicked in the ape's grasp.

"No!"

Kong placed Ann high on a small ledge just inside the cave and then turned toward Jack, who was cornered on the ledge, nowhere to run. Kong charged. Jack rolled to the side as massive fists smashed down around him. The giant gorilla raised a foot and stomped down, Jack diving clear just in time.

Jack lay on the ground with Kong rearing above him, no chance of escape. The creature's eyes blazed with deadly intent. He raised his foot again, ready to crush Jack like a bug.

The cave echoed with a scream of terror and pain.

Kong spun around, while Jack scrambled to safety. Both of them stared at the ledge where Kong had left Ann. The terapusmordax had found her, and were whipping around her in a frenzy, sharp claws lashing her. She cowered against the rock face behind her, trying to protect herself.

With a furious roar, Kong abandoned his attack on Jack and charged at the bat-things. As he snatched Ann from the ledge, cradling her to his chest, the frenzied creatures struck at both Kong and Ann like a swarm of giant bees. Kong roared and thrashed out at them.

There were too many of them, tearing at his flesh. Kong put Ann down against the rocks so that he could use both hands to attack the vicious bat-things. With every sweep of his arm, he hammered several of the terapusmordax to the ground, but others clawed his head and body.

Jack seized his chance. He rushed along the edge of the cliff toward Ann, under the cover of an overhang. Kong had his back turned, fighting to protect Ann, even as Jack raced up behind him and grabbed her hand. He led Ann toward the only possible escape route.

The ledge.

At the edge they paused for only a heartbeat. One thousand feet above the jungle floor, they glanced into one another's eyes. No choice. Jack grabbed a vine and

Ann wrapped her arms around his shoulders, and he began to lower them both over the edge of the dizzying drop.

Hand over hand, he climbed down, dangling high above the ground. From above came the boom of Kong's roars as he fought the winged vermin. Jack looked up to see Kong stagger onto the ledge. Several terapusmordax clung to the giant gorilla's back, clawing at him. Kong drove himself backward, slamming into the stone face of the mountain, crushing them.

The surviving bat-creatures wheeled away, hissing angrily. They fluttered back into the cave, as though preparing their next attack.

No! Jack thought. *Just a little more time!*

Too late. Kong looked around for Ann and saw that she was gone.

Jack and Ann were no more than sixty feet down the vine. He began to swing them toward the rock face so he could get a handhold, get off the vine. If they had to climb down, they would find a way. But they had to move fast before—

As one, the two of them began to rise. Kong was pulling on the vine, drawing them back up toward the ledge, lifting Jack and Ann toward him like a fisherman reeling in his catch. Ann tightened her grip on Jack's shoulders as bat-things swooped and soared around them.

Kong would have them both if the terapusmordax didn't pluck them off the vine first and make a meal of them. One of them darted down and reached its claws toward Jack's head.

Without thinking, Jack simply let go of the vine with one hand and grabbed his attacker's taloned ankle.

"Hang on to me!" he shouted.

Ann clung to him for dear life as he grabbed the bat-thing's other ankle, releasing the vine completely.

Their weight was too much for the terapusmordax. They dragged it down, descending rapidly. The bat-thing furiously flapped its wings but was unable to stop its spiraling plunge past the cliff face.

Up above on the cliff ledge, Kong roared with anguish.

The terapusmordax creature wobbled crazily in the sky, rapidly losing energy. Jack looked down. A fast flowing river ran now only fifty feet below, and he released his grip.

Ann screamed as they plummeted through the air and then splashed into the river. Immediately, the current grabbed them and swept them into the rapids and then down a small waterfall.

Moments later, coughing up water and gasping for breath, they surfaced in a less tumultuous part of the river. Half-drowned, they swam to the muddy riverbank, hauling themselves out of the water. They sprawled face down in the mud, too exhausted to move.

"Jack?"

"I'm here."

"Did he follow us?"

"I think it's safe to assume he will."

Ann rolled over and looked at him. Even now,

ragged and covered with mud, she was so beautiful he felt his spirits lift just to look in her eyes.

"Thank you."

"For what?" he asked.

"Coming back."

He looked at her. His throat tickled as though he had to cough, or like there were words waiting there that he couldn't seem to say. Jack glanced away.

"I didn't think you would."

He hesitated a moment before replying. "Neither did I."

A lightness touched her face, and it extended to her voice. "At least we can have a conversation now, without things turning hostile."

Jack looked at her, lightly touching her cheek. Ann reached out to him and it seemed to him that the moment was suspended in time. There were so many thoughts and words and feelings churning within.

He pulled away. Whatever it was inside him that clamored for release, he couldn't let it out. It just wasn't the way he'd been built.

But she had to know, after all. He had come for her, hadn't he?

And perhaps she did know, but then he could find no way to explain to himself the sting in her eyes when he pulled away, and the way she seemed to close off to him, then.

From above came a distant roar.

Jack stood. Ann scrambled to her feet. Neither of them seemed able to look at the other. They looked up at the mountain, silhouetted against the waning night, and could see Kong quickly descending from his lair at a reckless pace, roaring again in rage.

Ann could do nothing but run. Worn down, emotions frayed, her mind roiled with confusion. There had been no real hesitation in her when Jack appeared. She had given up the idea of a rescue, had resigned herself to her fate, and when she saw him and saw that escape was possible, her heart had soared.

He had come for her. She might get off of this hellish, violent, lost isle. One day, she could set foot upon the shores of America again.

Yet even as she ran, lungs aching, throat rasping, legs like stone, she felt a shadow of guilt upon her heart. Kong had been alone for who knew how long. He had kept her alive. When he could have killed her, he had protected her and taken her in.

Her survival was a miracle, and of course she would never have chosen to stay. But he was the loneliest creature she had ever encountered, and a great gulf of sadness opened within her when she thought of him now.

Even as she ran from his fury, even as his roars filled the jungle.

Branches whipped at her face and she raised her arms to protect herself. The undergrowth scratched at her legs as she ran. Jack was beside her, his mere presence compelling her onward. A hundred times she wanted to ask how much farther, but she dared not, for she didn't want to know the answer.

And then, through a break in the jungle ahead, she saw the wall.

They burst from the trees and just ahead was the grotto carved with the faces of ancient gods, the place where the villagers had set her out for Kong on an altar.

The thunder of Kong's roaring reverberated all around them and birds exploded from the trees, flocks of them flying away in terror.

Between the wall and the grotto was a deep chasm. The altar to which she'd been tied was part of a structure that bridged that chasm . . . or it did when it was down. At the moment, it was raised, and hung just out of reach.

"Drop the bridge!" Jack shouted. "Carl!"

Ann ran, arms and legs pumping, but a terrible dread filled her as she looked to the top of the wall and saw that it was deserted.

"Help us!" she cried. "Please! Anyone!"

Another roar thundered through the jungle behind them, louder than before. Growing closer. Ann cast a nervous glance over her shoulder.

Trees crashed to the ground and now they saw him. Kong smashed his way through the jungle, moving toward the grotto.

Again Ann looked up at the deserted wall, desperate. She felt numb, her face slack.

"They've gone."

Jack stared at the top of the wall. "Carl!"

Dawn was lightening the sky. Carl Denham hid behind the wall and listened to his friends calling, heard the terror in their voices, and did nothing. A small group huddled nearby. Preston, Jimmy, Bruce, and Captain Englehorn. He could feel the heat of their stares.

"Drop the bridge!" Preston snapped. "Do it now, for Christ's sake!"

"Not yet," Denham muttered. "Wait."

Another roar filled the dawn sky, so loud, so close that it shook the wall. A sailor with a machete hovered near the rope that held the bridge up, ready to cut it at Denham's command.

"Wait . . ."

Preston's face was red with anger. Incensed, he stepped forward. "No, Carl."

Denham shot him a withering glare, but Preston didn't flinch. Ann and Jack's cries for help resounded from the other side of the wall.

"You don't make the rules," Preston said. "Not anymore."

Preston lunged forward and snatched the machete. He sliced through the rope, staggering back in pain as it flicked back, slashing him across the cheek.

Denham looked through the hole set into the massive gate just in time to see the bridge drop, at the very moment that Kong exploded from the jungle. The monstrous gorilla saw Jack and Ann and charged forward.

The two raced across the bridge, getting to the other side just as Kong leaped the chasm. They barely made it to the hole in the gate, as Kong began to smash the bamboo defenses set up around the wall, the whole village echoing and shaking with his fury.

23

DENHAM FELT A STRANGE calm settle over him. In the back of his mind he knew that he ought to have been paralyzed with fear, or fleeing in utter terror. Meanwhile, the gigantic gorilla hammered on the ancient wall and it shook with his efforts. His roars split the sky like furious thunder. The defenses the villagers had built on the other side of the wall—bamboo stakes sharpened to spear points—were nothing to the creature, who tore through it in seconds.

Preston, Englehorn, and some of the others had stared angry disapproval at Denham while he listened to Jack and Ann shouting for help, for rescue, but he couldn't allow anyone to interfere with the plan now. If they could only have trusted him . . . which they should have, because now Jack and Ann were safe.

They ran through the small hole in the gigantic gate. From his vantage point he could see Ann looking around wildly as they raced into the village, leaving the wall behind them. Jack's features were set in a grim mask.

Denham strode right past them and went to the gate. The monster—Kong—slammed his fists again and again on the gate, shaking the timbers, the whole structure quivering. The roaring of Kong jarred Denham's bones.

In wonder, Denham stared up at the wall, imagining the ancient mystery behind it, and elated at the prospect of bringing that same feeling of awe and wonder to the world.

He glanced over his shoulder and saw Ann and Jack approaching the rocks, where several clusters of sailors hid, grappling hooks ready. Preston lay to one side, a rag held against his bleeding face. Englehorn carried a large bottle of chloroform.

"What are you doing?" Ann demanded. She was scratched and bloody, clothes filthy and torn, her hair matted, and yet she was still beautiful, regal, and when she spoke many of the sailors sat up straighter and averted their eyes guiltily.

Denham was glad she was alive, that she and Jack were both safe. But he was even more pleased that the sailors were more concerned with Englehorn's orders than they were with looking good in front of this woman for whom they all had such affection and respect.

Then another roar—louder than anything before— echoed across the village. A momentary pause came in the battering of the gate.

"Get ready!" the captain shouted.

The gate rocked with Kong's assault, wood cracking, the splintering noise like gunshots. Denham backed off, running for cover. There came another blow, and then another. On the next, at last, the bar across the gate snapped in two, giant timbers cracked, and then Kong exploded through the gate with savage power.

Denham watched the sailors, about to give the word.

And he saw a remarkable thing. Kong stood, gazing around as though nothing he saw could threaten him, eyes searching until they located Ann. The moment he saw her, the giant gorilla seemed to deflate just the tiniest bit, and if Denham could have believed it, he would have said it was relief in the monster's eyes.

Ann gazed at Kong in despair. The monster reached tentatively toward her.

"Bring him down!" Denham called to Englehorn. "Do it!"

Englehorn gestured to his crew. "Now!"

The sailors leaped from their hiding places like soldiers charging up from the battlefield trenches, throwing grappling hooks onto Kong—the hooks sinking into his flesh even as they hauled on the ropes, trying to immobilize him.

Jack had been so concerned with Ann, and focused on the gorilla, that he had barely noticed all the sailors, had not quite realized what was going on. Now a look of disgust and anger crossed his face.

"No!" Ann cried.

"Are you out of your minds?" Jack shouted, turning on Denham. "Carl!"

Englehorn pointed upward and Denham looked up to see the sailors that were on top of the wall getting into position.

"Drop the net!" the captain shouted.

A huge net from the ship rigged with boulders was shoved over the side of the wall. The net dropped over Kong and he was dragged to the ground by the boulders. That was all they needed to immobilize him.

Denham turned to Englehorn. "Gas him!"

Ann was walking toward them now, shaking her head, tears streaking her face. "No, please. Don't do this."

She started for Kong, but Jack held her back.

"Ann, he'll kill you."

"No, he won't."

Denham stared at them in disbelief. Whatever they'd gone through in the jungle, he figured it had addled Ann's brain.

Kong tried to get up. Englehorn cocked back his arm and hurled the bottle of chloroform, which shattered on the ground right beneath the gigantic gorilla's face.

"No!" Ann screamed.

As he tried to push himself up, Kong breathed in a noxious cloud of chloroform.

"Keep him down!" Englehorn shouted to his crew.

The sailors atop the wall had more rocks, not only the ones they had used to weight the net. Now they rolled those boulders to the edge and tipped them over, huge stones tumbling through the air. Several hit Kong in the head, one after another.

Ann tore herself away from Jack and rushed Englehorn, grabbing his arm as he prepared to throw another chloroform bottle.

"Stop it! You're killing him!"

The captain ignored her, turning instead to Jack and shooting the writer a dangerous look. "Get her out of here! Get her out of his sight!"

Of course, Denham thought. He could see it now, could see it in the way that Kong's eyes were locked on Ann. As long as she was near, he would fight them that much harder. Hell, from the look of it, Denham thought it almost seemed like Kong wanted to protect *her* from *them*.

Jack grabbed Ann's arm. Despite the chloroform and the ropes and the blows to his head, Kong opened his mouth and let out a thunderous roar. The battle scars all over his face stretched and shone sickly, and his razor teeth seemed all the more threatening.

"Do it!" Denham snapped at Jack.

But he hesitated. Ann stared up at Jack.

"Let go of me."

Denham could see Jack was torn. But then Ann glanced toward Kong, and the danger was just too much to ignore. Jack pulled her by the hand toward the other side of the village, toward the tunnel that would lead down to the cove.

She shouted at Jack, struggling to break his grip.

Kong exploded with anger, frenzied in his efforts to get to Ann. Abruptly he rose, tearing at the net, ripping it to pieces. Sailors swung haplessly from the ends of the ropes, tossed through the air.

Denham was rooted to the spot. This whole damned trip had been cursed, fate against him at every turn, but he had been sure he could salvage something from it, both for himself, and for the greater good, to let people touch the mystery that still existed in tiny pockets of a shrinking world.

Now it was all falling apart.

"We can't contain him!" one of the sailors shouted, running toward Englehorn.

"Kill it!" the captain ordered.

Denham flinched. "No!"

Englehorn rounded on him. "It's over, you goddamn lunatic!"

"I need him alive!"

"Shoot it!" Englehorn commanded, ignoring him.

Kong rampaged through the village now. Sailors who still held the ends of grappling ropes and bits of net were tossed aside. Kong crashed into ruins, knocking ancient stone buildings down and trampling the huts of the villagers.

Astonished, Denham saw a lone figure stand his ground in front of the monster. It was the boy, Jimmy, a Tommy gun gripped in his hands. Denham could not escape the familiarity of the image, for it reminded him of Hayes's last stand against Kong at the log chasm. A chill ran down his back.

Not the kid. After all this, not the kid.

He started to run toward Jimmy, maybe to knock some sense into him, but Englehorn beat him to it. The captain grabbed Jimmy by the collar and pulled him away, shoving him down the path toward the tunnel that led to the cover. All the sailors were running that way now. Denham saw Bruce practically shoving Preston toward the tunnel and onto the ancient steps.

"Jimmy, get out of here!" Englehorn shouted. "Get to the boat! All of you! Run!"

In all her life, Ann had never felt such anguish. Her fear was gone, now, and only sorrow remained. She and Jack hurried down the treacherous steps inside that burial chamber as fast as they could. Twice she stumbled and had to catch herself.

Then they emerged onto the rocky shore of the cover. Side by side, they ran for a whaler that was waiting for them. Several sailors scurried about, shoving the prows of the boats away from shore. Others shouted at their shipmates, who were coming behind Jack and Ann, running for the boats.

But at the water, Ann stopped short.

She wouldn't leave, simply could not allow Denham and Englehorn to destroy Kong. The creature terrified her, and yet on another level, she felt a connection to him that would never be severed. He had protected her, and she had seen a gentleness in him that the others would never be able to understand. He was not a monster, but an animal. A thinking, feeling animal, following his instincts and emotions.

So many men had already died. Why couldn't they just leave the island, leave Kong to his home, and go?

Jack grabbed her waist and went to lift her up into the whaler. Ann fought him, pushing his hands away.

"Get in the boat!"

She could not. Her heart was breaking. The idea that she was the cause of Kong's suffering tore at her.

"No! It's me he wants. I can stop this!"

An explosive bellow rolled out over the ocean. Kong rampaged through the village until he was on top of the cliff through which the tunnel had been dug. Then Kong started down, over the edge, toward the cove.

A few yards up the shore, Jimmy stood his ground once again, Tommy gun in hands, watching Kong descend.

Jack saw him too. He swore under his breath and turned to Bruce, who was already in the whaler.

"Take her!"

Right then, Ann despised them both. Jack passed her to Bruce as though she was an errant child, forcing her into the boat. She struggled against them, but to no avail.

"Let me go to him!"

Englehorn leaped into the whaler. "Row! Get the hell out of here!"

Bruce held her tight, so that Ann could only watch as the sailors began to row toward open water, and the *Venture*. Jack grabbed hold of Jimmy, and he half-dragged the kid down to the water and forced him into the second boat, climbing in after him.

Jimmy raised his Tommy gun.

"Jimmy, no!" Jack shouted.

The sailors pushed their boat away from shore. Denham and Preston were in that second whaler as well. As Ann watched, Carl tore the lid off a crate and raised up a bottle of chloroform. Like Jimmy, he was not ready to leave yet.

Denham cocked his arm back to throw the bottle.

Jimmy pulled his arm away from Jack, steadied

himself in the boat, and fired a burst from the Tommy gun. Bullets punctured the air, some of them striking Kong. He flinched, but nothing more. Then he bellowed and charged in fury, rushing at the water.

Ann didn't have time to scream. She stared in horror as Kong brought his fist down on the bow of the whaler. Denham was flung into the water, bottle of chloroform still clutched in his hand.

A huge form towering above them like the Colossus of Rhodes, Kong reached down and lifted the whaler out of the water. Men shouted in terror as they spilled into the ocean. Jack and Jimmy were thrown out with the rest, flailing as they hit the surf.

Kong flung the boat against the stone face of the cliff that loomed above the cover and it smashed into kindling.

Jack surfaced, holding onto Jimmy, who choked and coughed up sea water.

Then Kong turned toward Ann's boat, and looked directly at her.

"Go back!" she said, pushing herself up, waving him away.

Kong paused at the sound of her voice, as if sensing her fear for him.

"Hold her!" Englehorn snapped.

Bruce grabbed her and held her tightly as Englehorn raised a harpoon and fired it at Kong. It struck the giant gorilla in the knee. Kong staggered back, roaring in pain, and sank down in the water.

Ann could only sob, trying to pull herself away, shaking her head in denial. Englehorn stood, loading a second harpoon.

Nearby Denham scrambled onto a rock, holding the chloroform bottle.

"Wait!" he shouted at Englehorn.

The captain ignored him, intent on killing Kong with his next harpoon. Ann was not sure which of them she wished would succeed, whose intended fate for Kong would be more merciful. Kong started crawling painfully toward the boat, still pursuing Ann. Englehorn had almost finished loading.

"Leave him alone!" she shouted.

Jack was floating in the water, holding an unconscious Jimmy up to keep the boy from drowning. Denham steadied himself on his rock as Kong lumbered past him in the water on all fours. With a grunt of effort, he hurled the chloroform bottle. It smashed against Kong's face and the animal began choking on the gas.

As the creature succumbed, he reached plaintively for Ann.

She felt nothing but cold inside, a dreadful knowledge that his awful fate was only beginning here on the coast of Skull Island. Ann had failed to help him, to stop this from happening.

Horrified, she could only turn away as Kong slumped into unconsciousness. She saw Jack in the water, watching her, and she began to shudder with tears.

Denham waded toward the unconscious Kong, a look of gleeful triumph on his face, and he looked around at the others who had survived the journey.

"The whole world will pay to see this. We're millionaires, boys! I'll share it with all of you. In a few months his name will be up in lights on Broadway. 'Kong! The Eighth Wonder of the World!' "

24

TIMES SQUARE. THE BEATING heart of New York City, rightly called the crossroads of the world. On that winter's night, it was alive, teeming with the bustle of humanity. Groups of serious men moved together along sidewalks, the smoke from their cigars and pipes redolent in the chilly evening air. In other parts of the city, the Depression still gnawed at thousands, but in this place there gathered so many of those who had no such concerns. Couples young and old strode arm in arm, clad in formal attire, across an urban landscape made somehow innocent by a blanket of newly fallen snow.

All of them, it seemed, were making for the same destination.

Preston stood across from the Alhambra Theatre, its colorful lights reflected in the soft snow. The excited, curious crowd converged on the venue. Cabs pulled up to the curb. A long line had formed and scalpers sold tickets outside the door.

He gazed at the glittering marquee, the words there forcing a parade of difficult images through his mind. Preston shuddered once, and he was not sure if it was in relief to be standing there in Times Square at all, or dread at the prospect of entering that theater. For to enter would be, in a way, a return to those days and nights he would rather forget.

Upon the marquee, giant letters announced KING KONG THE EIGHTH WONDER OF THE WORLD! Billboards outside the theater commanded passersby to *Relive the adventure of the century! See Miss Ann Darrow offered to the beast!*

Preston had no interest in doing either.

Yet he could not turn away. Coming here tonight felt very much like the conclusion of something, and he believed that when the curtain fell on this evening's exhibition, he might at last be able to put the past behind him.

Perhaps tonight he would even be able to sleep without nightmares.

He reached up and idly traced a finger along the scar on his cheek. And then he started toward the entrance.

In her dressing room, Ann sat alone, numb and disconnected. As she put on her stage makeup, she felt strangely hollow, her mind drifting to thoughts of things far away, of disappointments and things that might have been.

The lobby teemed with people chatting and laughing, as though all the troubles of the world outside the theater had never existed. Preston thought Denham would be pleased. This was precisely what he wanted to provide for an audience—an escape from mundane reality into mystery and excitement—and the show had yet to begin.

The area around the cloakroom was crowded with people handing hats and coats to the check-in girls. From the balcony above, Preston watched it all. He searched the crowd for Denham, and after a few moments spotted the director, his employer, greeting Zelman and the other investors, all of whom had young girls like starlets hanging upon their arms. All of the men acted quite pleased to see one another, considering that before the *Venture* returned with Kong, the investors would gladly have seen Denham thrown in jail.

As if feeling the attention upon him, Carl glanced up. He looked at Preston, expressionless, then turned his back, mustering a brilliant smile for a waiting photographer.

The audience exploded in uproarious laughter.

On stage, the actors moved through a set built to look like a hotel lobby. Paul Thatcher, the actor playing Drew, pulled Harry Gorman to one side. Gorman was in the role of lovelorn Edgar . . . and in this scene, he was dressed in drag.

"Look at yourself. Look what you've become!" Drew said. "No woman is worth this."

"This woman is worth it! I've got to win her back," Edgar replied. "I don't care what it takes."

"Who do you think you are, Dolores del Rio?" Drew demanded. "She's not gonna buy it for a second."

Edgar pointed to a large bowl of fruit that sat on a

decorative sideboard. "Shut up, and hand me the grapefruit."

Drew sighed and did as he was asked. Edgar shoved a large grapefruit into his brassiere. The audience erupted in a fresh wave of laughter. The theater was small and arty, French in design, but their guffaws and giggles rose to the rafters.

Jack ought to have been thrilled. He sat a few rows from the front, right behind a woman who was paying more attention to the program for *Cry Havoc* than she was to the play itself, as if she were looking ahead to see how much longer she had to sit there.

Not that it bothered him. In many ways he felt the same. But despite his own and the heavyset woman's restlessness, the majority of the audience were having a grand time.

On cue, two attractive young women entered the hotel lobby set up on the stage. The actress playing Jayne had golden blond hair and startling eyes, and Jack was the first to admit she looked a little like Ann. Perhaps more than a little. He had convinced himself it was coincidence.

Jayne was hustled along by Thelma, her confidante.

"From the top. Tell me everything, every little detail!" Thelma demanded.

The two women sat on a sofa to stage left even as Edgar sat in an armchair nearby, pretending not to know them.

"So he took me to a fancy French restaurant," Jayne said.

Thelma studied her. "French, huh?"

Edgar, his feminine attire outrageous on him, leaned over and interrupted in his best falsetto.

"What a wonderfully generous, romantic gesture! Sounds like a fabulous young man."

Thelma frowned at him/her. "Excuse me?"

"Oh, I'm sorry. I couldn't help but overhear."

Ignoring the intrusion, Jayne continued. "Anyway, about halfway through the whore derves, he clutches my hand—"

"He clutches your hand?" Thelma asked, voice rising in disbelief.

"It felt like the right thing to do at the time!" falsetto Edgar chimed in, bringing a ripple of laughter from the audience before he corrected himself. "For him, I mean . . . It must have!"

Again, Jayne ignored him. "He's looking into my eyes—"

"And that's when he told you how he felt?" Thelma asked.

"No. He never said it."

Thelma looked horrified. "He never said it!"

Falsetto Edgar was frantic. "He probably thought he didn't *need* to say it."

The audience laughed, but suddenly, Jack didn't think it was very funny. Not funny at all.

Thelma spun and glared at Edgar, in his ridiculous wig and dress and grapefruit breasts. "Then how does *she* know that it's real?"

"He said it was not about the words," Jayne went on.

Thelma threw up her hands. "Please, if you feel it, you say it. It's really very simple."

Jayne shrugged. "He said we'd talk about it later. Only there *was* no later. It never happened. I just had this stupid idea that maybe, this one time, things would actually work out. Which was really very foolish."

Jack shifted uncomfortably in his seat and then abruptly stood. Part of him was flinching at the incredible breach of theater etiquette. It was his show, after all. But he didn't allow himself to consider his course of action any further. He stepped into the aisle, turned his back on the stage, and headed for the exit, making his way past surprised audience members.

"Men!" Thelma said, up on the stage. "They'll give you the world. But they let the one thing that truly matters slip through their fingers. All for the sake of three little words!"

"The three hardest words in the English language," Edgar snapped, barely able to maintain the falsetto.

As Jack left the theater, the audience broke into fresh laughter. He strode outside into the cold winter night and turned up his collar against the icy wind. He glanced once at the billboard above that advertised CRY HAVOC, *a new play by Jack Driscoll*.

Then he turned and started walking toward Times Square.

Denham waited quietly in the wings of the Alhambra Theatre. The auditorium was filled to capacity, nearly two thousand people. The excitement in the air was palpable. Yet here, backstage, he had a moment of calm, and he allowed himself at last to feel pride in what he had accomplished. Out of disaster, he had brought something extraordinary.

From the darkened area behind the curtain he heard a weak, rasping growl, the sound of Kong breathing.

Her hair perfect at last, Ann pulled on her costume, moving slowly, unable to summon an ounce of enthusiasm for the performance she was about to deliver. Her memories of the vibrant life and color and music of vaudeville seemed so distant to her now.

Jostled by people on the busy sidewalk, Jack hurried into Times Square and stepped off the curb. Horns beeped but he ignored them, darting between cars, straight toward the theater and the enormous marquee promising the Eighth Wonder of the World.

A spotlight swung back and forth across the closed curtain as if searching for something. Denham took his cue and walked across to center stage. The crowd erupted into applause as the spotlight locked onto him. His smile was so wide it hurt and he waved to the audience, basking in their acclaim.

It felt to him like arriving at last at a destination toward which he had strived all his life.

"Thank you! Thank you! Thank you! Ladies and gentlemen, I am here to tell you a very strange story. A story so strange, it is beyond all belief. But, ladies and gentlemen, seeing is believing! And what you are about to see is living proof of our adventure. An adventure in which seventeen of our own party suffered horrible deaths! Their lives lost in pursuit of a savage beast, a monstrous aberration of nature!

"But even the maddest brute can be tamed. Yes, ladies and gentlemen, as you will see, the beast was no match for the charms of a girl . . . a girl from New York, who melted his heart, bringing to mind that old Arabian proverb. 'And, lo, the Beast looked upon the face of Beauty and Beauty stayed his hand . . . and from that day forward he was as one dead . . .' "

Ann felt brittle and cold in her white velvet gown. She sat in her dressing room, staring into her mirror, at the sadness reflecting back from her eyes.

A soft knock came on the door. "You're on, Miss Darrow. Five minutes."

Ann stood.

Denham felt flushed with the heat of the spotlight and the moment. He faced the audience, raising a hand as though he was about to perform some act of magic.

Yet wasn't he, in a way? He was about to reveal to these people that the world still held magic, and mystery. And if by that revelation, some of the mystery was lost, that was the price of showmanship, the cost of discovery.

"And now I'm going to show you the greatest thing your eyes have ever beheld. He was a king in the world he knew but he comes to you now . . . a captive!"

Denham lifted his arms. "Ladies and gentlemen, I give you *Kong,* the Eighth Wonder of the World!"

The band began to play, music filling the theater.

Ann arrived in the wings. The stage manager turned toward her, face alight with anticipation.

Jack stood at the back of the balcony, looking out over the darkened theater. The music swelled. He watched Carl give a dramatic flourish of his hands and the curtain slowly rose to reveal Kong sitting slumped and unresponsive, his wrists manacled to a steel scaffold. Other manacles and chains secured his ankles, neck and waist. There came a collective gasp from the audience. Jack couldn't blame them. Kong's sheer size was overwhelming.

His own response to the sight of the beast was something else, something he hadn't expected. Pity. And Kong did look pitiful there, so different from the majestic thing he had been on Skull Island.

But Jack did not allow himself to be fooled. The sadness of the creature did not diminish the brutality of which he was capable.

A look of utter euphoria crossed Carl's features as the reactions of two thousand people washed over him.

Kong's head lolled as if he was barely aware of his surroundings.

"Don't be alarmed, ladies and gentlemen," Carl said, ever the gallant host. "It is perfectly safe. These chains are made of chrome steel!"

After the moment it had taken the audience to recover from the sight of the beast, they erupted in sudden, wild applause.

As though he were a college professor—a particularly patronizing instructor—he reached out and put his hand on Kong's leg, demonstrating the current harmlessness of his captive.

"Observe if you will, I am touching the beast. I am actually laying my hand on the twenty-five-foot gorilla."

Kong's foot twitched slightly, causing Denham to jump back in fright. It ought to have been funny, even a bit ridiculous, but Jack was not amused. Denham signaled to the stage hands in the wings. Offstage, one of them began to crank a winch. The chains at Kong's wrists tightened, drawing him up to his full height.

The audience gasped again.

Jack started forward, quietly made his way down the shadowed aisle, even as Carl turned to face the audience again.

"And now we have in the auditorium tonight a surprise guest. The real life hero of this story. The man who hunted down the mighty Kong!"

Jack felt a sick twist in his gut as he watched the spectacle unfold, his mind full of images, memories, he wished he could forget.

"The man who risked all to win the freedom of a helpless female!" Denham went on. "A big hand for . . . Mister Bruce Baxter!"

Jack smiled thinly.

Bruce strode on stage dressed as the great white hunter. The costume was ridiculous, but the audience exploded with applause and whistles. Carl shook Bruce's hand, clapping him on the back as if they were old friends. Bruce turned to acknowledge the adulation of the audience.

A pulsating drum beat began to fill the auditorium.

Carl raised a hand to quiet the audience. They were eating out of his hand, now, and he lowered his voice. "Ladies and gentlemen, imagine if you will an uncharted island. A forgotten fragment from another time. And clinging to life in this savage place, imagine a people untutored in the ways of the civilized world. A people who have dwelt all their lives in the shadow of fear. In the shadow of . . . Kong!"

A line of dancers dressed as absurd native costumes right out of the very sort of back lot safari films Carl despised appeared from either side of the stage. They danced to the beat, playing to Kong, who stared impassively at them.

In the balcony, Jack stared transfixed at the stage.

From behind him came a quiet voice. "He was right."

Jack turned to find Preston standing beside him.

"About there still being some mystery left in the world," the younger man went on softly. Preston stared down at Denham on the stage. "And we can all have a piece of it. For the price of an admission ticket."

Jack stared at Preston, at the scar that ran down his cheek.

"That's the thing you come to learn about Carl," he said. "His unfailing ability to destroy the things he loves."

Once upon a time, Carl Denham had been one of his closest friends. It was unlike Jack to say such things aloud, even after all Carl had put him through. But Preston had been equally close to the man, and had come to the same, unpleasant conclusions.

Down at the front of the theater, Denham strode to the front of the stage.

"Please remain calm, ladies and gentlemen, for we now come to the climax of this savage ritual. The sacrifice of a beautiful young girl!"

The crowd erupted into wild cheers, and Jack had the idea that their applause would have been no less enthusiastic—perhaps even more so—had they been about to witness an actual blood sacrifice.

The lights dimmed, the drum beat increased, and the native dancers fell to their knees in worship as a platform rose from beneath the stage.

"Behold her terror as she is offered up to the mighty Kong! A big hand folks for the bravest girl I ever met! Miss Ann Darrow!"

Jack wanted desperately to turn away. After all she'd been through, he was sickened by the thought of Ann being up on that stage. The entire voyage home she had barely spoken to him, to anyone, and he could not imagine how lost she must have felt. But to agree to this? He would never have believed it if he wasn't seeing it with his own eyes.

The platform rose, and upon it, a dramatic silhouette of a woman dressed in a white silk gown. She was tied to a wooden altar, her back to the audience.

Kong roused just a bit, a sudden flicker of hope in his eyes. The tiny figure tethered to the altar looked up into the face of the giant gorilla. Kong grunted, flinched back, and though he was not human, there was a look that could only have been confusion on his features.

Jack didn't understand.

Until he focused on Ann.

And realized that it wasn't Ann at all, but a woman in a blond wig, dressed to look like her.

Kong roared, no longer simply hanging in his chains. His eyes were alight with fury. Jack stared at him, dread certainty forming in his chest.

Fake Ann thrashed around, screaming unconvincingly. "No! No! Help me, no!"

Kong stared at her with mounting confusion and anger.

Jack turned to Preston.

"Where is she?"

25

THE TINY VAUDEVILLE THEATER filled with slow, dreamy
music. The line of chorus girls danced across the stage,
all identically dressed in dove white, each of them
holding a feathered fan in front of her face.

The main act was Charlie Almond, one of the best
tap dancers she had ever seen. The audience was wild
for him, cheering, barely noticing the chorus line. But
that was the point of the chorus, to be a beautiful moving background for the main act.

Ann held her fan like a mask, and when the chore-
ography of the number required her to sweep it aside,
revealing her face to the audience, she did her best not
to see them, not to see the theater at all. When she had
returned from her seaward journey, she had thought
that a return to the stage would heal her, that it was all
she needed. But she had been wrong. The lights and
the crowd and the smells and the music all served to
remind her of the life and vaudeville family she'd had
before she ever met Carl Denham, and the naïve girl
she'd been in those days when she dreamed of being in
one of Jack Driscoll's plays.

That time was lost to her. She wasn't even that girl

anymore. For just a moment, in the midst of the catastrophic events on Skull Island, she had imagined that all would be well if she and Jack could just have found peace and solace in one another's arms. Ann knew she could have escaped into Jack . . . if only he had been able to escape into her, as well.

But he couldn't love her enough to truly let his guard down.

And now she was here, doing the only thing she knew how to do. But being a chorus girl was different from vaudeville. It was a competition to these girls, and the competition was brutal. There was no family camaraderie here.

The audience clapped as Charlie Almond danced, and the chorus girls moved behind him, shaking their feathered fans, merely window dressing now.

It made no difference. The crowd's disregard could not touch Ann's heart, for it was not really here, but somewhere far away.

Jack glared at Preston, who turned away, shifting uncomfortably. Several people in the balcony urged them in hushed whispers to sit down.

"Where's Ann?"

"I've no idea," Preston said. "I heard he offered her all kinds of money and she turned him down flat. I guess, in the end, he didn't need her."

The words were cold, but it was clear Preston did not mean them that way. There was regret in his eyes.

On the stage, photographers pushed forward, flash bulbs popping. They called out to the false Ann, trying to get her attention. The strobing lights from the cameras agitated Kong further. The massive gorilla flinched, and then thrust his head and upper body forward, a roar erupting from his jaws.

"Come on, Denham!" shouted a reporter. "How about one with you and the big monkey?"

Jack looked on as Denham signaled to Bruce to join him. Behind them, the fake Ann continued to feign terror. She was one of the worst actresses Jack had ever seen.

"Here's your story, boys," Carl announced. " 'Beauty and the man who saved her from the beast.' "

One of the reporters turned the focus on Bruce. "How did you feel, Mr. Baxter, when you were on the island?"

"Well to be honest with you, I had some anxious moments . . ." Bruce began, and the gathered members of the press hung on his every word, grim-faced and eager. Then Bruce grinned. "For a while there it looked like I wasn't going to get paid."

That got a laugh.

"But as it turned out," Bruce continued, "Mister Denham here has been more than generous and—"

Kong threw himself against his bonds, the chains shaking, metal grinding upon metal. Again he roared, the bellow echoing through the theater. Jack could feel it in his chest like the thundercrack of fireworks exploding.

He glanced at Preston and saw that the other man was just as unnerved as he was.

Down on the stage, Carl was unaffected.

"Let him roar!" the director called. "It makes a swell picture!"

From the balcony Jack stared at Kong, who was breathing hard through his nostrils. He could feel Kong's mounting anger, could practically see it building inside the beast with volcanic pressure.

A terrible certainty filled him and he turned to Preston. "We have to get these people out of here."

Preston stared at him, brows knitted together. He shot a glance down at the stage, and Kong let out another bellow and began to throw himself forward, tugging his arms, straining his bonds. Jack thought Preston might have cursed under his breath, but then he turned toward the people seated around them in the balcony.

"Sir, excuse me, sir . . . you have to leave." He grabbed the arm of a fortyish, well-dressed man.

"Everyone has to leave," Jack added, raising his voice and looking around, spreading his arms so they would notice him. "Head to the exits."

The man angrily shook off Preston's hand. "Are you kidding me? Do you know how much I paid for these tickets?"

From a couple of rows back, another man called to Jack. "Get your own seat, buddy. You ain't having mine."

Over Kong's roars and the shouts of reporters, a scream split the air like a gunshot. Jack and Preston both turned. The fake Ann was no longer acting. Her screams were quite real. Kong had broken free of one of the manacles on his wrists; one of his hands was free.

And the audience, most of them anyway, thought it was just part of the show. Confused, maybe a little nervous, they started to applaud.

"Get out of here *now*!" Jack screamed to them. "*Go!*"

He and Preston were grabbing at people. Some of them began to rise from their seats at last, finally realizing something might actually be wrong, that they could be in danger.

Then there came another deafening roar. Jack glanced down from the balcony just in time to see the expression on Carl's face as he looked up and understood what he had done. Yet there was no fear or regret on Denham's face. Only awe. Only a childlike wonder.

Emboldened by having freed the one hand, Kong redoubled his efforts. In seconds he had torn free of the rest of his bonds, chains snapping, metal tearing, bolts lifting from the floor. Journalists and photographers started backing away, snapping pictures as they retreated. Flashbulbs popped, and for a moment Kong cowered back, shielding his eyes.

Roaring in defiance.

They were only infuriating him further.

But at last the audience realized this was not part of the show and any comfort they'd taken from Carl's reassurances evaporated. Screams echoed through the auditorium and as one, a wave of humanity rose up from their seats and began to scramble and shove and stampede for the exits.

On the stage, Kong tore off the restraints around his waist, and was completely free. The panic in the theater rose to a terrified crescendo. Yet as Jack tried to hurry people up the steps toward the balcony exit, he glanced back and saw Carl standing in the middle of the theater, still mesmerized by the spectacle of Kong's unleashed power.

The fake Ann tethered to the altar shrieked again for help. Kong leaped across the stage and picked her up, and for a moment Jack thought he might only hold her. But it was his fury at the deception, at the dashed hopes he'd had of seeing the real Ann, that had set him off to begin with. With an agonized scream, he hurled the poor woman and the altar across the wide auditorium, into the crowd.

"Go, go, go! Move!" Jack shouted as he and Preston herded people toward the doors.

And only now did he feel fear for himself. His skin prickled with the awareness of death's proximity. His throat was dry and his pulse hammered at his temples.

Kong swung from the stage into the front-row seats, stomping and crushing the slower moving patrons as he moved through the theater, trying to find his way out. Just below the edge of the balcony he stopped, as though sensing something, or catching a scent, and he looked up.

For a fleeting moment, Jack locked eyes with Kong.

It was time for him to get out of there *now*, to get as far away from Kong as possible. But the gorilla had other intentions. Kong grabbed hold of the boxes on the side walls of the theater and swung himself upward, scaling them easily. From the upper boxes, he leaped to the balcony.

Where he landed, a portion of the balcony gave way,

crumbling under his weight. Dozens of people plummeted to the floor below, screaming as they fell, the cries ceasing abruptly upon impact.

As Kong struggled to rise, Jack turned and raced for the door, pushing through the stragglers. At the exit, he turned and looked back, filled with a mixture of dread and awe.

Kong roared and hurled a plaster cornice across the length of the theater, up into the remains of the balcony, straight at Jack. At the last second, Jack ducked through the door as the cornice smashed into the wall, shattering on impact.

He joined the stampede going down the stairs, having lost track of Preston but assuming the other man was in the midst of the exodus as well. Halfway down, Jack spotted an open space on the stairs below and leaped over the banister, dropping to the steps. There were screams all around him. Women were being half-carried by their male escorts. A heavyset man had sat down on the stairs, unable to go on, and people flowed around him.

Then Jack was in the lobby. The whole building shook with Kong's roars and the pounding of his mighty fists.

He emerged from the theater amidst a rush of panicked people who fled in terror. Horns blared. Cars screeched and shuddered to a halt, or collided with a crumpling of metal. Jack started across the street, into the center of Times Square, and he glanced back just in time to see the façade of the Alhambra Theatre explode onto the street, showering pedestrians and cars with bricks and steel.

Kong seemed to burst from the guts of the theater and landed in the road. Jack stared up in horror. Eyes ablaze with ferocity, Kong headed straight for him.

And Jack understood that he was going to die.

With an anguished roar, the huge gorilla stumbled past him into the bright lights of Times Square. Jack was astonished to still be alive—Kong had not seen him.

The beast spun around, throwing up his arms, growling a challenge to the world, fighting the terror and confusion that must have filled him as he faced the strangeness of the city, of cars and trucks and trams, of bright lights and thousands of screaming people.

Again and again, Kong spun around, and Jack could see the fear and anger and frustration in him. It was as though he was searching for something in the streets, in the crowds.

Then, with terrifying speed, Kong reached out and snatched a blond woman from the crowd. Even as the woman's screams lifted above all others, Jack understood.

"Oh, Jesus," he said under his breath.

He's searching for Ann.

Kong had no idea the size of the city, the number of people. He could not have understood that finding Ann here would be like locating the proverbial needle in a haystack. But what chilled Jack to the bone was his certainty that Kong would keep looking, and that people would keep dying, until the beast found her.

Ann emerged from the shabby old theater.

She had just committed one of the most unprofessional acts of her life—walking off stage in the middle of her performance—but somehow it didn't really faze her.

Clad only in her chorus dress, Ann shivered. The winter night was merciless against her skin. Sirens screamed and echoed off of the buildings as three police cars careened down the street, racing past her.

Ann followed, running to the intersection, and looked up the street. Several blocks away, in Times Square, pandemonium had erupted.

She was well aware of what performance had been scheduled to take place there this evening.

Chest tight, pulse racing, Ann ran toward the chaos.

Kong circled Times Square snatching up any woman with blond hair, desperately looking for Ann. Dodging bits of flying debris, Jack tried to push his way toward Kong through crowds of fleeing people. As Jack watched, the great ape stomped on a car, killing all the occupants.

Shouts of alarm drew Jack's attention. People were pointing, and only then did he see the tram heading straight for Kong. The giant gorilla thrust out an arm protectively and his fist punched through the tram's windows. Startled, the beast drew his arm back, with the tram firmly attached. Jack could hear the screams of the dying and the terrified inside.

Like a cornered animal, Kong seemed to go into a blind panic. He flailed his arms and swung the tram through the air, smashing it into buildings in an attempt to get it off. Kong staggered out of Times

Square, caroming off of buildings, shattering glass and buckling walls.

Most of the area was now clear of people. Cars were abandoned, doors hanging open, cluttering Times Square. Jack dared not stop to consider how many had died, either at Kong's hands, or trampled underfoot by other men and women fleeing the scene.

Kong headed south along Broadway and Jack knew he had to follow. In the middle of the road was a stopped cab. The driver was too awestruck, too shocked to run or drive away. The man stood just outside his door watching the scene with his mouth agape.

Jack jumped into the back of the cab and gestured toward Kong.

"After him—go!"

The man stared at him incredulously, then raised his hands in surrender. "It's all yours, buddy!"

Jack scrambled into the front seat of the cab, threw it into gear, and headed down Broadway after Kong. He cut the wheel to the left to swerve around a huge, crumpled piece of the tram that had fallen, then had to cut it the other direction and weave around other parts of the tram that were tearing loose and plummeting to the street from Kong's fist.

As he righted the wheel, he looked up to see that Kong had stopped. He had no choice but to accelerate. Jack floored the gas and the cab shot through Kong's legs. He held his breath, eyes wide, when he saw the building dead ahead. Gritting his teeth he twisted the wheel and the cab spun around, nearly toppling over before it settled on the pavement. Jack's foot was on the brake and he stared out through the windshield and saw that the cab was facing straight at Kong.

The gorilla threw back his head and roared, pounded his chest, and then glared down at a car full of people that was in his path. Kong raised one fist up and Jack saw what was about to happen.

He hit the horn.

The blare of the cab's horn made Kong pause, and then turn. The winter wind whipped through the taxi, but it was a more profound cold that filled Jack now, an ancient terror that went down to the bone.

Kong looked through the windshield, right at him. There was no question in his mind that the gorilla would recognize him. He had done so once already tonight.

With a snarl that revealed black gums and huge, sharp teeth, and stretched gleaming scars on his horrid face, Kong started after Jack.

As he moved, panicked drivers coming up Broadway honked and tried to swerve around him, crashing their cars into one another. Vehicles collided with the cab, rocking Jack in his seat, but he hung on to the wheel. A useless gesture. With the cars that had piled up around him, there was no way he was driving out of there.

He tried his door, but it would not open. Frantic, Jack looked around and found he was wedged in by cars on either side. His throat was dry and felt closed off. He looked around, trying to figure some other way out of the taxi.

A huge hand came down into view just ahead. Jack

started, threw himself against the seat, as though he might somehow pass through solid objects and escape. Kong lifted the car directly in front of him. The beast raised the vehicle high above his head and then, with a roar that shook the glass in the cab windows, hurled it into a building, where it exploded in flames and shards of glass and metal.

Kong bent down and his huge eyes stared through the side window of the cab. But the beast had just cleared Jack a path.

Jack hit the gas. Wheels spinning wildly, a cloud of burning rubber behind him, Jack sped up the road, weaving in and out of the path cut by Kong's destruction. Pulse thumping in his head, he looked in the rearview mirror and saw Kong bounding after the cab on all fours, loping along with a speed that crushed any hope he had of escaping.

But he'd damn well keep trying.

The cab shot like a bullet across an intersection. Dozens of abandoned cars filled the streets, along with others whose drivers were still shouting angrily, trying to figure out how to extricate their vehicles, unaware of what was going on nearby. Jack swerved up onto the sidewalk, the only clear passage ahead.

Screaming, pedestrians scattered, leaping from his path. As he shot past them, he saw that most of them weren't paying any attention to him, but were looking behind him. Jack could see the primal terror etched in their faces and knew it reflected his own.

Kong was in hot pursuit.

Jack scanned the street, searching for any chance,

something small enough to at least slow Kong down. His fingers tightened on the wheel and he narrowed his eyes as he spotted a tiny alley off to one side.

Gunning the engine, he pointed the cab toward the alley's mouth, afraid it might even be too narrow for the vehicle. Then he shot into the alley, rearview mirror snapping off the cab, paint scraping on the walls. The alley was barely wide enough for the cab.

Jack looked over his shoulder to see Kong at the mouth of the alley, roaring with frustration.

The cab erupted from the other end of the alley into the midst of Herald Square. Kong's rampage had not reached this far south as yet and he heard screeching brakes and blaring horns. Cars slewed to one side as drivers tried to avoid collision.

Then he could drive no farther. The traffic was moving, but slowly. Jack twisted around in his seat, looking out every window for a sign of Kong's approach.

The beast dropped from above, landing on the street right in front of him, impact buckling pavement. Once again Jack swerved onto the sidewalk and steered the cab wildly, scattering pedestrians in all directions.

Kong followed. Jack swung the cab through a couple of tight turns, keeping track of the huge gorilla's pursuit. Then he came around a blind corner and slammed the cab straight into a fruit vendor's stall. Out of control, blinded by the ruined stall on the hood, Jack crashed the cab into a building, the impact throwing him forward so that his head struck the windshield.

Dazed, he shook himself, looking around. The windshield was shattered. He ignored it. As he turned in his seat again, hand on the door, about to get out to continue his flight, Kong rounded the corner and bounded right past the cab, which was hidden now safely beneath the rubble of the wall and the wrecked fruit stall.

Kong paused, glancing around for the cab, and roared in frustration.

Then Jack saw the beast freeze, there in the middle of the street.

No, he thought. *No, it's impossible. It can't be . . . unless she saw the chaos, knew what was happening . . . of course she'd come to try to help . . . of course she'd come to him.*

Disoriented, shaky on his feet, he climbed out of the cab and his worst fear was realized. There, in the street, was Ann. Kong inclined his head as though unsure that she was real, that he had found her at last.

But it *was* her. The real Ann, this time. She walked toward him. Kong roared and took a step nearer, then stopped. Ann stopped as well, and for a long moment they just stared at one another.

A small, soft smile lit her angelic features.

Kong reached out and gently lifted her off the ground, his eyes never leaving her face. Ann held tightly to his hand as Kong turned and carried her off, disappearing into the night.

26

THE TROOP CARRIER RATTLED, engine growling, as it sped through the New York streets. In the bed of the truck, Sergeant Bissette rubbed a hand across the light stubble on his jaw and stared in disgust at the fear he saw in the faces of the soldiers under his command.

"Listen up! This is New York City and this is sacred ground, you hear me? It was built for humans, by humans, not for stinking, lice-infested apes! The thought of some mutant gorilla crapping all over the streets of this fair city fills me with disgust."

Private Hautala, a new recruit, was pale and wide-eyed. Bissette merely glared at him.

"So this is how it's gonna be; we find it, we kill it, we cut its ugly head off and ram it up its—"

He saw Hautala's eyes widen, saw the kid's face contort with terror, and as the sergeant spun to find the source of that terror he saw the gigantic gorilla looming up beside them, and the fist driving down toward them.

It struck the front of the truck like a piledriver. The troop carrier flipped into the air, men and helmets and weapons scattering everywhere. Sergeant Bissette hit the ground at a bad angle, splintering his leg, but had no time to even let out a cry of pain before the truck's cab crashed down on top of him, pulping flesh and bone.

Ann clutched Kong's fingers, holding tightly as he scaled another building and then bounded along rooftops at high speed. A searchlight swept across the sky, light splashing upon buildings, and then it locked onto Kong from below. Ann turned away from the glare of the light and looked back the way they'd come to see army vehicles racing along the quiet streets. Soldiers on an armored transported fired at Kong. Right behind them was a truck carrying a mobile searchlight.

The streets teemed with these vehicles as the army flooded into the city to hunt for Kong. Ann knew she ought to have been terrified. Bullets whizzed around Kong, all too close to Ann. Yet she felt a curious calm, surrendering herself to forces she could not control. Denham had set it all in motion, and she would never forgive him for that. In the midst of this cruel, unforgiving, and unfamiliar landscape, Kong had gathered her up as his lifeline. Bereft for so long of any tribe or family, he had almost adopted her as family and tried to protect her.

Ann felt sure that Kong had seen Jack's rescue of her as an abduction. In his limited capacity, it was obvious he still believed she belonged with him. And now, in this terrifying place, he was trying to protect her again, even as he sought some refuge, some sanctuary for them both.

But this was not Skull Island. There was nowhere Kong could hide here, and no enemy he could defeat that would not bring more.

Kong leaped across the street as though it was some canyon, ten stories high. He landed on the opposite rooftop and bounded away. Another searchlight found him, and then a third. The army was closing in. Machine gun fire ripped past them as Kong leaped another great distance across the street. Ann shut her eyes, not wanting to see anymore, not wanting to feel the dreadful inevitability that was all around them now.

Then Kong paused, and she opened her eyes. Armored cars and mobile searchlights converged on them. Kong had run out of rooftop. Ahead of him, across the chasm of 34th street, rose the sheer wall of the Empire State Building.

Jack understood why Ann had given herself up to him. Somehow she had been in the area, had seen the chaos erupting, and had known that her presence might calm Kong. She had been trying to stop the rampage, to keep anyone else from being hurt, Kong most of all. But the sight of her being scooped up into his hands again was like a knife in Jack's heart.

How had it come to this? He felt that there had been a moment, back in the jungle, when he could have changed the course that had led them here. If he had just told her all of the feelings that were in his head and his heart, the things he kept caged inside of him, maybe the voyage would have ended differently. Denham and Englehorn and all of the others had commended him for his courage on Skull Island, but Jack knew the truth.

He had been a coward.

For his physical safety, he cared little. Flesh and bone would mend, or not. Ann's safety had been far more important to him than his own. But he had been unwilling to let her in close, to let her really know him. Emotionally, he had not been willing to take that risk. It was just not the kind of man he was, not the way he had been put together.

Driscoll men were stoic, and all his life he had equated that quality with strength.

But the second that passed between them in the jungle, the moment when he could have spoken the words to her, he knew that was all wrong. His father and grandfather had been wrong, and he had learned by their example.

If only he'd spoken up, he and Ann might not even have been in the city tonight. She might have been spared this.

Jack was convinced that the moment in the jungle had been his one opportunity. If anything happened to Ann now, there might never come another. So once again he was determined to save her, to rescue her from Kong, but this time was different, for in doing so he would also be rescuing himself.

Police and military vehicles were all converging in one direction. Jack ran along the street in pursuit. A mobile anti-aircraft gun screeched to a halt on 34th Street. Kong clung to the side of a building several stories up, right across from Empire State Building. Hundreds of guns were aimed at him.

Ann looked so tiny and fragile in his hand.

What are they thinking? They'll kill her if they fire!

A short distance ahead of him, an army commander shouted to his men. "All units, stand by to fire!"

Kong roared defiantly as the anti-aircraft gun's barrel swung toward him.

Another officer ran up to the commander. "I can't give that order, sir! The ape's holding a girl—"

The commander rushed past the officer. Over the shouts and sirens and groaning engines, he could barely make out the man's words, but they chilled him.

"Then I guess it's her unlucky day," the commander said. Then he pointed at Kong and shouted to his gunners. "Take aim!"

"Sir!" the other officer said.

"Shoot to kill!" the commander barked. "Fire!"

Jack froze. It couldn't end like this. Ann would be killed instantly. Kong, high on the side of the building, was a sitting duck.

A sudden bloom of fire erupted from the gun barrel, artillery speeding straight toward Ann and Kong. The beast leaped across 34th Street just as the missile slammed into the wall where he'd been a second before, exploding glass and metal and stone into a shower that rained down on the street below.

Kong smashed into the side of the Empire State Building. More glass rained down twelve stories to the street as Kong used windows for hand and footholds. He was one handed, his other still holding Ann protectively to his chest. Jack shuddered with relief to see that she was unhurt.

Then Kong placed her carefully on his broad shoulder. She grabbed hold of his fur. Jack stood amidst the noise and confusion and could only stare helplessly as Kong began to climb.

Jack had to save her, no matter what it took, or what it cost. He looked around, and then he saw that all eyes were turned upward, all attention on Kong, and the dark entrance to the Empire State Building was unguarded.

The night sky to the east had turned a cobalt blue, a hint that dawn was not far off. Ann felt the chill of the winter night cutting through her and she pressed herself more tightly to Kong's body, clinging to his shoulder, both for safety and for warmth. Though she'd felt resigned to whatever fate held for them, fear shot through her now. The ground seemed so far away. Kong continued his ascent and the wind plucked at Ann, tried to tear her off of him and drop her hundreds of feet to the street below. With every motion, every shift of his body, she felt as though she might be shaken loose.

But Ann did not scream.

She was frozen, just wanting to hang on, praying that she did not fall.

Higher and higher Kong climbed. Soon they were one thousand feet above the street, the dizzying drop yawning beneath Ann. Then, at last, Kong reached the observation deck and gently put Ann down.

Ann could only look at Kong, wishing they were both far from here, wishing he was still back on Skull Island, in his lair. It would have been better if Jack had never come for her. What good had come of it?

Kong regarded her carefully as though checking to see that she was all right. Ann was fine, but the gigantic ape had dozens of small wounds. Blood seeped slowly from those injuries, matting his fur.

Then he turned away, sitting down on the observation deck and staring out across the city. There was an ache in her heart as she remembered him sitting just that way on the ledge of his mountain lair, looking out over the jungle. To Kong, this building must have seemed the closest thing to that he could find. He thought he was bringing her somewhere safe, a sanctuary.

The sadness in her, watching him there, was deeper than anything she'd ever felt before. Kong only sat there. To the east the sun was rising, casting a soft glow over the tops of the buildings below them and glinting off the waters of the East River.

Kong looked down at her and gestured with his hands, touching his heart, then spreading his arms wide. Ann looked at him, confused, and he repeated the gesture.

Then she remembered, and understood.

"Beautiful . . . " she whispered.

She stood beside him and looked out, trying to see the city as he did. Here, so high above the squalor and noise and confusion, it seemed quiet, almost peaceful.

"Yes. Yes, it is."

Jack raced into an elevator and hit the uppermost button. Nothing happened. The elevator was shut down. He stepped out, back into the lobby, and nearly ran into a white-haired security guard.

"You can't go up," the man told him.

Jack pushed past him and set off at a run. He rounded a corner, found the service elevator, and stepped inside. This time, when he pressed a button, the doors drew slowly closed.

A buzzing roar filled the sky, destroying the beauty of the dawn. Ann looked up, startled, heart pounding once more, and saw four biplanes coming in low over the downtown business district to the south. The cold wind blew around her, whipping her hair across her face, and she pushed it away as she watched the biplanes approach. Two-seater planes, with mounted guns.

Kong shifted uneasily, watching their approach. He couldn't possibly know what they were, but he glanced at her and must have seen her agitation. Perhaps in sensing the fear in her, he realized they were predators. Or perhaps it was only the buzz of the engines that roused him.

The planes began to circle.

All along, Ann had felt a strange connection, as though she could sense what Kong was feeling. It seemed to her now that the bond was mutual.

One by one, the planes dipped the wings and began to dive toward the observation deck, aiming directly for Kong. He shifted slightly, protectively, though he could not have known what was to come. By instinct, he pushed her toward the wall behind him.

Kong roared at the planes as if issuing a challenge.

At last Ann found her voice. "No!" she screamed, at the pilots, at Kong himself, and at the world.

The four planes came at Kong from different directions and their machine guns began firing, tearing up the sky, the noise rupturing the dawn. Kong roared and snatched at planes as they darted by. Bullets tore into his flesh and he flinched with each impact, more blood spilling, dripping from his fur.

Kong grabbed hold of the wall and began climbing again, higher up the narrowing structure toward the uppermost level. There was another observation deck there, surrounded by glass, and above that, the dome and the pinnacle of the building. Ann stared first at Kong, then at the planes, amazed that he had left her behind.

Then she realized that was precisely the point. The bullets had hurt him. By climbing higher and leaving her behind, he was attempting to draw the planes away from Ann, still trying to keep her safe. But she could not allow that. The only chance he had of survival was if Ann could get in the way, could make the pilots and gunners of the planes see her. Maybe they would hesitate, retreat, and try to come up with another plan of attack.

Desperate, she ran to a ladder on the observation deck, and began to climb. The ladder led to the steel dome at the top of the building, and continued upward. The wind whipped at her, icy fingers tugging at her, but she tightened her grip and continued on.

Kong broke the mooring mast off of the pinnacle of the building and brandished it as the planes came in for another pass. The giant gorilla leaped into the air, smashing at the plane. The mast struck it, tearing metal, impact like cars colliding. The crippled plane spun out of control, plummeting toward the street, but Kong was falling, too.

Ann gasped and watched as he tumbled through the air, one hand still clutching the top of the building. He smashed against the dome, but managed to hang on. Then he dropped down to the upper observation deck, the highest level of the building, and caught himself by smashing one fist through glass windows, scattering shards that fell a thousand feet, glittering in the dawn's light.

The impact shook the whole structure and Ann's ladder gave way.

With a scream, she dangled precariously in mid-air, trying to keep her grip on the steel rungs. She stared at her fingers as though she could force strength into them by sheer will alone, pulse racing, pounding in her ears.

She saw her fingers slipping, but could do nothing.

Ann fell, only the winter wind beneath her now.

Kong caught her in his leather hand, cutting off her scream. For just a moment, Ann felt safe. Then she saw the three remaining planes circling behind him, preparing to dive. Kong reached through the broken windows and put Ann inside the closed observation deck. She tumbled roughly to the ground.

They looked at one another and in his eyes she saw

no more confusion, only a reflection of the same sadness she felt.

Before she could stand, another burst of gunfire raked the building. Windows shattered. Glass flew all around her and she raised her arms to protect her face. Bullets slammed into Kong's back and he arched his body and roared in pain.

Jack burst through the doors of the observation deck only to be greeted by a hail of bullets. He dove to the floor as they perforated the wall above his head.

When he looked up, he saw Ann stagger to her feet and run for a small stairway that led up higher still, to the dome.

The planes circled again and came in for an attack just as Kong reached the peak again. Bullets strafed him but he barely flinched. As the planes zipped by him through the air, he reached out and got hold of a wing. Its momentum nearly pulled him from the building, but he turned and flung it away, redirecting that momentum, tossing the plane into another, the two of them exploding in mid-air, wreckage tipping end over end as both flying machines fell away toward the ground.

Ann saw the whole thing as she came up through a hatch onto the dome. Kong stood there, holding the top of the dome, watching the planes warily. Blood soaked his fur. He was weakened from his wounds. An ordinary animal would have fled. Instinct should have demanded it. But he was cornered, with nowhere else to go, and another powerful instinct had taken over, the need to protect her.

Ann could do no less than try to protect him as well.

She ran to him, there on the edge of the dome, and raced between his legs to the edge of the building. Other planes had arrived. Reinforcements. They were coming in for another attack run and frantically she waved at them, screaming as loud as she could.

"No! No!"

But they came on, with no indication that they'd seen her. Gunfire tore into Kong and he staggered back against the dome and slid down, leaving a smear of blood behind. Ann crawled to him, buffeted by the wind. Kong grasped the side of the building, holding on. Ann clutched his fingers, hugging them, trying to comfort him. She felt hot tears on her cheeks and tasted their salt upon her lips.

Kong slowly lifted her in his hand, studying her, and then his gaze shifted and he looked to the east, to the rising sun.

Slowly he lowered her to the building, keeping her safe, close to the dome, shielding her. To Ann, all sound seemed to fade away except the wind, which had subsided to a gentle breeze.

In his eyes now she saw no fear, no confusion. Only tenderness. Then slowly the light faded from his eyes and was extinguished.

Kong toppled back, tumbled over the edge of the building, and disappeared from sight. Ann stared at the place where he'd been, the sunlight warm upon her face, the tracks of her tears suddenly cold in the breeze.

She moved to the edge and stared down at the street below, the empty places inside of her filling with despair. For a brief moment she wanted nothing more than to follow Kong. What place was there for her in a world so cold.

Then, suddenly, she became aware of Jack beside her. "Ann . . ."

Slowly, she turned to face him, her grief still trapped inside her.

"Why are you here?" she heard herself say.

It seemed to her that a kind of mask fell away from his face, that some distance between them was bridged. Ann felt as though she was seeing him for the first time.

"Because I love you."

Ann stared at him, paralyzed. Fresh tears spilled from her eyes, hot tears of anguish and grief and of hope. Slowly she rose. Hesitantly, she went to him.

Jack gently embraced her. She wrapped her arms around him, and they held one another as the dawn light washed over them.

Excited crowds gathered to stare at Kong's body. A swarm of journalists converged on him, light bulbs flashing. Two photographers climbed onto Kong's chest, cameras aimed right at his face, jostling for position before a policeman dragged them off.

"Come on, boys, move on! Show's over!"

The National Guard had arrived and began to push the onlookers back. One of the photographers stared up the long length of the Empire State Building at the extraordinary distance Kong had fallen.

"Why'd he do that? Climb up there and get himself cornered? The ape musta known what was comin'—"

"It's just a dumb animal," said the other, snapping a picture, flashbulb popping. "It didn't know nuthin'!"

"He knew," Carl Denham said as he pushed through the crowd. He couldn't tear his eyes off of the face of Kong, serene in death. Dread crept through him as the realization struck. "He knew how it would end."

"What does it matter?" the second photographer said. "The airplanes got him."

Denham did not even look up. He could only stare at Kong. "It wasn't the airplanes," he said.

"It was beauty killed the beast."

CHRISTOPHER GOLDEN is the award-winning, bestselling author of such novels as *Wildwood Road, The Boys Are Back in Town, The Ferryman, Strangewood, Of Saints and Shadows,* and the *Body of Evidence* series of teen thrillers. There are more than eight million copies of his books in print. Working with actress/writer/director Amber Benson, he co-created and co-wrote *Ghosts of Albion,* an animated supernatural drama for BBC on-line, which will soon become a book series from Del Rey. He has been listed among the top ten favorite writers by the readers of *SFX Magazine* in the U.K. three times since 2000, and his novels have been published around the world in nearly a dozen languages, including French, Italian, Czech, Chinese, and Russian.

With Thomas E. Sniegoski, he is the co-author of the dark fantasy series *The Menagerie* as well as the young readers fantasy series *OutCast.* Golden and Sniegoski also wrote the graphic novel *BPRD: Hollow Earth,* a spinoff from the fan favorite comic book series *Hellboy.* Golden authored the original Hellboy novels, *The Lost Army* and *The Bones of Giants,* and edited two Hellboy short story anthologies.

He has written or co-written a great many novels and comic books set in the worlds of the television series *Buffy the Vampire Slayer* and *Angel*, and also wrote the very first X-Men novels, a fan favorite trilogy entitled *X-Men: Mutant Empire*. His work in comic books has included tales of such characters as *Wolverine, Batman, The Punisher,* and *The Crow*.

Golden was born and raised in Massachusetts, where he still lives with his family. He is currently at work on a dark fantasy trilogy for Bantam Books entitled *The Veil*.